W9-BWD-762

AIRTIGHT CASE

Other books by Beverly Connor in the Lindsay Chamberlain Series:

A Rumor of Bones

Questionable Remains

Dressed to Die

Skeleton Crew

AIRTIGHT CASE

A Lindsay Chamberlain Novel

BEVERLY CONNOR

Cumberland House
Nashville, Tennessee

Published by Cumberland House Publishing, Inc., 431 Harding Industrial Drive, Nashville, TN 37211-3160.

The characters and events in this book are fictitious. Any similarity to real persons, living or dead, is coincidental and not intended by the author.

Library of Congress Cataloging-in-Publication Data

Connor, Beverly, 1948-
Airtight case : a Lindsay Chamberlain novel / Beverly Connor.
p. cm.
ISBN 1-58182-123-9 (alk. paper)
1. Chamberlain, Lindsay (Fictitious character)--Fiction. 2. Women archaeologists--Fiction. 3. Women forensic anthropologists--Fiction. 4. Excavations (Archaeology)--Fiction. 5. Tennessee--Fiction. 6. Great Smoky Mountains National Park (N.C. and Tenn.)--Fiction. I. Title

PS3553.O5138 A77 2000
813'.54--dc21 00-055486

Printed in the United States of America
1 2 3 4 5 6 7 8—05 04 03 02 01 00 99

In memory of my father, Charles Heth, for his belief in me. And my uncle, Arthur Heth, who told me Jack Tales and took me fishing and hunting for arrowheads in the mountains of Kentucky when I was a little girl.

Acknowledgments

Thanks to my dentist, Carlos Wilbanks, for his advice on teeth, to Michael Bedenbaugh for talking to me about log cabins, Diane Trap, Judy and Takis Iakovou, Marie and Richard Davis, and Larry MacDougald for their criticism and advice. A special thanks to my husband, Charles Connor, for everything.

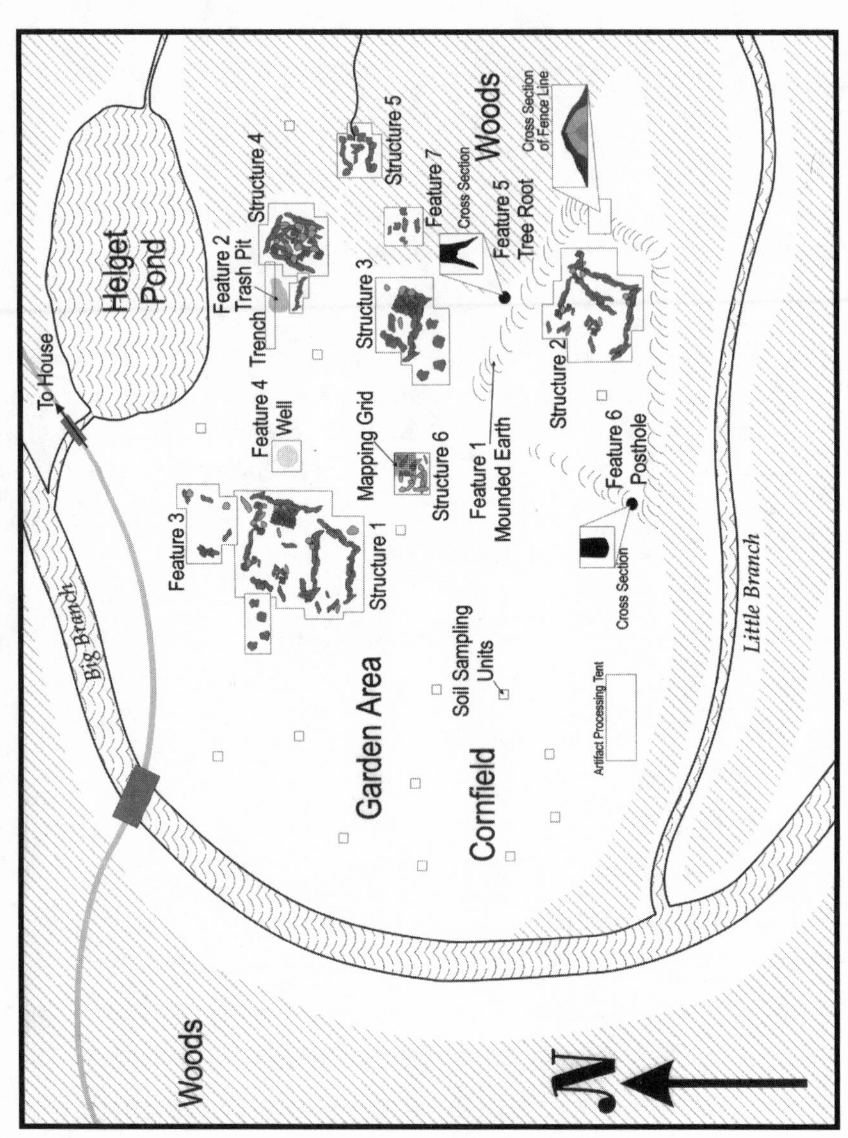

Author's Note

The Gallows Farmstead site and the towns of Kelley's Chase and Mac's Crossing are fictional.

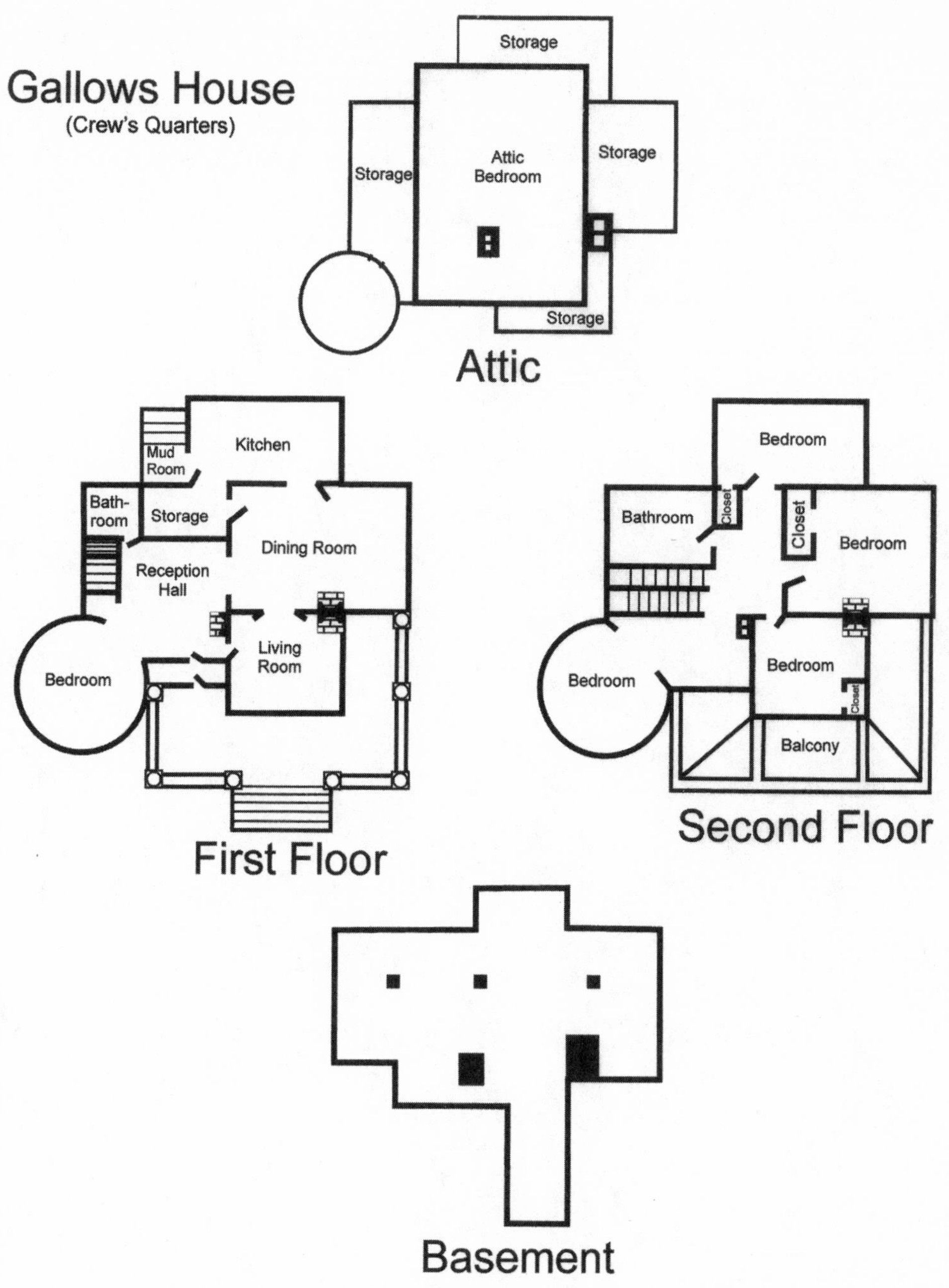
Gallows House
(Crew's Quarters)
Storage
Storage
Attic
Bedroom
Storage
Storage
Attic
Kitchen
Mud
Room
Bath-
room
Storage
Dining Room
Reception
Hall
Living
Room
Bedroom
First Floor
Bedroom
Bathroom
Closet
Closet
Bedroom
Bedroom
Bedroom
Closet
Balcony
Second Floor
Basement

AIRTIGHT CASE

PART I

◆ April 2 ◆

Chapter 1

THE SUN SHINING through the window onto the mirror made her reflection faint and ghostly. She stepped closer, examining the face, the hair, the eyes. A stranger. She took a strand of long chestnut brown hair in her fingers, observing with detachment how the sunlight brought out deep reddish undertones. She looked back at the face, the stitches on her forehead, the bruise on her cheek—black, blue, just a hint of yellow. She reached out and touched the mirror, as if the image were not of her, but some other suffering woman standing before her, disappearing under the light. The woman in the mirror was flat and cold under her fingers. That was her. That's how she felt. She turned at the sound of footsteps on the clay tiles of the sunroom.

"Miss, I have some good news."

The nurse, the dark-haired one with a pronounced overbite, stood with her hand grasping the elbow of a man. Both grinned at her. Silly grins, she thought with fleeting unkindness.

"We know who you are," continued the nurse. "You're Lisa Christian. This is your fiancé, Mark Smith."

The fiancé was a few inches shorter than she with dark receding hair and sparkling dark eyes. His white-and-gray-striped shirt was open at the throat, revealing a gold chain resting among black chest hairs.

She turned the name that was supposed to be hers over in her mind. Lisa Christian. The name was as much a stranger to her as the reflection in the mirror, as the man standing before her—as everything. She stepped back as he tried to embrace her.

"Lisa, it's me—Mark. I've been looking for you for two days. We've all been worried and looking for you."

This man, this Mark Smith, held out a hand and took hers, turning it over, examining her fingers. "You've lost your ring. It don't matter. I've found you. That's what matters."

"He's here to take you home, Miss Christian," said the nurse.

"I don't know him."

"Of course." The nurse patted her arm. "Your memory'll come back. Being at home'll help. You'll see."

"I'm not going anywhere with someone I don't know."

"Well, honey . . ." The nurse smiled at her as if she had made a joke. "Right now you don't know nobody."

She willed herself to stay and not run. She wanted so much to run back to someplace safe. But that would make her look foolish. And she couldn't afford to look foolish, not if she wanted to be taken seriously. They already talked to her as if she were a child.

Odd. There were so many things she knew, like how the Indian actors on the TV western last evening were really Italians and not Indians—that the horse in *The Black Stallion,* which came on afterward, was indeed Arabian, as advertised. Strange that she knew these things but didn't have a clue about the important things—like who she was.

She looked down at her tanned hand that this stranger calling himself Mark Smith, her fiancé, had released, and she wondered why there wasn't a white, untanned band around her finger.

"Here, Lisa." He handed her a small framed photograph of himself and the stranger named Lisa she had just been observing in the mirror. In the picture she was looking at the camera, smiling, her arm threaded through his. It wasn't a particularly good photograph of the two of them. He was looking off to the side, frowning at something out of camera range.

"Isn't that nice, Miss Christian?" asked the nurse, looking at the photograph.

"I brought you some clothes, Lisa." He handed her a short lavender wisp of a dress.

She didn't like the way the name *Lisa* sounded when he said it. She didn't like the dress. She handed it back. "One of the nurses loaned me some jeans and a shirt."

Mark tossed the dress into a plastic bag. "I'd like to leave soon. It's a long drive home."

"I'm not going with you," she said.

He gave a short laugh. "Of course you are, honey. You need to be home, in your own apartment."

"No."

"You're being discharged," the nurse said. "You've got to go somewhere."

"If there was no one to claim me, where would you send me? Would you put me out on the street?"

The nurse looked flustered. "Well, no. But this is a very small hospital . . ."

"Of course she's coming with me." Mark Smith took her hand again, and she pulled it away again. "I just need to talk to her."

"He's paying your bill," offered the nurse.

"The doctor said my memory will return in a few days. Surely, I can stay until then."

"Why don't you get changed and we'll talk about it." Mark smiled as he spoke. She noticed that his molars had gold fillings.

She walked back to her room, trailing the two of them behind her. "I'll only be a moment," she said, turning to stop Mark inside the doorway.

"It's nothing I've not seen before." He grinned again.

"You must understand, I don't know you."

"Why don't you wait out in the hallway, Mr. Smith?" the nurse said. "We'll be out in a minute."

He raised his hands as if giving up, and backed out the door. "Sure, I'm a sensitive kind of guy."

When the door was closed, she took the donated clothes out of the metal bureau drawer and removed her robe. She slipped the jeans on under her hospital gown.

"Mark is a real good-looking guy, Miss Christian. If you don't want him, I'll take him."

"You've got yourself a deal." She pulled the T-shirt over her head and slipped on the shoes that had been loaned to her but didn't fit just right.

"I'm going to get you a wheelchair," the nurse said.

"A wheelchair?"

"You have to leave the hospital in a wheelchair. It's hospital regulations. I'll be right back."

Lisa stared hard at the face in the mirror. *Remember, remember,* she silently yelled at herself.

"You look great." Mark had reentered her room. She hadn't heard him.

"You didn't knock." She didn't look at him, but at the strange face in the mirror.

"Sorry, force of habit." His little laugh was annoying.

"I'm not going with you."

Abruptly, he was by her side, gripping her arm hard. "Don't be stupid. You're coming with me, and that's that."

"Let go of me."

"Come on, dammit."

"Let go of me. I have to go to the bathroom."

"All right then. I'll be right here. Three minutes and we're out of here."

He let go of her arm and she ducked into the bathroom and locked the door. Her bathroom was shared by the next room. She didn't think he knew that. She turned on the water and flushed the toilet and opened the connecting door. The elderly woman in the adjoining room was asleep, making a wheezing sound with each breath, while a monitor sounded the regular beep of her heart rate. Lisa tiptoed across the room to the door, looked out briefly into the hallway, and sprinted across the hall to the exit door. She ran without stopping down the two flights of stairs and out the door, onto the sidewalk. She stopped outside the two-story hospital to catch her breath.

She was in the small Tennessee town of Mac's Crossing. Two days earlier a trucker had found her bruised, covered in mud, and walking down the highway. He had been kind, lucky for her. Since then, she had spent two days in the hospital, not knowing who she was or what had happened. Two days of constant fear churning acid in her stomach.

Running down the stairs had felt good. She wanted to run some more, but where could she go? She forced herself to walk down the sidewalk from the hospital as if she knew where she was going. She passed a man standing at the curb smoking a cigarette. He grabbed her arm.

"Now where do you think you're going?"

Chapter 2

"LET GO OF me!" She tried to pull the stranger's bony hand off her arm.

He was as tall as she was, perhaps about her age. He was thin and sinewy, with cornflower blue squinting eyes and dirty blond thinning hair. He scowled and gave her arm a hard shake.

"Get in the car!"

She pulled and twisted, trying to get away, but the more she pulled against his grasp, the tighter he dug his fingers into her upper arm. He threw his burning cigarette to the ground. She saw his free hand rising toward her. She had to get loose. Reflexively, without thinking, she hit him under the point of his nose with the heel of her hand, hard enough to make blood flow down his face.

"Damn you, bitch!" He jerked his head back, wiped his nose, and panicked at the sight of his own blood.

"You need help, miss?" A large woman in a silver Cadillac stuck her head out of her automobile window.

"Call the police and tell them a man is molesting people coming out of the hospital," she shouted.

Trying to feign innocence, the stranger relaxed his posture. She felt his grip on her arm loosen. She stomped the top of his foot nearest her, pulled away from him and ran, not stopping until she was out of sight between two buildings.

She ducked into a door and leaned against the wall, trying to compose herself, taking deep breaths. The gray-green walls and tile floor looked like another hospital, perhaps a doctors' building. To her left she saw a men's room. The women's room should be just beyond it, she reasoned, and forced herself to walk slowly down the corridor to the door marked WOMEN.

She examined her bruised and swollen face in the restroom mirror. It was still a stranger's face. The adrenaline running through her veins, causing her heart to pump like a jackhammer, did nothing to clear out the fog in her brain. "I need help," she whispered to the stranger in the mirror.

She turned on the faucet and splashed cool water on her face. *Think,* she told herself. *How can I find help when I can't tell my enemies from my friends? If I just had a place to stay for a few days—until my memory returns.*

That's it. Find a safe place. Where? Where can I go? A person with no money and no memory has no credibility. If I show up someplace looking like this, people will call the police and I'll be back in the same predicament. She combed her fingers through her hair to make it look less disheveled.

Think, think, think. She hammered the sides of the porcelain sink with the same ferocity her heart hammered in her chest. *Stop, be still, and think.* She closed her eyes. When she opened them again, she smiled into the mirror, trying on faces that looked confident. She heard the door to the restroom opening. They were looking for her. Why didn't she think of that?

She ducked inside a stall. A woman and a little boy walked past. It wasn't the men. But the damage was done. Her heart was racing again. Her ears rang from the rush of adrenaline. She stayed in the stall, breathing slowly, until some measure of calm returned. She wondered if she could stay here—dodging the custodian—and sleeping . . . where?

She left the stall and went to the door, where she stood for several moments, summoning the courage to open it. She pulled the door toward her just enough to see, and peeped out into the hallway. Neither Mark Smith nor the skinny cigarette-smoking man was there. Only a woman walking toward the bathroom. She might be one of them. *Don't panic. She's probably a patient. No, she's not carrying a purse. Perhaps she works here. Good,* she thought. Her brain was working—not well, but maybe it was coming around.

She walked past the woman and smiled, almost leaning into the wall with relief when the woman didn't reach out and grab her. She walked to the front of the building, stopping in the lobby to read the index. It was a doctors' building, but there was nothing here to help her, only pediatrics, ear-nose-and-throat, gynecology, and urology. She didn't have any of those problems.

Outside again, the sun was bright on her face, traffic moved back and forth, people came and went. She understood what it all meant, but it was as if it were the first time she had ever seen it. She put on the confident face she had practiced and walked with purpose down the sidewalk in the direction of the business district, looking for sanctuary.

She passed people, glancing at each face, hoping for one she recognized, praying with every encounter that they weren't enemies. Sometimes they nodded back at her. Mostly, they showed alarm at her stitched and bruised face, but all were aliens. Or, she was the alien with nothing that made her a part of them—no shared history, no remembered events, none of the cement that holds a people together. She was adrift, detached from the world, looking at all of them through a glass barrier.

The business district was a parallel row of buildings on each side of a main two-lane street. There was a shoe store, a clothing store, a drugstore, a department store, a hardware store. She stopped in front of the hardware store and stared at the window display: tools, shovels, hoes, rakes. They leaned against a bale of hay and looked like weapons. The shovel was pointed.

Couldn't shave with that.

Why had that odd thought popped into her head? It didn't even make sense. You don't shave with a shovel, you shave with a razor. She shivered and left the window, heading for the department store.

She walked up the steps and in through shiny glass doors. A cool breeze hit her face, smelling like good perfume. She stopped to think, pretending to examine a blouse hanging on a rack. She had to do something about her appearance—couldn't go around looking like a vagrant. If she found someone to ask for help it would be best to look more like she didn't need it.

She had to have a name. People always ask for a name. The men were hunting for Lisa Christian. She would make up another one. Linda. Linda Chambers. That was as good a name as any. And a story—she needed a story.

Linda Chambers walked into the cosmetic department where two women were working the counter. One was fiftyish, and one looked barely out of her teens. She chose the younger one to approach.

"Can I help you?" asked the woman whose name tag read Tiffany. Tiffany cringed at the sight of her face. "Wow, that looks like it hurts."

"It's mainly sore now. I had a car accident. I want to look at some makeup samples, something that will kind of cover the bruises."

Tiffany smiled. "We have some heavy pancake makeup."

"I don't necessarily need to hide the bruises, just make them less noticeable and me more presentable." She stepped back and looked across the store, craning her neck.

"Looking for someone?" Tiffany asked.

"My boyfriend. I lost my purse in the accident and I can't buy anything until he gets here. I think I lost him when we passed the hardware store. He'll find me. Anyway, do you have some samples I can try?"

Tiffany showed her several colors of foundation and helped her pick out a shade that went with her skin.

"Can I try it?"

"Sure. Just let me know when you're ready." Tiffany went to help another customer.

"Thanks."

She quickly applied a thin coat of foundation over her face, smoothing out her skin. She used samples of lipstick and mascara, lightly touching up her lips and lashes. The bruises still showed through, but the effect of the makeup was to make her look less homeless, more credible.

"How did it do?" asked Tiffany, returning.

"I think this color is fine. What do you think?"

Tiffany agreed.

"I'll be back. I'm going to look at the shoes while my boyfriend catches up." She left the counter, wondering if she had fooled Tiffany. Probably not, but at least she looked a little better.

She passed by the shoe department, heading for the exit. In a mirror she saw the man who called himself Mark Smith, her fiancé. She ducked behind a rack of hats. Did they know she came in here, or were they just looking everywhere for her? Why here? Were they using the same logic she was? Maybe one of those faces she passed on the street told him she came in here. *Have you seen a woman with a battered face?* She stood out. Don't panic. Her gaze darted around the store. At the end of the aisle, she saw the skinny man enter the door she had been about to exit.

She moved farther behind the rack, wishing she had a disguise. She could put her hair up, but she didn't have a bobby pin to her name. She pretended to try on a wide-brimmed straw hat. Maybe she could disguise herself just while she was in the store.

Mark's eyes were scanning every woman in the store. The skinny man was about to walk past her. She was stuck. If she tried to leave, they would see her. All she could do now was to keep them in sight and try to hide as they came her way. Surely, they wouldn't try to abduct her in a crowded store.

Why not? She was the one who had lost her mind.

Chapter 3

FROM HER HIDING place behind the racks of hats she watched Mark Smith systematically survey the people in the store, looking for her. He caught the eye of the clerk, Tiffany, who had helped her at the cosmetic counter. She chewed on her lower lip as Tiffany approached Mark. She watched Tiffany speak, Mark nod, Tiffany wave her hand in a broad gesture. She didn't have to hear their conversation to understand that Tiffany was telling him that she had been in the cosmetics department making up her face and was now somewhere in the store . . . waiting for him.

She wanted to fold herself over and pretend she was invisible. She wanted to be unconscious so she would stop feeling the panic that rose from her stomach and stung her throat. She wanted to know what to do. Was there anyone in the faces of strangers around her who would help her?

She snatched the hat off her head, suddenly realizing that she was the only person wearing one. It was then, perhaps attracted by the sudden movement, that Mark's eyes shifted in her direction. He must have recognized her even through the rack of hats, because he started in her direction.

She bolted into the aisle behind the racks of hats and almost ran into the skinny man. To her good fortune, he was looking the other way, searching down an adjoining aisle. She turned sharply on the ball of her foot, a move that oddly carried with it a faint familiarity, and walked quickly across the room to doors painted with the words "Employees Only."

"Can I help you?" An older woman in glasses, carrying a sheaf of papers stopped and looked at her, frowning.

She stared at the woman a moment, trying to find that calm face she had practiced.

"I'm supposed to see someone," she stammered.

"For what purpose?"

"A job."

"You need to go upstairs . . . are you all right?"

"I feel faint. Nervous, I suppose. Is there anywhere I can sit down?"

"Not here. You need . . ."

"Is that a door to the outside?" She pointed to a door at the end of the hall.

"Yes, to an alley, but you can't . . ."

"If I could just go outside before I throw up." That convinced the woman to allow her to go down the hall and out the alleyway door.

She ran down the alley and out to a sidewalk. She turned and hurried into the drugstore where she stopped behind a display of greeting cards.

The two men came out of the alley and looked up and down the street. The skinny one took off walking briskly up the street away from her. Mark came pushing through the front door of the drugstore, looking straight ahead down the aisle. She didn't move.

He headed toward the rear. Maybe he thought she had gone out the back, the way she did in the department store. She waited for him to reach the back of the store, dashed for the front door, ran across the street in front of a car and darted into an alley, chased by an angry blast of a car horn.

If there was just someplace she could go that would be safe. Somewhere she could sit down and rest, someplace where they wouldn't look. The other end of the alley opened onto a street lined by a row of white houses with wide porches, newly painted and converted to offices. She stood against the back wall of a brick building, reading the signs on the other side of the street, searching for some clue or place of refuge, or sanctuary . . . something.

The fog in her brain was getting worse instead of better. She closed her eyes a moment, then opened them again. She looked back to one of the houses. It was divided into two businesses: an attorney on one side and a detective on the other. Maybe they could help.

She crossed the street and stood in front of the offices, trying to make herself go in. Which one? The detective, she decided. He could find out who she really was. No, the attorney. He could protect her. She looked behind her for Mark or his accomplice.

A man with long, straight black hair and skin the color of sienna was getting out of a new midnight blue pickup truck less than fifty yards away. He was looking at her and she saw recognition, alarm perhaps, in his face. He started toward her.

She turned and ran as fast as she could down the driveway beside the house, across a narrow street, across a field, into thick woods, stopping only when she tripped over a root and fell to the ground. She crawled to her knees and scooted for cover, her back against a big tree.

She laid her head on her arms and cried. When her tears stopped, she raised her head and wiped her eyes with her fingertips. The black smear of mascara on her hands told her that her attempt to look normal and sane had gone for nothing. Now she probably looked like a mad woman.

She was in a pine and hardwood forest. It smelled clean. Maybe this was a safe place. She stood, leaning against the huge tree, and peered into the thick woods. At first they were inviting, but the invitation invoked a rising horror within her that moved upon her like a dark smothering shadow. There was a terrible secret in those woods. Her heart beat so fast she thought it would come out of her chest. She couldn't get her breath. She was suffocating. She sank to the ground, paralyzed with fear, her throat too clenched even to cry.

She didn't know how long she stayed crouched on the ground. She didn't even know if she had passed out and come to. She didn't know anything but overwhelming fear covering her like some wicked hand reaching into her mind. But she managed to rise to her feet again and forced herself to breathe normally.

The doctor said her memory would return in a few days. It had been how many—two, three, already? Her memory might return tomorrow. She could stay in the woods until then. But something was in the woods. Something was also out in the streets.

Better the devil you know than the devil you don't, an inner voice said. *Why?* another voice whispered. *What could there be in the woods worse than the men chasing you?*

Who was the third man? A friend of Mark's? Friend or foe?

And why had she been so afraid of Mark? Because he said he was her fiancé, someone she was supposed to marry, yet she was repelled by him. But he did have a picture of the two of them. She had looked happy.

But it wasn't really you, her inner voice said. *You knew that.*

She looked at her hands. Her fingers were long and slender, longer than those of the woman whose arm was threaded through Mark's in the picture. And the woman in the picture was shorter than Mark.

It might have been my face, but it wasn't my body. He isn't my fiancé. Then, who is he?

She wiped her face again with her hands and ran her fingers through her hair. The sun would be setting in an hour or two.

I've really no choice but to make a place in the woods to spend the night.

She walked deeper into the thick of the woods and began to look for a place to build a shelter. She found it both strange and comforting that she knew how. In a small thicket of scrub trees she bent half a dozen saplings in a circle toward one another and wove their tops together to form a dome shape. She interwove broken limbs and laid leafy branches on the outside of the dome until it was covered in a protective matted layer.

She sat in the shelter on a soft pile of moss, her arms around knees tucked under her chin. Night came, slowly at first, like a circling bird, then descended quickly, and it was dark. Through the opening of her makeshift structure, she could see the moon like a bright shiny silver dollar peeking through the trees. It was going to be a cool night, maybe too cool. She wasn't dressed for the mountain outdoors at night.

She didn't move, and hardly thought—what would she think about with the empty pockets of her mind? Instead, she listened. Owls, tree frogs—not crickets—she knew the difference. Wind in the trees. Good sounds . . . frightening sounds.

What . . . what . . . what was on the edge of her brain trying to get in? Why would sounds be frightening and comforting at the same time?

Don't force it, the doctors had told her. But what did they know? Nothing, if they were going to sign her out to an impostor.

She breathed slowly so that the sound of her own breath wouldn't resound in her ears, so her heart would slow, so she could listen.

A twig broke. Deer? Soft crunching in the forest litter.

Not deer, too loud for deer.

Footsteps. Man. Her heart pounded, filling her ears with the reverberation of her pumping blood.

Listen. Not steady footsteps. Starting . . . stopping . . . searching.

She felt silently around her on the ground for a stick, a weapon. Why hadn't she thought beforehand to find a weapon?

"Lindsay!"

A man's voice with a strange subtle accent . . . not foreign. Familiar. Who was Lindsay? A dog? Someone lost? She was lost. Who was Lindsay? Lisa, Linda, Lindsay. Coincidence?

"Lindsay! It's me, John. I know you don't remember . . ."

The voice had the soothing, subtle modulations of an Indian voice—another mysterious thing she knew. Through the opening in her shelter, she saw a distant shaft of light . . . bobbing, sweeping.

"I'm not going to hurt you."

How do I know? An old riddle forced its way into her head. Something half-remembered. What was it, exactly?

There are two tribes, the Blackfoot who always tell the truth, and the Whitefoot who always lie, but you cannot tell which is which. You meet one from each tribe at a fork in the road. You need directions. How do you ask the right question to get you where you want to go? What is the answer? Which road is not the right road? No, that's not it. No time to reason it out, the man is coming closer.

"Lindsay, can you hear me? Are you in the woods somewhere?"

She stayed very still, wondering what to do. Take a chance that he's a friend? *What if he's not? What if he's that terrible thing in the woods?*

The light swept across her shelter.

"Lindsay!"

The man calling himself John rushed toward her. She grasped her hand around a dried twig, a sorry excuse for a weapon.

"Oh, Jesus, Lindsay."

"Don't come any closer," she said quietly.

He squatted at the entrance and shone the light in the interior, but not on her face.

"It's all right." He shone the light on himself.

She watched his face for a moment before her gaze swept over his faded blue jeans and black shirt. He wore beaded bracelets on his wrists. He shifted, revealing an oval beaded belt buckle.

"Lindsay. It's me, John. I won't hurt you."

"I was trying to decide if you're the lying Whitefoot or the truthful Blackfoot."

He laughed gently. "Right now, I'm a very relieved Cherokee."

He stood and slowly took a pocketknife from his jeans. She moved back into the shelter. She couldn't make it past him, but maybe she could break through the back. He tossed the knife to her. She grabbed it and opened the blade. He squatted again and pushed the flashlight, handle first, toward her and moved back. She grabbed it and shone it in his eyes. He squinted.

"You said you're Cherokee, but the beadwork is Shoshone."

The corners of his mouth turned up in a grin. "Yes. Some friends gave them to me. You know that. You are remembering."

She shook her head. "I seem to know things. I remember nothing." She spat that last out like a bite of sour apple.

"I'm going to sit in here with you. I'll move slowly." He worked his way opposite her, staying at arm's length. "Nice shelter."

"I must live in the woods," she said.

"Actually, you do, but in a house. Your name is Lindsay Chamberlain. You're a professor at the University of Georgia's Archaeology Department. You're also a forensic anthropologist and do consulting work for law enforcement people."

"Lindsay Chamberlain. Linda Chambers. Maybe I am remembering," she whispered. "Who are you?"

"My name's John West."

"Are you a professor at the university, too?"

He laughed. "No. I own a construction company."

"Why have you come looking for me?"

"You're my girlfriend . . . most of the time."

"Do I have a family?"

"Your parents are in Europe. We haven't called them. Your brother, Sinjin, is on his way from California. He's a firefighter, a smoke jumper."

"A smoke jumper? That sounds dangerous."

"It doesn't come close to being an archaeologist."

Lindsay Chamberlain cocked her head and narrowed her eyes at John. "This has happened to me before?"

"Not like this. You've never lost your memory of who you were, but you've had some scary adventures."

"How did you know to look for me?"

"You went to a conference in Knoxville last weekend, something about primitive technology. We argued before you left, and I hadn't seen you for a couple of weeks."

"Argued? About what?"

"It doesn't matter now. I wanted to talk to you, so I called the UGA Archaeology Department looking for you. They said the conference at Knoxville ended two days ago, but that you hadn't come back to campus yet. I called Harper Latham, a faculty member friend of yours on campus. She said your plans had been to leave the conference, spend a few days with a friend of yours named Jane Burroughs in Asheville, North Carolina, and then come back to Georgia. You were supposed to call Harper from Jane's to let her know when you would be arriving back in town, and the two of you were to meet and have dinner together. You hadn't called, and Harper was worried."

"Harper is a nice name."

"She's a good friend. Harper called Jane in Asheville, and Jane said you never arrived at her place. Harper called Derrick . . ."

"Derrick?"

"He's an archaeologist friend of yours. He was at the conference in Knoxville with you." John hesitated a moment. "You dated him before me." He hesitated again. "You were engaged."

Derrick. She tried to remember.

"Derrick said you had left Knoxville two days ago, and he said you also told him you were going to Asheville to visit Jane Burroughs."

"Were Derrick and I, were we . . . well, seeing each other again?"

"No. I hope not."

"You said I was your girlfriend most of the time . . . is that because of Derrick and me?"

"No. It's because you and I argue about your work."

"But you came to find me."

"Of course."

"How did you know where to look?"

"That was part of the problem. We thought you might be somewhere between Knoxville and Asheville, but that's a huge area. We know you well enough to know that you probably wouldn't take the interstate highways, and there are hundreds of miles of mountain roads between Knoxville and Asheville, by a dozen different routes. We called local sheriffs and police, the highway patrol in three states . . . everyone we could think of. There were no reports on anyone fitting the description of you or your Explorer."

"I drive an Explorer?"

"Yes."

"Where is it?"

"They haven't found it yet. We tried to find you, Lindsay. It's hard to get the authorities to look for an adult, particularly one with a certain reputation for independence and adventure."

"What reputation?"

John just smiled. "Then, this morning the FBI called your department head. The sheriff's department here in Mac's Crossing had submitted your fingerprints for identification. The FBI has your prints on file—apparently, because of the work you do—and they made a match. Harper called me from campus to tell me where you were, and I came to Mac's Crossing to get you. When I arrived at the hospital, you were gone. They still hadn't gotten the word on your identification. They told me how you had been found wandering down the middle of the highway, and the condition you were in, and about your memory loss, and they said you had run away from the hospital. I knew something must have happened."

"Someone else tried to claim me."

"Yes. They told me about that. I called the local sheriff to report you missing. Because of some glitch, he had just received the FBI fingerprint match and hadn't yet notified the hospital. That's why they didn't know who you were. Do you know the man who was posing as your fiancé?"

Lindsay wanted to trust John. His stories hung together like the truth, and she desperately needed to trust someone. She put down the knife. "No. But he called me Lisa Christian. A lot like Lindsay Chamberlain."

"So, he knows who you are."

"It would seem so. How did you find me in the woods?"

"When you ran from me earlier, I went the wrong way looking for you. I thought you would run toward town and buildings. When I couldn't find you there, I retraced my path and saw the woods, and realized you would feel safe in the woods. Your father and uncles took you fishing and camping weeks at a time when you were a little girl." He paused and reached for her hand. "Let's go home."

She moved her hand from his reach. "The woods are dark now."

"We have a flashlight. We'll be able to see the town lights in a short distance."

"No, there's something terrible in the woods. I don't know what, but I know it's there."

John was silent for a long moment. He lowered his head and shook it again. "You want to stay all night in the woods. My ex-wife wasn't this much trouble."

"I'm afraid."

"I know. Okay. We'll stay the night. If you get cold, I'm here."

John settled in the shelter, trying to make himself comfortable. Lindsay stuck his knife in the ground beside her. Off in the distance they heard an owl screech.

Chapter 4

WHEN LINDSAY AWOKE, John was stretching and kneading his lower back. His long black hair fell across his shoulders, his Indian profile silhouetted against the bright morning light shining through the opening of the small makeshift shelter. He looked strong, and she had been asleep and defenseless. He could have harmed her if he had wanted, but he hadn't. That was a definite positive.

"I can tell you one thing." He turned his face toward her. In the shadows created by the sunlight shining from behind him, the only features visible in his face were the white teeth in his smile. "Knowing how to sleep in the woods and wake up refreshed isn't genetic."

"Do we ever camp together?" Lindsay asked.

"No. I'm not a happy camper. I like a soft bed and a roof over my head." He held out his hand to her. "Let's get out of the woods and go see the sheriff."

"The sheriff? Why?" She felt a return of uneasiness.

"He has his men keeping an eye out for you. He needs to know you've been found safe."

Talking about it brought back all her fears of yesterday. "Let's just go."

"We really need . . ."

In the closeness of the small enclosure, Lindsay suddenly felt confined . . . trapped. She scrambled from the shelter and stood in the open, drinking in the air like it was water, surveying the woods around her.

"I don't know who to trust. I just want to go home. I'm taking a chance trusting you."

"All right." John held up his hands in a gesture of surrender. "I'll call his office from down the road a ways. We don't have to see him." He extended his hand to her.

Lindsay stared at it for several moments before she took it, and they walked hand in hand out of the woods. Every few feet, she looked over her shoulder to see if the thing that cast a shadow over her sanity was pursuing them.

John squeezed her hand softly. "It'll be all right. You're safe now. I'll keep you safe."

"You don't know from what, and I'm not able to tell you."

"I will still keep you safe."

She hoped that it would be true. It didn't take long to leave the asylum of the woods. As they walked out into the open field, the dew-covered grass brushed her ankles and the dampness soaked into her socks. She shivered. How long could she have lived in the woods without turning wild, she wondered. With no memory and no resources, what would she have become—a forest creature, sitting on her haunches eating raw meat?

As they approached the row of converted offices, Lindsay spotted the midnight blue pickup parked on the street. It had dark tinted windows—good for escaping the town unseen. But if John West turned out to be a villain, no one could see her inside. She examined his profile. The movement of her head caught his attention, and he looked at her and smiled.

"We're out of the woods." He smiled again, as if that were a joke.

He took his remote from his jeans pocket and pointed it at the truck as they approached. Lindsay heard the clicks of the doors unlocking and wished he could point the remote at her and unlock her brain. Trying to remember was dizzying, frustrating—it made her want to cry. She climbed into the truck and slammed the door shut. John climbed into the driver's side.

"I need to call your brother and tell him you're safe and coming home." He reached for the cell phone mounted on the dashboard.

"Let's get out of town first."

He looked at her a moment. There was what might have been gentleness in his eyes. "All right." He started the truck. "Fasten your seat belt."

They were silent riding out of town, but Lindsay noticed John glancing over at her. What was he looking at . . . or watching for?

"I have to stop and get gas." He slowed down as they neared a convenience store.

"Why?"

"I'm almost empty." He pointed to the gauge.

"Can't we get farther out?"

"It'll be okay . . . nothing to be afraid of." He turned off the highway and drove up to the gas pumps. "I won't be long. You can sit in the truck with the doors locked."

Lindsay didn't take her eyes off him as he pumped the gas, and her gaze followed him to the store to pay. He looked relaxed. Everything seemed almost normal. But she lost sight of him after he went inside, and she felt panic swelling in her.

What if he doesn't come out? What if he calls the sheriff and they come and get me?

She broke her stare from the store and looked at the keys dangling from the ignition. She could take the truck and leave, get out of town fast, go someplace safe. Did she know how to drive? Surely, she did. John came out of the store carrying a sack and a couple of drinks, and she abandoned any thoughts of leaving him behind. She unlocked the door and he slid into the driver's seat, handing her a Dr Pepper.

"Do I like these?" She snapped the can open.

"Sure do."

Lindsay took a long drink. He was right about that. Another mark in his favor.

"I got you a sausage and biscuit." He handed her the paper bag.

The smells coming from the bag made her mouth water. How long had it been since she had eaten? Twenty-four hours? She pawed through the collection of other things John had bought: Reese's Cups, Moon Pies, and peanuts.

"Do I like all of these?"

"You like the candy. I like the Moon Pies." He took one from the bag and tore open the wrapper. "We both like the peanuts."

She unwrapped the sausage and biscuit and took a bite. "I'm glad I didn't have to catch and cook my breakfast."

"That doesn't bear thinking about." He followed a bite of Moon Pie with a long drink of Coke.

A car—familiar, like a roach or a snake is familiar—drove into her field of view and parked in front of the store. *Is this what John was waiting for? Is this why he chose this place to gas up the truck?*

She shook, wanting to throw open the door of the truck and run. But they would catch her. Right now they didn't even see her. Her faux fiancé got out of the car and hurried into the store, not even glancing in their direction.

She stole a glance at John. He started the truck and was putting it in gear, ready to ease away from the pumps. He seemed not to notice her would-be kidnappers. Maybe it was a coincidence that Mark Smith and the skinny man with the cornflower blue eyes showed up here, now, at this place.

Lindsay knew she should tell John who they were, but he would want to call the sheriff, and she couldn't chance it. Even if the sheriff wasn't in on whatever there was to be in on, they would all know she was here.

John was looking at her. "Are you all right? Are you sick?"

She shook her head. "I'm just anxious to go home, wherever that is, and sort myself out. Please, let's go." She lowered her head so she was not visible inside the truck as John drove onto the highway. It was a while before her pulse slowed and her stomach settled.

They rode in silence. They were all the way to Interstate 24, and Lindsay had eaten her sausage biscuit, the Reese's Cups, and the whole bag of peanuts before John spoke.

"I do need to call your brother. He's at your house waiting to hear something."

"I understand the reasoning." Food made her brave. She could think again. Maybe it would fuel her memory, too.

John punched a series of numbers into his car phone, put it to his ear, and started speaking almost immediately. Her brother must have been waiting by the phone.

"Sinjin, John here. She's fine. Like the doctor said, she doesn't remember anything. But she's okay. Yeah, I found her late yesterday, but couldn't call until now."

Lindsay could hear the relief in John's voice as he spoke.

"No, she doesn't know anyone. But small things seem to be coming back."

He paused and Lindsay could hear the distant voice on the other end. No words, but a voice. An unfamiliar voice.

"About four and a half or five hours. Hold the phone a moment. Lindsay, I'm going to have Sinjin call the sheriff in your county. He's someone who knows you. You trust him. We'll let him call the sheriff in Mac's Crossing and tell him you've been found and you're safe."

She nodded and listened to John explain things to her brother. *Sinjin's a strange name.* She wondered how he got it.

"Five hours? That long before we get there?" she asked.

"It's about 280 miles."

"I was a long way from home."

"Yes." John picked up the phone again. She fought the urge to put her hand on his to stop him.

"Who are you calling now?"

"I need to call Derrick. He's worried, too."

"You and I must have a very civilized relationship, for you to be so considerate of my old boyfriend."

"We do—as long as we aren't fighting about your work. Derrick's an all right guy."

John called Derrick and told him everything he had told her brother. He paused and handed the phone to her.

"He wants to talk to you. He understands you don't remember him."

Lindsay took the phone and put it to her ear, almost afraid to speak. "Hello?"

"Lindsay. I—I just wanted to hear your voice. John says you're well, except for—"

"I'm fine, except for a few bruises. Really. I'm sorry I worried everyone."

All these people, she thought, so worried for her, and she didn't know any of them. The conversation didn't last long. With no memory, there wasn't much to say. She replaced the phone and looked over at John, wondering what their relationship was like. He cared.

She believed that now. She heard the worry in his voice—unless he was really worried about her regaining her memory.

"What are you thinking?" he asked.

"Why do you ask?"

"You're sitting there staring at me. I just wondered if you trust me yet."

"Almost. I'm sorry I've brought everyone such anxiety. You say I've gotten into trouble before?"

He sighed and waved a hand in the air. "There have been times when you've been out doing what you do, and . . . if I had discovered you were really with another man, I'd have been relieved."

"Oh . . . I'm that bad at getting into trouble?"

He nodded. "You've been in deep trouble before—shot, kidnapped, stabbed, lost in a cave, lost at sea in a hurricane—all really frightening and dangerous things. But, as bad as those things were, you've always come through with your intellect intact, never lost your memory this way."

His jaw clinched and his grip tightened on the steering wheel. "The thing that worries me—really worries me this time—is what could have happened that was so terrible you don't want to remember?" He took her hand in his and looked at her. "It scares me. It scares me as much as when we discovered you were missing."

Chapter 5

LINDSAY WAS SNATCHED out of a disturbing dream by the bouncing of the truck. John had turned from the highway, and they were heading down an unpaved wooded lane. A strip of uncut grass grew in the center of the pastoral road between two narrow tracks worn bare by the travel of vehicle tires. The road seemed to disappear into a green wood ahead.

"Where are we?" she asked.

"Home. Your home. This is your property."

Home? It didn't look familiar, but it felt right. She rolled down the window and inhaled fresh woods smells. She wasn't frightened. Perhaps her memory was coming back after all, in parts, the sensory zones in her brain becoming unfrozen one at a time. The feelings—what she liked, disliked, feared, made her feel safe—maybe those feelings were truly hers, hers before the . . . before whatever happened.

"This is lovely. I live here?"

"It's yours, all right. Thirty-six beautiful acres."

He stopped the truck at a silver farm gate. Lindsay jumped out and opened it for him to drive through. Ahead of them was a wooden fence where a black horse pranced up and down the fence row, flagging his tail, talking to her in throaty rumbles and high-pitched whinnies, his ears listening for a sound from her.

She closed the gate and walked to the fence, drawn to the powerful horse. The huge stallion trotted to her and stood pawing the ground, shaking his head, his glossy mane shimmering and rippling with the motion, his big brown eyes fixed on her. His black coat was not the colorless black of darkness, or ink, but the blackness of a crow, or John's hair—with hues of dark blue and a shine that reflected in the sun. He talked to her in deep guttural tones. She stretched her hand out over the fence to him. He nuzzled her palm. His nose felt like fine velvet.

"That's Mandrake." John had gotten out of his truck and joined her at the fence. "He's your horse."

"I ride?"

"Quite well."

"All this is mine?"

"Yes. This is where you belong."

Where she belonged. Her place of mooring. What had John said when she asked him why he had hovered and watched over her every time they had stopped during the long trip back? He said he was staying close because one of the doctors had told him that people with amnesia are prone to wander off. With no memory, there is no place to dock. They're afloat in a perplexing, unfamiliar world with nothing or anyone to hold them.

Mandrake, in a burst of stallion energy, turned and galloped across the pasture. Was this where she was supposed to lay anchor and not drift away from?

John drove them down the quarter-mile-long winding driveway overhung by tall sheltering trees. This place was soothing and seductive. She felt safe for the first time within the span of her memory. Why didn't these woods frighten her? Did she remember home?

They crossed a creek and rounded a curve in the driveway, and ahead was a log house nestled among the trees. She looked hard at it, as if staring would bring out the memory of it. Nothing. She wanted to pound the dashboard with her fists in frustration, but she was afraid that acting crazy would be cause for John to take her away to someplace else.

Two people came out on the porch and rushed down the steps as they pulled to a stop in front of the house. A man a little older than she, and an attractive woman about her age.

"That's your brother, Sinjin," said John. "The woman is Harper Latham. She's a friend, the one I told you about."

A brother and a friend. Roots. Enough to hold her down? She

got out and walked toward them. *Strangers. Damn.* They were strangers—but only to her. She saw the keen look of concern in their eyes, as though they wanted as much as she to clear the fog from her mind.

"Lindsay." The man had short, chestnut-brown hair, the color of hers. His unshaven face, plaid shirt, and jeans made him look like a logger. He was taller than her by three or four inches—and she was tall, almost six feet. *Must have tall genes in the family.* He had blue eyes, too, but his were lighter, cooler than hers. Height, hair, and eye color were where the resemblance stopped. His facial features looked nothing like hers.

What if this was all a trick to get her to trust them and let her guard down? What if they were playing on her need to belong somewhere and feel safe?

"You're Sinjin?" she asked and saw a brief look of pain sweep across his face and disappear.

"Oh, Lindsay." Lindsay turned her attention to the woman, searching her hazel eyes for some sign of familiarity. Harper was five or six inches shorter than Lindsay with chin-length auburn hair and distinctive features. A memorable face. Why couldn't she recognize it? Or anyone? She hated the unrelenting unfamiliarity of virtually everything and everyone she met.

Sinjin stepped forward and put his hands on her shoulders as if she could recognize his touch. "Harper made a pot of chicken-and-vegetable soup. It smells really great. Why don't you come in and eat something?"

Lindsay nodded and walked with them up the steps to the cabin door. She stopped in the threshold and gazed at a painting of a woman from some past age looking over her shoulder at whoever enters this house. It had soothing, subtle hues. Had she selected it to welcome guests into her home, or to welcome herself after a hard day? She followed Sinjin into the living room, her eyes desperately searching for something familiar. The room was furnished with simple oak and leather furniture. A painting of Mandrake hung over a rock fireplace. Cozy, warm. She liked it. It rang no bells.

"I'd like to clean up first," she said, without looking at anyone.

Sinjin, John, and Harper exchanged glances before Harper spoke. "Shall I show you where your room is?"

Lindsay shook her head. "Let me try to find it." She walked back to the entrance hallway. There was a door opposite the living room and a staircase. *Which way? Fifty-fifty. Flip a coin?* She put a hand on the stair railing and forced herself not to look back for reassurance. She started up the stairs. Steep stairs. Had to be, with the narrow dog trot. *Dog trot? Where did that come from? A memory?*

No one said anything as she climbed, and she heard someone start up the stairs behind her. Up on the balcony, she looked down at John and Sinjin, still following her with their eyes. They smiled at her, relieved, perhaps, that she had chosen correctly. But then, there had been an even chance that she would. Maybe more than even. From the balcony it wasn't hard. There was only one door, and it led to a bedroom.

I have simple tastes, she thought as she looked at a quilt-covered white cedar bed in the corner of the room. There were a desk, a bookcase, a night stand, and a chest-of-drawers, all of white cedar. Atop the chest-of-drawers, across from the foot of the bed, sat a television—its remote control on the night stand. The room didn't have carpet, but shiny hardwood floors with green-and-white wool rugs. *It's good,* she thought. *I like it.*

"Why don't you look around your room?" suggested Harper. "Maybe something will tickle your memory. Come down when you're ready."

Lindsay nodded, still looking at the fan pattern in the bedspread, wondering if she had purchased the quilt or if someone in her family had made it. How odd it felt, almost dizzying, to be cut loose from all connections to the past. John said she had been an archaeologist. There must be some irony in that.

Harper left her alone. She stood for several moments staring at each piece of furniture in turn. Her gaze passed a closet. There first. An image out of the corner of her eye startled her as she opened the closet door—herself in the full-length mirror on the back of the door.

The closet contents were neatly arranged. Shoes were in little pigeon holes at the bottom. She squatted, pulling some of them out. Running shoes, loafers, heels—a few fairly high. Somehow that seemed odd. She didn't think of herself as the high-heeled shoe type. She stood and examined the clothes on the racks. Tweedy pantsuits, sweaters, and blouses seemed to be the preferred style. But there were also jeans and T-shirts.

Several garment bags hung near the end. She unzipped the first one. It contained a long-sleeved evening dress of blue silky material with a sequined bodice. Very elegant. The next bag held a short black dress with a full skirt and spaghetti straps, along with an almost identical red one, only with rhinestone-festooned straps. So, what was she before she became an archaeologist, a hooker? Her mind went back to the little lavender number her faux-fiancé had wanted her to wear. Maybe he knew her better than she had imagined.

She shivered, closed the closet door, and sat on the bed, frustrated at not being able to remember. But, more distressing than the inability to remember was the fear flowing through her like slow-moving hot lava, turning her insides to raw nerves. She squeezed her eyes shut to stop the tears that were about to erupt. When she opened them, her gaze rested on the bookshelf. Another place to mine for memories.

Most of the books were about archaeology and physical anthropology, but on the bottom shelf was a neat stack of photo albums. Recorded memory cells. Lindsay grabbed the top one and flipped through the pages. The photos were of a dig—one in the ocean—inside some structure built in the water. There were several photographs of John and some of Harper. They filled her with relief. *John and Harper are who they say they are.* She rushed over to a collection of framed photographs on the back corner of her desk. Strangers, except for one: Sinjin with his arm around her shoulders. Safe. Here was a safe place.

Lindsay pulled another album from the stack. Another archaeology site. Her eyes darted from one photograph to another, looking for things she recognized. She stopped at a group of guys shoveling. *Shovel shaving,* her mind said so clearly it was almost aloud. A memory. Her joy at having a real memory was short-lived, as hot black fear flooded her stomach, making her drop the album. Something about the photo. She sat bent over for several seconds before she picked up the album and returned it to the shelf.

She made her way to the bathroom to the shower.

It felt good to be clean. Good to have seen photographs of John, Sinjin, and Harper. But the guy, Mark Smith, who said he was her fiancé, had a photograph, too. These could be doctored like that one. "No!" she shouted, "I've got to have a safe place with no doubts."

"Lindsay? Are you all right?" It was Harper knocking on the door.

"I'm fine. I'll be right down." *Harper must think I'm crazy.*

"No hurry. I just came up to check."

She dressed in jeans and a sweatshirt and hurried downstairs to be greeted by the aroma of chicken soup. They were all standing in the kitchen. If Harper had told them Lindsay had been talking to herself, they showed no sign of knowing it.

"You look better." Sinjin touched her hand as she passed.

"I feel a lot better. I had a memory fragment," she said. They all looked up at her, wide-eyed and hopeful.

"Not much. Shovel shaving. I saw a picture in one of the albums, and I knew what they were doing."

"That's great," said Harper, smiling as if she had said she had invented penicillin while she was showering.

"It's not much, though," repeated Lindsay.

"It's something." John pulled back a chair for her at the table. "I think you've been having quite a few."

They sat down at the table that Harper had prepared with four bowls of her homemade chicken-and-vegetable soup and a large round of flat bread sitting in the middle between them. Lindsay took a spoonful of soup—warm, comfort food. Perhaps this was all she would need to get well. Food and home.

"You have an appointment tomorrow with a neuropsychiatrist," said Sinjin.

Lindsay nodded. "They treat people who have lost their mind?"

"You haven't lost your mind," he said, a little too emphatically, Lindsay thought.

"Perhaps not *lost,* but I've certainly seriously misplaced it."

They all laughed. "Your personality is intact," said John, tearing off a piece of the bread.

Fry bread, Lindsay thought. John must have made it. *Now, how did I know that? Another memory association?*

Harper left not long after they had washed the dishes. She kissed Lindsay on the cheek. "Call if you need me. I won't be leaving for Spain for about a month."

"Thanks for being here. I'm sorry I don't remember you."

"All the research says you'll remember in a few days." She smiled. "You're a very research-oriented person, so that should fill you with hope."

Lindsay watched from the porch as Harper drove down the long driveway.

"Maybe you should go through all the albums," suggested Sinjin. The three of them sat on the porch looking out over Lindsay's woods.

She nodded, but was a little afraid. What if she should see something that scared her again? She wanted to stay away from that.

"Is that the stable down there?"

"Yes. I'll be staying there tonight. John can have the guest room."

"I'll stay in the stable," offered John.

"Wait," interrupted Lindsay. "Neither of you should have to sleep in the barn, for heaven's sake. Can't someone sleep on the couch?"

Sinjin laughed. "You have a bedroom with all the amenities in the stable, in case you have to stay all night with Mandrake. It's quite comfortable."

"I sometimes sleep with my horse?"

"If he's sick. You're very fond of him, and he's very valuable. Ellen, your mother, would have your hide if anything happened to him."

"My mother, not yours?"

Sinjin shook his head. "I'm your half brother."

Lindsay felt a stab of disappointment. She didn't know why. It must have shown on her face, for Sinjin grabbed both her hands.

"But we're close. I'm going to stay here until you're recovered. So is John."

John nodded. "You have lots of friends. They'll visit you when you're ready. Many people want you to get better."

But there are a few who don't, thought Lindsay.

She went to bed early, bidding John and Sinjin good night from the stairs. She found a nightshirt in the chest-of-drawers and settled into what felt like a down mattress.

She awoke just as the sun was coming up, while it was still twilight outside. She dressed and started down the stairs. The smell of bacon, fried apples, and hot bread rose from the depth of her house. *John?* She grinned and bounded downstairs.

"Sinjin, John." She was still grinning as she walked into the kitchen. "My two main men. What a nice surprise. What are you doing here?"

They both stared at her.

"What?" she said. "Did I forget to put my clothes on?"

"You recognize us?" asked Sinjin.

"Yes, of course." She laughed. "Are you supposed to be disguised?"

John raced over to her and put his arms around her, picking her up off the floor and kissing her. Sinjin dropped the skillet on the counter and it skittered across the surface, knocking a potted plant to the floor, breaking the clay pot and scattering the dirt and plant.

"Oh, I'm sorry . . ." Sinjin went for a broom.

Lindsay squatted, taking the plant and root ball into her hands. "It's all right."

The smell of fresh damp earth saturated her senses until it was the only aroma in the room—as if the room were filled with freshly dug soil. Her heart pounded. She dropped the plant and stared at the black dirt on her hands. She backed away and crouched in the corner, shaking.

"What, Lindsay? What?" John and Sinjin came to her, squatting in front of her, pulling her hands away from her face.

Lindsay took great gulps of air and wiped the back of her hand across her mouth, as if that would make her breathe easier.

"They tried to kill me. They thought they had. They buried me in a hole in the ground. Oh, God, they buried me alive."

PART II

◆ July 5 ◆

Chapter 6

LINDSAY STOOD NEAR Helget Pond surveying the site, a patchwork of square holes dug out of a grassy landscape, each revealing various arrangements of rocks and other unearthed objects. Like detectives studying a crime scene, archaeologists reconstruct past events using only what is left: those things that are not destroyed, or fail to rot or erode, or that get left in some protected place, or are cherished and passed down through the generations. Those things are the only clues, presenting the archaeologist, like the detective, with the challenge of turning biased data into a representative truth. Now, with only scattered parts of foundations remaining, the Gallows farmstead looked as if it had been constructed entirely from rocks. The buildings, the house, barns, fences, corncribs, smokehouse, and springhouse actually had been built from large hewn timbers cut from the surrounding forest. Only the foundations and chimneys were made of stone.

Lindsay took a long drink of water from her water bottle, then poured some of it over her head and let the cool drops trickle down her healed face. She looked longingly to the east where but a few hundred yards away the forest was still as thick, lush, and cool as it had been almost 170 years ago when this farmstead was settled. Directly east were the Great Smoky Mountains, Lindsay's favorite place in the world, heaven-on-earth, a place where Francisco Lewis, head of the Division of Archaeology and Anthropology, thought Lindsay could rest and heal.

"After all," he reminded her, "you were planning to spend a few days for me at the Gallows site anyway, before . . ." *Before. . . before the incident . . . a mere three months ago . . . it seemed like a lifetime . . . it seemed like yesterday.*

Like everyone else, Lewis had let what happened to Lindsay go unnamed. It was just as well. Easier not to think about if it didn't have a name—only a number on an open case file that was at a dead end. Dead end. That almost described her, if things had been a little different.

But if Lewis had thought a stay at the Gallows farmstead was going to be restful, it was because he hadn't met the site director, Claire Burke, who at that moment was bearing down on Lindsay like an angry goat. Lindsay had a strong urge to run for the cover of the forest. She could make it, too; her legs were longer. But she was saved when Claire caught site of Adam Sterling and veered toward him as if he were a Claire magnet.

"What are you doing?" Her words were clipped like small bursts of machine-gun fire. "Not what I told you to do." *Ratta tat tat.*

"This site's older than we thought, dammit." Like everyone else, Adam's tolerance for Claire's dictatorial ways was wearing thin. "This trench needs to be deeper. Look at this pit profile. I'm not to the bottom."

Lindsay could hear his loud voice even where she was. He stood, holding his shovel in one hand, sweat dripping from his face and arms. Byron Rogers, looking hot and red-faced behind his long beard, climbed out of the shallow trench from behind Adam and lumbered toward the water barrel, eager to take a break while Claire and Adam went a round.

"You're wasting time and money. It's not older." Claire scowled. "You've read the proposal, or you should have. We have clear documentation of the age of the farmstead. And that looks like pit bottom to me. Now you'll do what I say, or you can find . . . "

". . . a job elsewhere," Lindsay whispered to herself. She'd heard Claire's threat many times.

"Documentation, shit. Marina identified clay pipes and salt-glazed stoneware that she said . . ."

"A couple of artifacts from an older period mean nothing. They could have been family heirlooms."

Adam's teeth were clenched and his muscles taut. "Claire, I know how to read a profile. I know what I'm doing. I'm not some freshman who wants to be an archaeologist, and I don't make stupid mistakes."

Lindsay saw Erin look up at Adam from her digging, probably feeling the sting of his words. Sharon looked up briefly and continued to work. Bill, her husband, stopped and listened. Joel, absorbed as always in what he was doing, never looked up.

As much as she hated to, Lindsay felt compelled to intervene. She set her water bottle down and walked over to Adam and Claire. *I'm a glutton for punishment,* she thought to herself.

"And what do you want?" Claire snapped before Lindsay could speak. "To give us wisdom from on high? I think we can do without advice from someone still recovering from a nervous breakdown."

"I didn't have a nervous breakdown. I think proof of that is my ability to stay here. Claire, what Adam is doing is not unreasonable. He's right about the parameters of the pit. The layers are subtle, but they are there. Why don't you talk to Drew? You and she might want to look at the artifacts Marina has identified and . . ."

"I'm not changing the research design in the middle of the excavation."

Adam threw his trowel down and it stuck up like a knife in the bottom of the trench. "Claire, are you really that dumb? I'm not talking about changing the research design. I'm talking about following it. Jesus, Claire, what does it take to get through to you?"

If the daggers in Claire's eyes had been real, Adam would be bleeding. She worked her mouth back and forth, as if her tongue was looking for words. "Don't you ever . . ."

"Come on, Claire," interrupted Lindsay, "you know the design has to be flexible enough to incorporate new information."

"Listen, Miss High-and-Mighty, when you university archaeologists get multimillion-dollar grants to dig sites, you have time for extras. But in contract archaeology, we have to be lean and efficient."

"And accurate."

"There's nothing inaccurate about my work." She turned to Adam. "It's my way or the highway, smartass."

"I have a contract," he said.

"Which says you'll do what you're told." Claire turned on Lindsay again. "Do you think you're levelheaded enough to map Structure 6?"

"Yes, I can do that. But Erin has found a cache of animal bones, perhaps I could . . ."

Claire's chin was raised in the air. A sign she wasn't to be moved. "We don't need you at this site. You're here because Drew says we have to take you—some kind of favor. But I don't have to give you *any* assignments. You can either map Structure 6, or you can go take a nap at the house. Which will it be?"

"Structure 6 it is then," said Lindsay.

Claire smiled at her victory, turned on her heels, her chin still in the air, and headed toward the artifact tent, probably to have it out with Marina. Adam dropped the shovel and raised his middle finger at her retreating back.

"This site is a pile of shit," Adam said to Lindsay.

Lindsay looked in the ditch, and felt dizzy. She sat down and forced herself to take hold of the shovel that leaned against the side of the ditch. Dark images were trying to break into her consciousness. She closed her eyes. Person or persons unknown weren't going to take away her love of archaeology. She wouldn't allow it. She forced her vision to clear.

"The excavation is really not bad," she said. "You guys are doing a good job."

"Thanks, but you know . . ." He heaved a heavy sigh. "It doesn't matter."

"Claire seems to bring out the worst in all of us," Lindsay said.

"What is this nervous breakdown business?" Adam took up his trowel and began scraping the sides of the trench smooth.

"On the way home from Knoxville three months ago I was attacked and left to die in the woods. I was without my memory for several days. It was amnesia due to trauma, not a nervous breakdown. I think the attack might have been some kind of serial thing." She waved her hand as if that got rid of it.

Adam's jaw dropped. "You serious?"

Her friend Harper, John, her brother, all told Lindsay she was denying what had happened, pushing it too far back in her brain.

But far back was where it belonged. *Don't unpack that trunk, leave it in the attic,* she told herself every time her mind wandered in that direction and threatened to pull the memories to the surface.

"I don't know much about what happened. The case is still open, and I'm leaving it to the police."

"What the heck are you doing here in archaeology hell?"

"Francisco Lewis knows I like the Smokies. He thought it would be restful."

Adam gave a short laugh. "Restful? Restful would be excavating in a minefield. Rumor says you're here gathering information for the company on how we're doing."

"If that were true, I think Claire would treat me better."

"You don't know her."

"Lewis wanted me to come take a look several months ago. The president of Sound Ecology is a friend of his. But I wasn't given instructions to spy. I think Lewis just wants to know about the site. He likes to get his fingers in everything. As if building a museum isn't enough, now he's decided he's interested in farmsteads."

"I've heard that about him. What's he really like?"

Lindsay shrugged. "Probably like the rumors you've heard. He denies nothing. Actually, I'm thinking about cutting this vacation short. I'm not needed here, and I'm kind of tired of putting up with Claire's abuse."

"I don't blame you. But when Drew's here, things are better. She's the only person Claire will listen to. Probably because Drew has the power to fire her butt."

"When is Drew coming?"

"This week, I hope. She's principal investigator on several of the Sound Ecology sites, and some of the others are more urgent because they're due to be flooded soon." Adam stood back and looked at the ditch bank in front of him. "What about it? Should I continue with this profile?"

Against Claire's wishes? Lindsay thought. She wished the crew wouldn't keep asking her advice. It only made Claire worse.

"You aren't to the bottom of this feature." She sat on her haunches and pointed toward the bottom layers of dirt. "This layer's simply interrupted by soil of a similar color and texture as the pit wall. But it's different. There's been some kind of soil disturbance into which layers of rubble were added over the years."

"I think so, too." He glanced toward the tent. "I guess, I'd better take it up with Drew. If she ever shows up."

The rumble of an engine approaching nearby brought their heads up toward the sound.

"Hey, what the hell are you doing?" shouted Adam, jumping up as a big red pickup truck drove across the site, its giant tires rolling over and crushing into the ground a corner of Feature 3. The front of the truck stopped at his trench.

Lindsay heard another voice screaming in the distance. Claire was flying across the site like a banshee. Lindsay stood staring, amazed, as a short, square, potbellied man with a receding hairline and black mustache climbed down from the truck with a folded piece of paper in his hand.

"You're destroying valuable artifacts," yelled Adam. "Are you crazy?"

"Who the hell are you, you sorry bastard? Get that truck . . ." Claire stopped. Even she was at a loss for words.

The man marched over to Lindsay and handed her the paper.

"Drew Van Horne, this is for you."

"I'm not . . ."

"I've been parked over in the woods watching, girly. You're obviously in charge, and you're obviously the illusive Miss Drew. Consider yourself served."

"But I'm not . . ."

He turned to go, but while he was talking to Lindsay, Claire had climbed into his truck and now began backing slowly out of the excavation in the least damaging path.

"What? Hey!" he shouted, running after the truck.

But Claire made it to the dirt road and took off, disappearing in a cloud of dust. Lindsay watched in surprised admiration. The man, whoever he was, stood in the middle of the site waving his arms.

"That bitch stole my truck! That bitch stole my truck!"

Chapter 7

"WHO WAS THAT?" The little potbellied man looked from one to the other, as if all the crew were in a conspiracy against him. "Is she going to bring my truck back?"

"I don't know," Lindsay told him. "I was too busy trying to figure out how even a casual observer could think I'm in charge here."

He turned to Adam—who was still dumbstruck and staring openmouthed at the dust settling on the road—and demanded that Adam tell him who took his truck.

"I don't know, either," said Adam. "I was concentrating on what kind of moron would drive a big-foot pickup across an archaeological excavation. Do you know what you've done?"

He looked around at the ground. "Rocks and holes, just rocks and holes."

"No, not rocks and holes," Adam shouted. "History, delicate history preserved in the ground—probably your history—and you've destroyed a portion of it."

"Where's she taking my truck?"

"Are you listening?" asked Adam. "Your truck isn't nearly as important as this site. You understand that?"

"If she damages my truck, you all are going to have to pay for it."

"We'll deduct it from what you owe for damages to the site," said Lindsay.

"I don't owe you nothing. It's just rocks and holes, dammit. I'm not going to pay for rocks and holes."

Lindsay ignored his protestations and scanned the legal papers she'd been "served." Drew was being sued by an Alfred Tidwell for the wrongful death of his aunt Mary Susan Tidwell, and she was accused of stealing valuable documents belonging to the Tidwell estate. That answered why Drew was so scarce. She was avoiding a process server. Lindsay had been at the site for a week and hadn't once seen the principal investigator.

While she was reading the summons, Adam had managed to learn that the fuming little man was Broach Moore, a bounty hunter, process server, and repo man.

"Here," Lindsay said, shoving the papers back at him. "I'm not Dr. Drew Van Horne. I'm Dr. Lindsay Chamberlain. And don't you ever call me girly again."

"Let me see some identification."

"No."

"Then you keep these papers."

"Fine, I'll deliver them to the sheriff tomorrow and let him deal with it. I *will* show *him* ID."

"You're really not Drew Van Horne?"

"No. I'm not." Lindsay turned her back and walked over to Feature 3 to see what kind of damage he had done.

"Hey!" he shouted at Lindsay. "How am I going to get back to my office?"

"You should have thought of that before you came," said Adam.

"I did. I brought my truck. I need to use the phone."

"Highway 129's down that dirt road. I'm sure you can find a lift," said Adam.

"I'm not walking back."

"Suit yourself. I'm sure we can find you a room in the house."

"I'm not staying in that house."

Lindsay ignored the bits of conversation and surveyed the damage to the scattered stones. At least two large flat stones were broken and others had plowed a three-foot-long furrow in the dirt from the force of the big truck tires. The air was filled with the aroma of fresh earth released by the disturbance to the soil. A shadow moved across the feature, and Lindsay looked up to see tall, willowy Erin joining her in examining the damage.

"Do you have . . ." Lindsay hesitated, searching for the word. ". . . drawings . . . drawings or photographs? I don't recall seeing anyone working on this feature since I've been here."

"No drawings. Claire said drawings would be redundant. I'm an artist. I was hoping to be able to do some drawings here, but it seems that we are overrun with artists—Marina, Joel, and now me. And Claire doesn't even want drawings." Erin paused a moment and looked wistfully over at the artifact tent and then at the south end of the site. "Marina does the photography. She sometimes lets me do some artifact drawing with her. She's taught me a lot about artifact illustration. She's done textbooks and everything."

"Has Marina taken photos of this section?"

"I don't know. I haven't seen any of the pictures."

Erin lowered her voice to a whisper. "What's Claire going to do with the truck?"

"She'll probably park it out of sight down the road and walk back to the house. Isn't that guy . . . Trent working on this feature? Where is he?"

"He's sick today."

Stoned, thought Lindsay. "How about the crew members working on it with him? Where are they?"

"Claire found another structure in the woods. She put them on that, I think." Erin nodded in the direction of the tree line. She shook her head. "I really thought archaeology would be different from this. I mean, I really wanted to be an archaeologist."

"I've never worked on a site with as much hostility as this one," said Lindsay. "Most digs aren't like this."

"Is it because it's a private company?"

"No, it's not that. I've consulted with several private archaeology companies. None have been like this one."

Claire was part of the problem, thought Lindsay, her controlling, abusive personality. But there was something else about this site that Lindsay couldn't put her finger on, and it troubled her. It was as if some evil hung in the air. Something that made the wind rush hard through the trees, whipping the crowns back and forth. Something that brought the darkness with it. Lindsay heard the blood rushing in her ears with each beat of her heart. She turned and looked at the forest. There was no wind in the trees, and it surprised her. Was the storm she felt in her mind, hovering on the edge of her sanity? *Don't think about it,* she said to herself. *Ignore it and it will go away. Don't build it and they won't come.*

"Don't judge archaeology by this experience."

"I'll keep reminding myself." Erin tapped one of the rocks with her fingers."What is this, do you think?"

Lindsay stood and stepped back, looking at the area. Only a portion of the feature was excavated. The several wooden stumps, frequently used as lunch tables by the crew, were from trees that had been cut down only a few years before. Here and there bunches of long, slender daffodil leaves stood above the grass and weeds. She noticed a thorny, long-stemmed shrub low on the ground, and picked out several more scattered about. Lindsay stepped back again.

"I believe it's a cemetery."

"A cemetery? The documents we have say the family is buried at Wild Grape Hollow Cemetery at the Primitive Baptist Church."

"Look at the berm around the feature." Lindsay indicated a gently raised strip of ground.

"I see it. Kind of like the mounded earth around the barn," said Erin.

Lindsay nodded. "The kind of berm made by years of dirt washing against a fence. I think this feature was fenced in. It also has daffodils and antique roses."

"But flowers wouldn't be here from that long ago, would they? The records date back over a hundred years, and they make no mention of a graveyard. It would have been abandoned more than a hundred years ago," objected Erin.

"That doesn't matter. Antique roses and daffodils are hardy plants. They sustain themselves indefinitely. There's another indication, too. There's been a copse of trees on this spot for a long time. It's not uncommon that local people know of the presence of a graveyard, even when who's buried in it is long forgotten. When the surrounding timber is cut, the trees in a graveyard are always left standing. You can drive through the countryside and see little stands of tall trees alone on hilltops when the rest of the countryside has been clear-cut. Those are old cemetery sites that the loggers won't cut. I think this was one of those sites."

"But who would be buried here?"

Lindsay shrugged. "Some members of the family who didn't get themselves buried in Wild Grape Cemetery. Were the Gallowses slaveholders?"

"I don't think so."

"When it's excavated, we may find some stones that will tell something."

"Actually, I'm not sure it will be excavated. I think maybe Claire is cutting this area from the plan." Erin pulled a small twig from one of the antique rose vines.

"So much for not changing a design in the middle of a dig. I think I'll be glad to be leaving this place."

"Oh, no. Don't tell me that. You're the only nice person here. You, Marina, and Mrs. Laurens."

"I'm clearly unwelcome and, frankly, my abilities are being purposefully wasted."

"Hey, man, what's going on?"

Before Lindsay turned around, she caught a whiff of beer and body odor. Trent Rich approached them, looking as if he had just risen from his bed after a two-week drunk without changing, showering, or even combing his hair. He sniffed and wiped his nose on his bare forearm, then wiped his arm on his cutoffs. Lindsay and Erin stepped away from him.

"Getting a cold, man. I feel awful. Who's that guy over there?"

His eyes were so bloodshot, Lindsay was surprised he could see out of them.

"Someone looking for Drew," offered Erin.

"Well, good luck to him. What happened here?" Trent stared at the damage to Feature 3.

"He drove his truck over it," said Lindsay. "Do you have photographs of the feature?"

"Me? I just got here."

"No. I mean before it was damaged."

"No, it's not finished." Trent looked around. "Where's his truck?"

"Claire stole it," said Erin.

"Hey, way to go, Claire!"

"Trent," said Lindsay, "you don't look well. Why don't you go back to bed? We'll explain to Claire how bad you look."

"It's tempting, but I gotta earn my pay. Where's my crew?"

Erin pointed to the woods where the Adonis twins—as she and Kelsey sometimes called tall, blond, long-haired Powell Gavin and his short-haired blond brother, Dillon—were digging.

"They're working on another structure," said Erin.

"The woods, huh?" He eyed the area suspiciously. "I just hate this jungle, don't you? Maybe it's cooler over there." Trent caught site of his crew and ambled over in their direction.

"Is he on drugs?" asked Erin.

"It would be my guess," said Lindsay. "I'm taking a break—I'll be back in a few minutes."

Lindsay started for the house where her new Explorer was parked.

I must be in a coma and this is a nightmare, she thought. *No. I'm probably dead and this is hell. I was sent here for digging up John's ancestors.*

The thought of spending an eternity at this site was almost too dark a punishment to imagine. Why in the world had Lewis wanted her to come here in the first place? Then it hit her. Of course.

She doubled her speed, racing across a small bridge spanning the creek that fed Helget Pond and to the parking lot. She punched the number code into the keypad on the driver's door of her Explorer, opened the door, and climbed in. Fortunately, the cell phone had a good signal. She dialed the number for the UGA Division of Anthropology and Archaeology, muttering under her breath and drumming her fingers on the steering wheel as she waited for an answer. Kate, the division secretary, answered the phone.

"Kate. I want to speak to Lewis, now."

"Is this Lindsay? How you doing? I think Dr. Lewis is with someone . . ."

"I don't care if he's with the President, I want to speak with him."

"Uh-oh, what's he done now?"

"Sent me here."

As Lindsay talked, she caught sight of Marina Ethridge on the front porch talking to someone in the shadows.

"Lindsay." The too cheerful voice came over the phone. "What can I do for you?"

"Lewis, did you send me here to investigate a crime?"

Chapter 8

"HAVE YOU FOUND a crime?" Lewis asked.

Lindsay could imagine him sitting behind his polished French provincial desk trying to look innocent. She was in no mood for it.

"Let's not fence, Lewis. A woman's family is accusing Drew of murder and theft. You must have known about it when you first suggested I spend time up here."

"Yes, I did. Keith York and I were in school together. His company, Sound Ecology, could be held liable if, well . . ."

"If one of his employees committed murder?"

"Or stole something. I don't really think she killed anyone. Even the authorities say it was a heart attack. The woman was old, with a history of heart disease and two previous heart attacks. Keith is worried mainly about the accusation of theft."

"And you told him, 'No problem, one of my faculty members is a detective.'"

"That, and that he would be getting an expert at the department's expense. They have made use of your talents there, haven't they?"

"Yes, as the village idiot. Look, Lewis, they don't want me here. They don't like me, and I've had more restful times in faculty meetings."

As Lindsay talked, she watched the conversation, or at least one side of it, going on between Marina on the front porch and someone in the shadows. Marina gestured with some intensity. The person stepped for a moment into the sunlight. It was a woman Lindsay didn't recognize, possibly the elusive Drew. Whoever it was stepped back out of sight again.

"I know you love the Smokies," Lewis was saying in her ear.

"Yes, I do, and I can enjoy them without working here. I just called to tell you I'm quitting."

"I wish you wouldn't. Just as a favor to me, find out if there is anything to the accusations. You don't have to do any real detective work. Just talk to the sheriff and a few people. You're good at that, and you know those law enforcement types."

From her rearview mirror, Lindsay saw Broach Moore in the distance, ambling toward the house, his hands in his pockets.

"I'll give it a week, and if I'm not having fun, I'm leaving this place."

"I knew I could count on you. What quality of work are they doing?"

"I don't like to critique another archaeologist's work."

"What do you mean? You do that all the time. I just read a letter by you in *American Antiquity . . .*"

"That was different. I wasn't spying on them."

"York is hearing some rumors about that site."

"If it's important to him, tell him to get his butt down here and take a look for himself."

"He can't. Is Drew doing a fair job?"

"It's not being excavated the way I'd do it, but it's not bad . . . yet. I'd fire a couple of people and sit the site director down and have a talk with her. By the way, I've never met Drew. She's been conspicuously absent . . . avoiding a process server."

"Indeed? Can you find out about that?" Lindsay didn't need to ignore the question, for Lewis continued on as if she had agreed. "The site's had a frequent turnover of staff from the very beginning."

"I'm not surprised."

She watched Moore crossing the bridge. He stopped and looked over the side at the water below. He seemed reluctant to cross. Maybe he was looking for a troll, she thought.

"The site director is one of the most unpleasant people I've ever worked with."

"You're good with unpleasant people. Is there anything you need?"

Lindsay rolled her eyes. "I'd like to read the proposal and look at the historical documents."

"They won't let you? Do you want me to call—"

"No. I'll work it out. As I said. I'm only giving it a week."

"Fair enough. Call if you need anything."

"Sure."

Lindsay put the phone back in its cradle and got out of the Explorer. The sound of the door closing brought Marina's head around. She saw Moore on the bridge and pushed whoever she was talking to farther into the shadows. It had to be Drew. Lindsay stepped in front of Moore, blocking his path.

"I assume that you still need a ride to town." Lindsay reopened the driver's-side door and started to get in.

"I need my truck."

"Then, you don't need a ride to town?" She started to get back out.

"Yes—wait—yes. You'll take me?"

"Hop in."

He climbed in and settled into the seat. Lindsay started the engine before he had a chance to change his mind, or catch site of anyone on the porch.

"I'm going to report my truck stolen."

"I doubt it's been stolen." Lindsay drove out of the gravel parking area and over the bridge. "It's probably parked somewhere where it can't do any more damage. And before you say it was only rocks and holes, it wasn't. That's like saying the original Declaration of Independence is only paper. You may not understand it or care, but we get information from what we're finding in those holes. The kind of rocks those are and how they are placed, plus their shapes and sizes, tell us how foundations were built here a hundred years ago, the size of the structures, and if the materials were hauled in, quarried nearby, or were simply found at the site. And rocks aren't the only thing. Just under the surface there are bones, dish sherds, and the remains of farm implements."

"I'll bet you're a lot of fun at a party. Look, lady, you're right. I don't appreciate what you all are doing. I appreciate my truck. It cost me $35,000."

Having recently had to purchase a new vehicle herself, Lindsay was sympathetic, but not enough to stop trying to press her point home.

"And that may have been a cemetery you drove over. You may have broken irreplaceable headstones with inscriptions."

Moore looked at Lindsay wide-eyed. "A cemetery. Oh, damn." He shook his head back and forth. "Oh damn. What the hell are you all doing digging in a cemetery?"

"We're identifying all the features of the farmstead that used to be here. And I don't know that it was a cemetery. It may have been."

"You going to disturb the dead?"

Lindsay regretted saying anything. She only wanted to make him understand the impact of his behavior, and now she may have simply made it worse.

"I just said it might be. I don't know. If we find gravestones, we'll probably leave it alone."

"You'd better. Living in Gallows House and digging up the dead to boot . . . I wouldn't want to be in your shoes. No, sirree, that's just asking for trouble."

"What about the house?"

"It's haunted. Everybody knows that. That's why Cal Strickland can't sell it—How long you say you been here?"

"Just a few days."

"Maybe you ain't heard or seen nothing yet, but I'll guarantee you, before the month's out, something'll happen that'll make you wish you was someplace else."

I wish that already, thought Lindsay. The single-lane dirt road leading from Knave's Seat Cove was shaded by the dense crowns of old hardwoods. After a mile it widened to two lanes and the heavy forest thinned out to a sparser woods. She drove on about five miles before the dirt road intersected with Highway 129.

"I'm taking you to Kelley's Chase."

"That's fine. There's a diner on the way owned by my cousin. I'll borrow her car. I'll tell you when to stop."

"Why do people say the Gallows House is haunted?"

Lindsay liked the ride into Kelley's Chase. She enjoyed looking at the peaceful, cool waters of the Little Tennessee River running alongside the highway and the mountains rising from the bank on the other side. It reminded her of the poem *Hiawatha*.

"Because it is. You watch the road and not the scenery."

"Have you ever seen anything?"

"In the house? Not me. I won't go near the place, leastwise at night. Didn't want to today."

"How do you know it's haunted?"

"Everybody knows. People's seen things in that cove for over a hundred years."

"The house is about a hundred years old. Are you saying the ghosts predate the house?"

"I'm saying it's a bad place."

"How do you think it got that way?"

"Some people say the cove's an Indian burial ground."

"I've worked on many Indian burials and have never witnessed anything supernatural."

Moore looked over at Lindsay, a frown on his face. "It's best to leave the dead alone."

"You haven't told me what people have seen at the house."

"Some's seen strange mists."

"This is the Smoky Mountains."

"You've got a point there. I'll have to give you that. Mostly, people has heard noises—tapping sounds, footsteps with no body attached to them."

They drove through a road cut, a profile showing layers of folded rock strata—millions of years of geological history displayed in one slice. Almost like going back in time. *That's what archaeologists do,* Lindsay mused to herself, *go back in time.*

"Old houses make strange noises," she said.

"They do, but settling sounds are different from what people say they've heard. Bad things happen to people who live there."

"Like what?"

"Death. Can't get any worse than that."

"All people die. I doubt if there is a greater number of deaths associated with the house than with other hundred-year-old houses."

"It's not just the house, it's the whole cove. The house just had the misfortune of being built there."

"What do you think it is about the cove?"

"Ghosts coming out of the fourth dimension."

Lindsay was silent a moment. "Fourth dimension? Are you putting me on?"

"No. It's all around us. They can see us, but we can't see them. Heard it on Public Radio. You don't know about the fourth dimension?"

"No."

"I listen to NPR during lunch sometime. Real interesting, but it can get kind of far out. They had this scientist on the same program talking about chaos theory. Boils down to 'one thing leads to another.' They had to have a rocket scientist to figure that out? You know anything about chaos theory?"

"No."

"For a scientist, you don't know much, do you?"

Lindsay sighed. "I guess not. I know about bones," she said in her defense.

"Bones?"

"I'm a forensic anthropologist as well as an archaeologist."

"Is that right? I've never seen you on the Discovery Channel."

"We can't all be in the limelight. Why does Alfred Tidwell think Drew had something to do with his aunt's death?"

"Why you asking me?"

"That was what was in the subpoena."

"I never look at them. I just deliver them."

"Did you know Mary Tidwell?"

"Met her once. Crazy old lady. Bought a kid-goat from Jeb Simpson up at Calderwood and wouldn't pay for it. I was supposed to repossess it. Borrowed my brother's old truck and went to her place expecting a little goat," Moore said, gesturing with a hand held above the floor of Lindsay's SUV.

"Damn thing was as big as a cow. Never knew they got that big. Had horns that long." He demonstrated with his hands a size that Lindsay was sure was exaggerated. "Had eyes as red as the devil's. He stomped, spit, reared like a horse, and then peed on his beard. I couldn't get back to my truck fast enough, and that old lady cackling at me all the way like it was the funniest thing she'd ever seen." Moore stopped and laughed. "I guess it was."

Lindsay laughed with him. "Must have been a Nubian?"

"No, she was a white woman."

"No, a Nubian goat. I think males can get quite large. My vet has a huge one like that."

"He was large all right. A regular Billy Goat Gruff." *He was looking for a troll under the bridge,* Lindsay thought with a smile. "I decided right then, I wasn't gonna repo no more animals."

"Do you know if she had a lot of valuables?"

"You interrogating me?"

"Yes."

He nodded. "Thought so. That's all right. I might need a forensic person someday. Couldn't tell if she had anything that might be considered valuable. Might have. She was a hoarder, from the looks of the place. Yard like a junkyard. She didn't look rich herself, but you never know what some folks hide in their mattresses."

"Is the sheriff in this county a good person to talk to?"

"Can be. You investigating her death?"

Lindsay thought a minute, unsure of how she was going to explain her interest. "Anytime serious accusations are made against an archaeologist, it's looked into."

"You guys have some kind of union for that kind of thing?"

"Not exactly. I'm just interested in the truth."

"Uh-huh."

"The site employs a lot of people."

"I gotcha. You working for the people who's paying the money?"

"No . . . look . . ."

He waved a hand. "That's all right. I understand. I tell you what. You tell this Drew Van Horne to come out of hiding, and I'm sure all this will be straightened out."

"If I see her, I'll give her your message. Is that the diner ahead?"

"Ellie's Diner. That's it."

Lindsay pulled into the parking lot, and Moore opened the door. Before he got out, he handed her a card.

"You tell whoever took my truck to make an anonymous call to this number and tell me where it is. If there's no damage, we'll call it even."

Lindsay watched his short stocky figure go into the diner, and drove back to the site.

She looked at the big old Victorian farmhouse that the locals called Gallows House as if for the first time. The structure appeared both worn and substantial. It had been white at one time, but most of the paint had peeled away, leaving silver gray wood with uneven, curled, gray-white patches, like it had been a snake shedding its skin. The wraparound porch, along with the trees, kept the front and right side of the house in deep shade, making a perfect environment for a greenish mildew to grow on the walls. The rooms on the front left corner, two stories and attic, were round-shaped with a peaked roof, so that the house had the vague look of a castle. It looked haunted. Lindsay wondered if most old picturesque houses had similar reputations.

She mounted the porch and entered the front door. Mrs. Laurens, the site cook, had started dinner. The aroma of baked bread and roast beef wafted from the kitchen. Lindsay's stomach growled.

"You took him back to town?" Claire stood at the bottom of the stairs, hands on hips, glaring at Lindsay.

"I'm glad she did. He was about to come into the house."

Lindsay turned toward the voice coming from the dining room. She was finally going to meet the elusive Drew Van Horne.

Chapter 9

DREW VAN HORNE was sitting at the dining room table with her feet propped on one of the chairs. With neat, cropped blonde hair, her crisp new L. L. Bean shorts and shirt, and sunglasses tucked in the pocket of her leather vest, she looked less like an archaeologist and more like a tourist interested in archaeology. Only her well-worn work boots and tan skin gave any indication of outdoor work.

"Lindsay Chamberlain. It's good to finally meet you." Drew put out a cigarette in a glass ashtray and held out her hand for Lindsay to walk over and take. "Marina told me how you intercepted that process server. I appreciate it. This Tidwell thing is such a nuisance."

Marina sat opposite her, a counterpoint with worn cutoffs, a red Arizona T-shirt, and freshly washed dark brown hair slicked back and tucked behind her ears. Her freckled face broke into a sardonic smile. "He must have been good company."

"I'll bet," said Drew. "What did the two of you manage to talk about?"

Lindsay grabbed one of the chairs and pulled it out to face the two of them. Claire took another one and sat beside Drew, eyeing the boxes of artifacts on the table.

"Chaos theory and dimensional physics. I'm afraid I didn't acquit myself very well."

Drew and Marina laughed. "What?"

"He likes listening to NPR and watching the Discovery Channel, and thought that as a scientist, I might know something. I think I disappointed him."

"He mentioned me, I suppose?" Drew asked, lighting another cigarette and inhaling deeply.

"Only that if you turn yourself in to be served, everything could be sorted out quickly."

Drew blew a puff of smoke. "Yeah, right."

Lindsay took a card from her pocket and handed it to Claire. "He said if whoever took his truck would make an anonymous call and tell him where it is, he'd call it even." Lindsay sincerely hoped that Claire hadn't keyed it or knocked out a window.

Claire tossed the card on the table. "I'll think about it."

"You'd better call him," said Drew. "I'd prefer not to give him reasons to come around here."

Claire frowned, took the card, and slid it into the pocket of her shorts.

Lindsay stood. "I'm going to clean up before dinner."

"Before you go, have a look at these artifacts from Feature 2."

Drew handed Lindsay a box containing white sherds and stems from what looked like clay pipes.

Claire frowned. "There are no really diagnostic pieces."

Marina sighed loudly and turned in her chair to face Claire. "Not only are they diagnostic, I'll probably be able to tell who manufactured them."

Lindsay picked out a sherd decorated with a lion design. "Then you know the dates?"

Marina nodded. "White clay smoking pipes are as good for dating a historic site as potsherds are in Indian sites. That one is between 1730 and 1770. This one . . ." She picked out a piece of broken pipe bowl with a different design. "This is probably somewhere between 1780 and 1820."

"The Gallowses held the property from 1831 to 1869, is that right?" asked Lindsay.

"Yes." Claire's voice was a little too loud and Drew jumped. "Yes," she said again, more quietly.

"There are other older artifacts," said Marina. "Creamware . . ."

Claire's chin jutted forward defiantly. "Everything in the documents suggests that the Gallowses were the first to build on the property."

"What do you think, Lindsay?" Drew took another drag on her cigarette and watched Lindsay through narrowed eyes.

This isn't a difficult problem, Lindsay thought. She felt as if she were somehow being tested—or Claire was. "Doesn't one of the research questions concern the length of occupation?"

"Yes," Claire answered. "We have documents that show the Gallowses built the farmstead."

"And also artifacts that suggest it was occupied earlier. You have to deal with the conflicting data in some way."

Claire sat stiff in her chair, glaring at Lindsay.

Why is she so angry? Lindsay wondered. It occurred to her, as she looked at her white-knuckled hands gripping the sides of her seat, that Claire was also scared. Of what?

"What would you do?" asked Drew.

"What would I do?" Lindsay repeated. "I'm assuming funds are limited. You've got good horizontal excavation for each of the buildings." She saw Claire relax ever so slightly. "Dig a few more deep vertical trenches. That should expose the occupation layers." *My ARC 101 students could do this.*

"I'm not going to change the design," Claire snapped.

She's scared of her judgment, Lindsay realized as she watched Claire's eyes dart toward Drew for confirmation.

Whether from inexperience or incompetence, Claire didn't understand when an alteration in excavation procedure fell within the boundary of a research design and when it changed the design. Why, then, was she hired as site director and why was Drew deliberately putting Claire in the hot seat when she knew perfectly well how to proceed?

"Claire," said Lindsay, "Adam isn't even to the bottom of the trash pit he's profiling in the trench. You can amend your excavation strategy without changing the research design."

"Draw up some plans, Claire." Drew smiled at Claire as if she were a child.

Lindsay had had enough of whatever game Drew was playing. She looked at her watch. "If I'm lucky, I'll be able to get to the shower before dinner."

Lindsay's room was on the second floor. Because she was a late arrival and all the other bedrooms were full, she was given the tower room all to herself. No one had chosen it because it had no door. Lindsay had tacked up a curtain across the opening and rigged another one around the mattress on the floor. However, even with the unfinished dull wood floor and unpainted walls, she'd had worse accommodations on digs. In fact, there were times when a room like this would have been a luxury. But here—and now—the easy access to her place of sleep made her nervous.

She took her towel and washcloth from the wooden crate she'd made into a night stand and opened her suitcase to get fresh clothes. She frowned as she searched through the suitcase. She wasn't sure, but she thought someone had rummaged through her clothes. Nothing overt was amiss, it just didn't seem to be the way she'd left it. She made a quick search of the various pockets in the suitcase. Nothing missing. She collected her things and went to the bathroom, glad she had the foresight to keep her money hidden in her Explorer.

Erin was emerging from the bathroom. "Just in time," she said, "but I'm afraid all the hot water's gone."

"That's all right, cold water is good for the hair."

The bathroom matched the rest of the house: old-fashioned and rundown. The toilet behind the door had been refurbished by adding a new seat. The pedestal sink was speckled with yellow paint from some long-ago attempt to brighten the walls, which had since been covered with a garish rose wallpaper. The tub was an antique, sitting off the floor on four clawed feet. At some point in its history, someone had added a spindly shower attachment that rose above a metal frame holding a curtain surrounding the tub.

Lindsay latched the door and glanced down at the keyhole below the brass knob, making sure the plug of putty still blocked the hole before she undressed and got into the shower. The water was ice cold, and the plumbing made sounds that she was sure were the source of the ghostly rumors. She washed and shampooed in record time. Covered in goose bumps, she dried, dressed, and was back in her room within ten minutes.

"Lindsay, can I come in?"

"Sure, Marina, I'm just hanging up my towel to dry."

Marina entered through the curtains with a folder under her arm. She looked around at the bare room. "I see you got the executive suite."

"It's not too bad. I have a good view." Lindsay gestured toward the window that looked out into the woods.

"I gather that you've not read the survey reports or the proposal. I thought you'd like to take a look. I appreciate your backing me up down there."

Lindsay took the folder and flipped through the pages. "I didn't realize that's what I was doing."

Marina looked around again as if perhaps a chair might have appeared. "Why don't you get yourself one of the chairs from downstairs? It's bad enough that you don't have a door."

"That's all right. I just sit on the mattress. Tell me something. Claire seems out of her depth. Why is she site director?"

"Because Drew's a softy. Claire washed out of the master's program at South Carolina at the time that Drew had a temporary teaching position there. Drew said it was just because Claire doesn't test well, that all she needs is a chance to show what she can do."

"Is this Claire's first site experience?"

"She's done fieldwork. I think she wouldn't be bad as one of the excavation supervisors. But a whole site's too much for her abilities, and she substitutes bossiness for competence. I can't tell you how many times she's come into the artifact lab and tried to give me orders. She once came into the darkroom while I was developing. Today she tried to tell me I was wrong about the eighteenth-century artifacts—like she knows potsherds from turtle shells." Marina shrugged. "Anyway, I'm glad you're here, though I'm not sure why. No offense to you or the rest of the crew, but being a part of the field crew seems beneath you. That didn't come out right. I mean, why aren't you principal investigator at a site somewhere?"

"I've been recovering from an injury I received a couple of months ago. Francisco Lewis, my division head, thought this would be a vacation."

"Why didn't he send you to Club Med? This place sucks."

"He thought that since I love the Smokies, this site would be perfect."

"Claire's been telling everyone you were put on leave because your work was suffering."

"She's saying what?

"Claire's inclined to put her own twist on information. Most here don't pay much attention to her. Which, I suppose, only adds to her frustration."

"Nevertheless, I'll have to tell her to stop spreading those rumors." Lindsay looked through the papers again. "I appreciate these."

"Sure. I didn't think you had seen them. Eco Analysts did the initial survey work about four years ago. Then they went out of business. We used most of their data." Marina looked at her watch. "It's about time for dinner. Mrs. Laurens made a pot roast to die for."

Lindsay laid the reports on her mattress and went with Marina downstairs. At the bottom of the stairs Broach Moore was serving Drew with papers.

Chapter 10

DINNER WAS STRAINED that evening. Not that the presence of anxiety with the evening meal was a significant change. Every day at suppertime the twelve crew members, plus Mrs. Laurens and her husband, sat crammed together on a collection of scavenged mismatched chairs at the long makeshift table constructed by the crew. Normally, Claire sat at the end, engaging in what she termed *debriefing,* but what Lindsay called ambushing.

From her vantage point at the head of the table, Claire's gaze would move from face to face, selecting her target for public rebuke over real or imagined mistakes—Erin for prying up and moving foundation stones in order to excavate under them, Kelsey for flirting, one of the twins, Dillon or Powell, for manhandling the equipment. Erin would grow red with embarrassment. Kelsey would tell Claire it was none of her business. Dillon would give her the finger.

Often the target was Joel, his brown straight hair hanging halfway in front of his glasses, sitting hunched over eating as she criticized him for his slowness. Joel was a careful excavator. His profiles were always smooth and straight. The artifacts he unearthed stood out clean and distinct against the brown soil. Joel never responded to Claire. Lindsay had thought him timid, but after talking with him on the site, she realized he simply loved excavating. Dealing with Claire was the cost of doing his job—the same way that divers occasionally have to deal with sharks.

Good excavation takes time, which is what Adam told Claire in Joel's defense, often standing, leaning in her direction with the palms of his hands on the table. Claire's response was her usual lecture on how they didn't have the luxury of wasting time the way university archaeologists do. On the last remark, her gaze would invariably shift to Lindsay. Lindsay wondered where the barbs were directed before her arrival.

Only Byron and Trent were safe. Byron, not only because he was large, but also because he had the ability to cast her an insane scary glare from behind his long beard and hair. Trent, because, for some reason that escaped all of them, Claire appeared to be in love with the lanky, concave-chested addict.

Most mealtime interactions ended with a loud argument between Claire and Adam on how the site should be excavated. Lindsay wondered why everyone didn't have ulcers. It was no wonder they had a high turnover of crew. If it weren't for Mrs. Laurens's good cooking, the meal wouldn't be at all worthwhile.

This evening, Drew sat at the head of the table, Claire to her right. The reappearance of Broach Moore had cast a shadow over what everyone thought should have been a peaceful meal, with Drew present to control Claire. The crew stared at their plates, eating silently for the first five minutes.

"How did he know you were here?" Claire asked Drew, while staring at Lindsay.

"He probably came here looking for his truck, peeked in the window, and saw her," said Adam.

Sharon, the peacemaker, spoke up in her soft voice before Adam and Claire could get started. "Bill and I ate at Ellie's Diner for lunch. The waitress there said Alfred Tidwell's lawyer was the only one he could find who would take the case."

Though Sharon Kirkwood's master's was in history, her experience was in archaeology. She supervised the excavation of the house foundation. Bill, her clean-cut accountant husband, was taking vacation time as a volunteer. They stayed in a small motel on the outskirts of Kelley's Chase.

Bill nodded in agreement with his wife. "She said the lawyer's a shyster. The only reason he took the case was to milk Tidwell for what he can get. I imagine the company will supply you with a lawyer. After all, if you were to be found guilty of something, they could be held responsible, too."

"I'm not guilty of anything," said Drew.

"I wasn't suggesting that you are, but . . ."

Trent fixed his bloodshot gaze on Lindsay. "It's odd that the process server came back. Do you have any ideas why? You were with him."

"No, I don't. When I left him at the diner, he seemed content to let Drew come to him. The only logical explanation is that after I let him out, he may have received information about Drew's whereabouts."

"I wonder from whom," said Claire.

"Give it a rest, Claire," said Marina, glaring at her.

"If it were I," said Lindsay, "I could have saved myself a trip into town and just pointed the way to the house after he crossed the bridge."

"This just gives you a reason for denial," insisted Claire.

"Why would I go to all the trouble? No one was around. I could have just whispered to him that Drew was in the house."

"I understand you're a faculty member at the University of Georgia," said Bill. "Why are you working for a private company as a crew member?"

Lindsay could see in their faces that this was something they all wanted to know. Whether from eagerness to change the subject or curiosity, she couldn't tell.

"My department is paying my salary. They sent me here for a vacation." Everyone laughed, especially Bill.

Mrs. Laurens passed around extra helpings of roast beef, mashed potatoes, and squash casserole, which kept everyone occupied for a few peaceful minutes.

"Why did you have a nervous breakdown?" asked Kelsey.

"I didn't. But I've heard that a rumor is going around to that effect. I'm going to have to find out who's slandering me and put a stop to it." Lindsay directed her attention to Claire as she spoke.

Claire's face broke into a mock innocent expression. "Talk to your boss."

"I don't have a boss. If you mean the division head, he told you no such thing."

"Tell them what really happened," said Adam. "It's far more interesting." He winked at Lindsay and smirked at Claire.

Lindsay held her breath and gripped her fork hard. Adam didn't know what he was asking. He thought he was helping shut Claire up. Slowly, Lindsay let out a breath, hoping no one would notice her fear. Perhaps she should tell them what happened. It wasn't as if she hadn't told the story before: to John, to her brother, to the police, to Derrick, to Lewis, to the doctors. Each time, the telling of it had been hard. Each telling made it more a part of her history, made it *her* story, and she didn't want it. But it was her story and always would be.

Do it, a voice told her. *Telling takes away its power over you, eventually.* She wasn't completely convinced by her inner voice. Her throat tightened, but she spoke, quietly at first, making a conscious effort to open her mouth and talk. She began the story with the same objectivity as she would in giving a scientific paper, as if it had happened to someone else, as if her story was just a story.

"I went to the Primitive Technology Conference in Knoxville and gave a paper on tool markings on ancient animal bones. After the conference was over, I was driving to visit a friend in Asheville before going back to Georgia. We'd worked on sites together and I hadn't seen her for a while. Halfway between Newport and the Cherokee National Forest two men in a pickup truck ran me off the road. I didn't see their faces. They wore masks."

Lindsay took a drink of tea, letting the sweet, cold liquid slide down her tight throat, hoping her hand wasn't shaking, but she could hear the ice clinking in the glass as she drank. The people at the table stared openmouthed at her.

"I tried to fight them off. I tried to run into the woods. Then . . ." She shrugged. "Then, nothing. One of them hit me with something, or perhaps tried to shoot me and the bullet creased my head." She touched a thin red scar on the side of her forehead. "I don't remember. If the blow is hard enough, you don't remember getting hit. It was never recorded in my memory."

"My God," whispered Erin.

"They apparently thought they had killed me. My next memory was waking up choking on dirt. They had buried me, and I had to claw my way out of the grave. Fortunately, it was a shallow grave."

Shallow grave, thought Lindsay. How many had she excavated in her career? And now, she had excavated her own . . . from the inside. How ironic.

"That would sure make me have a nervous breakdown," said Sharon, after a long pause during which the only sound was the creaking of the house, like the gentle rattling of old bones.

"But that wasn't the result," Lindsay said. "The head injury and the trauma of the attack caused me to have amnesia. I didn't know who I was or where I was. A truck driver found me wandering down the highway and took me to the hospital in Mac's Crossing, the nearest town. After a couple of days, a strange man tried to claim me by showing a doctored picture of me and him together to the hospital personnel. Fortunately, I was able to escape. The FBI established my identity from my fingerprints. My boyfriend, John West, came looking for me and found me hiding in the woods in the dark. He took me home to Georgia, where I recovered my memory the following day."

Lindsay waited for the sensation that the dark fear surrounding her was lifting with this telling of the story. But as with the other tellings and retellings, this recounting of the experience didn't change anything. She still felt like she was smothering in a grave.

Everyone was still, perhaps afraid to speak. Claire stared at her food, twirling her fork in the mashed potatoes. Drew's face was frozen into a concerned frown. Adam, who had unwittingly opened this can of worms, stared at the table, as if watching them squirm about. Mrs. Laurens broke the choked silence.

"What a frightening experience. I'd be at home with my doors locked. You must be a strong girl."

"I just don't want them to win."

"Do you have any idea why they attacked you?" asked Marina.

"I think it was random. Maybe they've done it before. I don't really know. The police are at a dead end."

"That's a terrible thing to have happen," said Drew. "And here I've been worrying about a little process server."

"You said someone tried to claim you," said Kelsey. "Was it the one who attacked you? You mean he came after you?"

"I believe it was one of the men who attacked me—there were

actually two of them, the other one was waiting outside the hospital. I assume they wanted to make sure I didn't recognize them. They were never found. I couldn't describe them, and apparently the nurse at the hospital was no help. Unfortunately, after I recovered my memory, I could no longer remember much about what had happened during the time I had amnesia."

"Aren't you scared?" Kelsey asked.

"Not now," Lindsay lied. She was terrified.

Mrs. Laurens rose to get dessert. Chocolate cake, in honor of Drew's visit.

"It's a wonder you didn't go completely crazy," said Powell.

"I'm getting accustomed to adventure." Lindsay tried to give him a convincing smile.

"You mean similar things have happened before?" Bill pushed his plate forward to make room for dessert.

"I've been shot, stabbed, kidnapped a couple of times, and lost in a cave. Being buried alive was a piece of cake." *That's right,* her inner voice told her. *Laugh at your fears and they will go away—someday.*

Everyone laughed. They thought she was kidding.

"You're serious," said Bill after a moment.

"Unfortunately, it's true."

"Exactly how do you get into these . . . adventures?" he asked.

"I'm also a forensic anthropologist. In the course of identifying skeletal remains, I sometimes become entangled in the solution of the crime."

"What, exactly, does that mean?" Dillon asked.

"It means she doesn't mind her own business and gets into trouble." Lindsay could see she hadn't enlisted Claire's sympathy.

"Claire," said Kelsey, "what is wrong with you?"

"I just call things as I see them."

"You're just rude . . . and jealous," said Adam.

Trent leaned forward and glared at Adam. "Now listen here, don't you . . ."

"You're just sucking up to Lindsay because you want to apply to graduate school at UGA," Claire said to Adam. "Don't think everyone hasn't noticed."

"Stop this," said Drew. "Obviously, Lindsay's been through a lot, and I'd like to eat Mrs. Laurens's wonderful cake in peace."

"Amen," said Powell.

Dinner ended after the cake. As usual, several of the women asked Mrs. Laurens if they could help with the dishes. And as usual, she refused.

"Jimmy and I can do them," she said, smiling.

Lindsay imagined that dining with the crew was enough for her, and washing dishes alone with her husband was a relief.

As Lindsay started to climb the stairs to the second floor to her room, she heard Drew's voice ring out from the living room. "I love it!"

Lindsay walked across the hall and peeked in. Sharon and Bill were there about to hang a photograph next to the site map.

"Now that's beautiful," said Lindsay when she saw the object of Drew's praise.

Bill smiled broadly. "It is, isn't it?"

The twenty-five by seventeen inch photograph was a wide panorama of the crew working on the site, with a hazy view of the mountains in the distance. She had remembered him taking photographs, but had no idea he was such a good photographer. The neat thing about this one was the ghostly superimposed cabins and outbuildings—as they might have been.

"Bill is really good," said Sharon. "I've tried to encourage him to chuck the accounting business and take up photography, but no deal."

"The photography probably wouldn't be as fun if I did it for a living. Besides, I like accounting. As long as there are things to count, there'll be a need for accountants."

"Bill comes from such a conservative family. I'm not sure they know what to do with an archaeologist among them." Sharon gazed at her husband with obvious pride.

"How did you do it?" Lindsay asked. She looked closer at the crew. "In fact, how did you get yourself in the photograph?"

Bill laughed. "Magic, my dear. Actually, the cabins are the ones in Cade's Cove. The picture of me is one I made with a timed delay. I used a computer to combine all the images."

The phone rang. Drew answered it and settled into a far corner with her back to them, talking in low tones.

"What I'd love to do is to write a book about the site and use this as a cover," Sharon whispered. She peeked through the dining room and hallway door. "That is, if the site turns out decent. Claire just doesn't have it, and I'm afraid she's going to mess the whole thing up."

"It would make a lovely dust jacket," said Lindsay. "I'd love to have a copy of this."

"Sure," said Bill. "I'm glad you like it."

"It's wonderful."

Lindsay left them in the living room and took a chance that Claire would be alone in the bedroom she shared with Drew.

Claire stood looking at papers spread out on a table beside the door to the second-floor balcony off her room. The fading sunlight shone through her permed light brown hair like a halo.

"Claire," said Lindsay, "I need to speak with you."

"Do you?"

"Yes. I don't know what I did to offend you, but whatever it was, I apologize."

She blew across the surface of the mug of hot tea she held in her left hand. "You came to apologize?"

Lindsay couldn't see Claire's face clearly because of the setting sun shining through the trees, so she came into the room and stood in front of her.

"That, and to tell you to stop telling people I've had a nervous breakdown and that my work has suffered because of it. If you got that mistaken impression from somewhere, I can understand. If it's malicious, I'm afraid I'm at a loss. Whichever, it has to stop."

"I believe they call what you had *hysterical* amnesia." She emphasized the word *hysterical* as though Lindsay had been found screaming in the woods.

"Don't fence words with me. You may think you're being clever, but I take my reputation seriously and will defend it seriously."

Claire's dark eyes narrowed. "Are you threatening me?"

"I don't threaten. Nor do I bluff. I'm trying civil conversation first. If that doesn't work, then I hope you have extra funds in your personal budget for an attorney."

"I suppose you want special treatment, too."

"No. I want you to stop spreading rumors."

Claire balled up her fist at her side. "You people think you're so important, sitting up there in your clubhouse judging who can get through the gate and who can't."

"What are you talking about?"

"Nothing."

"Prelims? Is that what you're talking about?"

"Get out of here. If you want people to think nothing happened to you, fine. I'll go along with your charade."

"Why are you so angry?"

"Get out. This is my room and I didn't invite you."

Lindsay turned to leave, but looked back. "We all admired you making off with the truck today. You should have seen the look on the guy's face."

Lindsay left before Claire could respond, passing Trent on the way through the door. "Is she bothering you?" she heard him say as she turned the corner to the hallway that led to her room.

She's angry with me because she didn't pass her prelims? Lindsay shook her head. *If I had any sense, I'd leave right now. Why in the world did I tell Lewis I'd give it another week?*

She knew why—it was the way everyone treated her, even her friends. They made her feel incompetent, that she needed a rest—as if she could no longer think—and her ability to think was who she was. Lewis had trusted her to do a job, treating her injuries as if they were no big deal.

Lindsay sighed, kicked off her shoes, and stretched out on her mattress with the folder Marina had left with her earlier.

Chapter 11

THE SMOKY MOUNTAINS are ancient. The rocks forming the tops of Mount Le Conte and Clingmans Dome had their origins beneath an ocean more than a billion years ago. A creeping collision of continents caused massive strata of rock to thrust over one another, fold, and tilt upward, forming the Appalachian Mountain chain, of which the Smokies are a part. Through the eons, the continents broke apart and separated again, leaving a segment of the long Appalachian chain on the North American continent and a segment in the British Isles and Europe.

The Smokies were tall in their beginning, as tall as the brand-new Rocky Mountains are today. But the effects of wind, rain, ice, heat, and cold worked like a sculptor's chisel, carving deep ravines and leaving tall peaks. Where the artist's chisel sculpted through older, harder Precambrian rock of the high ground, it exposed younger, softer Paleozoic limestones and shales that had been overridden by the thrust fault.

Over time, the erosive effects became more like the fingers of an artist, smoothing the sharp edges and working down the mountains into gentler hills and valleys. The Paleozoic layers became the coves—valleys surrounded by higher and older Precambrian rock formations. The ceaseless weathering of the limestone in the coves created deep, fertile soils, making perfect homesteads for farmers like the Gallowses to settle.

◆ ◆ ◆

Lindsay reached for a Dr Pepper in her ice chest and popped the tab, sending a tiny mist of fizz over her bed. She took a long drink before continuing to peruse the results of the Gallows farmstead survey by Eco Analysts.

Eco Analysts had not skimped on their work at the site. Before the company went under they had produced maps of the topography, the current vegetation, the distribution of surface artifacts, and a map based on their survey with metal detectors. They also had taken an aerial photograph and produced ground-penetrating radar profiles. The results of the survey with the metal detectors were particularly impressive, producing a prodigious number of hits around the area identified as the barn. A large version of their artifact map on the living room wall downstairs had the excavation units marked as black squares.

Lindsay pulled out the Cultural Resource Management report. CRM reports are often dry, and sometimes only a cursory exercise to fulfill the legal obligation that they be produced. This report, however, was a detailed description of the method and discoveries made in the initial culture survey. Lindsay looked to see who had written it and noted several of the current crew among the authors—including Claire.

She spotted another interesting name in the acknowledgments. The late Mary Susan Tidwell had been one of the informants who supplied the survey team with anecdotal information and led them to documents archived by the local historical society. Copies of those documents also were in the folder—Josh Gallows's will, his deed to the farmstead, a church membership role, pages from a diary written by Hope Foute, wife of the local physician, and a copy of the record page from the Gallows family Bible. The CRM contained enough information to produce a reasonable history of the area, the family, and their farm, even without the data the archaeologists were currently recovering from the ground.

Knave's Seat Cove, location of the Gallows farmstead, was a smaller version of the popular Cade's Cove located in the Great Smoky Mountains National Park. The valley, lush in the summer, harsh and often inaccessible in the winter, was, for a period of time, home to several self-sufficient families. Josh Gallows bought his three-hundred-acre parcel from Clarence Foute in 1836 and moved to the property with his wife, Rosellen, and Elisha, his eight-year-old son from a previous marriage. Together, with the help of their neighbors, they built a house and barn.

According to information contained in his will, by the time Josh Gallows died in 1857, he also had built a smokehouse, a spring-house, and two other unnamed outbuildings. Listed among his property were eight cows, two horses, seven pigs, a loom and tackle, flax wheels, a hunting rifle, and several kinds of animal traps, all of which he left to his only surviving offspring, Elisha Gallows. Those possessions suggested that Josh Gallows had grown flax, from which he had made linen, that he raised farm animals, and that an important part of his livelihood came from hunting. He had not been a slaveholder, but kept from two to three hired hands at any one time.

"He grew flax," Lindsay whispered to herself. "Where were the fields?"

The research questions underlying the Gallows farmstead archaeological excavation concerned site habitation and techniques used in the construction of buildings. The excavation site proper was small—about three acres—but Lindsay was curious about where the entire three-hundred-acre farmstead had extended. The original farmstead was cleared in 1838. Now, trees grew over it in abundance. How long had it remained in cultivation? Perhaps there was a clue in the trees.

The vegetation maps showed that except for the side bordering on the national park, the woods immediately surrounding the excavation site were mostly immature pines mixed with hardwoods of no more than twenty or thirty years of age. These fields could have been in cultivation until relatively recently. Or, they could have grown to mature forests and been cut several times since the last habitation of the farm. *How long is forest succession in this area?* she wondered to herself. She didn't really know.

She had seen the old growth stands in dense wilderness areas of the Smokies where the toppling of a giant tree can open as much as a quarter of an acre to the sun. There was none of that old growth here. Two-thirds of the Smokies have been logged, some as recently as seventy years ago. Those areas have grown back a succession of pines and softwoods to dense forests of tall hardwoods of a hundred feet or more in height. None of the trees around the Gallows site came close to that.

Lindsay got up to look out the window. Although her room didn't have a door, it did have intact pane glass windows. Most of the other windows in the house had succumbed to the rocks and bullets of vandals and were now covered with clear plastic and duct tape, or completely boarded up. The round shape of her bedroom with its three windows allowed her a panoramic view of the woods, about the only perk the place served up.

In the fading light, the mountain laurel, rhododendron, and groves of devil's walking stick were deep green against the dark hardwoods looming behind them. She noticed Mr. and Mrs. Laurens lingering in the parking lot, talking to Erin. Before Mrs. Laurens got in her car, she shook a finger at Erin. She shut the door and Erin walked away with her head low and her arms folded under her breasts. Odd, thought Lindsay, what an intimate personal gesture a scolding is. She wondered if Erin and Mrs. Laurens knew each other before meeting at the site.

Lindsay shifted her gaze to the view of the site. In her mind's eye, she rebuilt the house, the barn, the outbuildings. It looked like there were two springhouses, one completely excavated, and the newly discovered one. She could barely see anything of the woods except a dark tree line; however, she would bet that the flax fields were across the Little Branch Creek. Soil samples would reveal if there were flax pollen there. Perhaps she'd take soil samples from the woods, just to satisfy her curiosity.

She stretched back down on her mattress, turned on the brass lamp sitting on the floor beside her bed, and took up the CRM report again. The legal documents indicated that the Gallowses were a reasonably prosperous farming family. The entries from Hope Foute's diary and the page from the Gallows Bible revealed a more personal story. Josh Gallows's wife, Rosellen, had confided in the doctor's wife who, fortunately for interested historians, kept council with her journal.

Hope Foute described Rosellen Gallows as a big-boned, doe-eyed girl, scared of her own shadow, who hated moving from their home in Maryland to the mountains of Tennessee. She was afraid of Indians and dreaded the harsh existence as a farmer's wife. Her husband's assurances that the government was "taking care of the Indian problem" did not allay her fears. Nor did her temperament improve as seven of eight children born to her died within their first year. Following the birth of the eighth child, Mrs. Gallows was in such an exhausted state that her husband worried she couldn't care for the new baby boy, and the child was taken in and nursed by Mrs. Foute's daughter. Indeed, Rosellen's ill health must have lasted a while, for the child wasn't returned until the age of two. He died six months later. Hope Foute wrote that Rosellen Gallows had two more pregnancies that ended in miscarriages. Afterward, Rosellen fell into deep melancholia and died of heart failure.

Lindsay touched the photocopied page from the Gallows family Bible with the tips of her fingers. The name of each child born to Rosellen Gallows was written in a neat, flowing hand. Rosellen had signed the bottom of the page. It was a sad little page and pitiful to think about Rosellen herself, sitting down and recording the birth and death of each of her children. Infant mortality was high during that time and in that place, as a cursory inspection of the old cemeteries eloquently reveals.

Josh Gallows's health and fortunes took a downward turn after the death of his wife. Due to the onset of gout, he was unable to hunt or to run his farm successfully, even with the help of hired hands and his son, Elisha. He died in 1857 of heart failure. Elisha sold the property and moved away.

The cove community was almost decimated during the Civil War. Only a few of the old families still remained when Elisha Gallows returned in 1882 with a wife and two children. He bought back a portion of his family's original homestead and built Gallows House near his former home—the house that was now temporary accommodations for the archaeology crew.

There was a separate page in the folder on the topic of ghosts. Mary Susan Tidwell reported that her great-great-stepgrandmother, Rosellen Gallows, had reported several instances of seeing apparitions in the woods and hearing voices.

No mystery there, thought Lindsay. Between probable post-partum depression and the trauma produced by the loss of her children, the poor woman's already fragile mental state was primed for hallucinations. The apparition was likely the white tail of a deer, or perhaps a hunter, or simply her own grief manifested in some ethereal shape.

Hope Foute, the doctor's wife, reported seeing a woman in white fleeing through the woods when she was a child. *Rather clichéd,* thought Lindsay. Mary Susan Tidwell herself said she saw something white on the stairs on several occasions as a little girl while visiting her grandmother in the house built by Elisha Gallows. Miss Tidwell was related to the Gallowses. Interesting.

Many of the area's older residents were quoted in the report as saying that Knave's Seat Cove had a reputation as a bad place. Some said the gate to hell was in the cove, though no particular incident was cited that might have been responsible for attracting malevolence, and the area had no more murders or premature deaths than any other place. One informant told a sketchy story of a young girl drowning herself in one of the cove's ponds, her body never found. A woman from the historical society writing an article for the local paper one Halloween blamed the manifestations on Rosellen, not so much because she lost so many babies, but because the last one had lived for two years with another family and then died when returned to Rosellen's care. She suggested that perhaps Rosellen couldn't leave the earth because of a guilty conscience.

Lindsay wondered why the writer of the article hadn't mentioned the ghosts seen by Hope Foute or Rosellen Gallows herself. It didn't escape Lindsay's notice, either, that the only people to have seen the ghosts were children and a woman of questionable mental stability. Mary Susan Tidwell, when asked about the ghosts, said they were simply souls who had left things undone. Lindsay imagined that everyone who died must leave things undone. When in life do you have everything finished? Had she died in the woods after the attack on her, she'd have left a surfeit of things undone.

Lindsay rose and stretched. If it weren't for Claire, this would be a great site. Nothing to beat a good ghost story. She finished her drink, dropped the can in the brown grocery bag she used for recycling, and stepped over to the window. The sound of someone coming through the curtain behind her startled her.

"Lindsay? It's me, Drew. Can I come in?"

"Sure. What can I do for you?"

"We really need to do something about a door for you, don't we?"

"A door would be nice."

"I'll see what I can do. Cal Strickland said we can make only minimal changes."

"It seems to me that refitting a door wouldn't constitute a change."

"I believe he's the one who removed it. Anyway, I came to apologize. I know that sometimes Claire is difficult to take. But you have to understand what a difficult time she's had."

Lindsay had paragraphs of responses to Drew's particular defense of Claire, but she said nothing. Drew looked around the room.

"You need some chairs, too, don't you? There are some extras in the living room. Why don't you take one?"

I will, thought Lindsay, *but it's only a problem when I have company.*

"Claire could be a good archaeologist. She only needs self-confidence. That's why I gave her the job as site director."

"The needs of Claire came before the requirements of the site?"

Lindsay hadn't meant to say that out loud. A confrontation with Drew was the last thing she wanted. And, as many of her friends would remind her, it wasn't really any of her business.

Drew smiled thinly. "No. I'm still principal investigator, and Claire isn't incompetent. You know how some faculty are. They consider themselves to be gatekeepers more than teachers. At South Carolina I wasn't on the graduate faculty, so I couldn't do much more than give Claire moral support. She froze up during her prelims, and the committee was very sarcastic about her abilities."

"Drew, this is none of my business. If you're satisfied with Claire's work, then that's all that matters."

"There's a rumor that you're here to evaluate our work on the site."

Drew stood with her back against the wall. She slid down the wall and sat on the floor. Lindsay sat down cross-legged in front of her.

"It's not true. That doesn't make any sense. Why would this site more than any other need some archaeologist from Georgia to pass on it?"

"You weren't sent here to spy on us?"

Lindsay thought for a moment on how to answer that. The moment lasted too long to deny, and Drew narrowed her dark eyes. Lindsay opted for the truth, rather than some clumsy attempt at avoiding the question.

"I didn't come here to spy. I came here under direction from Francisco Lewis to help out at the site. Today I spoke with Lewis. I asked if he had any ulterior motive for sending me here. He and Keith York are friends. He said York is concerned about the Tidwell accusations—not that he believes the accusations, but he doesn't want rumors to get out of hand. Lewis, as is his way, told York I could come take a look. As is also his way, he didn't tell me until I'd been up here a week. I'm not a spy, and I believe Lewis and York simply thought I could help in some way. Lewis seems to think I'm good at damage control."

"Are you?"

"I don't think so. I don't know any of my colleagues who would call me diplomatic."

A hint of a smile played around Drew's lips. "But you do have a knack for solving things. I've read about you."

"It's what we archaeologists do, isn't it?"

"I didn't kill that Tidwell woman, and I didn't steal anything of hers."

"As far as I know, no one but Alfred Tidwell thinks you did, and from what Sharon and Bill said at dinner, he's probably just trying to get a settlement."

"The only papers any of us saw were from the historical society, and they have the originals." Drew leaned her head back against the wall and looked at the ceiling. "Maybe he thought those papers were hers."

"Have York get you a lawyer."

"My husband's a lawyer. He said he'll sort it out."

"Then it's on its way to being solved."

"I don't want a public record of these accusations against me." Drew stood up. "Did you tell that process server, Broach Moore, I was here?"

Lindsay stood. "No, I didn't. Why on earth would I? I have my own problems."

Drew focused on the woods in the distance, as if trying to see something that made sense to her.

"Maybe it was Mr. Laurens or his wife who tipped Moore off. They live in the community. Maybe they thought it was their duty."

"Maybe Adam was right," Lindsay suggested. "Perhaps Moore came back looking for his truck and just saw you. I can tell you, he loves that truck."

Drew shrugged. "Maybe. Look. I'll tell Claire to lay off you. I know she's not easy to get along with." She pulled back the curtain and started to leave, hesitated, and turned back to Lindsay. "I'd prefer you not investigate this Tidwell business. After all, it isn't your or Lewis's concern, is it?"

"No it isn't. I didn't really plan to do anything but talk to you anyway. This was not my idea. There is one other thing."

"What's that?" Drew let the curtain drop.

"Trent. It's obvious that he stays in some kind of altered state of awareness. You really need to have a talk with him."

"Have you seen him using drugs?"

"No. But this is a big house. I have a theory that some of the knocking and tapping sounds are Trent going either to the attic or the basement. I know others at the site are concerned about it. If this thing with Tidwell does end up in court, it won't help your case if a member of the crew under your supervision is caught buying or using drugs."

"That's a good point. I'll speak with him." Drew smiled and left.

Lindsay hoped Drew would remember to see about a door. Maybe John would build her one. She sat back down on her bed and studied the maps. As she leafed through the ground-penetrating radar profiles, an anomaly jumped out at her. It was in the profile that sliced through the trash pit—where Adam was digging a trench. Something large and solid about four feet deep. She carefully examined the other profiles and found a similar pattern at the same depth in the slice through the feature she believed to be a cemetery. Lindsay circled the suspicious shapes. She had an inkling of what they might be. She had seen a radar profile with a dense signature like this before. This kind of discovery was far more interesting than whatever drama Drew and the local community residents were playing out.

She thought about showing the anomalies to Drew, but decided against it. Right now, Drew was probably too focused on her legal problems to appreciate the possibilities. Tomorrow would be soon enough. Instead, Lindsay changed into her nightshirt and slipped under the covers with a book she'd been wanting to read, an autobiography of a female forensic anthropologist. *Maybe I should write a book,* she thought as the room grew dark, leaving only a small circle of lamplight at the head of her bed.

She didn't know how it happened, but suddenly it was pitch dark and she was lying on something lumpy. She couldn't breathe. She strained to take a breath, and jerked with a spasm of coughing. Something grainy was in her mouth . . . Dirt? Was it dirt? She tried to spit it out, but couldn't. It was harder to breathe, and her head ached. She could die from the pain. She wanted to hold her head in her hands, but her arms were pinned. Some heavy thickness covered her entire body. She felt paralyzed, unable to move. She panicked, tried to cry, but choked on whatever was in her mouth. She was blind, or in the dark, or her eyes were closed.

Open your eyes.

Darkness.

Open them!

Glittering shafts of light danced for a moment, then were gone, then were back and gone again. There was a small hollow of space around her head, a small place that wasn't covered by the heavy thickness, but the space was disappearing. Every struggle to move made the space smaller.

You have to move. You have to move.

She lifted and pushed her right arm with all her strength . . . until she felt . . . a breeze. Something fell on her face. She felt panic.

Move. Move. Hurry. Struggle harder.

She rose from her grave.

Lindsay jerked awake grappling with the sheet covering her head, gasping for breath. Her heart beat so fast and hard her hand went to her chest to hold it. She stayed in that position, frozen with nauseating fear.

Oh, God, don't let me relive this every night.

Her breaths were as ragged as if she were still . . . still there. She gathered the strength to get out of bed and slip on her shoes. Shaking from head to foot, she grabbed her robe and slipped it on as she stumbled through her curtains and down the hall.

The bathroom door was closed and she saw a thin strip of light coming from under it. Someone was there. *Damn. What time is it? Why don't people stay in bed?* she thought irritably as she started downstairs to the bathroom on the first floor. The stairs were dark. Why hadn't she thought to bring a flashlight? She walked slowly, keeping a hand on the wall. Except for the creaking, the dark confined space reminded her of the cave she'd been lost in. The stairway was like the long cave tunnels she had wanted to lead upward, but invariably led down.

It's a staircase, she told herself over and over. *A staircase. You know where it leads.*

The tiny bathroom at the bottom of the stairs, thankfully, was unoccupied. She fumbled with the light switch and made a mental note not to drink anything before she went to bed at night. She wished she had brought some aspirin with her. Her head was splitting.

Lindsay crossed over to the sink and turned on the faucet. She glanced into the mirror over the sink and jumped back. She would have screamed if she had any breath in her. It wasn't her face staring back at her. It was the face of a girl with flaming red hair, freckles, deep green eyes, and features contorted in terror.

Chapter 12

LINDSAY STARED AT the face, not moving, not realizing that she was holding her breath until her lungs forced her to gasp for oxygen. She closed her eyes and rubbed her eyelids with the tips of her fingers. When she looked in the mirror again, her own face stared back at her, pale and frightened.

God, what was that? Lindsay reached out and touched the mirror. Was it a trick of the light? How could the light have changed her image to such a ghastly reflection? A ghost? *There's no such thing as ghosts.* Insanity? *No, not that, please.*

She shook as she washed and dried her hands, avoiding looking in the mirror again. At the bottom of the staircase, she stopped cold. Unable to walk back up the dark narrow stairs, she turned and ran out the front door of the house to the safety of her Explorer.

The metal door handle of the truck was ice cold to the touch. The upward pressure of her grasp on the handle caused the interior light of the vehicle to come on. She pulled on the door. It was locked. What was the door keypad code? Her mind was blank.

Stop and think . . . Fox . . . the dental formula for a fox.

Her finger flew over the keypad. The door unlocked with a loud click. Once inside the safe chamber, she slammed the door behind her, belatedly worrying about waking up the household. But the windows were all still dark.

In the relative safety of the SUV, she started to cry. Her sobs were checked by some deep-seated inhibition against displaying weaknesses. If someone saw her run out of the house, it wouldn't do to have red swollen eyes in the morning.

Why do I care? What's wrong with me?

She wiped her eyes, feeling alone and needing to talk to someone friendly. But who? Her friends and family would only worry; her enemies would use it against her. Everyone would think she had lost her mind.

She should talk to John, but his company had been awarded a big project that required his full attention. He couldn't be worried with holding her hand. Her brother would want to come get her. Her good friend Harper was gone to Spain. Her parents didn't know the whole story. There was no one.

She thought of Derrick. Perhaps she could talk to him—Derrick, her ex-fiancé, at one time her best friend. The usually unflappable Derrick had come close to yelling at her.

"Lindsay, dammit, you just barely escaped permanent damage to your brain—your brain, Lindsay!"

As if that were worse than death. Maybe it was worse for her, and maybe she had come close to dying so many times that Derrick was used to that danger. No he wasn't. It was why he'd left her.

"You're a danger junkie, Lindsay," he had said to her. "You've made danger an intellectual pursuit. I just can't take standing by, watching you go from one peril to the next."

What would he say now? That he'd warned her. That she'd finally done it. No, she couldn't talk to Derrick.

Get a hold of yourself, said that inner voice that was the core of her. *You just saw something. People do that. It's not a big deal. The doctors said your brain is fine. The scans found nothing wrong. Do your work here, or go home, one or the other, but don't fall apart.*

She opened the sleeping bag she kept tucked behind the driver's seat and let the back seat down. When she finally settled into the fleecy warmth, she fell asleep thinking those thoughts over and over.

Don't fall apart.

She was awakened by the ringing phone. Why was the phone ringing in her room?—it didn't have a phone. She wasn't in her room. It was her car phone. She stretched forward and grabbed the phone.

"Yes?"

"Lindsay, is this you? My old eyes must have made a mistake. I was calling Emily. I'm sorry if I disturbed you."

It was George West, Cherokee elder and John's father. Lindsay rubbed her eyes and looked out the window. It was still dark out, even the house was still and unlit. She settled back deep in her sleeping bag.

"You didn't disturb me. I'm glad you called."

"And how are you?"

"I'm fine. I . . ."

She fumbled through an account of her middle of the night experience, feeling silly when she had finished.

"So, you had a vision."

"A hallucination, I imagine."

There was a pause. Lindsay saw a light come on in the window of the second-floor room where Drew and Claire slept. The house was waking up.

"What were you doing before your encounter in the mirror?"

"I'd awakened from a dream . . . about what happened to me."

"And before that?"

"I was reading about the history of the site. Normal archaeological information . . . there was some stuff about ghosts. The, uh, house I'm staying in is supposed to be haunted."

Lindsay heard a car. Mrs. Laurens's old Buick was rounding the curve to the side parking lot. She was arriving to make breakfast.

"So you read about ghosts, dream about your ordeal, then see something strange in the mirror in the middle of the night. If that happened to John, what would you tell him?"

"That the play of shadows distorted his features and he saw his fears. Apparitions in mirrors are fairly clichéd ghostly stuff that taps into childhood fears. His subconscious expected to see something scary in the mirror, and he did."

"Why can't you tell yourself that?"

"I don't know."

"Maybe you can't because you are afraid that your mind is no longer reliable and you feel guilty for allowing yourself to get hurt. You think?"

"I suppose."

"John works with a lot of complex machines. Sometimes when one is moved to a new place it has to be recalibrated. And sometimes the machine is working right, but the operator misreads it. Either way, it's not the machine's fault. It's doing what it's supposed to. Maybe your brain is not failing, but working the way it should."

Lindsay was silent.

"You have had visions before."

"I can mentally reconstruct an archaeological site to its original condition, but that's because I have data and understand what it means."

"Maybe you just don't know what this means yet."

"You think it means something?"

"It means something. Maybe just your fear. But that doesn't mean your brain's not working."

"Thanks, George. I'm glad you called."

"I'm glad I did, too. Take care of yourself."

Lindsay was smiling when she got out of the Explorer and walked up the steps to the house. As she opened the door, she realized she had left it unlocked. She tiptoed past the guys' bedroom—the round room directly under hers. The stairs were much less foreboding this morning. She managed to make it up to her room without passing anyone, without having to explain what she was doing running around in her robe. *Not that it should matter,* she thought, as she slipped on her work clothes and went back downstairs.

She poured herself a glass of milk for breakfast.

"Are you sure you don't want anything solid? How long will that glass of milk last you, working out there?" Mrs. Laurens was making pancakes for the crew, several of whom were in the dining room eating.

"I'll be all right. You know anything about the rumors of ghosts around here?"

Mrs. Laurens took a hot pancake off the griddle and put it on a paper towel to cool.

"Don't believe in ghosts myself, but Cal hardly likes to come here. Says he hears things in the house. I'd be worried if I didn't hear tapping and creaking in an old house like this. As far as I know, he's not seen one. We'd have all heard about it." She folded the pancake up in the paper towel and handed it to Lindsay. "Here. Eat this on the way to the site. You're going to need something."

Mrs. Laurens reminded her of her great-aunts. Lindsay grinned as she accepted the blueberry pancake and took a bite. It was sweet, warm, and aromatic. "Thanks," she mumbled on her way out of the house into the early morning.

She shivered as the cold mountain air penetrated her sweatshirt. Tall, thin Erin, dressed in cutoffs and a sweatshirt, came up beside her. "It's cold this morning." She rubbed her hands together.

"Nice and brisk." Lindsay finished her pancake and stuffed the paper towel in her pocket.

"If you say so." Erin shivered.

"Hi, guys."

"Adam." Lindsay pulled the profile pages from under her sweatshirt. "I've got something to show you."

"The radar profiles? What about them?"

"Just two of them. Look here and here." Lindsay pointed to the dense object echo on each of the profiles.

"I kind of remember those. Claire says they're rocks."

"Perhaps. But they may be something else."

"Wait—this one's in my trench line. Someone from the initial survey must have planned the trench here to find out what that is."

Lindsay nodded. "Likely."

"What is it?" Erin looked at the ground-penetrating radar images on one of the pages. "I don't see how you can tell anything."

"I'm almost to that depth," said Adam. "We'll probably find out today. Any ideas, Lindsay?"

"Yes, but only because there's one here, too." She shifted the pages so that the Feature 3 profile was on top.

"So. What's special about this place?" asked Adam.

"Let's see what you find today."

Adam nodded. "It's nice . . ." He looked over his shoulder. "It's nice to start out the day looking forward to something besides Claire on a tear, or Trent on a drunk."

An early morning fog was coming off Helget Pond, shrouding the bridge. Fogs at excavations are eerie, the way they hover near the ground over the leavings of the past, like the spirit of artifacts, ghosts of things gone by. She shivered as they passed through the mist, making each of them momentarily invisible. Their footfalls on the wooden planks sounded loud in the early morning stillness.

"Anyone ever see *The Incredible Shrinking Man*?" asked Adam.

"Yeah," said Lindsay.

"What's it about?" asked Erin.

"A guy went through a mist like this. Started shrinking until he was nothing but a molecule." Adam made a gesture with his hands.

"Nice thought," Erin replied.

Lindsay helped Erin take the plastic coverings off of Structure 3, and Adam tended to his trench as some of the other crew drifted onto the site. When the plastic was folded and off to the side, Lindsay crossed to the processing tent, passing structures and features that she mentally raised from the surrounding rock and dirt into images of a smokehouse, corncrib, barn, and fence.

The twenty-foot by forty-foot tent was the shape of a Quonset hut—constructed from a series of metal rods curved into arcs and covered with weatherproof material.

"Anybody home?" Lindsay called out at the door. Someone always stayed in the structure overnight, guarding the artifacts from thieves.

"Me," Joel yelled. "Come in."

Lindsay entered through the door flap to the interior where a series of long rough-hewn tables lined one side, and equally unfinished shelves and cabinets lined the other. Sacks and boxes of artifacts, brought in for Marina to process, covered almost every surface, as did a coating of dust. Joel was coming from his makeshift bedroom behind a wall of tall shelves at the far end of the tent, pulling on a green, black, and white plaid long-sleeved flannel shirt over his T-shirt and cutoffs. A cold Pop-Tart stuck out of his mouth.

"I need the mapping equipment, today," she told him.

Joel pointed to the cabinets. "The grid's standing against the side there. Sorry to hear about your troubles," he mumbled. "But this is a great site, isn't it." Joel's enthusiasm never failed to surprise Lindsay.

"Let me show you something," she said.

She spread her profiles out on a table. Joel bent over them, his hair falling forward in front of his face.

"Something's there," he said.

"Maybe," agreed Lindsay. "We'll find out today. Adam said he's almost to that depth."

"If Claire doesn't pull him off onto some other project. Do you know she stopped the crew in the middle of their work on Feature 3 and put them on something in the woods that wasn't even in the initial survey?" Joel brushed Pop-Tart crumbs off the page and turned his attention to the radar profile in Feature 3.

"I think I might know what this is." He glanced sideways at Lindsay. "I think Feature 3's a cemetery. Have you seen the flowers and berm around it?"

"Yes, and I think you're right."

Joel looked up from the profile and grinned. "Uh-oh," he said as he looked out the gauzy tent window. "Bogey at twelve o'clock. Can I take these?" He stuffed the ends of the folded pages in his cutoffs.

"Sure." Lindsay looked up to see Claire and Marina walking toward the tent.

"I'm working with Adam today," Joel said. "Just so Claire doesn't decide to reassign me, I'm going to slip out the back door before she sees me."

Before Lindsay could say anything, Joel headed to the sleeping area behind the bookcases and, presumably, out the back way. She picked up the mapping equipment and started through the door.

"And where are you going with that?" asked Claire, standing in front of her. Marina rolled her eyes.

"You said you wanted Structure . . ." She had to think a moment. "Structure 6 mapped."

"You haven't done that yet? Yes, I do. Try to have it done before lunch." Lindsay resisted the temptation to salute. Like Joel, she hurried out before Claire could think of any other little insults.

"Really, Claire . . . ," Marina said before Lindsay was out of earshot.

Structure 6 was possibly an outhouse. Lindsay thought it should be excavated and the fill floated to separate the contents for analysis. The most amazing kind of minutiae can be found in an outhouse. Pollen, tiny seeds, carbonized plant remains, bones, and the staple of all archaeology—things lost. However, Claire thought a map of the foundation stones and a soil sample would do. Maybe . . . no, she was in enough trouble with Claire already because some of the crew now and then came to her for advice.

Lindsay put down the equipment beside the collections of stones that formed more or less a rectangle. The mapping grid was a one meter by one meter wooden frame strung with wires every tenth of a meter so that inside the frame were one hundred small squares, all one decimeter by one decimeter. She placed the grid over the right-hand part of the feature with the right corner of the grid adjoining a previously mapped wooden stake. She sat down beside the grid, took up the clipboard and graph paper, and began to draw and record the rocks inside the grid.

Thirty minutes later, she got up to stretch and move the grid over one meter. The early morning cold was gone and sweat was already forming on her brow. She took off her sweatshirt, tied the sleeves around her waist, and resumed her task.

Mapping was actually relaxing. Drawing was a quiet, solitary pursuit, and she couldn't complain about the soothing sound of Big Branch Creek in the background and the smell of fresh air. So far, the day was quiet, which meant no arguing—probably a benefit of Drew's presence on the site. Drew was excavating with Sharon and Bill on Structure 1, the main house—formerly a log cabin.

Occasionally, Lindsay heard phrases like "two-pen construction . . . maybe two springhouses . . . is this one of those pipes?" come wafting across the site from various directions, intermingled with the sounds of trowels clinking on rocks, dirt being sifted through screens, and the squeaking of wheelbarrow wheels. She smiled to herself when she heard Trent's high-pitched voice from his excavation in the woods. "Really, I heard the ghost go past the door last night . . ."

At one point, she looked up to see Powell dancing across the site toward the drinking water wearing a Walkman, his Adonis blond hair blowing in a mild breeze. He grabbed Kelsey, whirled her around a couple of times, and continued on his way. Now that Drew had been served with her papers, maybe she would stay at the site a while and things would stay calm.

Lindsay glanced at the sun to estimate the time and rose from her sitting position, stretching each leg. It was still well before lunch and she didn't look forward to finding Claire for her next assignment.

"Yo, Lindsay," Adam shouted from his trench. "Come look what we've found."

Chapter 13

"I'LL BE DAMNED," said Powell. "I thought this was a trash pit."

Bill, Drew, and Sharon reached the trench just ahead of Lindsay and stood staring. In the ditch Joel and Adam squatted on either side of their find. Joel brushed the surface with a whiskbroom. Byron sat cross-legged like a giant bearded guru on the bank above with a shovel across his knees. Sticking out of the trench cross section were the head and shoulders of a wedge-shaped coffin.

"It's metal," said Byron.

"Lead," said Joel.

Lindsay climbed down into the trench to get a closer look just as Claire arrived.

"What is it?"

"A lead coffin," answered Drew.

"I'm willing to bet there's another one in Feature 3," Lindsay said, shielding her eyes from the sun while trying to include both Drew and Claire in her gaze. "It showed up on the radar profile."

"Who said you could look at the profiles?"

"Claire," said Byron, "enough is enough. You thought they were big rocks."

"This is a real find," said Lindsay. "If the interior hasn't been compromised, there's a possibility of retrieving a sample of very old air."

"No kidding?" said Joel and Adam together.

Bill pushed up the wire-rimmed glasses slipping down his nose and took another look at the dirt-stained receptacle. "Old air? How?"

The other members of the crew noticed the congregation around the trench and drifted over to have a look. However much archaeologists say that patterns indicating behavior are more important than spectacular artifacts—spectacular artifacts still draw their attention.

"NASA has already worked out the protocol," Lindsay said.

"NASA?" said Claire. "Like we can call them down here. Just who's going to pay for it?"

"I think I can find the money. There's a lot of people who would be interested in an air sample. This could be a major find."

"Think of the publications you can get out of this, Claire."

Adam wanted this, Lindsay could see. Enough to hold out bait for Claire.

"You say you can get funding?" asked Drew.

"I believe so."

"Good. Keith ought to love this."

Lindsay thought she heard a hint of resentment in Drew's voice as she said the president of Sound Ecology's name. It was understandable she might feel that way, since he had apparently asked his friend Francisco Lewis to send Lindsay to check up on her.

"If it's that important," Claire said, "then I'll personally supervise the excavation of the coffin."

The glances Adam and his crew exchanged with one another conveyed their displeasure at the idea. Lindsay almost felt sorry for Claire, having the respect of no one, when respect was something she desperately wanted. Claire was her own worst enemy, and now Lindsay was about to make her more angry.

"We have to stop excavating until the arrangements are made. Re-bury this coffin until then. Everything has to be coordinated, and I don't know when we can get the experts here. I believe some of the tests have to be done while the coffins are still in the ground."

Oddly, at least to Lindsay, her taking charge didn't make Claire angry. On the contrary, Claire took it like she was about to be a part of something special—the site director of a significant find. She ordered the trench to be filled in without argument or deferring to Drew.

Lindsay breathed a sigh of relief. Now to go make the arrangements. She walked back to the house to make some phone calls.

The phone sat on a scratched-up end table beside a wine-colored Naugahyde sofa. Getting up off Naugahyde was like pulling off a Band-Aid the way it stuck to her legs, so she pulled up a chair and dialed the number of the office of the UGA Division of Anthropology and Archaeology. Luck was on her side. Francisco Lewis was in. She admired Bill's photograph of the site hanging on the wall as she waited for Kate to put her through to Lewis.

"Lindsay. How are things? Better I hope."

"A little. I have a favor to ask."

"Shoot."

"I need some money for some extra analysis."

"Why are you asking me?"

"Because you owe me for putting me in this hellhole."

"Keith has a budget. You know about the shortfall because of the semester debacle . . ."

"Lewis. Don't give me that. I'm not asking you to build a cofferdam around the site."

"What are you asking?"

"I need you to call NASA and arrange for them to send a special team to analyze a couple of coffins for us. If you could coordinate this with the Armed Forces Radiobiology Research Institute, it'd be great."

Even with the phone held away from her ear, Lindsay could hear Lewis's laughter clearly.

"This is a joke, right? NASA?"

Lindsay explained what they had found and what she hoped to gain from the analysis.

"Antiquated air," he mused. "Do you know how old?"

"No, not now. The last family to live on the farmstead, the only family for which we have documentation, dates from around 1836 or thereabouts. The first non-Indian settlers at Cade's Cove didn't come until the early 1800s. But we've found artifacts that seem to point to a much earlier occupation of this site. To add to the puzzle, the only lead coffins I've read about were found in the North and East, and are artifacts of wealthy families. But, except for the presence of the lead coffins, this appears to be a typical frontier wilderness farm homestead. Interesting, huh?"

"Lindsay, I can always count on you to make a site more interesting."

"Then you'll help?"

"Of course. You knew I would."

"I'm not sure who you call, but ask Kerwin in Archaeology. He's familiar with the work done at St. Mary's, Maryland, and will know who to contact. It was on their coffins that NASA developed the protocol for extracting air."

"I'll let you know as soon as I set things up."

"Thanks."

"Sure. How's the little investigation coming?"

"Lewis, you're asking me to spy on people I work with."

"No, I'm not. I'm asking you to clear up a situation that might unfairly impact the ability of Keith York to win contracts. You'll be doing me a big favor. After all, this thing you're asking me to set up is no small favor."

"I know. But you just love to arrange stuff like this." Lewis didn't say anything. "Okay. The only thing I know now is . . ." Lindsay paused, trying to think of what she knew. "Drew says the supposedly stolen documents belonged to the historical society and were returned to them after copies were made. No one, not even the Tidwells, knows what any other documents might be." She let out a resigned breath. "I'll find out more."

"Thanks. I appreciate your help in this."

"Where is your friend Keith, anyway?"

"He has an opportunity to do a series of digs in China that he's been interested in for years. He's working on negotiations for that."

"He has his irons in pretty far-ranging and diverse fires."

"Yes, he does, and he doesn't want any scandal."

"I can't guarantee a specific outcome."

"I'm aware of that. But I know you'll do what's best."

Best for whom? Lindsay didn't have to wonder long. "I think the whole thing's a nonstarter. One of the crew overheard some locals express the opinion that the entire situation was instigated by Alfred Tidwell's lawyer in hopes of earning a fee or a percentage of a settlement. That seems to be his reputation. No other lawyer would take the case."

"That says a lot, right there. I'll pass that information along."

"Sure, I wouldn't want Keith to think I'm out here doing nothing."

"Before you go, an Athens detective came by today hoping to see you. They're cooperating with the Tennessee authorities on your attempted murder. They still don't know anything, but they heard about some argument you got into at the conference and want to know the details."

Attempted murder. The words caused Lindsay to have a period of momentary dizziness. She shook her head to clear it.

"What? They think some crazed postmodernist followed me from the conference and attacked me on the road?"

Lewis gave a short laugh. "I think they're just tying up loose ends. I have a phone number for you to call."

"Lewis, I really don't have time to speak with him. This can't be any serious lead. No one at the conference would have done that to me."

"Probably not, but he did say they want to try and establish whether the attack was aimed specifically at you, was opportunistic, or was part of a pattern of attacks. He didn't go into details."

Lindsay took down the number and stuck it in her pocket. "I'll call him when I get a chance. We're likely to get busy here in a few days."

"You doing okay?"

"Yes, I'm fine."

"Good. Take care of yourself. Antique air. I like that."

The discovery of the lead coffins meant dinner that evening was a blessed relief. Claire was in a good mood. No doubt, she saw that the professional respect and recognition she craved were finally within her grasp.

Adding to the good cheer of the household, Mrs. Laurens made roast chicken, a sweet potato soufflé, green beans, homemade rolls, and apple pie for dinner. Amid the clatter of utensils, all the talk was about the find. What was it? Who was it? What did it mean?

"I'd like to know who's in the coffin. Aren't the Gallowses supposed to be buried in town in a church cemetery?" Dillon asked of no particular person.

"The artifacts suggest the site was occupied before the Gallowses," Marina said, not looking at Claire.

"Why isn't there any documentation?" asked Powell.

"Not everything gets saved," Byron answered, reaching for a second helping of sweet potatoes. "I hope you made lots of this, Mrs. Laurens."

"If I'm not used to your big appetites by now, I shouldn't be here. There's more of everything in the kitchen."

"The farm was bought from Clarence Foute," Byron continued. "Must be his family."

"The Foutes are buried in the same cemetery," said Drew. "We don't have any documentation that there were structures there before the Gallowses occupied the land."

"What happens now, Lindsay?" Adam asked.

"First of all, keep in mind that the people Lewis is contacting might not be able to come immediately. Several agencies will be involved, and they'll have to coordinate with each other. When they come, they'll set up a tent with special equipment to x-ray through the lead and to extract the air from the coffin. I don't know all the details."

"Why the x-ray?" asked Erin. "I mean, after they get the air out, we're going to open the coffin, aren't we?"

"They have to locate the remains inside the coffin so when they drill a hole they don't damage anything."

"Which brings up a touchy subject," said Drew. "Let's keep this quiet until it's done. We don't want a circus here."

"Wait a minute," said Bill. "They can't x-ray through lead—I hope. That's why my dentist puts a lead vest over me when he x-rays my teeth."

"He's right," observed Byron. "Superman couldn't see through lead."

"It's not exactly a traditional x-ray," said Lindsay. "It's some kind of gamma ray process. Very high-tech stuff."

"Do you think Dr. Lewis can really set it up?" asked Claire.

Lindsay nodded. "He lives for this kind of thing."

Mr. Laurens rarely spoke at dinner unless the talk involved building or fixing something. He knew about wood and tools, however much to the contrary might be suggested by the missing first joint of his ring and little fingers on his left hand from the injudicious use of a saw. However, when a topic was of sufficient interest to puzzle his sensibilities, he spoke up.

"Exactly what are you going to do with this stale air once you get a hold of it? I can't see much use for it."

"You got a point, dude," said Trent. "Just what's all this for, anyhow?"

"If the seal on the coffins hasn't been broken, and the coffins are as old as we think, the air inside predates the industrial revolution. One of the questions we have about the environment is the seriousness of the greenhouse effect. Data on the composition of preindustrial atmosphere will help in answering those questions. People who study such things have also developed methods of studying gases trapped in bubbles inside glacier ice frozen thousands of years ago."

"What about the people in the coffins?" asked Mrs. Laurens. "There'll be some who don't think it's right to dig up the dead."

"It's like finding someone who has been lost and forgotten," Lindsay said. "I treat them with the greatest respect to discover as much as possible about their life. The bones tell me things about how the person lived and died. It's like an autopsy."

"Well, what *I'd* like to know is," said Kelsey, her lips curved up in one of her flirtatious smiles as she delicately sipped her tea, "who's supposed to be haunting this place? Trent says he heard a ghost go past the guys' bedroom early this morning. And I know I've heard things. I was taking an afternoon nap last week and I could have sworn there was a presence in the room with me."

"Kelsey, you got Erin and Marina sharing the room with you," said Adam. "You reckon it was one of them?"

Kelsey made a face at him. "No. They weren't even in the house at the time."

"It was probably a dream, then," he said.

"I wasn't dreaming," said Trent. "I distinctly heard footsteps go past the door, and when I peeked out, nothing was there, I'm telling you. It's just like people said—disembodied footsteps."

"Trent, there's so many reasons I could give for your hearing things," said Adam. "But I'll only remind you, we live in a house full of people. Besides, I didn't hear anything."

"You were sleeping—the sleep of the dead, I might add." Trent laughed at his joke.

"What do you think, Lindsay? Do you believe in ghosts?" asked Claire.

"No, I don't."

"So you aren't afraid in this house?" she asked.

Lindsay wondered if Claire had seen her run out of the house last night. The window to her bedroom was above the front parking lot. If she had, why wouldn't she clue Trent in?

"I didn't say that. I certainly believe in people." Lindsay's face broke into a grin. "Particularly an archaeology field crew who've been known to succumb to temptation and play an occasional joke."

"I believe in ghosts," said Erin. "I think sometimes people who die suddenly leave unfinished business."

"Don't you think almost everyone who dies leaves some unfinished business?" Lindsay asked. "It's the living who're left with the real unfinished business. Rumors of ghosts come from the living trying to deal with that business. It seems to me that if all the reasons given for ghostly presence were true, we'd be overrun with them, especially in war zones."

"I agree," said Adam. "I don't believe in ghosts, either, and I've never heard or seen anything in this house that would convince me otherwise."

Erin was unwilling to let the subject go. "What about all the people who claim to have seen ghosts? You think they're imagining it?"

"Not necessarily imagining it." Lindsay recollected the twisted frightened face in the mirror. Did she believe it was a ghost? No. Did she believe she imagined it? Probably. "I believe it's our brain's job to make sense out of input, even when the input is incomplete—the way it does when it fills in the visual image where the lack of photoreceptors creates a blind spot in our vision. I think when we see a flash of something, get a whiff of an aroma, or hear a fragment of sound, our brain tries to match it with something that makes sense, and we think we've experienced a whole when there was really only a part, or nothing at all. Add guilt or fear to the equation and the result can be a ghost."

"Do you analyze everything?" asked Kelsey.

"Pretty much," Lindsay answered.

"That kind of makes sense," said Drew. "I've read that musicians who've gone deaf sometimes, out of the blue, hear whole symphonies playing. I think the explanation is that the brain is getting some kind of input and is filling in the rest out of what is familiar, or calling up old memories."

"Kind of like persistence of vision," Adam agreed. "We see what our brain tells us makes sense. Will someone pass the platter of chicken down this way?"

"I can't believe that souls are allowed to get stuck here on earth and wander around in confusion," said Mrs. Laurens, passing the platter down to Adam. The phone rang and she rose to answer it.

"It's for you, Lindsay," she said on returning to the room.

Lindsay took her tea with her to the living room and hesitantly picked up the receiver. "Yes. This is Lindsay Chamberlain."

"Dr. Chamberlain. This is Detective Barclay in Athens, Georgia. How are you?"

"Fine." Lindsay's heart beat faster on hearing that he was a detective. Had Lewis given him her number?

"I just need to ask you a few questions in relation to our investigation into the attack on you. Do you have a couple of minutes?"

"Yes. Go ahead." She wished she could say no.

"Do you know a Harold van Deevers, Celestine Molesky, and an Arlene Lautaro?"

"Yes. They're archaeologists."

"I understand you had words with Ms. Molesky and Lautaro at a conference at Knoxville, Tennessee, before you were attacked last April, and before that, you wrote a letter to the editor of *American Antiquity* criticizing Mr. van Deevers."

"You don't suspect any of them? Archaeologists always have words with one another at conferences. It means nothing. And I didn't criticize van Deevers, I criticized his article. If you look at several issues of *American Antiquity* you'll find that it's common for peers to comment on articles through letters to the editor."

"So, you don't think it could have been any of them who attacked you?"

"No, not at all. From what I remember, the guys who attacked me were thugs."

"You said they wore masks."

"Yes, they did. But, they were male, for one thing, and they walked and moved like young thugs, not like someone . . . educated."

"Educated people walk differently?"

"Come on, Detective, you know that. Children emulate their role models. Go watch people walking in and out of jail and then go watch people walking in and out of a symphony, and see if you can't tell a difference."

"I take your point. We're just trying to eliminate anyone of your acquaintance. Although someone you know could have hired one of these undereducated thugs."

"The people you're asking about wouldn't do that. We argue over theories. That's not enough to kill someone over. I've never ruined anyone's reputation, no more than they have mine."

"Like I said, we're trying to eliminate suspects. Our best theory right now is that somewhere along the route, maybe somewhere you stopped, you attracted the attention of the perps—young woman traveling alone. We're trying to match the M.O. of your case with missing persons and other attacks in the area."

"I've told the investigators in Tennessee and in Athens everything I can remember."

"Have you had anything suspicious happen to you lately?"

"No."

"The reason I'm asking is that they tried to take you from the hospital. That suggests that they could try something again."

Lindsay gripped the receiver, suddenly angry at the detective. "I believe I was probably an opportunistic target. They left me for dead, I got away, I can't identify them, and it's over."

"That's probably true. We just have so few leads. The conference thing was a long shot."

"I appreciate your work, Detective. I'm sorry I can't be more help."

Just as Lindsay hung up the phone, it rang again. She jumped, almost dropping her tea, and let it ring a second time before lifting the receiver.

"Yes?"

"Is this that dig up at Knave's Seat?"

"Yes."

"I'd like to speak with a Dr. Chamberlain."

"This is she."

"Dr. Chamberlain, this is Alfred Tidwell. My aunt, the late Mary Susan Tidwell, did some work with you all a few months back."

Chapter 14

"I BELIEVE MISS Tidwell served as a consultant about local history," Lindsay replied. "However, I wasn't here at that time."

"I know," Albert Tidwell said. "That's why I'm calling you. I need to talk with somebody with an unbiased point of view. I was wondering if you would talk with me."

"Mr. Tidwell, I really . . ."

"Just hear me out. Can you come to the diner outside of town for breakfast? It won't take long."

Lindsay agreed—in order to keep her promise to Lewis, she told herself. But at the first opportunity, she'd have to tell Drew about it. She wasn't going to secretly investigate the people she worked with. *God, how do I get into these situations?* She pressed her fingers to her eyes.

Mrs. Laurens was serving dessert when she got back to her seat.

"You all right?" asked Erin.

"Yes. Detectives updating me on my case. Nothing new, though."

"What was the other call?" asked Claire.

"That was for me, too. Similar thing." She took a bite of the apple pie and ice cream in front of her. "This is great, Mrs. Laurens. It's a real treat to have such good food at an excavation."

Mrs. Laurens smiled. "It's a treat for me to cook for a group so easy to please."

After dinner, Lindsay sat on the porch in a rickety rattan chair, her feet propped on a wooden box, as she stared out into the woods and listened to the birds. What did Trent call it? The jungle. It was a jungle. The thickets of mountain laurel and rhododendron were so dense they could only be penetrated by animals like the wedge-shaped black bears. Add the myriad bird and animal cries, and the place felt primordial. Lindsay found it also fiercely beautiful. Even in the fading light, she could see the white rhododendron blossoms against the jade leaves and the towering hardwoods.

The woods are lovely, dark, and deep, she thought, pulling from deep in her memory Robert Frost's fitting description. The trees and shrubs were like a deep emerald curtain to a hidden place, a secret wilderness, concealing rare wild animals.

What did Rosellen Gallows see when she looked into these woods from her log house—woods that were lovely, dark and deep—or did she see monsters? Did she dread getting up each morning to the never-ending tasks of farm life—cooking and preserving food, spinning and weaving cloth, making clothing, rendering lard, making soap, hauling water, worrying every year about the crops, worrying each time her husband went hunting, each time she got pregnant? Or did she dread the night and look forward to the work that would take her mind off her fears?

Until recently, Lindsay could not understand anyone fearing the woods. Now she could almost put herself in Rosellen's fearful shoes. There was something in the woods to be afraid of. She shut her eyes and listened to the evening sounds, willing away the evil. She was so tired of being afraid.

Maybe she shouldn't will it away, but confront it. There was a time, not long ago at all, when she would have argued with anyone who cautioned her against running headlong into danger to investigate a murder. Now, she avoided even talking to the police about her own close brush with death.

She knew about crime scenes—not so different from archaeological digs. Maybe she should mentally examine her own. Perhaps the mental energy would push out the fear before it took root in her brain forever. She made herself return in her mind to the incident.

She'd left the conference in Knoxville after the last presentation—Derrick demonstrating a primitive fire piston. They'd said good-bye, and he'd kissed her cheek and told her to take care. She hadn't, had she?

She had chosen the scenic route to Asheville, along 411 and 25. At no time during the trip had she noticed anyone following her, or seen anything suspicious. It took less than an hour to reach Sevierville where she stopped to buy a bag of chocolate fudge for Jane Burroughs. Lindsay didn't recall seeing anyone who seemed to be watching her. But, she wasn't looking.

After Sevierville she had been on the road about twenty minutes when it happened, on a lonely stretch of highway at the northeastern cusp of English Mountain. An old green truck, a much lighter shade than the emerald green of her Explorer, came roaring past on her right, veering into her side. The impact caught her completely off guard, and she skidded across the road and drove headlong into the ditch.

It had happened so fast. She tried to slow it down in her mind, but it was still too fast. Her air bag deployed, hitting her in the face. She reached up and touched her cheek, now healed, where it had been burned from the friction of the bag.

She'd barely caught her breath when she saw a glimpse of someone in her side mirrors. Somehow, she knew it wasn't an accident. She knew to flee. She opened her door and ran into the woods. The sound of her own heart pumping in her ears was so loud she couldn't hear them behind her, and she didn't want to chance a look. It would slow her down. She would have to take her eyes off her flight path. There was a shot and a chip of bark flying off a tree. She ran faster and was winning the race—until an old piece of rusted barbed wire grabbed her ankle and pulled her down.

They were on her so quickly. One pointed the gun at her, screaming epithets under his ski mask. He didn't like the woods. He hadn't wanted to chase her—didn't want to break a sweat. He wanted it to be easy, her to be a willing victim. Running her off the road had been fun. This wasn't fun. The other one pulled at her, trying to get her to her feet. Then what?

Lindsay folded her arms across her chest, holding in her heart. She felt as if she were still running in the woods, still out of breath, still scared. But what had happened next?

Next they were somewhere else in the woods. She sort of

remembered being half dragged, threatened, hit with the gun—trying to formulate a plan. After that was the big blank spot, the gray nothing, the place where nothing existed until she awoke, clawing out of the ground.

Don't panic. You're on the porch in a place surrounded by people—of whom only a few are mildly hostile. The bad guys don't know where you are. It was random anyway. Was it? What do I know? If this were a story told to me by someone else, what would I make of it? Think about that.

The perpetrators were not well educated. They were white and young—late twenties, early thirties? Not forties. Not teens. Height? She didn't remember.

They were not professional. Why? Because they were so disorganized. Disorganized. That's another thing. Disorganized crime scene.

She was buried very shallow. Had to be to have gotten out. They were in a hurry, were interrupted, or it didn't matter if she were found. Then why bury her at all? They wanted to conceal the crime, but for some reason were in a hurry. Okay. That's something. The authorities probably had already thought of this.

Was it random? Was it some serial crime? There were two of them. Not common in serial crimes. The Hillside stranglers were two cousins.

But what if she was their specific target? Why? She didn't believe for a second that one of her colleagues would hire assassins. It was almost too ludicrous to think about.

Maybe it was connected with her forensic work. But she wasn't even working on a case at the time, and hadn't for at least a month.

Could it have been something she was about to do? She was on her way to visit her friend, Jane Burroughs, and then go home to Georgia. In a couple of weeks, come here.

It swept through her like a tidal wave. It would have knocked her out of the chair, had it been solid. Could it be here? Someone thought she was coming to investigate the death of Mary Susan Tidwell and wanted to stop her?

No, surely not. Lindsay shivered. If that were true, then the perpetrators did know where she was, and her enemy could be someone she worked with and ate with every day. *Go home.* That's what she should do. Just go home.

She opened her eyes. A man with honey brown hair to his shoulders and dark eyes was standing in front of her, reaching a hand toward her. She screamed. Not loud, just a shriek, and he vanished.

"What?" Adam came out onto the porch, holding a sheaf of papers. "Anything the matter?"

"No," she said, staring into the thin air where the man had stood. "I'm sorry. I thought I saw a snake." She lied. What could she say? Sorry, just the resident ghost? Or worse, sorry, just hallucinating again?

"A snake? What kind?"

"Black—kind of long and black."

"Probably harmless. They eat the poisonous varieties. I wouldn't worry."

"Thanks. I won't. Sorry I disturbed you."

"You didn't. I was just looking at the printouts of the profile. I can't think about anything but the coffin. I hope Lewis can get those people to come."

"He probably will."

"Hey, guys." Kelsey Calabrini came out onto the porch and pulled up a chair. "Did I hear somebody yell?" She combed her fingers through her short dark hair.

"Me," said Lindsay, starting to feel really embarrassed.

"She saw a snake."

Kelsey lifted her feet and sat cross-legged in the chair. "Ugh . . . where?

"I may have been mistaken. I was dozing in the chair."

"Probably a black snake," said Adam. "They're harmless."

"So . . ." Kelsey unfolded her legs and stretched them out in front of her. "You think there's another coffin?" It flitted through Lindsay's mind that Kelsey had studied ballet. She had dancer's legs.

"I think so." Lindsay was relieved to change the subject before her lie spun itself into a really tangled web.

Kelsey leaned forward and whispered, "Claire seems really happy. I hope your Lewis guy can come through."

"Lewis will come through." She had no doubt.

"Uh, Lindsay." Adam cast his eyes out to the site. He seemed embarrassed.

"Oh, go ahead and ask her," said Kelsey. "For heaven's sake."

Adam frowned at Kelsey. "Lindsay, Claire said I was sucking up to you. I wasn't. I want you to know that."

"I haven't felt sucked up to the whole time I've been here."

Adam's lips turned up into almost a smile. "But one thing she said is true. I've been thinking for a long time about applying to graduate school at UGA."

"And you want me to recommend you?"

"Yeah, something like that."

"What area are you interested in? Historical?"

"Not necessarily."

"I've seen your work. It's very good. How's your GRE?"

He waved his hand in a noncommittal motion. "All right, I guess."

"Your GPA?"

"Much better. I graduated UT with a 3.8."

"It sounds like it shouldn't be too much of a problem. When I get back, I'll write you a letter of recommendation."

Adam let out a breath of relief. Kelsey stood up and put her hands on his shoulders and her lips to his ear. "See, that wasn't so bad." She laughed and bounced into the house.

"Thanks. I really appreciate this."

"It's no problem. We are always on the lookout for dedicated students."

The light was fading fast, and Lindsay had already slapped two mosquitoes. She stood, stretched, and announced her intention of getting to bed early.

In her room, she pulled out her book and read herself to sleep. The night brought no more surprises. No bad dreams, no quick trips down to sleep in her vehicle.

Lindsay opened her eyes and looked at her clock. 5:00 A.M. Almost time to get up. Her mind wandered to the man who had stood in front of her on the front porch. Was that her imagination? Had to be. She didn't believe it was a ghost, however much it looked and acted like a ghost. Things that look like a duck, walk like a duck, and quack like a duck are not always a duck. Sometimes it can be a goose.

What was going on in her brain? Maybe later on in the day she'd call George West and tell him about it. Now, she had to get dressed and go meet with Alfred Tidwell.

She had meant to do only the bare minimum necessary to satisfy her word to Lewis. She hadn't really believed there was anything to the accusations against Drew, but now, after taking a walk through her memory . . . Even the smallest possibility that the answer to what happened to her lay here with Drew had to be taken seriously. Maybe whoever was after her was after Drew as well—or maybe Drew was involved.

Ellie's Diner, a white-shingled shack on the outside of Kelley's Chase, was already open for business when Lindsay drove into the gravel lot. Three cars were parked in front and another was driving up. It was a small restaurant, five tables and four booths and a counter with six stools. Most of the customers were sitting at the counter. One man and woman sitting side by side in the far booth looked up expectantly when she opened the door. Must be the Tidwells. As she walked over to them, the man rose and held out his hand.

"I'm Alfred Tidwell. This is my wife, Sugar. You must be Lindsay Chamberlain."

Alfred Tidwell looked to be in his mid-fifties, with gray wavy hair and a weathered complexion. He had wrinkles around his lips like he had smoked all his life. The kind of lines that in women made tiny channels for lipstick to seep into and feather the boundaries of their lips. The last joint of the index finger and middle finger of his right hand were stained a deep nicotine yellow.

His wife, Sugar, probably wasn't a smoker. Nothing about her lips, teeth, or fingers indicated that she had anything to do with cigarettes. She was a thin woman with fine hair, dyed dark brown and pulled up in a large loose bun on top of her head. She had startlingly large blue eyes behind black cat-eye glasses.

Lindsay shook Alfred's hand and slid in opposite them. "Yes, I'm Lindsay Chamberlain. How did you come by my name?"

"Let's just say we heard about you."

"What, exactly, did you hear?"

"That you might be an objective party in a position to help."

"Objective, yes. I'm not sure about the help part."

"Just the same, I'd like you to just listen to what I have to say."

"All right."

A waitress came over and looked at Lindsay, her pencil poised over her order pad. She said nothing, as though her intentions should be clear.

"I'll have pancakes, bacon, orange juice," said Lindsay.

The Tidwells ordered the sunrise special.

"My aunt," began Tidwell, "was always her own woman. She liked to save things, and she liked to go to flea markets and yard sales." He shrugged. "It was her money. She earned it. She could spend it like she wanted."

"What did she do for a living?"

"She was a schoolteacher. Never married. Had only herself to worry about. She lived all her life in the house her and her brother—my daddy—grew up in."

"What makes you think someone from the archaeology site killed her?"

"I say it, 'cause it's true." He held up a palm. "I know what the doctor says, and the sheriff, and I ain't saying she didn't have a heart attack. But that don't mean somebody couldn't of brought one on."

"Is that what you think happened?"

"Yes, I do. Sugar does, too, don't you, Sugar?" Sugar nodded.

"And you think Drew Van Horne is the one who brought on her heart attack?"

"I do."

"Can you tell me why you think that?"

"Aunt Sue died March 5 in the evening. This Horne woman was with her all morning and afternoon, taking her places."

"Taking her places?"

"Having my aunt show her old places around here. Says it was some kind of historical research."

"That's what she was paying your aunt to do," said Lindsay.

"I know. But she was old and not in good health. She had no

call to keep her out all day. People who saw her told us how tired she looked—plumb worn out, they said."

"Mr. Tidwell . . ."

"I know, that's not a whole lot to go on. That's why no lawyer, except that Mayhew, would take the case. I know we can't take that to court. But there's more. It was raining all day and it was cold. Miss Horne got Aunt Sue tired and sick, then brought her back, and while she was sleeping, went through her things, stealing her papers."

"What's missing?"

"We don't know, exactly. Aunt Sue was one for keeping things to herself."

"How do you know anything was stolen?"

The waitress brought three plates of breakfast. Three sunrise specials—it seems a sunrise special was pancakes, bacon, and orange juice. Lindsay spread the butter on her pancakes and poured maple syrup over them.

"Ellie makes good pancakes," said Sugar.

"Aunt Sue always said she had valuable papers. Said we'd be surprised at what'd been handed down in the family and what she'd found over the years. She said we was to split everything—me and my sister, Bonnie. Right now, things are up in the air, because Bonnie's . . . well, Bonnie is Bonnie." He pounded the table with the flat of his hand. "But Aunt Sue said she had valuable papers in a safe. We found the safe and there was nothing in it." He gave the table one last slap, punctuating his last statement.

"Mr. Tidwell . . . ," Lindsay said again.

"I saw some papers once," said Sugar, leaning forward, whispering. "She showed me a stack of papers. They was all done up in some kind of plastic like. Looked like the kind of clear cover my grandchildren put over their school reports. She wouldn't let me touch them, even all done up. Didn't want me seeing what they was."

"Could you tell what kind of papers they were?"

"Letters, papers. I remember the name Beau something on one of them. They were real hard to read. That was all I could make out. They looked real old and speckled like."

"And none of these turned up?"

"The safe was cleaned out," said Sugar. "Was nothing in it."

"And that's not all," said Alfred Tidwell. "About twenty years ago, when Aunt Sue got around better, she used to go all over, looking for finds, as she called her things. Estate sales, old printing companies, and dead newspapers—she liked those. Not just here in Tennessee, but North Carolina, Virginia, and even up the coast once." Tidwell leaned forward and whispered, "She found a trunk filled with something. Wouldn't tell none of us what it was, but she was happy. Never showed it to nobody, but she told us it was her best find."

"You talked to the sheriff. What did he say?"

"Him? Huh. He's no help," Alfred said. Sugar started to speak, but he waved her away. "I know he's just doing his job. I know we got nothing. I'm not a fool. I know he can't arrest someone for carrying a person around in the wet and cold all day, and I know if I can't identify what was stole, there ain't nothing he can do. But there's got to be something somebody can do."

"What do you want of me?"

"To find out what happened."

Sugar finished her orange juice and set the glass down on the table hard. "There's people that says Miss Mary Susan was crazy. Crazy like a fox. Last year she sold one of those old Barbie dolls for five thousand dollars. Five thousand dollars." She slapped the table as her husband had. "She did things her way, all right, but she wasn't crazy."

"Is there anyone in your family Miss Tidwell might have confided in about what was in the safe? You said you have a sister, Bonnie. Might she know?"

"She don't know more than me and Sugar."

"Was an autopsy performed?"

"No. Sugar found her dead at home in bed and called her doctor. He said her heart gave out. Nothing looked wrong. We didn't find out 'til after she was buried about her being out all day and about her papers being missing."

"Would you ask the funeral home director to speak with me about her?"

"Sure. Does that mean you'll help?"

"It means I'll try to find out what happened."

The waitress brought the bill and Alfred Tidwell snatched it up. "We asked you here. I'll pay for it."

Lindsay left the restaurant and got into her truck. She waited a moment before starting the engine, wondering what she was doing. Why didn't she just go home? There appeared to be nothing whatsoever that she could do. No one but the Tidwells saw a crime here. They didn't even know if the woman had valuable papers or not. They certainly wouldn't be able to describe them well enough to claim them if they turned up in Drew's possession. Why, she asked herself again, was she doing this?

Because you think it may be linked to what happened to you, and you're tired of being afraid.

Lindsay started the engine and drove out of the lot onto the highway. She was almost to the turnoff for the cove when a black truck came roaring past on the right side so fast she felt her truck sway from the force of the wind.

Chapter 15

LINDSAY'S TRUCK SKIDDED to a stop and sat across the center line of the narrow paved road. She was shaking so badly it was hard to hold on to the steering wheel. A sudden chill and nausea swept over her. She opened her door and leaned out, feeling like she might lose her breakfast. A car appeared suddenly, braking hard and blowing its horn as it narrowly slid past on the left side. She thought she heard someone yell. She jerked herself back in and put her hands over her face.

"Damn!" She hit the steering wheel with the palms of her hands. She was so tired of the sound of her own heart pounding in her ears, she wanted to scream. Everything was falling apart—her sanity, her courage. Her own emotions had turned against her.

She whipped the Explorer around in a U-turn, running onto the shoulder. When she wrestled the Explorer back onto the road, she headed for Kelley's Chase. A string of rundown-looking businesses, selling everything from produce to car parts, rocks, and assorted junk, lined the road just outside of town. Kelley's Chase itself was no more than a courthouse, jail, library, post office, real estate office, and hardware store. Most of the main street buildings had been empty for a long time. She drove all the way through town and past the Romanesque revival–style red-brick courthouse, to the ancient two-story matching brick sheriff's office where she parked and sat, taking deep slow breaths, willing her heart to slow its beating.

When she finally calmed down and stopped shaking, she looked at herself in the mirror. Convinced that she didn't look hysterical, she got out and went into the sheriff's office. The receptionist smiled and asked if she could help. *If only you could,* Lindsay thought to herself.

"I'd like to see Sheriff Ramsey. My name is Lindsay Chamberlain." Her voice sounded shaky to her own ears. She wondered how she sounded to the receptionist.

The woman wanted to know her business with the sheriff, as if she might not be able to interrupt him. Lindsay wanted to shout at her, *This is a small town. How busy can he be? Do you think this is a social call?* But she paused and spoke calmly. Maybe she couldn't control how she felt, but she could control her behavior.

"I want to report someone trying to run me off the road."

"I can take your . . ."

"I'll see Miss Chamberlain, Marietta."

Lindsay turned and looked to see Sheriff Ramsey standing in his doorway. He nodded to her. He could have been elected on his looks, she thought. He must have been at least six feet, six inches tall with a thick chest and arms and a square, pock-marked face framing a crooked nose. The voters probably thought he could handle anything that went down in this county. She walked into his office.

"Have a seat."

Lindsay pulled up a wooden chair in front of his desk. He sat down in a large brown leather chair and leaned back. *It's going to break one of these days,* she thought.

"I assume you're here about Mary Susan Tidwell? Her nephew Alfred called and paved the way for you. I just didn't expect you this soon. We just got off the phone."

"The reason I'm here now is to report that someone tried to run me off the road."

"Oh?"

Lindsay clasped her hands in her lap to hold them still. "I had just left the diner from meeting Alfred Tidwell and his wife when someone in a black Ford pickup tried to run me off the road. It looked like about a '97, but I'm not sure."

"Lots of young boys hot-rod along that road. Did they hit your vehicle?"

"No."

He shrugged. "Not much I can do about it, I'm afraid."

"I understand, and I would agree that it probably was joy riders, except for what happened to me recently."

Lindsay gave him a brief description of her attempted murder.

"Whoever tried to kill me also came up on my right side and ran me off the road. It was so similar to the last time. This felt like a warning."

She could feel tears threatening her eyes. *Don't cry,* she silently commanded herself. She raised her chin a fraction of an inch.

"That's different." He picked up the phone. "Marietta, call Martha and Rafe to be on the lookout for a late-model black Ford pickup truck, possibly a 1997, may be driving recklessly." He paused, raising his eyebrows. "You don't say? When was that?" He recradled the phone. "Seems Elaine and Phil McBride had their black 1997 Ford pickup stolen last night. Martha, one of my deputies, will check it out."

"Thank you. That would take a lot off my mind." She relaxed in the chair a little. *Everything can be handled and controlled,* she told herself. *They were probably joy riders.* She smiled at the sheriff. "Did you know Mary Susan Tidwell?"

The sheriff nodded and smiled before he spoke. "When I was little, we thought she was a witch. She always had all kinds of odd things around her place. Odd to little kids, that is. I think she kept us scared so we'd stay out of her yard."

"What do you think happened to her?"

"Died of old age. I know what Alfred thinks. Lord knows him and his sister Bonnie's been in my office enough explaining it to me. But there's just no evidence at all anyone tried to hurt her." The sheriff got up and pulled a file out of the drawer of an old metal filing cabinet and tossed it on the desk in front of Lindsay. "You can look at the file. When Alfred made his complaint, I talked to her doctor, the mortician who handled her body, everybody I could think of. Nobody saw anything suspicious. Her neighbor across the road saw the Van Horne woman drop Miss Susan off and leave immediately. She didn't even go in, much less leave with valuable papers."

Lindsay picked up the report and scanned the pages. He was thorough—looked in all the places she would have. No unusual marks on the body, a history of a heart condition, nothing out of the ordinary in the bedroom where she was found.

The sheriff sat back down in his chair. "Maybe this Drew woman did make Miss Susan so tired she died. If she did, it doesn't sound intentional. It's not exactly a sure-fire way to go about killing someone. She might've had to drive her around all year."

"What did Drew say they were doing that day?" As Lindsay asked, she came to the page in the file where he had recorded his interview with Drew Van Horne and Claire Burke.

"Miss Susan was showing her where some of the old places are —churches, homesteads—that kind of thing."

"Claire Burke was with them?"

"No, not with them. After Miss Van Horne saw Miss Susan to her house and left her there, the Burke woman came to visit Miss Susan. She said she knocked on the door and left when no one answered. She never saw her."

"Did Claire say why she went to see Miss Tidwell?"

"Something to do with a collection of farm tools. As I'm sure you know, Miss Burke is an excitable young woman. She's accused several people of what she calls 'looting' things they've found at the old farm place over the years. Seems as though she found out someone sold Miss Susan some rusty farm tools—plow parts, stuff like that—that was supposed to have come from there. Miss Burke wanted a look at them."

"Why isn't she named in Tidwell's lawsuit?"

"She never saw Miss Susan that day, as far as I can find out. On the other hand, several people saw the Van Horne woman with Miss Susan."

"What about the papers that are supposed to have been stolen?"

"I've done my best to find out what she had. That list is all I could find out."

Lindsay looked at the page he pointed to. The description of the documents was almost the same as what the Tidwells had told her. The only difference was an added notation that a relative had seen a letter from a place called Turkeyville.

"Where's Turkeyville?"

"I've no idea. One of Alfred's relatives seemed to remember

something about that from years ago. I located a Turkville, Kansas, on the map, but that's as close as I could find. As you can see, even if I found an incriminating stack of documents in someone's possession, I wouldn't be able to identify them from the sketchy descriptions Alfred and Bonnie gave me. The only way Alfred's going to get his property back is if someone comes forward with better information than this, or if whoever took them confesses."

"Do you believe Alfred's aunt had any valuable papers?"

He shrugged. "I don't know. Miss Susan was shrewd about her business. I'll say that for her. Sugar tell you about the Barbie doll?"

Lindsay nodded.

"Miss Susan had lots of deals like that. You ever watch the *Antiques Road Show*?"

Lindsay shook her head. "No, but my father watches it."

"Ever since my wife started watching it, she never throws a thing away." He laughed. "Miss Susan had all kinds of stuff that most folks wouldn't think was valuable. But she knew better."

"Her estate must have been large, even without the documents," said Lindsay.

"I've heard it was around a hundred thousand dollars. Maybe more, when all the junk is appraised."

"That's a lot of money."

"I'd be happy with it, but that's fifty thousand apiece. I don't know for sure, but Miss Susan is supposed to have told Bonnie and Alfred they were to split everything equally after she died."

"Did she have a will?"

The sheriff laughed out loud. "She had what they call a holographic will. When I first heard it, I thought the woman had made one of those holograms of herself, like Princess Leia in *Star Wars*. I couldn't puzzle why she'd do such a thing, but I sure wanted to take a look at it. Found out that just meant handwritten. I was disappointed." He laughed again and shook his head.

Lindsay decided she liked a man who could laugh at himself. She laughed with him.

"Tidwell mentioned he and his sister were having differences. But it seems clear what their aunt wanted."

"Bonnie has a way of reinterpreting things in her favor. Apparently, she thinks that 'split equally' means split equally between all the children and grandchildren. That's $25,000 for Alfred and $75,000 for her and her two kids. Alfred and Sugar don't have any children."

"That sounds like it's going to be a mess."

"I expect it already is."

"What was Miss Tidwell like?"

"Sharp. She marched to her own drummer. She never married and stayed healthy until the last five years of her life. My wife says that's why she was so healthy—she didn't have a husband worrying her to death."

"I'm not sure there's anything I can do for the Tidwells. I suppose he expects me to investigate Drew Van Horne."

"I expect so."

"Drew denies taking any papers. She says the only documents she looked at are held by the historical society."

"I can't prove any different," said the sheriff. "To tell you the truth, I haven't gone to look at the historical society papers. But, it occurred to me that if I could find a word in those documents that matched what the Tidwells remembered, I'd be able to convince them that Susan donated the papers to the historical society."

"That seems reasonable. Wouldn't the historical society have records of all the things donated to them?"

"I would have thought so, but they don't seem to have very good records."

"How about Miss Tidwell's insurance company? Surely she would have valuable documents insured. They would have a list of what they were."

"Miss Susan didn't believe in insurance."

"What?"

"I know. Sounds incredible, but she didn't. She said the money was better spent making sure her house had good wiring and a good burglar alarm."

"But still . . ."

"Years ago, she had a claim that wasn't resolved to her satisfaction. She felt she'd paid them money for years and they were cheating her. She decided she'd do without them."

"She must have made a record of what she had. Maybe it's hidden somewhere."

"You're welcome to look. Frankly, I don't have the time. If Alfred and Bonnie ever get the inheritance mess straightened out and go through the house piece by piece, maybe they'll come across some kind of record keeping."

Lindsay sighed. "I doubt there's anything I can discover, but I'll try."

"Good luck to you. I'll let you know what I find out about that stolen truck that tried to run you off the road. You know Elaine and Phil own the log house that came off the old farm you all are working on, don't you?"

"What?"

"The Gallowses' log cabin that was in the cove was moved and renovated by Elaine and Phil McBride."

"The original cabin was still standing?"

"You didn't know?"

"No, but I've only been here a little more than a week. Surely, Drew and Claire know."

"They do. As I said before, Miss Burke's rather excitable. She accused Phil and Elaine of looting. Naturally, they won't have anything to do with the archaeologists after that."

Lindsay put a hand to her face. "Claire."

"They're real nice people, and told me they had looked forward to contributing to the history of the county. They're members of the historical society and everything."

"Could we go out and see them? Could you take the call instead of your deputy?"

"I reckon. Since you're a new arrival, they might talk to you. Especially since their truck almost ran you off the road. People around here feel a sense of responsibility for the things they own. They'd feel real bad if their truck had been involved in hurting someone. You can ride with me. It'll be all right to leave your vehicle here."

Lindsay climbed into the four-wheel-drive Dodge beside Sheriff Ramsey and he set out for the McBride place.

"I appreciate this, Sheriff. I can't believe the log house still exists."

"They moved it about, let's see, about seven years ago. They thought the archaeologists would be eager to find out about it."

Lindsay didn't know what to say to him. Aside from trashing Claire, there wasn't much she could say. Instead, she asked about the other house—Gallows House, the one said to be haunted with the ghosts she didn't believe in. Yet she was at a loss to explain what she had seen, short of pronouncing herself nuts.

"Do you know anything about the house we're staying in? I know it was built by Elisha Gallows, but that's about all."

"That's about more than I know. Cal Strickland has occasionally rented the place out—artists, tourists, relatives. Nobody liked to stay there for very long. As I understand it, it needs work."

"What about the rumors about it being haunted?"

He lifted his shoulders an inch and relaxed. "It's an old house. All old houses are rumored to be haunted, aren't they? My wife says the round tower makes it look more mysterious than it ought. Offhand, I don't know of anyone specific who ever saw anything supernatural. Just heard stories about folks seeing and hearing things."

"What kind of things did they see?"

"Somebody saw something running through the woods once, and another time someone saw a ghost on the stairs."

"I read about that in some newspaper clippings." Lindsay had hoped he knew more.

"Yeah, that's where I read it, too. People always said it was haunted, but I think that was just a story started to keep people away. How's Mrs. Laurens and her husband working out? I recommended them for the job."

"They're great. Mrs. Laurens's cooking is the best part about the place."

Sheriff Ramsey looked over at Lindsay, eyebrows raised. "I been hearing stories that nobody gets along over there."

"That's a little exaggerated. Archaeology is hard work. When you're tired, nerves can get a little frayed."

"Uh-huh. You know, Mrs. Laurens's people've lived here a long time. She might be able to tell you more about the history of the place. I assume someone's asked her."

"I talked to her a little about it."

"That whole area back in the cove has a bad reputation. I'm not sure why. Just always heard the old folks say a lot of people died there. No idea who or why. Oh, I do remember my mother telling me about some kid drowning in the pond when she was a child. Never found his body."

"That's odd. It's a small pond, and bodies usually float eventually."

"You know it doesn't have a bottom, don't you?"

"No, I didn't."

"That's what I heard. I guess that means there's an underground river or cave down there."

"Karst topography," muttered Lindsay. "That makes sense."

"What's that?"

"Chemical weathering of the limestone underground causes cave and sinkhole terrain."

"Yeah, we got that here."

He turned onto a paved drive that wound up the mountainside. A cabin of dark brown square-cut logs was nestled in the mountain hollow against a steep backdrop of deep green foliage. Water cascaded down a stone-covered creek bed, its banks bordered by huge fanlike ferns. It looked primordial. Lindsay loved mountain creeks. They're idyllic, the way they flow over the rocks and boulders, polishing them smooth and round. Lindsay looked back down the winding drive and wondered how anyone found this place to steal a truck.

She stared back at the cabin. The house the Gallowses had carried out their tragedies and triumphs in still stood. This cabin, unlike hers, was a saddle-bag design—two pens side by side with a chimney between. The McBrides had built a two-story addition to the back and a separate garage.

Log houses of the period were built as a one-room square or rectangle called a pen. Their strength was in the joints of the four corners. So, when settlers added on, they added another pen. Like Lindsay, the McBrides had tried to keep the integrity of the original design as they added their extensions.

Phil and Elaine came out on the porch as she and the sheriff drove up. Lindsay guessed they were in their late thirties. Their appearance struck her as well groomed—clothes, hair, nails, all styled and manicured. Phil McBride had lost the hair on top of his head, but had neatly trimmed thick dark blond hair around the sides and back. He bounced down the steps, holding out his hand for the sheriff.

"Thanks for coming, Sheriff. I didn't expect you personally."

"No problem. I can't believe someone came up here and stole your truck."

McBride shook his head. "They didn't. It was at Jerry's garage. I explained that on the phone."

As he spoke, he looked at Lindsay expectantly.

"This is Lindsay Chamberlain," said the sheriff. "She's one of the archaeologists working at the Gallows farmstead."

The smiles on McBride's and his wife's faces froze. The sheriff hurried on.

"The person who stole your truck tried to run her off the road."

"She doesn't think it was us?" Phil McBride's expression was somewhere between surprise and hostility. His wife came down the steps to join him.

"No. She doesn't think that, and neither do I."

"Sheriff . . . ," began Elaine McBride. She laid a hand on her husband's shoulder and tucked a lock of smooth blonde hair behind her ear. Lindsay could see she was having trouble figuring out how to hospitably throw a guest off her property.

"I understand you caught a lot of flack about the house," said Lindsay. "I renovated an old log house to live in, too. And being an archaeologist, you can imagine some of the criticism I got. I'm really interested in your home, and the sheriff was good enough to bring me."

They looked at each other, and the husband put his hand over his wife's. Their faces unfroze and returned to the former friendly smiles. "Please come in." They stepped aside to allow Lindsay and the sheriff to enter first.

Before she entered the house, Lindsay paused and brushed a palm over the corners of the left pen, running her fingers over the full-dovetail notching, a style of making corners that allowed the square hewn logs to fit so tightly a knife couldn't have been forced between them. It was a style more typical of the eighteenth century. The opposite pen had half-dovetail notching and caulking in the spaces between the logs—a design often accompanied by siding, and common in the nineteenth century.

She entered a living room bedecked with charm and a look that matched the house. Antiques, period crockery, and blue willow plates decorated the walls. The furniture was made from cherry. A plush sofa and chairs upholstered with large blue and deep rose flowered designs sat in front of a rock fireplace. Several unburned logs were stacked on a set of brass andirons. Matching brass fire irons stood on one side of the hearth, and a bellows leaned against the rocks on the opposite side. A Kentucky rifle hung on the wall over the oak mantel. The room was about twenty by fifteen feet and part of the ceiling was open, revealing the roof beams. In one corner next to the fireplace, a set of stairs led to a loft.

"Nice," said Lindsay as she sat on the couch. The sheriff sat on the opposite end, and Phil McBride settled in one of the chairs.

"Please, let me get some refreshments." Elaine left the room before Lindsay could say anything.

While she was in the kitchen, McBride and the sheriff discussed the theft. There wasn't much to tell. McBride himself didn't know anything, other than that the pickup was gone. He eyed Lindsay as she rose to look at the various antiques. A framed plaque under glass caught her eye. Inside, a crumpled metal plate contained the number 1775. She looked over at Phil McBride and realized he had been waiting for her to find it. She smiled.

"Is this the date of the cabin?"

He grinned a huge boyish grin, nodding his head. Sheriff Ramsey rose to take a look.

Elaine brought in a tray of coffee and chocolate chip cookies and set them down on an end table. "She found the plaque?" Elaine looked as pleased as her husband as she poured coffee in blue willow cups.

"Where was it?" Lindsay asked.

"We found it between the logs, taking the cabin apart to move it," said Phil. "It's lead."

There was little question now about the earlier occupation of the farmstead and the date of the site. Lindsay wished she could tell them about the coffins.

"Cream and sugar?"

"Black," Lindsay answered.

"Elaine makes great coffee," said the sheriff as Elaine handed her a cup. "I've been trying to get her to bring a pot to the department every morning."

The sheriff was right. It had a rich nutty flavor, not bitter. She sipped on the coffee, still examining the lead date marker—neat numbers, probably drawn freehand.

"What's your cabin like?" asked Elaine, sitting on the other chair.

Lindsay turned back to her hosts and sat down on the sofa. "It was built in the late 1800s. The design is two pens with a dog trot between them. I turned the dog trot into a hallway, added a kitchen onto the back, and built a bedroom and balcony over the kitchen."

"You say you were criticized for renovating your cabin?"

"Some of the people in my department thought that what I did was inappropriate. I moved the cabin to my property, so even had it been on the national registry, it would have been taken off. It was in great condition and just seemed like it ought to be lived in."

"What do you think of ours?" asked Phil.

"I like it. The idea of just going from this room to the next and crossing a century is kind of neat."

"You know that phrase, *if these walls could talk*?" asked Phil. "These have."

The way he and his wife exchanged smiles, Lindsay could see the house held other surprises.

Chapter 16

Elaine McBride reached inside the drawer of the cherry end table and pulled out two hardbound scrapbooks. She handed one of them to Lindsay. On the cover was a photograph of the cabin, not as it is now, refurbished and modernized, but as it was when it sat at the Gallows farmstead before being moved and renovated. The first page, a sort of title page, contained a photograph of a second view of the cabin *in situ,* the new version below it, and a paragraph describing the cabin's provenance.

"These two scrapbooks are identical," said Elaine. "There are three, altogether. I made one for us, another for the historical society, and one for the archaeologists when I learned they would be excavating the site."

The pages cataloged in detail the dismantling and rebuilding of the cabin, obviously lovingly put together by Elaine. Lindsay imagined Elaine's excited anticipation of the reception of this information by archaeologists, and how Claire's reaction must have stung. Claire probably looked at the well-off McBrides with jealously and anger, as she did everyone who possessed things or qualities she didn't.

"This is invaluable data. Your photo close-ups are so clear I can see the details of the notching and tool markings along the logs."

As Lindsay turned the pages and commented on almost every photograph, she noted that both Elaine and Phil leaned forward slightly in their seats, again waiting for her to find something. She was beginning to catch their anticipation. She flipped to a page that showed what looked like a close-up view of hardwood flooring. The caption described it as a corner of the loft in the older pen.

Lindsay glanced up at the loft and down again at the photograph. Something in the photo caught her eye. She looked closer.

"Do you have . . ." She didn't finish, for as she looked up, Elaine had a magnifying glass held out to her. Lindsay took the glass and examined the photograph again. "Is this writing?" It looked like someone had scratched words into the floor.

The sheriff looked over her shoulder. Elaine and Phil grinned.

"Yes, it is writing. We did tracings, took high-resolution photographs, did some computer enhancements, and finally came up with our best estimate." Elaine had typed a transcription on the facing page.

Eda Mae
Gone all day
Wouldn't say
Which a way

"What?" said Lindsay and the sheriff together.

"The spellings aren't exactly the way they were in the scratches," said Elaine. "I changed them to the correct spellings to make easier reading. It took me a while to realize that what looked like an *f* on some of the words was actually an *s*."

Lindsay turned the page. Another close-up photograph. Another translation.

Cherry's gone a looking
Not at home a cooking

"Cherry, Eda Mae . . . do you know who they are?"

The McBrides shook their heads. "I've looked through some of the documents we have at the historical society and talked to a couple of the older society members and haven't found a clue. I don't know if this was done by the Gallowses or by the people who lived in the cabin before them, in 1775."

Lindsay looked up at the date plaque on the wall.

"It doesn't appear to be the same hand that did the plaque and the floor writing," said Phil.

"Go on, there's more," said Elaine.

Apparently, someone had scratched several little poems on the floor of the loft. Elaine had photographed and transcribed them all into the scrapbook.

Shot him dead
In the head

"That doesn't sound good," said the sheriff after Lindsay read the poem aloud.

"We can't tell the order in which they were written. But, if you look closely, you can see definite changes in the handwriting from one poem to the next. Some are neat, others look a little shaky, some are printed. Most, like that one, are rather dark. A psychiatrist would have a field day with those."

"This is interesting." Lindsay was able to read one poem from the photograph.

Bear chased Cally
Out in valley

"Bear? Cally-Kelley? Do you think that's how Kelley's Chase got its name?"

"That's what we think." Phil gestured elaborately. "Place names around here frequently describe events in people's lives. There's a place called Stocking Hollow in the Smokies. It seems that a hunter stopped there to spend the night. He removed his wet socks, hung them by his fire to dry, and fell asleep. Next morning, he discovered his socks had burned up . . . thus, the name for the hollow. Apparently, you didn't have to do a whole lot to get a place named for what you did."

The sheriff chuckled. "Phil is somewhat of an expert on names of places around here."

"Names can let you know what you're in for," Phil said. "Anything named after the devil, or hell—like Devil's Chute or Hell's Ridge—is going to be a rough place to traverse."

"What about Holy Butt? How'd that get its name?" asked the sheriff. "I've always wondered about that."

"Not for what it sounds like. A woman renamed the creek that ran by her house from Holly Creek to Holy Creek, thinking it was a much better name. Oddly enough, the name change stuck. The name change also carried itself over to the adjacent mountain peak, and Holly Butt—the old name of the peak—caught the unfortunate moniker, Holy Butt."

Lindsay laughed and turned the page.

Cherry bell
Bound to hell

"That's gloomy." She glanced up at Elaine.

"It gets worse," she said.

Made no sound
When she bound

The next entries were rather grim. Lindsay and the others frowned as she read aloud. The dark messages sounded odd, written in rhyming couplets.

Buried well
By the gate to hell

Not my sin
The hell he's in

"What do you make of those?" asked Lindsay after she read the final entry.

"Elaine and I've made up all kinds of stories. But basically, it looks like something bad happened—either someone did something or saw something and felt guilty enough to write it down, like a confession of sorts. But that last entry you read sounds like some kind of denial of responsibility."

"We thought maybe you archaeologists might come up with some documentation mentioning a Cherry or an Eda Mae."

"It's too interesting not to follow up on. What did the others say when you showed this to them?"

The McBrides exchanged glances. "We didn't get that far."

"I see. And no one in the historical society has any information—how about the library?"

Elaine shook her head. "There's some older folks I could talk to. We didn't find the scratches right away, so we haven't been looking for answers long. Phil's mother wanted us to sand the floors. I'm glad we didn't."

"All the scratches and dents were history to us," agreed Phil. "Elaine wants to start a project with the historical society where everyone who owns an old home does a similar history."

"Makes me want to put together a scrapbook of my home. Actually, I think when I get back, I'll take a magnifying glass to my floor."

"You can have that scrapbook," said Elaine. "It's yours, personally," she added.

"I understand. Thank you." Lindsay took another sip of coffee and took a cookie.

"Alfred Tidwell wants Miss Chamberlain here to investigate his aunt's death and her missing papers," the sheriff said. Elaine and Phil raised their eyebrows. "Phil here was Miss Susan's doctor."

Phil McBride took on a more sober expression. "Why did Alfred come to you? That seems odd."

"I'm not sure," said Lindsay. "Someone told him I would be objective. I don't know who, or exactly why."

"And are you?" Elaine picked up the coffeepot and offered everyone another round.

"I've reached my limit," said the sheriff. "Makes me hyper."

Lindsay declined, too. "I'm cutting down on caffeine while I'm working this dig. Thank you. In answer to your question, the president of the company that has the contract to excavate the site wants to know the truth about what happened."

"I don't mean to offend, but might you not have a conflict of interest?" Phil accepted another cup of coffee and grabbed a cookie from the plate.

"No, not really. We all want the truth."

"That's a little altruistic, isn't it?"

"My division head, Francisco Lewis, asked me to look into it. Lewis wouldn't have asked me if they wanted it swept under the rug."

"But why you?" The corners of Phil's lips turned up in a skeptical smile.

"In addition to being an archaeologist, I'm also a forensic anthropologist. In that capacity, I've worked with the courts and on criminal investigations. I like to consider myself a person of integrity, and I want to keep that same reputation with my forensic colleagues."

"So, you're *Dr.* Chamberlain, then?" said Phil.

"Yes, but I can't practice medicine."

That brought a round of chuckles and lightened the mood that the mention of Tidwell had ever so slightly darkened.

"I suppose you want to ask me some questions about Miss Tidwell," said Phil, getting to his feet. "I'll have to call Alfred. I believe you, Sheriff, but I still have to hear firsthand the family's permission. Meanwhile, Elaine can take you on the grand tour."

Phil headed up to the loft while Elaine led Lindsay and the sheriff on a tour of the house. The opposite pen was smaller than the 1775 side by about five feet in length, making it a fifteen foot by fifteen foot square. This was the room Elaine McBride used for her projects. Part sewing room, part craft room, it also doubled as a guest room. The worktable, wardrobe, chests, chairs, and futon frame were made of distressed pine with oxidized pulls and hinges. The futon cover was deep red and green tartan. Lindsay liked the room. She could have worked in these surroundings.

"We added a small bathroom." Elaine stepped aside, letting Lindsay look at the ceramic tiled sink and porcelain and silver fixtures.

"This is real nice," said the sheriff. "No wonder every time the women's club meets here, Leanne comes home and looks at log house magazines."

Elaine showed them the large modern kitchen and dining room they'd built on the back. "Our bedroom's upstairs. We put the new addition on the back so as not to interfere with the original design too much. Phil's study's in the loft," she told Lindsay. "Go on up and have a look. You can talk to him there. Remind him to show you the writing."

Lindsay climbed the stairs and emerged into a room that looked like a nook in a library: shelves of books, a library table, desk with a computer. Phil had just hung up the telephone.

"Come over here first," he said, as he turned on a corner lamp and removed a braided-rag throw rug from the corner. "We keep it covered to protect it."

Lindsay got down on the floor and rubbed her fingers over the scratches. Some letters were clear, others just looked like scratches. Elaine must have worked hard to figure out what was written. Lindsay stood. "This window . . . was it here, or did you put it in?"

"It was here. And about that size. We just put in the window framing and double panes."

"These scratches are a good mystery."

"Yes, I'm a little ambivalent about solving it. The idea of discovering the secret is intriguing, but once we do, then the mystery is gone. Now, speaking of mysteries, I really don't think we have one in Miss Tidwell."

"Alfred said it was all right for you to talk to me about her?"

"Yes, he was quite anxious that I do so."

"I don't suppose he told you why he selected me?"

"Yes, but he swore me to secrecy on that."

Lindsay raised her eyebrows and took the chair offered her.

"Nothing sinister, I assure you," he said.

"I suppose I'll find out, sooner or later. You say she had a heart attack?"

"Yes. She had had two before. When she had the second one, I wasn't sure she was going to make it. But, except for her heart, she was in good health."

"How was she mentally?"

"Nothing wrong with her mind. She was eccentric, but that was her right."

"You didn't find any sign at all that someone might have harmed her or induced a heart attack?"

"None whatsoever. No bruises, nothing. She died peacefully in bed. I know Alfred thinks this Van Horne woman took her around, trying to tire her out, or something. Frankly, I'm not sure what he thinks. But I don't believe her activities that day contributed to her death. It was simply her time."

"Did you know her personally?"

"Elaine and I bought several antiques from her. Several are around the house—the conductor's lantern on the mantel in Elaine's room, the rifle over the fireplace in the living room, to name two."

"Ever purchase any documents?"

"No."

"Ever see any?"

"No. Elaine and I talked about it when this whole thing came up. Tidwell came to my office—many times—with his suspicions and told me about the alleged theft. Neither of us knew of any historical documents she may have had."

"What do you think of Tidwell's claim about the documents?"

McBride shrugged. "I don't know. It's not out of the question that his aunt had valuable documents. She told us she loved old estate sales. She particularly liked buying old trunks and boxes no one had opened in years . . . which was kind of odd . . . she was a shrewd businesswoman. Didn't seem like she'd buy a pig-in-a-poke, but I guess there's a little kid in all of us."

"If you or your wife remember anything, give me a call." Lindsay wrote the house phone number on a piece of paper for him. "I appreciate your talking with me. And I'm sorry some people from the site were rude to you and your wife. Archaeology is like any other field. We have some people who are easy to get along with, and some who aren't very tactful."

"I appreciate your interest in our work, especially Elaine's. She put a lot of time in recording the history of the house." McBride opened a drawer and took out a CD jewel case and handed it to Lindsay. "Here's all the photographs from our restoration."

Lindsay turned the case over in her hand. "Thank you. This is very kind of the two of you."

They rose to go downstairs, when suddenly Lindsay turned. "Have you ever been involved in a postmortem?"

"I didn't see the need to have Miss Tidwell's body autopsied. It was very evident how she died."

"No. The question has nothing to do with the Tidwell case."

"Oh. In medical school I attended a couple . . . why?"

"I may be able to repay your hospitality."

"Now, that sounds very mysterious."

"It is, indeed."

Lindsay and the sheriff said good-bye to the McBrides, and he drove her to her SUV. On the way back to the site, she kept an eye out in her rearview mirror for anyone who looked like they might be following her, breathing a sigh of relief when she arrived at the site without incident. She parked the Explorer and went in to change clothes for work. On the way in, she met Claire, blocking the way up the stairs.

Chapter 17

"You finally decided to show up for work, did you?"

Claire's tone, as usual, was one of confrontation. She stood three steps up on the stairs, holding a file folder in her hand, unconsciously stroking the edges. Lindsay folded her arms, as though to remove the temptation to throttle Claire.

"I asked Adam to tell you I had errands to run."

Claire didn't move, and there was no way to get past her, short of shoving her aside. Her position on the stairs made her taller than Lindsay. The way she lingered there and her eyes sparkled, Lindsay thought she must enjoy the stature.

"And you think you can just take off whenever you want? We have work to do here, and you left me short-handed." She tapped the folder in the palm of her hand.

"Claire, not two days ago you told me I was unnecessary. Now you're telling me I'm indispensable?"

Claire didn't say anything for a moment, just dropped her arms to her sides and worked her mouth, the way she did when she was caught with no retort. Papers fell out of the folder and floated to the floor. With an exasperated sigh, she came down the last two steps to pick them up. Lindsay took the opportunity to get past her.

"I'm going up to change. Is there anything in particular you want me to work on?"

"We'll see when you get to the site."

Lindsay started up the steps. Claire called up after her.

"By the way, Dr. Lewis called while you were out gallivanting. He talked to Drew. They hit it off really well." She looked smug, as if getting along with Lewis was some kind of triumph.

"That's good. Has he made arrangements for the coffins this soon?"

"Some of them. He needed some logistical information about the site. I guess you didn't give him enough."

God, Claire, thought Lindsay. *Don't you ever get tired of this?*

She wondered how far she'd get if she tried to question Claire about her visit to Miss Tidwell's house on the afternoon of the day she died. Not far. She could try to trick her into talking about it, maybe get her mad enough to blurt something out.

And maybe I can be a glutton for punishment.

"Oh, and I also called a forensic expert from Tennessee. He'll be down to analyze the bones from the coffins." Lindsay didn't think it was possible for Claire to look even more smug than she had a minute ago, but this positively thrilled her.

"Who?" asked Lindsay.

"Dr. Nigel Boyd."

Lindsay smiled and continued up the stairs to change.

It was lunchtime when she got out to the excavation. The crew was already breaking up for lunch. She'd made herself a peanut butter and jelly sandwich and taken an apple from the kitchen, though she wasn't hungry. Her emotions were split about the prospect of talking with Drew. On the one hand, she was looking forward to telling her about the cabin. On the other hand, she'd just as soon not tell Drew in front of the crew that she was, after all, going to investigate Alfred Tidwell's claims against her. Damn Lewis. It was like dealing with the devil. He gives you what you want, but there's always a price.

Drew hadn't yet sat down to eat, but was looking over a cache of bones Erin had excavated and Marina was getting ready to photograph.

"Do you know what these are?" Drew asked when Lindsay squatted down beside her.

Lindsay scrutinized the collection of mostly long bones jumbled together like pickup sticks. "I see pig, deer, chicken, turkey, squirrel."

"Sort of what we would expect." Drew turned her head toward Lindsay, looking her in the eyes. "Adam said you had some errands?"

"Yes. That's what I need to speak with you about. I know I said I wasn't going to investigate this thing with the Tidwells, but Lewis, in his way, made it a condition for his help with the lead coffins. He and Keith York want you cleared. Everything I've been able to discover says Miss Tidwell died of natural causes and there were no documents to be stolen. The Tidwells can't even describe the documents they say their aunt had. I'm thinking that you're right, and the documents owned by the historical society are the ones Alfred Tidwell thinks his aunt owned. It may be that Miss Tidwell donated them and didn't tell her relatives. By all accounts, she was secretive."

Drew frowned and stared off into the distance. Her hazel eyes looked misty. "I'm supposed to be deposed next week by his lawyer. My husband is coming down. It'd be good to know what they have." She focused back on Lindsay. "Do you know why Keith is so dead set on pursuing this?"

"I think it has something to do with his China negotiations. He doesn't want any scandal to interfere. I'll be as honest with you as I can, but I don't want to be caught in the middle of this."

"Looks like it's too late for that." Marina snapped a final picture and unscrewed the camera from the mount.

"Yes, but I'd like not to get crushed."

Drew threw up her hands. "If it'll satisfy Keith. I want to work on the digs in China he's negotiating. He won't ask me if I'm under suspicion of being a murderer and a thief. Damn, I've made my reputation in historical documents. Now, to have those people . . . Damn them."

"The depositions will be the end of it," predicted Marina. "Like Lindsay said, they have nothing. That's because there is nothing. Don't sweat it. They're just opportunists."

They hadn't seemed like opportunists to Lindsay. Rather, like people who honestly thought they'd been wronged. But it was probably best not to say that. It was a good time to change the subject.

"I wasn't aware until this morning that the log cabin from here is still standing."

Drew shrugged. "Yes, but we don't have access to it—not even a photograph."

"Claire alienated the McBrides, the way she does everyone," said Marina, packing the camera in its case.

"I was just there," said Lindsay.

"You're kidding. Today?" Marina laid down the camera case and sat down beside them.

"Yes. You'll be happy to know, Marina, that in dismantling the cabin they found a lead tag with the date 1775."

"I knew it!" She shoved Drew on the shoulder. "Haven't I been telling you, Drew?"

"The cabin's that old?" asked Drew.

"Half is. The pen with the date tag was built using an earlier construction technique than the opposite pen. My guess is, the second pen was added by the Gallowses after they acquired the farm in 1836."

"So we have access to the cabin now. That's good." She smiled and the creases in her forehead smoothed away. "I understand that you think Structure 6 is an outhouse and ought to be completely excavated and the contents floated?" asked Drew.

"Chemically floated, yes."

"Because of the interest over the coffins, there's a chance we'll have some extra funds for more excavation. Maybe we can do the outhouse. I know that's what Powell wants to do. I think he wants to specialize in outhouses. He's one of those guys who gets excited over excavating coprolites. Let's go tell the crew the news. Joel and Adam will be thrilled. They've both been bitching lately about not having photographs of the log house."

Lindsay, Marina, and Drew sat down with the crew near Feature 3. Lindsay gave them the essentials about her visit to the McBrides and their cabin. She was disappointed to hear that all the initial rather gleeful responses were about how this development was going to anger Claire. Only Joel connected the rediscovery of the cabin with its impact on what they could learn about the site.

"This'll tie everything together," he said, wadding up his napkin and stuffing it down into his lunch sack. "It'll be a great focus for the questions about building construction technique, occupation, and time. Can we get photographs?"

"As a matter of fact, McBride gave me a CD filled with photographs of the cabin, both before and after the move and renovation."

"No, really?" said Marina. "That's unbelievable. He must have really liked you. Joel's right. The cabin and our friends in the lead coffins are going to make this a much more significant site."

"There's an added bit of information," said Lindsay. "There's a chance someone in one of the households was a poet of sorts."

"What? What are you talking about?" Claire walked up and sat down with the rest of the crew and opened her lunch sack. Drew filled her in about the log cabin as she took out her sandwich and unwrapped it. Before she took a bite, she looked over at Lindsay. "How did you get selected for such an honor?"

"Claire, what does it matter?" For a moment, Lindsay thought Joel was going to wad up his paper sack and throw it at Claire. The quiet, mild-mannered Joel appeared finally to be getting tired of her incessant abuse. "This is a great find, and all you can think about is what kind of mean shit you're going to say next. All of us are just a little sick of it. Drew, I don't understand why you let her do this."

"You're fired, Joel Markowitz."

"You can't fire me."

"Let's settle down," Drew said. "No one's fired. Lindsay was about to tell us something interesting about the house." Claire gave Drew the look of a hurt puppy.

"On the floor of the loft they found scratchings that turned out to be a series of poems—rhyming couplets."

"Poems?" asked Joel.

"Yeah, right. They've certainly got you fooled," Claire said sarcastically. "They probably did it themselves."

Joel stood. "Why don't you wait until later to tell us? Maybe we can all meet somewhere without Claire, so we won't have to listen to her running insults."

"You won't be meeting about the site without me. I am the site director, and I resent your . . ."

"No, Claire, you're a walking turd." Joel scowled. "You contribute nothing to the site. All of us have to work around you and your incompetence, and I'm sick of it." He turned to Drew. "Everyone knows Keith has been worried about the turnover of crew at this site, and we all know what's causing the turnover. When he gets back from China, I'm going to take it up with him." Joel stomped off toward the artifact tent before Drew could comment.

"Let's take this disk up to the computer," whispered Marina. "You can show me the photographs." Before anyone could object, Lindsay and Marina rose and took their lunches back to the house.

The second story of the house had four bedrooms and a bath. Lindsay's was the round room. Claire and Drew shared the front room, the one with a balcony. The large bedroom across from the bathroom was where Kelsey, Erin, and Marina slept. The fourth bedroom, the one adjacent to the bathroom and over the kitchen, was used as a storeroom and Marina's workroom. She had installed a tiny darkroom in the closet—an easy renovation, because the closet backed against the bathroom. Some of the more valuable surveying equipment was kept there, along with a desk and Marina's computer.

"I bring artifacts here to catalog sometimes," Marina said as she unlocked the door. "Sometimes I work late and don't want to be walking back to the house from the artifact tent in the dead of night."

"I can't blame you." Lindsay handed her the CD. "This is probably the spookiest site I've ever worked on."

As Marina booted up the computer and called up her paint program, Lindsay glanced around the room at the boxes of supplies.

"You have extra weatherproof tents?" asked Lindsay, reading the lettering on the sides of some of the boxes.

"Yes. In case we decide to dig through the winter, we can put a tent up over a feature and dig in relative warmth. It can get cold in the mountains."

On the shelf opposite the computer, Marina had stored reams of laser paper, a can of coffee, family-size tea bags, and a hot plate and toaster oven. Marina grabbed a ream of paper to refill the printer.

"You have a regular kitchen in here," Lindsay commented.

Marina grinned. "If there was room, I'd move my mattress in here. I spend enough time here. A couple of winters ago when we were doing survey work for Eco Analysts, I lived on hot chocolate in the evenings." She clicked on the image of the CD on her computer screen. "This disk has a lot of pictures on it. Some text files, too."

"That must be the poems and the descriptive narrative Elaine McBride put together."

"Oh, yeah, the poems. We'll print those out, too." Marina printed out pictures of a couple of views of the cabin before it was moved from the site. "Nice. I'm glad you made friends with the McBrides. I couldn't imagine how Drew was going to explain why we didn't have pictures of the cabin."

Marina exited the paint program, called up her word processor, and found a file called "loftpoems." When it came out of the printer, she snatched it up and laughed after reading the lines.

"What do you reckon these mean?"

"I have no idea."

"You're sure the McBrides didn't do this?"

"I examined the floor. The scratches looked old to me."

"You know there are ways of making things look old. Antiques traders do it all the time. The scratches could have been made to look old by being stained in some way—rubbed with nutmeats, or a drop of soy sauce. Here, let me look at a photo of the scratches."

Marina called up a couple of the floor photographs and looked closely at the images on the screen. She wrinkled her brow, changed the contrast, brightness, and smiled at Lindsay. "You know, I'd be inclined to think it's for real. Think we can verify this without alienating the McBrides again?"

Lindsay nodded. "I was thinking about going through the documents at the historical society, and while I look for something that might shed light on Drew's problem, I can look for the names Cherry and Eda Mae."

"Ask Mrs. Laurens, too. She knows a lot of the old stories around here. Maybe she's heard of one about a Cherry or Eda Mae."

Dinner was calm. Claire had little to say, and everyone else seemed lost in thought. Lindsay noticed Mrs. Laurens and her husband eyeing the group, probably wondering what had happened to shut everyone up. After dinner Drew called a meeting in the living room. *Damage control,* thought Lindsay.

Lindsay had to pass Trent to get from the dining room to the living room. The dark look he gave her was frightening. She sat down on an old cane-back chair in a corner of the room. Trent stood with his back against the wall, staring at her. Claire, Kelsey, and Erin sat on the couch, Powell perched on a window seat. Adam, Byron, Joel, Dillon, Bill, and Sharon found seats on the various chairs or floor pillows. With so many people, the room was hot and stuffy. Drew stood, her hands in the pockets of her khaki shorts, her head bowed.

"This hasn't been an easy site . . ." She paused until the snickers subsided. "But, with the discovery of the lead coffins and the help both in manpower and financing that we're going to get to excavate them, we all have a chance to make our mark—or at least fill out our vitae. So please, let's stop all of this bickering. We . . ."

She was interrupted by the telephone. Claire was closest, so she snatched it off the receiver.

"Yes, this is Claire Burke. I'm the one you spoke with." Claire's face changed to her self-satisfied look, which melted instantly into a frown. She was silent for a long while. "I . . . I . . . I don't think you understand. Yes, she's here."

Claire handed the phone to Drew. She sat with her head down, chewing her thumbnail and not meeting any of the puzzled stares in her direction. Lindsay shifted her gaze from Claire to Drew who, other than for a crease in her forehead, looked calm.

"Yes, this is Drew Van Horne. I was unaware. Yes, of course, I understand. I've been to Scotland; it's lovely there. Yes, she's here." Drew put her hand over the mouthpiece. "Lindsay, it's Nigel Boyd. He'd like to speak with you."

Lindsay rose and took the phone. She stretched the cord as far as she could away from Claire, until she was almost in Powell's lap. He moved to let her lean against the window seat.

"Hi, Nigel."

"Lindsay, are you all right? What the heck is going on down there?"

"It's a very long story, Nigel."

"Who is this Claire Burke? She called here this morning telling me about the lead coffins, and that I was the only forensic anthropologist available to work on the bones. I'm backed up here with remains found in a well, possible missing hikers found by some hunters, and the skeleton that may be the remains of an elderly man who wandered away from his nursing home last year. It was already going to be tight getting done before I have to leave for the forensic conference in Scotland, and then this came up. Luckily, I called Lewis to find out about the timing on the coffin thing, and he tells me you're already down there. What gives?"

"I'll explain over dinner sometime."

"Can't talk, eh? I'll be waiting to hear what kind of mess you've gotten yourself in this time." He gave an audible sigh. "I was very sorry to hear about the attack on you. I'm glad I didn't find out about it until you were found safe and sound. Would've worried myself sick. And to think I'd just seen you and Derrick. You two going to get back together?"

"No, don't think so. I'm still seeing John."

"The coffin thing sounds like an interesting project, but I'm happy to leave it in your very capable hands. I've been looking forward to Scotland."

"Have a good trip. We'll talk when you get back."

"Take care, Lindsay."

Lindsay hung up the phone and went back to her seat. Claire got up and rushed out of the room.

"Hey, Claire, what's the matter?" called Trent.

"I didn't know she'd done that, Lindsay. I'm sorry," said Drew.

"No harm done."

"Done what?" asked Adam.

"Let's just drop it for now," said Drew. "Lindsay, you were about to tell us about the scratches on the floor."

Marina passed around the photographs she had printed of the cabin and handed out copies of the poems.

"Did they take photographs of the floor?" asked Powell.

"Several," Lindsay told him.

"You think this is real?" Joel asked Lindsay.

"I believe the McBrides didn't do it. I don't know how to date the scratches. They could date from the late 1700s, or from the Gallowses' time, or they could have been made any time between the building of the cabin and now. It sat empty for decades."

"It's kind of weird." Byron stroked his long beard and scratched his head.

"Does anyone remember running across mention of a Cherry or an Eda Mae?" Joel asked.

They all looked at Drew, who shook her head. "I don't recall seeing either of those names, but at the time we were looking only for documents and information about the Gallows farmstead."

"I think I'll spend tomorrow looking, if that's all right," said Lindsay.

"They won't let you in the historical society archives," said Adam. "Claire's messed that up, too."

"I think Lindsay's made friends with the natives," said Marina.

The conversation drifted away from site business, so Bill and Sharon got up to go to their motel. Adam and Byron went to the kitchen to get a round of beers for everyone, and Kelsey put on some music and pulled the twins up to dance. Lindsay took the opportunity to go upstairs to see Claire.

The door was closed. She knocked lightly.

"What do you want?" Claire sounded as if she had been crying. Lindsay didn't wait for an invitation. She opened the door, went in, and closed it behind her. Claire was propped up on her mattress, an open book in her hands. "Come to gloat?"

"Claire, you really need to do a network analysis before you go off halfcocked again. I'm a forensic anthropologist. Nigel is a forensic anthropologist in a neighboring state—didn't you think we might know each other? In fact, we were in graduate school together."

"I suppose you couldn't wait to call him up."

"As a matter of fact, I didn't call him."

"Yeah, sure. Like I believe that."

"I didn't have to call him. He called Francisco Lewis to find out about the project. I imagine Lewis was very surprised when Nigel called. Claire, why don't you stop alienating people? You've got Nigel and Lewis thinking you're nuts. Why did you do that?"

"And you think you're a pet with Dr. Lewis?"

"No. You're missing the point. When the finding of those coffins is made public, and the professional papers and reports are published, it won't be my name on them that matters to Lewis. It's the connection to the University of Georgia that's important. Lewis is doing a lot of work and spending UGA money to bring NASA here. By bypassing me and bringing Nigel Boyd in to do the forensic analysis, you would have taken credit away from UGA. It wasn't a smart move."

"And you came to throw it in my face?"

"No, I came to offer you a proposal."

"Proposal?" asked Claire. "What could you possibly propose to me?"

"I would like some peace; so would the crew. I'm offering to co-author two papers with you with your name as primary author."

"And you think that would be attractive to me? I'm going to be coauthoring papers with Drew."

"No doubt. However, Drew and I have different expertise. Our articles appear in different journals. This is an opportunity to expand your vita. Go to Marina's computer and get on the Internet. Look up the UGA Department of Archaeology faculty and call up my vita. You'll find I have pages of publications, all in good academic journals, and in most I'm the sole author."

"And in return, you want what?"

"I want you to lighten up. Stop making little insulting remarks every time I open my mouth. Stop criticizing the crew during dinner."

"I suppose you want special treatment, too?"

"No. You can put me shovel shaving if you want. Just lay off your hostility. Think about it."

Lindsay didn't wait for an answer. If she forced Claire to make a decision right then, it would be no. However, if she let her think about it, there was a good chance she would go for it.

Instead of going back downstairs, Lindsay returned to her room. She lay on her bed with her eyes closed. It was the first chance she'd had to think about the incident with the truck that had zoomed past her that morning. Maybe it was an unfortunate coincidence. Maybe not. If not, whoever attacked her in the spring had followed her here.

Oh, God. How did they know I was here? Have they been looking for me? Did someone tell them? Who? Most everyone who knows that I'm here was told not to give out the information. That her attack was connected to something going on here now looked more likely.

She recalled Trent's dark expression. *What was that about? Did Drew talk to him about drugs, and he blames me? Am I in danger here—in this house, in this room without a door?*

Tears came to her eyes, spilling over and running to her ears. She reached up with the heel of her hands and wiped her eyes.

Damn, I hate this. I used to be so strong. Is this who I am now? A crybaby?

She could ask Erin, Kelsey, and Marina if she could share their room, but they were already crowded. Besides, she liked being alone, just not exposed. She looked at the curtain. A door would go a long way toward making her feel secure. If they could put in a darkroom, they could put in a door. She would ask Mr. Laurens to do that for her tomorrow.

She turned over and took a drink from her cooler. The house had a chill, and the cold drink made her shiver. She got out of bed and stood by the window, watching the mountain flora waving back and forth in the wind through the twilight. It looked like there was a storm brewing.

Storms are nature's way of keeping a good house. Rain washes dust from the leaves and replenishes moisture in the soil, and the wind clears out the dead wood. The forest after a rain is fresh, like new. That's what Lindsay's uncle used to tell her when a coming storm frightened her. The storm this night shook the house. Lindsay lay awake, watching the flashes outside her window and listening to the wind blow through every portal of the house, playing it like a reedless instrument. No one would be lurking about the house that night, she need only fear the people inside.

Why don't I just go home? It was her last thought before she fell asleep.

At first Lindsay thought it was the storm outside that had awakened her. It took several moments for her to realize that the storm was inside. Like loud crashes of thunder, violent sounds spewed up the stairwell from the first floor. She jumped up, slipped her feet into her shoes, and grabbed a robe. The noises had awakened everyone. Outside her room, the others raced with her down the stairway.

Chapter 18

AT THE BOTTOM of the stairs they all piled into the reception hall where all the guys were gathered in their underwear. Adam was holding onto a flailing Dillon. Byron was holding back Trent, who had blood running from his nose onto his chest. Claire started to go to him, but Drew reached out and grabbed her arm.

"What the hell is going on?" Drew shouted, looking from one to the other.

"You son of a bitch, I'm going to kill you!" Trent shouted at Dillon. "He's been stealing from me."

"Dillon?" asked Drew.

"Where is it? What did you do with my stuff?" Trent shouted.

"Gone, you stupid bastard!"

"Damn you!" Trent tried to lunge for Dillon, but Byron shoved him off balance, slamming him into the wall. Trent doubled over, trying to catch his breath.

"Stop this! Will somebody tell me what the hell is going on here!"

There were so many people crowded together, Lindsay was having trouble breathing. She hung back near the door, giving herself an escape route in case she had to flee. Dillon had calmed down enough that his brother and Adam let him go.

"Drugs. That's what's going on. That stupid shit's been going down to the basement to do his drugs."

"You're a liar!" shouted Claire.

"Duh . . . Claire." Dillon rapped his knuckles on his forehead. "Why do you think he's so pissed at me? I took his drugs and shit and got rid of them. If he wasn't doing drugs, then he'd have no beef with me. Get it?" Dillon turned and faced Drew. "We're about to get the attention of NASA, the army, and the news media. We don't need Trent getting us all in trouble because he's some kind of damned addict. You've not done anything . . ."

"I had no proof," Drew interrupted. "Now, let's everyone go back to bed and we'll sort this out in the morning."

"He's not sleeping in our room." Powell pointed an angry finger at Trent.

"Trent, why don't you sleep on the couch in the living room? We'll talk tomorrow," suggested Drew.

"This isn't finished." Trent was breathing hard, but the fight in him seemed to have evaporated.

"No," agreed Drew. "But we'll finish it tomorrow. Now, go to bed, all of you."

"Well," said Kelsey on the way back upstairs, "at least now we know who wears tighty whiteys and who wears boxers."

"You mean you didn't know already?" asked Marina, ducking before Kelsey could cuff her shoulder.

By morning the storm had stopped, leaving the cove soaked. Lindsay couldn't face breakfast with the crew, so she took a walk in the woods instead. Listening to the melodic sounds of birds and rushing water was more soothing to the soul than wind blowing through the house or the bickering of the crew. She hoped the freshly cleaned forest wouldn't hold the shadow that had dogged her. All the deadwood, dust, and sin would be washed and stripped away, leaving the pure forest she loved. It had, more or less. The canopy dripped water like rain falling and the forest litter was soft under her feet. She sucked in the mountain air as if it were life.

"Is this my lot in life, coming to drag you out of the woods?"

Lindsay laughed at the sound of John's voice. She turned and held out her arms. "Looks that way. What are you doing here?"

He pulled her into an embrace and a kiss. The smell of him was familiar and comforting—and safe. Maybe that's what she should do, maybe she should leave with John. Let the troublemakers solve their own problems. There were better things in life than this site.

"I talked to Dad last night. He asked me if I was taking good care of you."

"Oh? What did he say?"

"Only that. But when he says something like that, it lets me know that I'm not."

She kissed John again and held on to him. "I think tracking me down when I was lost and rescuing me from my would-be murderers a couple of months ago comes under the heading of taking good care of me."

He put her hands to his lips. "I just have a few hours, but I thought we could drive somewhere for lunch. Can you get away?"

"I'd love it, and today's a good day. It rained last night and the site's too wet to work. Drew wants to let it dry out a day. How did you find me out here?"

"I asked at the house. That's a strange bunch of people you have up there."

Water dripped on John's face, and Lindsay wiped it away with her fingers. "You've got that right. What did they do strange this time?"

"I went in—I thought it was all right not to knock—anyway, I heard talking and found everyone eating breakfast in the dining room."

"You must have been a surprise to them."

He caught her hands and held them to his chest. "No more than they were to me. They looked at me for several seconds. I think someone groaned, then this woman stood up and announced that Indians didn't bury their dead in lead coffins. I have no idea what she meant by that, but I agreed and asked where you were. Someone told me you'd just walked down into the woods toward the stream."

Lindsay laughed out loud. "We found some very old lead coffins. They must have thought you were here to protest us opening a burial." Lindsay kept hold of his hand and continued walking.

"You're expecting protesters? Wait, aren't we going deeper into the woods? You want to go back?"

"Someone will probably kick up a fuss . . . Just a little ways further—there's a small waterfall up ahead."

"You archaeologists don't like to leave people in the ground, do you?"

Lindsay leaned into him, pushing him off balance. "These aren't your ancestors, they're mine."

"I'm sorry I haven't been in closer touch." John put a hand on the back of her neck, under her hair, rubbing her skin with his fingertips.

"I just spoke with you last week. Besides, we do better this way. Did you have any trouble finding the cove?"

He shook his head. "Dogwood Cove's not hard to find."

"Dogwood Cove? Is that what you call it?"

"It's what you guys call it, too, you just don't know it. *Ka-nv-si-ta* is Cherokee for Dogwood. We've always thought that Knave's Seat is a corruption of that."

The sound of the falls grew loud as they got nearer, drowning out the other sounds.

"I like Dogwood better."

"We do, too. You been doing okay?"

"I'm all right."

"Is that true?"

"I'm . . . handling it."

"What 'it' are you handling?"

"Fear. I can't seem to get away from it. I'm scared of everything. Last night some of the guys got into a fight. It terrified me."

They turned a curve in the path and were at the falls, a four-foot drop of white water boiling over large boulders.

"Isn't this breathtaking?" She stood and looked at the falls for several moments. "Do you feel connected to this place?"

John looked for several seconds at the falls, the mountain laurel, and the thick canopy above him before he answered.

"Yes, I suppose I do." They walked to the edge of the creek, and he squatted and dipped his hands in the cold, clear water.

"My great-great-great-grandfather lived to the south of here. He had two brothers who lived up here in these mountains. There weren't many whites living here at that time, but like the rain, they were settling in low places where the earth was rich."

He stood up and dried his wet hands on his jeans. "They came here, not knowing how to survive the hard winters. My ancestors took pity on a family of settlers in the valley and gave them dried pumpkin to get them through the winter. There was also a quarrelsome white hunter who settled high in the mountains. He knew how to feed himself and his family and didn't need help.

"In 1838, the government drove my people from their lands and forced their relocation into the far West. My great-great-great-grandfather's land to the south, which he owned by deed and purchase, was also taken from him. He escaped with his family to these mountains to join his brothers and their families in hiding.

"He found when he got here that the man whose family my people had saved had repaid their kindness by turning them over to the soldiers and volunteering to help enforce their march to the west. The quarrelsome white hunter in the mountains hid and protected the other brother and his family and gave them food.

"When I was a kid and my father told me this story, I never understood how a man whose family you saved would not return the deed. I could only assume they didn't like dried pumpkin." John stroked Lindsay on the cheek with the back of his fingers. "These mountains hid my family. Yes, I feel connected."

Lindsay hugged him to her. "I'm glad you came."

They started back, arms threaded through each other's.

"I wish I could stay here with you."

"I need to get through this myself." She hesitated before adding. "I've apparently hallucinated a couple of times."

John stopped, gripped her shoulders, and turned her toward him. "Hallucinated? How? Have you called your doctor?"

"No."

"Why?"

"I'm not crazy."

"I didn't say that. But this is something your doctor needs to hear about."

"Your father said it may be a good thing. Or at least, not a bad thing."

"My father? You talked to him?"

"He called."

"My father called?" He said it as if that were another hallucination.

Lindsay explained the incident in the mirror, her running out to sleep in the Explorer, and his father calling in the morning on her car phone.

"Is that what he said—he thought he was calling Emily?"

"Yes. Obviously, read the wrong number."

"Dad's full of surprises. But I think you need to mention it to . . ."

"Well, I'm not going to."

"Okay. I give up—for now. Where's a good place for lunch?"

"How about freshwater trout?"

"Sounds great. I could go for that. You can tell me about your lead coffins over lunch."

Lunch with John was a welcome change from the zoo at the house and was over too soon. But it left her feeling safe as she drove to the local library to meet Elaine McBride. The library was one of the newer buildings in Kelley's Chase. The one-story yellow-brick building was in the middle of town, just off the main road near a real estate office and the post office.

Besides the main room with rows of metal shelves filled with books, and a couple of offices, the library had an auditorium, a computer room with two computers, and a room dedicated to the historical society. Elaine was waiting by the front desk when she arrived, talking to a young woman with thick brown curly hair and eyes the color of a Hershey's bar.

"Hi, Lindsay. This is Afton Phillips—one of the librarians."

Afton looked barely out of high school. She held out her hand and grinned, showing a deep set of dimples on a face that appeared to be in perpetually genuine good humor. "Hi. Mrs. McBride tells me you are new at the site."

"I've only been here about a week and a half or so."

"Must be fun digging in the dirt all day."

"It is. You'll have to come out some time and have a look at the excavation."

"Thanks. I'd love that."

Elaine led the way to the historical society's room, her heels clicking on the shiny green-and-white-tile floor. Lindsay's jeans and Archaeology Club T-shirt with the skeleton of a rat and the name *Rattus rattus* on the front were a stark contrast to Elaine's silk beige pantsuit and a gold chain neckless. Her blonde hair was pulled back in a small ponytail.

"You said you want to look first at the Hope Foute diary?" As she spoke, Elaine retrieved a spiral-bound notebook from the shelf. "This is a copy. Will that be all right? We have the original, but . . ."

"A copy is fine." Lindsay sat down with the document. "The records show that the Gallowses bought the land from Clarence Foute. So, something in his wife's diary may hold a clue to the writing on the floor. However, we have to realize that the writing could have occurred anytime between when the cabin was built and the present. Someone who owned the cabin before the Gallowses or someone in the Gallows household could have written it. Or someone could have come in the abandoned cabin and written graffiti on the floor."

"Oh, I hadn't really thought that it might have been done so recently." Elaine looked disappointed.

"If we're lucky, we'll come across something that will give us a clue. Do you know if this is the only volume of her diary? This is limited to the 1830s. Might she have kept a diary before that?"

"I don't know, really. It's the only one we have, but her descendants may have more."

"Where did the historical society come by the diary?"

"Hope Foute's granddaughter bequeathed it to the town. It was kept in a vault at the courthouse and forgotten for a long time. Then someone remembered seeing it and gave it to the society."

"Is there any way to contact other descendants?"

"I'll look into it." Elaine took out a notebook and began writing. "This is fun. It's like solving a mystery."

"Exactly." Lindsay started on the first page scanning the diary. For the most part, it contained information she had already learned in the survey reports. Hope Foute wrote about her husband's patients, her neighbors, her four children and sixteen grandchildren, and her older spinster sister, Faith Redmond, whom she cared for until she died. It was interesting and full of good information about the time and manners of the cove folk, but completely unenlightening about the mysterious floor carvings or any previous occupants of the Gallows cabin.

Elaine put on a pair of white gloves and began looking through old letters of the era.

"If you don't mind," Lindsay asked, "look for anything that has the word *Beau* or *Turkeyville*. Maybe we'll get really lucky and solve Tidwell's mystery as well."

"You think maybe Miss Tidwell did give her documents to the historical society?"

"Do you think that's possible?"

"Yes, I suppose it's possible, but she wasn't a person to give away something she could sell. Did Mr. Tidwell have any idea what the documents were about?" asked Elaine.

"None. Do you have provenance on all the documents here in the archives?"

"You mean, like where they came from?"

"Yes."

"I think we do. The librarian probably knows where they came from. I'll go ask if Miss Tidwell donated anything." Elaine was gone for about fifteen minutes. "Sorry I took so long. I had to call the head librarian. She's at home today. She said she didn't think Miss Tidwell donated or sold anything to the library or the historical society."

"Not quite an answer, is it?"

Elaine handed Lindsay an envelope. "This was left for you at the desk. They didn't see who left it. It was just lying in the chair when Afton came back from the bathroom."

The envelope wasn't sealed. Instead, the flap was tucked inside. Lindsay opened it and took out a page torn from a book. She stared a moment, then dropped it.

Elaine watched it flutter to the floor as Lindsay doubled over, holding her mouth to muffle a scream.

Chapter 19

"LINDSAY, ARE YOU all right?"

Elaine bent over to pick up the paper, but Lindsay put a hand on her arm. "No. Please. I need to find out if there are any prints on it."

"Prints?"

Lindsay straightened up. Her hands shook as she picked up the paper by a small corner and dropped it on the table.

"Fingerprints," she whispered.

Elaine looked at the paper that had been ripped out of a book—the title page to Edgar Allan Poe's short story "The Premature Burial."

"What does that mean?" Elaine's puzzled expression was mixed with concern.

"Please, will you call the sheriff for me?"

"Yes, of course."

Elaine hurried out to use the phone behind the main desk of the library. When she returned, Lindsay gave her the brief version of what had happened to her.

"Oh, my God," exclaimed Elaine. "Oh, my God. Is it one of those stalkers?"

"I don't know."

As they waited, Elaine fetched Lindsay a glass of cool water and sat with her. Neither of them said much until the sheriff arrived. When he strode through the door, Elaine seemed as relieved as Lindsay.

Lindsay reminded him of their previous conversation, and this time he wrote down the names of the investigators in Georgia and Tennessee who were working on her case.

"Have you had anything else happen?" asked the sheriff.

"Just the episode with the truck."

"Our truck?" asked Elaine. "This maniac stole our truck?"

"Could be," said the sheriff.

"Well, you have to catch him."

Afton stuck her head in the door. "Sheriff, the page was torn out of one of our books." Her throaty voice was vibrant with indignation. "You want that I should bag it or something?"

"I'll come take care of it, Afton. Thanks. Don't let anybody touch it. I need to know everyone who's been in the library today. How about you make me a list of the names of everyone you can remember . . . anyone who might have checked a book in or out, or anything else you can think of."

"Miss Chamberlain," said the sheriff, "could anyone at the site have done this as a joke?"

Lindsay almost laughed with relief. The notion was like a life preserver. "Yes, that's possible. That's probably what it is."

"You seem sure." He looked skeptical as he stuck his pen and notebook in his shirt pocket.

"It's not uncommon for the crew to play practical jokes on one another. Sheriff, if it's all right with you, I'll talk to them about it."

No good having the sheriff find out about Trent and what he'd been up to. Like Dillon said the evening before, that's the last kind of attention they needed. In fact, thought Lindsay, Trent was a likely suspect for this, the way he had eyed her at the last crew meeting, the way he seemed out of control. The fight with Dillon probably exacerbated whatever state he was in. She wouldn't put it past Claire, either. Lindsay willed this culprit to be different from the ones who had buried her. More than anything, she wanted that episode in her life to be over.

"I'm agreeable to that, for the time being," the sheriff said. "I'll let you know if we come up with prints, or anything else that might be helpful." He put the torn page and the envelope it came in into an evidence bag and went out to talk with Afton.

"We can meet tomorrow and continue with the documents," suggested Elaine.

"That would probably be better. How about after lunch tomorrow?"

"Great. In the meantime, I'll ask about other descendants of Hope Foute who might be in possession of more of her diary."

Lindsay drove back to the house, constantly checking in the rearview mirror. *It was just a tasteless joke,* she told herself. *Probably Trent. Possibly Claire.*

When she arrived in the house, everyone was already eating and all abuzz with news about the coffins. In one week, Dr. Alex Jarman, an atmospheric specialist from NASA, Dr. Guy Posnansky from the Armed Forces Radiobiology Research Institute, who was handling the gamma ray technology, and Dr. Juliana Skyler, a specialist in nondestructive evaluation, would arrive with their teams—bringing with them an army reserve unit. It didn't surprise Lindsay that Francisco Lewis would be arriving also. It would be like him to come and wring out every ounce of publicity he could. Actually, she welcomed his coming. She welcomed a yard full of military people milling around. She could stop worrying. The sick fear would finally go away. She would be safe.

"Dare I ask where . . . what's his name . . . Trent is?" she whispered to Marina.

"Out the door, thank God."

"How's Claire taking it?"

"Not bad. When Dr. Lewis called Drew, we all got happy again. Aren't we easy to please? It only takes a visit from NASA."

"Okay, listen up people." Drew tapped her glass with her spoon. "We're going to have to rearrange ourselves a little. The science teams are bringing their own accommodations. They'll be setting up in the cornfield, near the creek. Lewis will be staying with us. Claire and I are graciously giving up our room to him. We're moving in with you, Lindsay. You'll be happy to know that Mr. Laurens finished you a door today." Lindsay forced a smile. "They're going to be fencing off the main part of the site. I'd like to get Structure 4 finished before then."

The area just outside of Lindsay's round room was a space more or less comparable in size to the reception hall below it. It might at one time have been a sitting room off the round room. That was where Mr. Laurens hung the door, so that the curtain separating it from the bedroom was still there. What she had now was a very large bedroom. Lindsay didn't care. She opened and closed the door, locked it, opened it again and closed it. It was a good door, and it locked. The military were coming to the site, and she had a door. Life was good.

"Trying out the door?"

Claire was standing in her own doorway, adjacent to Lindsay's.

"Yes. Just basking in the luxury of it."

"I looked up your vita."

Lindsay met Claire's unblinking gaze. She had made it sound like an admission of something. Lindsay said nothing.

"I didn't know you were so widely published in so many areas."

That was definitely an admission of something.

"The thing I particularly like about archaeology," Lindsay said carefully, "is that it encompasses so many disciplines." Lindsay continued to examine the lock on her door, not looking at Claire, as if meeting her eyes too many times would break her sudden spell of civility.

"These are the topics I'm interested in." Claire shoved some papers into Lindsay's hand. She left, bouncing down the stairs before Lindsay had a chance to say anything else.

So, bribery works. Life was getting better. She looked at the folded sheets of paper and the printout of topics: comparison of farmstead excavation with historic documentation; comparisons of artifact patterns among structures; intrasite trade networks; mountain farmsteads versus hunting domiciles of the nineteenth century. Under each topic, she had made a brief outline and listed a partial bibliography. Not a bad list, none of burning appeal to Lindsay, but possibly interesting. She'd make some preliminary notes on each and share them with Claire.

Drew didn't waste much time moving herself and Claire into Lindsay's bedroom. Claire tried to bring the table for her laptop, but Drew wanted to leave it for Lewis. Like Lindsay, Claire put her mattress near an outlet and put her computer on the floor. Drew took Powell and Dillon to town and came back with a bed for

Lewis. He would be the only one in the house whose mattress sat on a bedframe and not the floor.

"You going to order flowers, too?" asked Marina, peeking into the room while Drew was making up the bed with a new bedspread.

"You know, Mrs. Laurens has a flower bed. I could ask her to bring some."

Marina rolled her eyes at Lindsay and poked her finger down her throat out of Drew's range of vision. Lindsay tried not to laugh.

"Lindsay, I'm glad you're here. Does Lewis smoke?"

Lindsay was tempted to say that he smoked a special Turkish blend and she could find out the number of his tobacconist in New York if Drew liked.

"No, he doesn't smoke."

"I understand people call him Cisco," said Drew.

"Some do." Lindsay smiled.

"And you call him Lewis?"

"Yes."

"What should I call him?"

"Whatever you like. They call him Francisco in the department."

"Francisco. I like that."

"Drew, I'd like to ask Dr. McBride to sit in on the analysis of the remains. I think it would be good PR, and it would be nice to have a local in on it . . ."

Drew nodded absently, surveying the room. "In case some issues arise about examining the dead. That's a good idea."

"A bowl of mints would be nice," Lindsay muttered.

"What?" Drew pulled her gaze away from the room and looked at Lindsay.

"Also, you have to inform the coroner. Have you done that?"

"Francisco said he would call the state archaeologist and ask him to arrange all the paperwork. What do you think of irises? They're Tennessee's state flower. They would look nice here in his room, don't you think?"

Lindsay went back into her room before she broke out laughing. Claire was typing away on her laptop.

"Is this guy that big a deal?" asked Claire.

"To some he is. He's great at getting grants. UGA loves him for that. He brings in a lot of good PR, gets UGA's name out there on the cutting edge of a lot of projects."

"Byron said he mostly publishes in popular magazines."

"That's not true. He does publish in the popular media, but he's also well published in juried journals. He likes being well known in both spheres—the public and among his peers."

"Why?"

Lindsay sat cross-legged on her bed. Odd, this was the first civilized conversation she had had with Claire since she arrived. Claire was being true to her word.

"Lewis likes to be a star."

Claire lowered her voice. "It looks like Drew's going to give him the star treatment."

Lindsay smiled. "It does seem that way."

"Is he hard to get along with?"

Not as hard as you, Lindsay thought so loudly she almost said it. "No. Not really. He's very personable. He'd make a good politician. You working on a paper?"

Lindsay was surprised Claire had jumped into the task so soon. That meant she'd have to jump into it sooner than she had planned.

"I've been working on one about trade networks among mountain settlers."

"Do you have anything I can read?"

Belatedly, Lindsay realized that was a good opening for a retort on Claire's part. But she didn't take it. The woman was trying. She handed Lindsay a folder with a printout of about thirty pages of copyedited manuscript. Lindsay stretched out on the bed and began reading, praying that it was good. Claire had already done quite a bit of literature review for the article. It must be one she'd already been working on.

Lindsay was surprised to find that it was a good paper. It needed work, but it was a good foundation. She told her, relieved for a chance to give her a genuine compliment.

"You write well."

"Yes, I do. My grades were always good in composition. If you don't mind, don't say anything about this. Everyone will accuse me of having you do all the work, and that's not the way it's going to be."

"No problem. You wrote some of the survey reports didn't you? I recognize your style."

"Yes. I can do the work. I just freeze up on tests. I always have, and you can't get through graduate school if you can't take tests."

"You got through undergraduate school."

"It was hard. I took as many courses as I could that relied mostly on papers."

"There aren't that many that don't have tests. Obviously, you can get through them. You couldn't have gotten into a graduate program in the first place, had you not had a pretty good GPA." Claire simply shrugged. "With several articles in good journals under your belt and having been the site director of this dig, if you want to go back, you can."

"I don't know. I hate jumping through hoops."

"Don't."

Claire looked up from her keyboard at Lindsay. "That's what graduate school is all about."

"A big part of getting through graduate school is learning how to be a student. It's a learnable behavior."

"I'll bet it was easy for you." Claire was coming close to dropping into insulting mode.

Lindsay wasn't sure how to answer her without making Claire jealous. Graduate school wasn't easy, but it wasn't hard, either. "I grew up in an academic environment, so it held few unknowns for me."

"My parents didn't think that either I or my brother should have an education greater than theirs."

Lindsay kept her eyes on Claire's article and tried not to show her surprise that Claire would share what must have been a private detail of her life with her. With that kind of background, school must have been very hard for her. Claire wouldn't welcome sympathy. Lindsay kept her mouth shut.

"What does Lewis look like?" Claire asked.

"Kind of Italian looking—hawkish nose, dark hair, dark eyes."

"Damn. Backup disk full. Do you have any blank disks?"

"I have everything on the hard disk."

"You mean you don't make backups?"

"Sometimes."

Claire shook her head. "One of these days, you're going to lose something."

"That's what people keep telling me. It just seems like a hard disk is more reliable than those tiny things."

Claire shook her head and rose from her sitting position. She bent over, stretching her cramped muscles. "Maybe Miss Gatekeeper left the storeroom open so I can get some."

Even with two roommates, Lindsay slept better than she had since she'd been at the site. The reality of a door gave her immeasurable peace of mind, which manifested itself in a good mood. It must have been catching, for everyone worked happily all morning.

The main task was to finish the units immediately adjacent to where the lead coffins were buried. Structure 4 seemed to be either a large smokehouse or maybe a small one-room cabin. It had a fireplace and measured about ten by seven feet.

"I have something here," said Adam, who was excavating the firebox.

"Oh, my God," said Sharon, looking over his shoulder. "Those look like human teeth."

Chapter 20

"HUMAN TEETH?" ASKED Erin. "What would they be doing in the firebox?"

The others looked at her and grinned wickedly.

"Lindsay?" called Adam.

Lindsay had heard snatches of the conversation, but was involved with Drew mapping Structure 1 and had tuned most of it out.

"Just a minute." She wrote down a number and laid down her clipboard and tape measure.

She and the others working on Structure 1 marched over to Structure 4 to see what the excitement was about.

"It looks like they're human," said Adam, rubbing the dirt off two molars.

"Could it be one of Rosellen Gallows's little babies?" asked Erin, torn between getting a closer look and stepping away entirely.

"No. They look adult to me," said Sharon, "like a rather large adult."

Lindsay took the teeth from Adam and turned them over in her hand. "Suidae, P2 and P3—Pig."

"Pig?" said Adam.

"They have teeth similar to ours." Lindsay grinned at him and put the teeth back in the palm of his hand. "Does that surprise you?"

"I should've guessed. Can you tell if they're from wild hogs in the area or domestic pigs?"

"Wild hogs weren't introduced to this area until the early 1900s. None were seen in the Smoky Mountains until the 1950s." Lindsay gestured toward where the barn originally stood. "They raised them."

She went back to Structure 1, smiling inwardly. *Not everything is sinister,* she thought.

"Claire," she said, "I'm meeting Mrs. McBride after lunch. I think I'll go shower."

Claire nodded and asked Powell to help her with the mapping. No argument. No smart retort. Lindsay was seriously considering bribery as a normal means of interaction with people. Powell raised his eyebrows at Lindsay as she passed, wondering, no doubt, about the mysterious change in Claire.

"You seem recovered," said Elaine when Lindsay met her after lunch at the library. "Did you find out who sent you that awful thing?"

"No. But it was probably a prank. Ready to go through some documents?"

"Sure." Elaine took several boxes of documents from the shelves and divided them between herself and Lindsay.

Many were hard to read—the ink was faded, or the handwriting was illegible. Lindsay scanned them as quickly as she could, looking for key words and phrases. "This is interesting. It's a letter from someone—it's hard to make out—the State of Franklin commissioned a survey of this area in 1784."

"You know, we—the historical society—need to copy some of these documents for the schools." She wrote a note in her notebook. "I visited the nursing home." She gave Lindsay a look that said she had found out something important and had been waiting for the right time to tell her.

"And?"

"I found out a tidbit of something. One of my husband's patients is a hundred and two. She's bedridden but is lucid most of the time. I read the poems to her, and we talked a while. Suddenly, she remembered something her grandmother used to say to her when she was little. 'You're gonna be like Eda Mae.' Or, 'You don't want to be like Eda Mae.'"

"Really? Did she say who Eda Mae was?"

"No. She said she never knew an Eda Mae. It was like saying don't be a Peeping Tom. I asked her what she was doing when her grandmother chastised her, but she couldn't remember. She really just added to the puzzle."

"Research is like that. If you aren't getting more questions than answers, you aren't doing it right."

"Phil suggested I put a letter in the local paper and ask if anyone has heard the expression."

"That's a good idea. Had your friend heard of Cherry?"

"No, she hadn't. I'm still trying to get a line on descendants of Hope Foute." Elaine hesitated a moment. "Phil had another idea about the writing."

"What's that?"

"A lot of people think Rosellen Gallows killed her children. Mainly, I think, because of the last one, the one who thrived with Hope Foute's daughter but died when he was returned to Rosellen. Anyway, Phil suggested that maybe some of the poems reflect Rosellen's guilt—or her husband's."

Lindsay thought about that for a moment. "Like maybe her husband killed the children, and Rosellen scratched out the poem, 'Not my sin, the hell he's in,' out of her guilt for not being able to save them."

Elaine nodded. "Or, her husband wrote them for the same reason. Were men more likely to be literate back then?"

"I believe so, but I'm not sure. Many women knew how to write. Hope Foute did. That's a good hypothesis. I'm not sure how we can verify it. What you and your husband are doing is a big help."

"I'm glad to do it. I'm going to get some more information from Miss Hill. That's the woman in the nursing home. She was born in 1899, so she may have lots of stories from her mother or grandmother."

"Did you ask her about the Gallowses?"

"Yes, but she didn't remember anything about them. She said she'd think on it. Her granddaughter says Miss Hill's like that. She can't remember something, then it will just pop into her head. Maybe talking to me will jog other memories."

"Didn't the initial archaeology survey team interview community residents?"

"Yes, but they found Mary Susan Tidwell early on. Miss Tidwell was jealous of her unique position. She liked being the one to give out information and kind of discouraged your people from using anyone else. She didn't mean any harm."

"I'm sure she didn't. No doubt she enjoyed the attention. I can't blame her. But the survey team should have known how to deal with informants to avoid that kind of situation."

Lindsay put a document aside and picked up another one. "When we leave here would it be possible to drop by your husband's office? I'd like to ask him something."

Lindsay lowered her voice to almost a whisper and told Elaine about the lead coffins and what was about to happen.

"I thought maybe he would like to assist in examining the remains."

Elaine was wide-eyed. "That's what you meant the other day about repaying him. Oh, yes, I know he'd love to. These were people who lived in our cabin, weren't they? He'll be excited to help."

"This has to be kept quiet."

"Folks will know, when all those people come to town."

"Yes. But we'd like to keep it under wraps until then."

"Phil's as interested as I am in information about our house. He'll really love this." Elaine put one box back on the shelf and got another one. "These really need to be cataloged, don't they? That would be another good project for the historical society."

"At least they have protective coverings." Lindsay picked up a letter and would have discarded it because the writing was so illegible . . . had not a word caught her eye. She took it to the copier and made an enlargement.

"What is it?" asked Elaine when Lindsay returned.

"It's a letter dated 1785, from a Michael Ellis, ordering a pewter plaque from a metalsmith."

"What does that mean?"

"Pewter is an alloy of tin, sometimes mixed with lead. It was used widely in the making of fine kitchen utensils and tableware. Perhaps, the same metalsmith also made lead coffins. And if he did, maybe there's information somewhere about who he made them for."

"I hate to rain on your parade, but that sounds kind of like a long shot."

"It is, but that's the nature of the beast. You look for clues and cross-check them."

"So, we're looking for anything about lead, too?"

"Or pewter, or any other product or process that uses lead. You said there may be records on who donated documents to the library?"

"I'll ask Afton."

Elaine stepped to the door and asked the assistant librarian to join them. Afton came in smiling, her brown curly hair bouncing as she walked.

"What can I do for you? No more morbidity, I hope."

"No," said Lindsay. "I was just wondering if you have a list of people who have donated documents to the library?"

Afton sat down and shook her short brown curls. "They were purged during the dark age of the library."

"Oh, yes, I forgot," said Elaine. "The madness of King George."

"What's the dark age?"

"The reign of George Henry McKinnon. He owns a hardware store and got himself elected to the city council. Our library's not part of the Tennessee library system. It's owned by the town. Miss Marella Oliver started it with her own money fifty years ago."

Lindsay relaxed from her efforts at deciphering the writing. This had the markings of a long story.

"About six or seven years ago the librarian retired, and the budget came under consideration. I was in high school at the time. George Henry had become head of the library committee. He decided that keeping track of books couldn't be too much different from keeping track of hammers and nails and applied the same principles of good hardware management to the library. Space is money, and anything that wasn't earning its keep—by being checked out—would have to go. So, he decided to have a book sale, and he ordered the people who worked here to locate all the books that hadn't been checked out in two years, to be sold—any of them," she added with emphasis.

"You don't mean . . . ," began Lindsay, and Afton and Elaine nodded.

"All the reference materials, the rare books that weren't allowed to circulate, and the archives. Fortunately, the idea had to go before the council. My dad came to the meeting. He's a farmer. Taught us kids to love books. Anyway, he stood up and told George Henry he was a damn fool. Didn't he, Miss McBride? He stood right up and said that. The sale was voted down."

"Many people missed the opportunity to get a good deal on encyclopedias, dictionaries, and some very rare manuscripts." Elaine folded her arms and grinned at Afton.

"I don't believe that," said Lindsay. "You're making that up."

"No. It's true," said Elaine.

"What happened to the list of donations?" Lindsay asked.

"A victim of the dark age. George Henry decided that a list of who had donated books and documents to the library was a sign of vanity. He had the whole list purged and ordered the crediting of donations to stop. Unfortunately, that list covered all the documents in this room. George finally went back to what he knew best, and we now keep track again."

Lindsay didn't quite know what to say. "I don't suppose you remember if Mary Susan Tidwell donated any documents to the library collection of the historical society?"

"I don't recall her ever donating anything. But I'll ask some of the people who used to work here."

Afton stood up to go. "Wait a minute," said Elaine, motioning her to sit back down. "Afton's great-great-grandmother is the woman I talked to at the nursing home."

"You visited Granny Hill? I'll bet she enjoyed that. She loves visitors."

"She's fun to talk to." Elaine pulled out the page of loft poems and handed it to Afton, briefly explaining where they came from.

"These are scratched in your floor? Wow."

"We're trying to find anyone who ever heard of a Cherry or an Eda Mae."

Afton screwed up her face, thinking. "Granny Hill used to tell us a lot of stuff. I wish I'd written it down. I don't remember a Cherry or Eda Mae."

"She said she thought she remembered her grandmother saying something about not wanting to be like Eda Mae," prodded Elaine.

Afton scanned the poems again. "'Eda Mae/Gone all day' . . . This is kind of like jump rope rhymes, in a way."

She tapped out a rhythm on the table and muttered almost to herself while moving her body to the beat.

"I had a little puppy/His name was Tiny Tim/I put him in the bathtub, to see if he could swim/He drank all the water, he ate a bar of soap/The next thing you know, he had a bubble in his throat/In came the doctor/In came the nurse/In came the lady with the alligator purse."

She looked up at Lindsay and Elaine staring at her. "Didn't you all jump rope?"

Lindsay shook her head.

"Some," said Elaine. "Seems I remember something about Cinderella dressed in yella . . ."

"That's one of them," Afton said. "Julie Ramsey, the sheriff's daughter, and I used to be on the precision jump rope team. We were pretty good."

"Amazing," said Lindsay. "I didn't think of children's poems. The poems were so dark, I thought it was some kind of disturbed adult. I'd forgotten that children's stories and rhymes are pretty grim."

"What's the date on these?" asked Afton.

"They're in the old part of the cabin," said Elaine. "But it could be anywhere from 1775 on until recent, I guess. But they look really old," she added quickly.

"Before the nineteenth century, jumping rope was a guy thing, and they didn't say any rhymes with it . . . did a few tricks, though. It was the girls who made it like flashdance. They already had these clapping songs and just applied them to the rope jumping."

"I never knew," said Elaine.

Afton stood and put a hand on her hip. "Just visit the library. We know everything."

"Interesting," said Lindsay. "Maybe you could investigate some of these rhymes. They may have been in popular use at one time."

"Good idea." Elaine fairly wiggled with delight. "I'll start with an Internet search tonight."

"I'll ask a folklorist at UGA," said Lindsay.

They reached the end of the day without finding anything else that shed light on any of their questions. Nor did Lindsay discover any definitive answer to her question about the source of the documents owned by the historical society. Her life these days seemed to consist of dead ends.

"I can continue looking through the documents, if you'll tell me everything to look for," offered Elaine, ". . . besides Cherry and Eda Mae."

"Look for documents between the dates 1770 and the time the Gallowses bought the property in 1836. Look for names that you recognize. Also, look for anything having to do with metalworks." Lindsay paused. "The Gallowses bought the farm from Clarence Foute, Hope Foute's husband. So, anything that has to do with that family. And if you should find anything that has Miss Tidwell's name on it, please alert me to that."

Elaine smiled. "You do all kinds of detective work, don't you?"

"Yep, that's me, Detective Chamberlain."

They put away the documents and rose to go. When Lindsay opened the door, she thought for a moment she saw Erin Blake at the front desk, then saw that it was a much older version of Erin.

"Who's that?" she whispered to Elaine.

"That's Bonnie Blake. Alfred Tidwell's sister."

Chapter 21

LINDSAY SMILED AS she approached the woman at the front desk and offered her hand in greeting. "Mrs. Blake, I'm Dr. Lindsay Chamberlain from out at the Gallows farmstead site. I wanted to tell you what a charming, hard worker Erin is. I know you must be proud of her."

The woman, tall, thin, and blonde like Erin, stood for a moment, wavering slightly, as if by some mysterious breeze. Her mouth stretched itself into a forced smile. "I . . . we are very proud of Erin. I thought, I mean, she didn't . . ."

Elaine and Afton exchanged puzzled glances. Lindsay turned to Elaine. "Would you mind asking your husband about the thing we talked about? I'll give him a call later this evening."

"Of course. Nice to see you, Bonnie."

"Yes, Elaine . . ."

"Mrs. Blake, may I speak with you a moment?"

"I suppose." She looked around her, as if searching for an escape.

"You can use the historical society's room," said Afton, leaning over the circulation desk, watching as Lindsay led Bonnie Blake into the room and closed the door.

"What's this about?" asked Mrs. Blake. She set her purse on the table and pulled out a chair, smoothing the back of her lemon yellow skirt as she sat down.

"Your brother asked me to look into the question of items missing from your late aunt's estate."

"Yes, I knew he was going to."

"He was rather vague about exactly what is missing."

"He would have to be. We don't know exactly. It's very frustrating. My aunt wasn't herself the last few years of her life—if she ever was. We really should have put her in a home several years ago."

"So, you're saying there may not have been any papers?"

Mrs. Blake tapped her long polished nails on the table. "Now, don't you put words in my mouth. I didn't say that. She had sense about the value of some things. She just . . . well, you should have seen her place. I tried to go see her as much as possible, but I just couldn't tolerate it. Things piled everywhere. Wouldn't throw anything away. Depression-era mentality, you understand. She had stacks of ancient empty ledgers she found in the attic of some long-ago bankrupt company. Nobody keeps books with those anymore. Rolls of old stained paper from God knows where. Boxes of mismatched flatware, old clothes, old shoes. It's a wonder the house didn't spontaneously erupt in flames."

"Did she say anything to you about her documents?"

"She said she had papers that would make Erin famous. She adored Erin, you see."

"How would they make her famous?"

Mrs. Blake shrugged. "Had something to do with Erin wanting to be an anthropologist or archaeologist—why anyone would choose a career digging in the dirt is beyond me. Though, you said you're a doctor?"

"No. I have a doctorate, so I get to use the title."

Bonnie Blake shrugged again. "You people are so vague, I don't see how you get anything done. I want Erin to be a lawyer. She's a smart girl. I mean, what do you archaeologists do?"

"We're sort of like historians."

"You write encyclopedias?"

"Some of us have been known to do that. We use various investigation techniques to find out what happened in the past."

"Then you are going to find out what happened to the documents?"

"If I can. The problem I'm having is that no one seems to know what the documents are that I'm supposed to be looking for."

"My brother's wife, Sugar, saw them. She spent more time with

Aunt Sue than we did. Sugar should have taken a better look when she had the opportunity. She's a case herself. Birds of a feather, I always say . . ."

"I appreciate your speaking with me."

"If you can find those missing documents, you'll be doing us all a favor. And please, steer Erin away from archaeology."

Lindsay left the library feeling great for the first time in months. Something about recognizing Erin's mother and interrogating her gave her a second wind, made her feel in control again, as if her brain was finally kicking into gear.

She arrived at the house to find it in a flurry of housekeeping. Joel, Powell, and Dillon were trying to scrub the worst of the green mildew from the wood of the front porch.

"The woman's gone nuts," complained Byron, carrying out a box of trash.

"Who?" asked Lindsay.

"Drew. I'm expecting any minute for her to tell us to paint the damn place before tomorrow. By the way, dinner is either in town or leftovers. Drew has Mr. and Mrs. Laurens helping clean up the place and baking cakes and homemade bread for this Lewis guy. You'd think he was God coming." *He probably thinks so too,* thought Lindsay. "Drew and Marina are in town looking for an Airwick or something."

"Is this guy king of some country?" asked Powell, splashing water and Clorox across the porch.

"Yes." Lindsay hopped across the wet front porch into the house and bounded up the steps to the second floor. Kelsey stood at the head of the stairs with a broom in her hand.

"I was just about to sweep the stairs. I think Drew should have hired one of those minute-maid services or whatever they're called."

"It looks like you've all got everything under control."

"That's because we stopped digging at lunch so we could come back and clean."

"Is Erin up here?" asked Lindsay.

"No. She may be downstairs."

Lindsay found Erin in the kitchen with Mrs. Laurens, who, judging from the aroma, was baking a cake.

"Erin, I spoke with your mother today."

Erin blanched and sat down in a chair, dishtowel in hand. Mrs. Laurens gave her a look that Lindsay had received from her grandmother on occasion when she was a little girl. The look that said, "I told you this would happen. Now that you've made your bed, you're going to have to lie in it."

"I'm sorry. Mrs. Laurens told me I should have said something when they were accusing you of reporting Drew's whereabouts to the process server."

Lindsay remembered the brief exchange between Erin and Mrs. Laurens she had seen from her window the evening Drew was served with the papers. So, that's what it was about.

"If your family believes that Drew may have been involved with your great-aunt's death, why did they allow you to stay here and spy?"

Erin straightened her body. "I'm an adult. I don't need their permission."

"Erin," said Mrs. Laurens, the way a mother or a grandmother might chastise a child.

"Since Mr. and Mrs. Laurens would be here most of the time, I convinced my parents it would be safe. You have to understand, if this hadn't been so important to me and my family, I wouldn't have let Claire blame you."

"Are you the one who suggested that your uncle ask me to investigate your great-aunt's death?"

"You seemed different from everyone else here. I thought if anyone would be fair, you would. Are you going to investigate?"

"So far, I can't find a thing out of place. Does anyone in your family know what documents your great-aunt was supposed to have?"

"You don't believe she had any, do you?"

"It doesn't matter what I believe. Right now, there is little evidence of what they were. Even if Drew were to be caught with a bunch of documents in her trunk, there's no way to prove they belonged to Miss Tidwell. Your mother said that your great-aunt told her she had something that would make you famous?"

"Yes. She told me that many times."

"And you have no idea what she meant?"

Erin slowly shook her head. "No. It was like it was going to be a surprise. I do remember that she read to me from these old pages when I was little. I'd forgotten about it until I heard the discussion about how older cabins had logs that were close together and later ones had spaces between the logs. I don't know if they were loose pages from a really old book or from her documents, but I remember when I was little thinking that it must be really old because of the color—kind of brown gold."

"What do you remember?"

"Something about a man who was really sick. He was staying in a cabin and it was freezing cold outside. There were spaces between the logs, and the wind blew through the cracks. That's about all I remember."

"That's something."

"It might not even be from the missing documents."

"Maybe not, but if they turn up, at least it's something that might give credibility to your claim."

"You aren't going to tell on me are you?"

"No." Lindsay took a loaf of bread and a jar of peanut butter out of the pantry.

"Let me fix you something." Mrs. Laurens dried her hands on her apron and turned toward the refrigerator. "You can't eat that for supper."

"This is fine. I'm not that hungry. I'll eat an apple with it."

"This guy, Lewis," said Erin. "Why is Drew making over him in such a big way? We had our big boss from Sound Ecology visit a couple of months ago, and he didn't get this kind of treatment."

"Francisco Lewis is the kind of guy who can do your career good, if he takes a liking to you."

"That explains why everyone is going along with Drew making them clean up everything. Lindsay, I'm really sorry about letting you take the blame on the process server business, especially since Claire's been treating you so badly."

"Forget it."

Erin laid her dishtowel across a chair and started out of the kitchen. "I'm supposed to help Kelsey scrub the sofa in the living room."

"Erin's a nice girl," said Mrs. Laurens. "Her family was countin' an awful lot of chickens when they hadn't even seen any eggs."

"What do you think happened?"

Mrs. Laurens opened the oven and tested the cake with a toothpick before she answered. Pronouncing it done, she put the two large rectangular red cakes on a cooling rack.

"Miss Tidwell taught me and my brothers when we were little. She was one of those favorite teachers. She wasn't easy, but she had that knack of making you interested in learning. She would bring things into class for us to look at. She had a coin that was part of a pirate treasure she showed us. That was particularly popular with the boys. I remember making a rubbing off it when I was in her class."

Mrs. Laurens took a bowl down from the cabinet and two boxes of confectioners' sugar from the pantry.

"Will you hand me the bricks of cream cheese and sticks of butter, over there on the table?"

"Red velvet cake? That's one of my favorites."

"Mine, too. I thought this Mr. Lewis might like it."

Mrs. Laurens emptied confectioners' sugar, butter, and cream cheese into the bowl. "Is Miss Van Horne likely to impress him, do you think?"

Lindsay got the idea that Mrs. Laurens thought not. "Lewis is impressed by people with the potential to do something for him. If she can, then he'll be impressed."

"Erin's always loved archaeology. She's friends with my granddaughter. I've known her family for years. I hope this experience won't end it for her."

"Her mother wants her to be a lawyer."

"Bonnie Blake means well for her children. She just doesn't know them very well. You asked me if I thought that Miss Tidwell really had valuable papers. I'm inclined to believe she did. Though, she said things sometimes I didn't always believe. She brought in a letter once, said it was 225 years old. I'd seen one 100 years old my uncle had that wasn't in nearly as good condition as hers, so I didn't believe it was that old."

"Do you know what the letter was about?"

"No, I don't remember. Miss Tidwell's family has always been around here. I guess you all know, she's related to the Gallowses, don't you?"

"Yes. I read that in the reports."

"I believed the letter was supposed to be written by someone in her family. But like I said, it didn't look that old."

After standing there for several minutes with peanut butter in one hand and jelly in the other, Lindsay made herself a peanut butter and jelly sandwich, and took a bite. "Do you think someone killed her?"

"No, I really don't. She was old and not in good health. It was her time."

"About those scratches on the McBrides' floor . . . Have you ever heard of a Cherry, or an Eda Mae?"

"There was a story my grandmother would tell sometimes about a girl named Eda Mae being haunted by a witch who would beat her up at night. Much like the Bell witch."

"You mean the Blair witch?"

Mrs. Laurens laughed. "Oh, no. There was a Bell witch in Tennessee long before there was a Blair witch. She haunted the John Bell family over in Robertson County, about thirty miles northwest of Nashville. Andrew Jackson himself had an encounter with the Bell witch. Everyone around here knows about her."

"What did the Bell witch do?"

"Pull on the bedcovers, make gnawing sounds on the bedposts, beat on the walls, whisper. She'd slap members of the family and houseguests in the middle of the night. That's mainly what Eda Mae's witch did. Slap her at night. In the morning, she'd have big red welts like handprints on her face. As far as I know, neither one ever killed anyone."

"What do you think it was?"

"Don't know about the Bell witch. As for Eda Mae's, these days you hear about bad things daddies do to their children. I kind of think it was from something like that. Of course, when I was a little, I thought it was a witch for sure."

"That's interesting. Eda Mae probably lived around here. I

don't suppose you know a family name?"

"No, I sure don't. Her story wasn't as well known as the Bell witch. I guess that's because somebody like Andrew Jackson never ran across her. It was one of those stories told to kids to scare them, like Raw Head and Bloody Bones."

"Yeah, I know Raw Head and Bloody Bones," said Lindsay. "My grandmother used to try to keep me out of the attic with them."

"Never really worked, did it?" Mrs. Laurens put the bowl under the mixer and turned it on.

"No. The attic was far too attractive."

When Lindsay entered her room, she heard the whirring sounds of Claire's hard disk. Claire was sitting on her mattress, hunched over her laptop, pecking away on the keys.

"I'm glad you're back," she said without looking up. "I have some things I want you to look at."

"Sure. I have something for you, too." Lindsay gave her the copy of the 1785 letter about Michael Ellis ordering a pewter plaque from a metalsmith. "I thought we might be able to run this down. The metalsmith got his lead from somewhere. Maybe he made coffins, too."

Claire examined the letter, drawing circles around several words. "Michael Ellis. We have another name we can investigate." She looked up from the page. "Can the origin of the lead from the coffins be traced to the source of the metal?"

"As in a spectrographic or chemical analysis?" Lindsay asked. "I don't know. We'll find out."

"There was a lead mine in Bumpass Cove in 1770. That's in the northeast corner of the state." Claire dug among the papers scattered around her bed and came up with a stapled copy of a journal article. "Here it is. It was owned by a William Colyer. Lead from the mines was used to make bullets for the Revolutionary War. The references say the ore was so rich they could smelt it over an open fire. Wouldn't it be great if we could match up the lead from the coffins to that mine?"

"Yes, it would. If not from some physical analysis, perhaps from documentation. Mrs. McBride is trying to run down descendants of Hope Foute. We're hoping that maybe other volumes of her diary survived." Lindsay took a pen and wrote a name on the edge of the article. "Here's my Gopher password if you'd like to do some research on the Web."

"Great." Claire looked at her watch. "If I can make it across the hall without getting caught by the cleaning police, I'll try to get in the storeroom to do some research."

Lindsay considered going downstairs to help with the cleaning, but lay across her bed instead, to read what Claire had done so far.

It was after midnight before Lindsay heard the house settle down to sleep. Claire came back from her Internet research with a handful of printouts and went directly to bed. Drew dragged herself in, looking completely worn out. Lindsay tried to work up some feelings of guilt for not helping out, but to no avail. She felt none. "The house looks good," she said. "Lewis ought to feel right at home."

"I hope this Tidwell thing isn't going to hang over me while he's here."

"As far as I can see, there's no real evidence that there ever were any documents. And everyone, from the doctor to the sheriff to the woman's family, believes she had a heart attack. I wouldn't worry."

Drew stopped. "The family believes she had a heart attack?" She looked over at Claire sleeping and lowered her voice. "Then, why all this fuss?"

"They're saying perhaps you kept her out all day, knowing that the stress on her might bring on a heart attack, and maybe it was intentional. They know it's a stretch. As to the missing documents, apparently she told them over the years she had some valuable documents of a surprising nature. When she died and no documents were found, they were disappointed. If I were you, I would try not to worry about it."

"God, I'm tired. Archaeology is a lot easier than cleaning. I guess that's why I became one. Eric, my husband, got the deposition put off. I'm glad I don't have to deal with that on top of everything else."

Lindsay reached over to turn out her light. Before she switched it off, she saw that Claire wasn't asleep. She was looking at her with an unfathomable expression. Lindsay switched off the light.

Chapter 22

LINDSAY GLANCED UP just as the shiny black Porsche stopped on the dirt road near where they were working.

"Who the heck is that?" asked Joel.

"Not a process server, for sure," said Adam.

They were excavating Feature 3, examining and recording the rocks, watching for gravestones. So far, they had found none. Marina had dug up the flowers that were in the path of the excavation of what they hoped was the second lead coffin. She had put the daffodil bulbs and antique roses in the buckets normally used in carting dirt to the screens to be sifted for artifacts.

The driver got out of the car and walked toward the group, who stood motionless, watching him cross the grassy divide. He took off his sunglasses as he approached and slid them into the front pocket of his light gray silk shirt. He held a large manila envelope under his arm and stopped at the edge of their excavation. He was impressive, as usual.

"This is Francisco Lewis," said Lindsay by way of introduction.

"Oh," said Drew, brushing the dirt off her shorts and smoothing down her hair. "I wasn't expecting you until later. I'm Drew Van Horne."

How like Lewis, thought Lindsay, *to keep people off guard.*

"Hi, Drew," he responded. "Fortunately, I was able to get away early."

As Drew tugged at her clothes, arranging herself to be presentable—a common reflex—Lindsay realized that Lewis lacked those nervous habits that betray a person's insecurity. That subtle sign of confidence, combined with the impact of his expensive clothes, gave Lewis a commanding air. Nevertheless, she was glad to see him, which had not always been her reaction to his presence.

Lindsay introduced all the crew: Marina, holding the buckets of plants; Joel, just rising from a group of stones; Adam, making a cross section of the berm surrounding the feature; Bill and Sharon, finishing up the house near Feature 3. The others, Claire, Powell, Dillon, Kelsey, Byron, and Erin came over from their tasks to meet Francisco Lewis—the man of the hour.

"I'm happy to meet all of you," he said, repeating each of their names as they were introduced. Lindsay knew he would remember all of them. "Drew has told me good things about her crew."

Out of the corner of her eye, Lindsay happened to catch sight of Claire raising her chin slightly. With someone like Claire, Lewis's compliment must have had a sting to it. However much Claire liked Drew, Drew was gone most of the time, leaving Claire to handle things every day—never mind how she handled them. She was the one who normally managed the crew.

Drew dropped her shovel. "Let me show you to the house."

"As I am early, I have a little company business with Lindsay." He took the envelope and opened it. "We're building a museum for the ship we excavated. Lindsay told you about the ship, didn't she?" He didn't wait for an answer, immediately turning his attention to Lindsay. "I have something to show you. The sculptor finished the facial reconstruction of the crew members we excavated." He pulled out several eight by ten color photographs.

"Wow." Lindsay stepped to get a closer look. "I have dirt on my hands. You'll have to show them to me."

One by one, he showed her each of the photos of the busts of the crew of the *Estrella de España,* a Spanish galleon that she and Lewis had had a hand in excavating off the coast of Georgia. The others gathered around to look at the lifelike reconstructions. They were fascinating to the crew, but to Lindsay they were mesmerizing. She recognized them—she had touched their bones and had told their stories from them.

"I'm thinking about a wax component to the museum." Lewis's voice brought her out of her trance.

"Wax?"

"You know that idea you had about building a replica of a galleon?" Lindsay nodded. "We may not be able to do that right now, but I was thinking about doing smaller sections of a ship as an environment for wax figures representing the crew we excavated—as though they were performing the work they did on the ship."

"I like that," said Lindsay.

"We need to discuss a couple of things so I can tell the builders." Lewis turned to Drew and the crew. "Let me get this business out of the way, and this evening we'll all go out to a restaurant. It's on me. Pick one you like."

With that, he turned back to his car. Lindsay followed, wiping her hands on a handkerchief from her back pocket. "I need to change. I'm too dirty to get in your car."

"It's all right." He took a stadium blanket from the trunk and put it over the tan leather seats, and Lindsay climbed in.

"Can I put in for a Porsche in my next contract?"

"Sure. You want that instead of a salary?" He started the car and drove up to the house. "I thought I did that quite well. I think I have a knack for stealth."

"What are you talking about?"

"I needed to speak with you alone without arousing suspicion. I wanted to show you the photos of the reconstructions anyway, so I pretended that's what I needed to talk about."

"Oh, no. You mean you really aren't going to do wax figures?"

"Yes, we are. I've already decided that, and got the ball rolling on it. But that's not something I'd need to consult you about."

"Lewis . . ."

"What?"

"Nothing."

He pulled in beside Lindsay's SUV, cut the engine, and shifted in the seat facing her. "How's your new vehicle doing?"

"Great. Runs like the old one."

"And you?"

Other than being terrified all the time and hallucinating . . . "I'm doing fine, too."

"That's good. I told the detective to call you. I knew you wouldn't call him. It's not like you to go into this avoidance pattern you've been in."

"So, you took control." Lindsay could feel the heat rising in her cheeks.

"You can take control any time." His dark eyes bore into hers as if he were issuing a challenge. She was silent. He continued after a moment. "So tell me what you've found out."

"I've talked with the sheriff, the family, Miss Tidwell's doctor, people who knew her, and Drew. No one but the Tidwells is suspicious of her death. Although they don't know what kind of documents are missing, her family insists she possessed valuable papers that were going to make them rich."

"So, Drew is in the clear?"

"Most likely. However . . ."

"However, what?"

"What aren't you telling me, Lewis?"

Lewis paused for only a moment. "Keith would have just brushed the whole thing off were it not that Drew is a fairly well known appraiser of historical documents . . . and her husband's a collector."

"What? And you didn't see fit to give me that information?"

"I didn't want to color your opinion."

"It would have changed how I approached Drew."

"Does it matter that much?"

"Yes. You thought it did, too, or you would have told me right off. Miss Tidwell's family were allowed only a glimpse of the alleged documents. She wouldn't show them to anyone, even her family. However, she probably would show them to an appraiser. She may have even told Drew that her family didn't know what she had."

Lewis closed his eyes tightly and made a face. "Damn, you're right."

"I would be more suspicious about her death, too, with what I know now."

"How's that?"

"If Drew—or anyone—stole the papers, the thief might think it was necessary to kill her to keep her from discovering the theft and filing a charge. If you're an appraiser and a professional archaeologist, your reputation is very important—important enough for some people to kill for."

"So, now you suspect Drew?"

"Not really, but I have to consider it. Her husband's a collector, you said? The things Miss Tidwell had may have proved too tempting for a collector who knew their value. Do you know what specifically he collects?"

"You suspect her husband, too?"

"Theoretically."

"He specializes in postrevolutionary documents. Will you continue on, then?"

"I don't really want to." Lindsay thought of the Tidwells . . . and Erin. The stolen property, if it was stolen, was theirs and they had counted on having it. They had asked her to look into it and she had agreed. "But, yes, I will."

"Good." He grasped her shoulder and gave it a gentle squeeze. "Be discreet."

"Of course."

"Now, I need to know a little about Tennessee history—I'll be asked questions."

"By whom?"

"The media. This find of the lead coffins is too important to go unnoticed, particularly with all the commotion that NASA and the other technical experts will bring, and I need to be able to converse intelligently about the cultural context, the historical significance, that sort of thing. I know the Native American history up to de Soto and the other explorers, so you can skip that part."

"Lewis, you're the limit. Are you asking me to give you a quick history lesson?"

"Yes."

"Now?"

"Please."

"Very well. Where do I start? Okay. Here's a concept to hang your hat on. The single most important thing that shaped the history of this whole region was the struggle between cultures over possession of the land and resources. The Indians had it, the settlers wanted it. By the way, the name Tennessee comes from the principal Cherokee town, *Tanasi.*"

"So, *Tanasi* converted into southern drawl became *Tennessee.*"

Lindsay rolled her eyes. "Another interesting tidbit is the name of this cove. John came to see me, and he called this Dogwood Cove. Dogwood in Cherokee is: *ka-nv-si-ta.* He believes that *Knave's Seat* is a corruption of that. I tend to agree."

"Sounds reasonable. Knave's Seat is a little hard on the tongue."

"History. Okay. Before the 1600s, Tennessee was occupied by Indians. At first, a few French and English fur traders arrived to establish posts for trading with the Indians—food, guns, blankets, axes, and such—for fur. Animal fur was the big lure and by the 1700s the good hunting brought more long hunters."

"Long hunters?"

"You've seen pictures of those guys in fringed buckskin clothing, leggings, and leaning on a rifle? Those were long hunters. Men who went on long hunting and trapping trips, staying out for months. Daniel Boone was one."

"I had an outfit like that when I was a kid. Coonskin cap and everything." Lewis gestured as if he were fitting the cap on his head.

"I'll bet you were cute. The trading posts bartered for furs from the Indians and long hunters, and sent the furs by pack trains or down the rivers by keelboats to Charles Town and New Orleans. American furs brought high prices in Europe, and the competition between the English and French for the Indian trade quickly escalated into a power struggle for the new territory."

"I know about the French and Indian War, in 1750—something wasn't it?"

Lindsay nodded. "It was a long war, lasted about nine years. The Indians were kind of caught in the middle. When it was over, the English had won."

"So how does this all connect to the farmstead?"

"I'm giving you background and context. Isn't that what you said you wanted?"

"Yes, don't get testy. Just continue."

"After the French and Indian War, the big deal was no longer fur trading, but land acquisition. English settlers from Virginia and

North Carolina began migrating across the mountains into East Tennessee, settling in Indian lands. At first they leased the lands from the Indians, but as time went on and the number of settlers increased, they settled wherever they wanted, with or without consultation with the Indians.

"So, by the early 1770s, the pioneers had built settlements along the rivers in the northeast corner of what is now Tennessee. This, naturally, brought all kinds of tradesmen, blacksmiths, craftsmen, miners, preachers, land speculators, surveyors, soldiers, politicians—you name it. I believe the first occupation of the farmstead, the lead coffin people, were in this group.

"Anyway, the influx of people put a lot of pressure on the Cherokee. Different factions among the Indians responded in different ways. One faction tried trading with the settlers and selling them land. Another faction resented this and, led by Chief Dragging Canoe, made their presence felt for the next twenty years."

"Interesting. I always thought of the Cherokee as peaceful."

"They were, unless they were provoked. In the beginning when the settlers were few, the Indians were very friendly. They brought them food to get through the winter."

"What linguistic family do the Cherokee belong to?"

"Iroquoian. Lewis, all this is in books. I could check you out a . . ."

"No. I just want something quick."

"Something quick, then. The settlers naturally wanted self-government . . ."

"How do you know all this stuff?"

"Lewis, I study about the sites I work on. Anyway, as you probably know, the British didn't like all this self-government business."

"So, we get to the Revolutionary War."

Lindsay was feeling closed in. She had decided against a Porsche. Too small.

"Yes, the Revolutionary War. Do you mind if we get out into the fresh air? Let's go into the woods. There's a beautiful place we can sit."

Before Lewis could object, she was out of the car. She took Elaine's scrapbook from her Explorer and headed for the woods.

"What's that?"

"Something I want to show you. You'll like it."

Lindsay led him down a path bounded by the deep green mountain flora. She breathed deeply.

"Isn't this great?"

She sat down on a large boulder, motioning for Lewis to sit beside her.

"I see why you like this place. It's quite beautiful. We won't get bitten by mosquitoes, will we?"

"No," Lindsay lied. "You need to get back to nature more. There are beautiful, timeless things here. William Bartram went through here exploring the southern Appalachians in the 1770s or thereabouts."

"I've seen historical markers for his trails all over the place."

"He passed near where I live in Georgia," said Lindsay. "He came through here, too, surveying, sketching, and recording everything he saw. He probably sat on this very rock, observing the plants and the animals that passed his way."

"Animals?"

"Bears, mountain lions, wolves."

"Here?" Lewis glanced around, squinting at the deep undergrowth.

"Don't worry, they're usually very shy. You know, historical archaeology can be seductive when you run across the writings and drawings of someone like Bartram who was a keen observer and appreciated beauty. Many of the species around us are the same ones Bartram saw and recorded over two hundred years ago—wild woodbine, magnolias, silver bell, rhododendron. Gregory Bald isn't far from here. The azaleas are in bloom there now. It's all so beautiful. It would seem that being amid such beauty would keep a person in a state of grace, charmed against evil." Lindsay shivered.

"Nature's impartial, so is beauty. Perhaps, Lindsay, you should take a more active role in the investigation of what happened to you. Even an insensitive guy like me can tell you're hurting."

Lindsay turned her head sharply in his direction. "I wasn't talking about me."

"Weren't you? My mistake. How about the history lesson?"

Lindsay breathed in the fresh air with its green woodsy smell. It was like cool water, refreshing. Here the smells were clean, the air pure. *Maybe I should camp out here. No, he's right, the forest wouldn't protect me.*

"Lindsay?"

"The settlers annexed themselves to North Carolina, hoping for protection." *It didn't come. They had to protect themselves. A lesson there.*

"Lindsay? Are you all right?"

"Sure. Fine. By this time, the Cherokee had had enough of their lands being taken, and they sided with the British. In July 1776, the Cherokee attacked the settlements. Under the leadership of John Sevier, the settlers successfully defended themselves and then went on the attack against the Indians, burning their towns to the ground."

"I didn't know the Cherokee were involved in the Revolutionary War. What was their interest?"

"Their land. The Cherokee were a very large tribe, and they were losing land left and right. The settlers became greater in number and more and more independent. The Cherokee didn't like it, and neither did the British, so the Cherokee thought their best interests would be served by siding with the British."

The wind started to blow through the canopy of tall trees. *The wind was blowing that night. I had forgotten the way the trees whipped back and forth. They tripped me. No, it wasn't nature, something man-made. Barbed wire. Traitorous barbed wire. Its only reason for existence is to constrain. That's what it did.*

The top outline of the mountains looming in the distance looked like tiny stiff fringe because of the dead Fraser firs throughout the high elevations.

"Ninety percent of them are dead, you know," she said.

"Who?" asked Lewis. "The Cherokee?"

"The Fraser firs." Lindsay pointed into the distance. "They're being killed by the balsam woolly adelgid. It's a European aphid that was accidentally introduced into the United States. Ironic, isn't it? Another European invasion with devastating results for the area."

"Anything being done to stop it?"

"The park service is planting seedlings. People are working on it."

"They'll probably find a solution. What happened after the revolution?" Lewis prompted.

"The settlers organized the State of Franklin but failed to get it ratified. This all happened in the late 1780s. By the way, did I tell you about the log cabin?"

"What log cabin?"

Lindsay explained about the McBrides' log cabin and the plaque and the older artifacts identified by Marina. She opened the scrapbook on Lewis's lap. "These are pictures of the log cabin as it looked when it was at the site and now."

"This is great. You say Drew didn't have this?"

"No. The McBrides were put off by the archaeology survey team before Drew could find out anything."

"I see. This Claire person?"

Lindsay nodded. "Unfortunately."

"So you believe the lead coffins are from that earlier occupation and not the later one?"

"The use of lead coffins was an earlier burial practice in the North. As far as I can discover, they weren't used here in the 1800s. By that time, settlers buried their dead in wooden coffins that were made and donated by members of the community. Often, families would keep wood, mostly walnut, on hand for that purpose. Besides, the Gallows family is buried in the church cemetery. They're all accounted for."

"So, who's in the coffins, and how did they get here?"

"What I think is that the lead coffins belong to a family who immigrated from the North in the 1700s. People generally want to be buried the way their parents and grandparents were buried. They were performing the burial practices they were familiar with. I also believe that the burials themselves either predate or postdate the Revolutionary War."

"Why is that?"

"Because the lead would have been needed for cannonballs and bullets during the war. Claire found an article about one of the first mines in Tennessee. It was a lead mine, and it's believed that the mine supplied all the bullets for the Battle of Kings Mountain in

North Carolina—that was one of the decisive battles of the Revolutionary War."

"You think the lead in the coffins came from there?"

Lindsay shrugged. "I don't think they schlepped the coffins all the way from wherever the settlers came from."

"Is there a way we can match the metal with its source?"

"Maybe, I don't know. I'll have to find out. Another interesting question is why a form of burial more typical of wealthy families is being practiced on a farmstead that has shown no indication of wealth. In the 1700s, the log cabin was one room and a loft. Nothing we've found so far indicates they had wealth."

"Are you sure?"

"Yes. We've excavated the house foundation. And we now have the house that came off the foundation."

"But you said that it was two—what do you call it—pens?" Lewis slapped a flying bug between his hands. "I thought you said there were no mosquitoes."

Lindsay drew her feet up and sat cross-legged. "There are two pens. The second pen was built much later. You can tell by the two different styles of building techniques. It's my guess the second pen was added to the house around 1836 by the Gallowses."

"Could the cemetery be attached to some other house not yet discovered? Like the Gallows House, the house the crew stays in, for instance?"

"The artifacts on top of the coffin predate our house. There could be another house foundation somewhere, but where? There's no indication I've seen of another house, and the initial survey was pretty good." Lindsay shrugged. "But the survey team did miss the log cabin that was moved. I don't know how they did that. Their informant knew about it."

"I wonder why they weren't told?"

"Mary Susan Tidwell was the main informant used by the survey team. Miss Tidwell was possessive about her status as their informant. Maybe she didn't want to tell them about the cabin. That would have pointed their attention away from her and toward the McBrides. Maybe she concealed the information to prevent loss of her standing. Informants have been known to do that."

"Didn't the survey team use a variety of informants? Did this woman hypnotize them away from everyone else?"

"I think she had such a wealth of knowledge it was just easier to deal with only her. You can ask Drew. I try to keep away from challenging their survey methods."

"How's your relationship with the site director? Claire? I know she tried to bring in Nigel Boyd to analyze the remains in the coffins, rather than using you. He was really pissed off when he found out you were already here."

"I know. He called. But Claire and I are getting along swimmingly now."

"How did you manage that?"

"Bribery."

Lewis laughed. "I'm glad to see I'm rubbing off on you. What did you offer?"

"First author on a couple of publications. It turned out that was something she really wanted. She's not a bad writer or researcher, she's just too inexperienced to be a site director."

"That's a big carrot you offered her. No wonder she took it. Are we about finished with the history lesson? As lovely as these woods are, I'm anxious to get back to civilization. That's a big spider's web in those branches over there," he said, pointing toward a giant web swaying in the breeze with the motion of the branches.

"It's going to be a cold winter."

"What?"

"A thick spider's web means a cold winter."

"Does it really?"

"The mountain folk think so. I've never run a correlation." Lindsay walked over and touched a strand of the web, gently vibrating it, trying to get the spider to come out. But it wouldn't show itself. "Must be on to me." She turned back to Lewis.

"Only about fifty more years of history. In 1789, North Carolina ratified the new Constitution of the United States and ceded its western regions, which included this area, to the federal government. They then called this the Southwest Territory. There was another land rush, and more land was taken from the Indians. In 1792 the Cherokee and Creek warriors attacked settlers in an effort to stop the squatters. The settlers formed a militia and counter-attacked the Indian towns, finally ending the raids. In 1796, Tennessee became the sixteenth state. This is the world the people like the Gallowses settled into.

"At the time, all the manufacturing, like forging tools, spinning cloth, making soap, tanning hides, milling grain, sawing lumber, and making whiskey, were done on the farmsteads like the one we're excavating. I'll have to take you to the mountain farm museum. It has a rebuilt farmstead, much like this one."

"Good. We'll all go. We have a few days before everyone arrives."

"I think most of the crew have already seen it, that and Cade's Cove, too. Anyway, about the only industry outside the farms was ironwork. Early on, metalworking was brought to the region by craftsmen from Pennsylvania—which is where the earliest settlers on our farmstead may have come from. These men built furnaces and forges to process the iron ores and supplied farmers and blacksmiths with the metal.

"Meanwhile, the Cherokee in north Georgia and Tennessee had been peacefully farming their own farmsteads. They wrote their own constitution and started Cherokee language newspapers. Many were better educated than the white settlers. But this didn't stop the state of Georgia from confiscating their lands when gold was found, nor did the Supreme Court decision protecting Cherokee sovereignty stop Andrew Jackson from ordering the army to forcibly remove them to a reserve in Oklahoma in 1838. The confiscated land was quickly sold to settlers."

"The Trail of Tears," commented Lewis.

Lindsay nodded. "Almost two-fifths died of exhaustion, exposure, and starvation. A few managed to escape into the Smoky Mountains, becoming the Eastern Band. John's a member of the Eastern band."

"How is John? I imagine his construction company's been receiving a lot of business since he built the cofferdam around the shipwreck."

"It has. In fact, he's got more work than he can get to. I feel guilty that he had to come haul me out of the woods."

"Lindsay, we are all very grateful that he did. When you hear of someone missing under those circumstances . . . well, the outcome is not usually good. You know that. All the archaeology faculty, even Kenneth Kerwin, was deeply worried."

Lindsay tried to smile. Lewis was getting too close to her open wounds. How was she going to keep the fear tucked away safely inside if people insisted on wanting to talk about it? "Kenneth?" she replied, trying to sound like that was funny.

"Of course, now he's aggravated you're working in his territory—a historical site. He wonders why I didn't send him."

"Did you tell him you didn't want an archaeologist as much as a detective?"

Lewis chuckled. "I can just see him dealing with some of the people you have described to me on this site. We'd probably be up here hauling him out of jail. I can see the headlines now: Archaeologist Goes Berserk, Trowels Entire Crew to Death."

Lindsay tried to laugh with him. "I guess we'd better get back. I think Drew had Mrs. Laurens fix a big meal in your honor. She's a great cook, and she made a red velvet cake."

"That's fine with me. We can go out to dinner anytime. What's this?" Lewis stared at a page in the scrapbook.

Lindsay laughed and the black cloud drifting over her dispersed into the forest. "Poems scratched on the floor of the Gallows cabin loft. Elaine McBride and I are trying to track them down. Marina thinks there's a good chance they are contemporary with the earliest part of the house."

"What do you think they mean?"

"They could be children's rhymes. You know how dark those can be."

"Interesting. I wonder who would write them on the floor? I appreciate your history lesson, even though it was a little biased."

"Biased? What do you mean?"

"I detected a slight bias in favor of the Indians."

"Lewis, I'm shocked you would accuse me of being anything but objective where history is concerned. That's . . . What in the world is going on now?" In the distance, Lindsay saw the field crew crossing the bridge in the midst of a heated argument with a stranger.

Chapter 23

"JUST TELL ME, is it true that you're going to dig up bodies from a cemetery?"

The questioner was a young man in jeans, T-shirt, and a long-sleeved shirt worn as a jacket. His brown hair was tousled by the wind. In his hand he had a pen poised over a pad of paper. Adam was poised to yell at him for encroaching on his personal space. Drew was asking him to leave. Lindsay's first thought was to wonder if Claire was going to steal his car. She looked at his black pickup truck and almost flew over to grab him by his shirt front.

"Where did you get that truck? Does it belong to the McBrides?"

"What? No. It's mine. What are you doing? Let me go." He was beginning to look a little wild-eyed, and tried to pull away, but Lindsay held fast, aided by the adrenaline pumping through her body.

"Not until you tell me what you were doing Tuesday at 8:30 A.M."

"Tuesday? Tuesday . . . I don't know . . . I was at the newspaper office. What's this about?"

"Do you know a truck was stolen from the McBrides?"

"No. Who are they? Who are you?"

Lindsay looked again at the truck. It was a small black Toyota, not the truck that had passed her, not the McBrides' truck. Lindsay loosened her grasp, and he pulled away.

"You people are crazy." He almost ran across the bridge to his truck.

"That was a strange approach, but effective," said Adam.

Lindsay glanced over at Lewis. He stared at her, as did all the others, with open amazement on his face.

"The McBrides' truck was stolen. For a moment I thought that was it."

"Did you develop some kind of bond with them?" asked Kelsey.

Lindsay looked at Kelsey, realizing suddenly that her behavior must have seemed bizarre. "They're nice people."

"They must've been," said Kelsey.

"What did that reporter want?" asked Lewis.

"Someone told him about the lead coffins," said Drew. "He wouldn't say who."

"He had a bad slant to his questions," said Joel, "like we're grave robbers or something."

"We need to have some discussion about how to deal with the media," said Lewis. "I'll write an article for the local paper."

"I like Lindsay's approach," said Byron.

Lewis took a suitcase from the trunk of his car and started toward the house with the others. He stopped at the steps and looked up. "Nice place. A lot nicer than some of the places I've stayed on digs."

"It comes with ghosts," said Powell.

"Yes," agreed his brother, Dillon, "we hear them knocking about occasionally. Mostly at night."

"They were very active when we first got here," said Kelsey. "But they've sort of calmed down. Used to us, I suppose."

"They've been real quiet since Trent left," said Adam.

"Ghosts. This should be interesting," Lewis said.

"Your room is upstairs," Drew told him.

As they ascended to the second floor, Lewis leaned over and whispered in Lindsay's ear. "You want to tell me what that was about?"

"Not particularly."

Lindsay hurried to her room and gathered up her clothes and towel. She was surprised to discover that the bathroom was empty.

A warm shower—it had been a while since she'd had anything other than a cold one. The warm water was a comfort. She wanted to stay. She'd like to have a bath and just lie back in the tub and soak. But she hurried through the shower, to give the others a turn. Kelsey was waiting at the door when she opened it.

"It's about time." Kelsey brushed past her into the bathroom.

"Sorry, I thought I was hurrying."

Dinner was the most civil it had ever been. Claire ate in silence. From the corner of her eye, Lindsay noticed Claire stealing occasional glances at her. She wondered if she had committed some offense, real or imagined, against her.

It was Lewis who did most of the talking, explaining in detail what was to happen when the NASA team arrived. Lewis was good at rekindling people's spirits. Soon, everyone was talking, asking questions, speculating about the coffins and the site. Lewis held his own. The brief history lesson Lindsay had given him had taken hold so well that you'd think Tennessee history was his specialty. Lewis could go a long way with a little data.

"So, Lindsay, what was that thing with the reporter about?" asked Powell.

Lindsay had managed to avoid the question all the way through dinner. She thought she was home free when Mrs. Laurens had cut the red velvet cake.

"I almost had a collision yesterday with a reckless driver in a black pickup. It turned out the truck was stolen from the McBrides. I thought it might have been the reporter." Had that sounded innocent enough? No. They all stared as if there had to be more. "My SUV is brand-new."

"Ah," said Bill, "you're one of those people who park in the farthest parking space just so you don't get dinged, I'll bet."

"Anyway, it was a chance to manhandle him," said Byron. "Did you see his face? Good job."

Lindsay had to laugh. She *had* seen his face, and his wide-eyed, openmouthed expression of dire surprise and bewilderment was indeed funny.

The meal ended with Lewis telling the crew to refer all questions about the coffins to him. Most of the crew drifted along with Drew and Lewis to the living room. Lindsay went to her room, expecting to be alone. Claire was upstairs in the hallway. Lindsay had the impression she had come from Lewis's room. She shrugged it off. Perhaps Claire forgot something when she moved, or maybe she had just imagined it.

"You aren't downstairs with the others?" asked Lindsay.

Claire shook her head. "There's a lot of stuff I need to be doing up here."

"Me, too."

"You and Lewis seem to know each other real well." Claire followed Lindsay into their room.

"He's my division head."

"Division?"

"When he came to the University of Georgia, he combined the Departments of Anthropology and Archaeology into a division. Sort of made us all one department, but not exactly. Each has a separate chair. He's head of the whole thing."

"Why not put them all together in one department?"

"Archaeology and anthropology have different needs and concerns, and the anthropology faculty outnumber us. We archaeologists don't want to get outvoted every time we have a conflict in our interests."

"There's a lot of politics in universities."

"Whatever gave you that idea?"

Lindsay wished for the first time that they had a television set. She would like to watch TV. She would like to occupy her mind with something every moment, no matter how trivial.

"He acts like he's your friend."

Lindsay thought that was an odd way of putting it. "I suppose he is, most of the time. I didn't think we would get along when I first heard he was coming to UGA, but things have worked out, so far."

"What were the two of you doing in the woods?"

Another peculiar question. "Discussing the ship display and the wax figures he was talking about." Lindsay hated to lie, but what choice was there? *I can't just say, "Gee, Claire, we were talking about your and Drew's possible homicidal tendencies."* "He wanted to see the photo album with the pictures of the cabin."

Lindsay knew that must have hurt, since Claire was the one

who had alienated the McBrides from the archaeology project. She had a strong urge to sit Claire down and ask her why she acted the way she did—explain to her that she was her own worst enemy. But why break the peaceful bliss she had achieved? She pulled out a novel instead. Claire got out her papers and computer and was soon pecking away at the keyboard.

"Where do you come down on the ghost thing?" Lindsay asked after a while.

Claire looked up from her work. For a moment Lindsay thought she looked like she might cry.

"Here, or in theory?"

"Both."

"I think there could be ghosts. I don't disbelieve in them. I kind of think this place is haunted. There've been a lot of noises that can't be accounted for. Sharon doesn't want to admit it now, but four or five months ago she was in the house alone upstairs. She told Kelsey later that she had heard voices—no words, just voices. She thought some of the crew had come back to the house and she went down to look. No one was there. Even Mrs. Laurens and her husband hadn't arrived yet. That's really why she moved to a hotel when her husband got here."

"She denies it now?"

"Not really denies it, just laughs it off, as if it was really a joke."

"Has anyone seen any ghosts?" Lindsay completely understood why Sharon might be reticent. No way was she going to admit to seeing anything out of the ordinary.

"No, not that I know of. You see anything?" Claire asked.

Lindsay smiled and shook her head.

Claire went back to typing on her laptop, Lindsay to her reading. Occasionally, they heard laughter drifting up from the floor below—Lewis charming the crowd, no doubt.

"Do you believe that Rosellen Gallows killed her children?" asked Claire. "Some of the people in town think that's who haunts these woods. Rosellen or her babies."

Lindsay thought a moment. "No, not really. Infant mortality was so high, it's not really suspicious, like it would be today, that all her children died."

"If you were looking for something suspicious, what would you look for?"

"I'd first go through Hope Foute's diary more closely to see if there is a clue there. I'd look in the church cemetery to see how many other families lost several of their children. I'd try to discover if there was an epidemic of any kind around that time. If I could, I'd look at the bodies."

"You think people are going to protest us excavating the coffins?"

"A good chance. Nobody but us archaeologists likes to dig up their ancestors."

"I'd like to watch you examine the bones. I've never really had a chance to work with bones."

"Sure. You're entitled. You're the site director."

Claire focused her attention back on her work. "I think that's being taken away from me. The site doesn't need Drew, Dr. Lewis, and me."

"It does need a site director. Don't bow out. Lewis may be handling the coffins, but there's still the whole site that needs to be excavated, and Lewis doesn't want to be in charge of that. He's here for the glamour stuff. Besides, Drew told me that Lewis may get funding for some extras, like excavating the outhouse, or whatever." *What am I saying? I must be crazy, trying to talk Claire out of giving up, rather than buying a tank of gas for her car.*

"It sounds like they're having fun down there," said Claire after a burst of raucous laughter drifted up from downstairs.

"Who's playing the guitar?" Lindsay asked. "I haven't heard that before."

"It's one of the Adonis twins—Powell or Dillon . . . the one with short hair . . . showing off. He used to drag that thing out every evening."

Until you put a damper on things, I'll bet. Lindsay listened to him play. "Dillon is the one with the short hair."

Lindsay went out to the hallway and sat on the steps. Claire followed and stood behind her, leaning against the wall. He was playing "In My Room."

"He gets very loud. I hate loud music, but that one's kind of nice. I do like some guitar music," said Claire, defending her musical taste.

"That's not just a guitar he's playing. It's a Fender Telecaster."

"What's that?"

"A very famous electric guitar designed by Leo Fender. In the early fifties he designed the Telecaster, and later made improvements with the Fender Stratocaster—though not everyone would agree the Stratocaster was better."

"Analogous to a Stradivarius, then?"

"Well . . . not as expensive or as old, but a fine instrument nonetheless. My brother has a Danny Gatton Signature Fender Telecaster. It sounds as if Dillon likes Danny Gatton, too. He's playing several pieces from his CDs."

"Who's Danny Gatton?"

"According to my brother, he was the greatest guitar player in the world."

"Was he?"

Lindsay nodded, rocking back and forth. "Yeah, I think so."

"Is Dillon good? Sometimes it's hard for me to tell."

"Pretty good. Not as good as his guitar, but don't tell him I said so."

"So, he's not as good as this Gatton fellow?"

"Not even close. But don't tell him I said that, either. I think I'll go downstairs. Want to come?"

Claire shook her head. "No. If we're getting more money, I think I'll work on what to do with it."

Lindsay descended the stairs into an impromptu party of a kind she'd been to many times before, but never at this site—the crew letting loose after a hard day at digging.

Dillon moved out to the porch with his guitar. Its cord snaked through the front window where the boards had been removed. On the porch someone had supplied a tub of ice filled with bottles of beer. Lindsay took one and opened it with the bottle opener tethered by a string to the handle of the tub. She took several gulps. It was ice cold and sent chills down her body.

The advantage of having a party in the middle of the woods is no neighbors to be disturbed by boisterous behavior. The voices and music were loud, possibly from relief—like an inrush of helium into everyone's spirits, causing them to rise upward in joyful, chaotic racket. Adam and Joel accompanied Dillon on the guitar by beating out the rhythm of the music on various surfaces.

The porch chairs were taken by Erin and Marina. Lindsay sat on the steps with her back against a post, feeling the sound of the music vibrating through the wood, and watching some of the crew dancing to Dillon's rendition of "Elmira St. Boogie." Sharon and Bill were doing a respectable variation of the Mamba. Kelsey, with her exposed midriff rippling under her short T-shirt, and Powell swayed and rocked in their own freestyle.

With a bottle of beer in their hands, Drew Van Horne and Francisco Lewis looked like kindred spirits, leaning against the open door frame. Each dressed more like old-style aristocratic archaeologists—with their neatly pressed khakis, leather belts, crisp tucked-in shirts, and styled hair—than the working-in-the-dirt variety. What surprised Lindsay was the deferential manner in which Drew interacted with Lewis. Occasionally, above the din, Lindsay heard a twitter of girlish giggling—Drew laughing at some Cisco cleverness.

Dillon played "Proud Mary," and Adam abandoned his upturned bucket and pulled a protesting Erin out of her chair. Lindsay felt a hand on her shoulder and warm breath in her ear.

"Show them how it's done," said Lewis, and he pulled her to her feet.

It had been a while since Lindsay had danced—at the *Estrella* site, with Lewis on the barge, if she remembered right. John didn't dance, and she hadn't danced with Derrick in what seemed like years.

Why not, she thought. As she and Lewis danced, she realized she missed it. Not the demanding competition that she and Derrick used to be involved in, but the melody of movement. It was like riding a horse—the metamorphosis from being who you are to the thing you are doing, going to a place where there are no problems.

"Wow," shouted Adam over the music. "You've done this before."

"A little," Lindsay shouted back.

Lindsay saw Drew through the window talking on the phone,

holding one hand over her free ear. She wondered how Drew heard anything at all, with the noise. She only took notice because, before Drew turned her back, her face was contorted in anger.

Dillon played "Popcorn," not a tune often danced to. Sharon and Bill dropped out. Kelsey and Powell stopped. Kelsey started again, trying to get with the rhythm. Lindsay—and Lewis, too, if the truth were told—understood both the science and art of dancing. They could make the steps, turns, and spins flow easily with the music. To Lindsay there was a little science in all art. Beyond possessing a body of knowledge, art can be expressed by the physics of movement or color, the chemistry of paint, or the mathematics of music. All great artists are conscious or unconscious scientists, just as there is a little art in all science, as witnessed by any elegant research design or creative hypothesis. Whoever first put the arts and sciences in the same college probably understood that, too.

As Lindsay and Lewis danced, she realized that there was medicine in dancing, too—a magic elixir to calm her tattered nerves and soothe her exhausted spirit. When they finished, Adam held out his hand to her.

"How 'bout it, Lindsay?"

They danced to a piece with a Spanish beat that Lindsay didn't recognize. Afterward, she danced with Powell and with Lewis once more, stopping occasionally to take a swallow of warm beer. Once she caught a whiff of the unmistakable pungent odor of marijuana and looked around to see who was smoking. No one on the porch. Then the aroma was gone.

That's when she saw Drew through the window, arguing with Erin in the living room. She couldn't hear what Drew was saying, but she could see that Erin was in tears. So, Drew had found out who Erin was. Drew would fire her. Lindsay wished she wouldn't. She pulled Lewis closer. After getting a quizzical smile from him, she whispered in his ear, asking him not to let Drew fire Erin.

"What are you talking about?" he shouted over the music.

Lindsay led Lewis off the porch, away from the intensity of the noise, and they stood eye to eye while she explained about Erin being the grandniece of Mary Susan Tidwell.

"And you knew about Erin?" Lewis asked.

"I only just learned about it. Erin's a good kid and really wants to be an archaeologist, against the wishes of her mother."

"She may want to quit after this," said Lewis.

"Maybe. But let it be her decision."

With the activity of the dancing, Lindsay hadn't noticed the evening growing cool. Now shivering in the mountain breeze, she hugged her arms around her shoulders.

"This isn't my site," he reminded her.

"Oh, yes it is."

"You give me too much credit."

"I probably don't give you enough."

"I have to keep up appearances. Why would I ask Drew to do me this favor?"

"Because it will look good in court. Erin's family can't really think Drew or anyone here killed their aunt if they're willing to allow Erin to stay here. Besides, Erin is a descendant of the Gallowses. It would make good copy."

"She is? I didn't know that. You're right. Good answers."

"That's what I'm here for." Lindsay looked beyond Lewis across the way to the site. A glow had caught her eye. "Oh, my God. The artifact tent. Is it on fire?"

Chapter 24

LINDSAY RAN TO her SUV, and Lewis followed, yelling to the others. Soon a parade of vehicles raced across the bridge and down the dirt road toward the site. She had no idea how they would put out the fire when they got there. *Water from the river, pumped by the flotation pumps . . . but they're in the tent.* She turned onto the site, skirting the edge, heading toward the fire.

"It doesn't look like the tent is burning." Lewis had the door open before she came to a complete stop.

The fire was behind the tent, between it and the wooded area that bordered Little Branch Creek. Lindsay grabbed a flashlight, jumped out of the vehicle, and followed Lewis, the others close on their heels. The smell of gasoline and wood smoke stung her nose.

"It's a bonfire," said Adam. "Who the hell would do such a thing?"

Someone had piled dead wood behind the processing tent, doused it with gasoline, and set it ablaze.

"Why would someone do this?" Kelsey held her arms across her bare middle and edged closer to the fire.

They all stood for a moment under the starry sky and watched the flickering blaze, already beginning to die down.

"I don't like this." Sharon looked up at her husband, and he put his arm around her shoulders.

"Just some prank," he muttered.

Lindsay shone the light around on the ground, looking for anything that might be a clue.

"What's that?" Joel pointed toward the tent.

In the flickering light of the fire they saw that the visitors had spray-painted black capital letters across the back of the tent. "LEAVE THE DEAD ALONE!" it read.

"Well, shit," said Byron. "First that little pissant reporter, and now this."

"What should we do?" asked Marina. "Call the sheriff?"

"No." Drew shook her head and turned to Lewis. "I think Bill's right. It's a prank. We've all had experiences at sites."

"I'll talk with the sheriff tomorrow." Lewis brushed his hands together, as if the matter were done. "He'll probably be more helpful if we don't get him out of bed in the middle of the night. In the meantime, how about a couple of you guys staying in the tent tonight?"

"Come on, girls can stand guard duty, too," said Kelsey. "I've stood guard over sites before."

Lewis shrugged. "Whoever. Decide among yourselves. You have cell phones or something to keep in touch with the house?"

"Yeah," said Byron. "We got walkie-talkies, too."

Powell and Marina brought shovels from inside the tent. "Everything looks okay in there," she said. "Maybe they just wanted to leave a message."

They handed out the shovels and the crew shoveled dirt over the dying fire.

"So, how about it?" Lindsay heard Kelsey ask Powell. "You and me take the first watch?"

"They aren't going to have their minds on guarding the artifacts," Marina whispered to Lindsay.

"At least they'll be awake if anything happens."

"You all act like this kind of thing is common." Erin stood by Lindsay, leaning on her shovel. With the fire out, the only light was Lindsay's flashlight.

"Not common," Lindsay told her as they made their way back to the cars. "Mostly, you have to guard sites from pothunters . . . people trying to steal artifacts. This is a little different. But don't worry, in a few days there will be a whole passel of people here."

"I may not be here." Erin's voice dropped. "Drew's husband found out about me."

"Do you want to stay?"

"If people won't be mad at me."

"Lewis can probably work something out. He'll want local people working at the site now. It'll make us less outsiders."

The fire had effectively broken up the party. Sharon and Bill drove back to their motel. Kelsey ran upstairs to get clothes and blankets for her and Powell's stay in the tent. Lindsay remained downstairs with Drew, Lewis, and Erin. Lewis had driven back with Drew, during which time he had made a pitch for Erin.

"Erin, you could have said something. This is like a family here, and you broke that bond," Drew told her.

Lindsay raised her eyebrows at that, but said nothing. Hardly a family. Erin for her part, didn't have anything to say, either. There was nothing she could say that wouldn't give Drew information on what her family was thinking. And defending herself at this point would only aggravate things.

"Good, it's settled then. Erin will stay on, and we'll put this behind us and work together on the upcoming project."

Occasionally, Lindsay truly admired Lewis, the way he assumed agreement with his position. They went upstairs to bed. Lindsay was tired, but for the first time in a long time she felt safe. It was a relief to look forward to something besides getting through another day with a knot in her stomach.

Drew was already in the room changing into her nightshirt. From the rise and fall of her breathing, Claire appeared to already be sound asleep. Lindsay tiptoed in and changed her clothes. She'd be able to fall asleep quickly, too, she thought as her head hit the pillow.

When Lindsay awoke, Drew and Claire had already gone. She hurriedly put on her clothes and went down to the dining room. As she crossed the reception hall she heard Lewis in the living room talking on the phone to the sheriff. She peeked in just as he was hanging up.

"What did he say?"

"Essentially, that there was nothing he could do, though he was nice about it. He said he'd have a deputy put our road on his route. He also said that some people have pretty strong feelings about digging up graves."

"I suppose since nothing was destroyed or stolen, the only

crime was vandalism. Not really a priority." The living room had been picked up from the party the evening before. *Probably Mrs. Laurens, bless her.*

"I'll get going on an article for the paper. Perhaps if people understand what we're doing, we'll get fewer protests like the one last night."

"Sounds like a good plan. Do you think last night had anything to do with the reporter kid who was here yesterday?"

Lewis shrugged. "Feeling guilty?"

"No. But it did occur to me, he might want to retaliate somehow for the way I treated him."

Lewis grinned. "Could be. As a rule, guys don't like to be beat up by a girl."

"I didn't beat him up," Lindsay protested. "Just roughed him up a bit."

"Last night—before the fire—was quite enjoyable. You looked like you were having a good time, too."

Lindsay looked out the window to avoid Lewis's eyes. "I was. Things are getting better."

"The sheriff told me about the stolen truck and the page out of the library book."

Lindsay shifted her gaze back to Lewis. "Did he?"

He put a hand on her shoulder. "Why didn't you tell me?"

She shrugged. "Probably unrelated pranks." *I hope.*

"They found the McBrides' truck."

"They did? Where?"

"Abandoned on a dirt road. Hadn't been stripped or damaged."

"Did they dust for prints?"

"He didn't say. Lindsay, there will be military personnel here tomorrow. I'll have them keep an eye out for anything unusual. They will anyway, but I'll explain our special circumstance."

Our special circumstance, thought Lindsay. Odd choice of pronoun—but comforting in a way. She felt less alone. "I appreciate your support. I really do."

"Good. Make it easier when I need to ask for another favor sometime."

Mrs. Laurens had made a breakfast of blueberry pancakes, ham, scrambled eggs, and fried apples. Everyone was chowing down by the time Lindsay and Lewis got to the table.

"I think it was that reporter guy," said Dillon. "Definitely hostile to our position."

"What about Trent?" asked Kelsey.

"Oh, yeah, Trent. I forgot about him." Dillon handed the platter of pancakes to Lewis. "Better get some before we have seconds." He turned back to Kelsey. "Trent's a possibility, but why would he hang around here?"

"For Claire?" asked Kelsey.

Lindsay looked around for Claire and noticed that she wasn't there. "Where is Claire?"

"Haven't seen her," said Adam. "I think it was probably someone local who thinks we're grave robbers."

Lindsay turned to Mrs. Laurens, who had just come in with an extra platter of fresh scrambled eggs. "Did Claire have an early breakfast?"

"Not unless she was up before I got here."

"She was gone when I got up," said Drew. "Probably at the processing tent."

"She left in her car early this morning. About three o'clock, wasn't it, Powell?"

Powell nodded. "About that."

"And what were you two doing up at that time?" asked Marina, grinning, eliciting laughs from around the table.

"Guarding the fort," said Powell. "Like we were supposed to."

Lewis changed the subject to the tasks to be done before the scientists arrived. It was as if he had turned on a switch sending a spark of electricity to their seats. They stopped talking about the adventure last evening and gave him their full attention.

"There are some things we have to get done today. Ground preparation around the units to be excavated, and locating spots for the other tents and trailers that will be coming in. Lindsay, haven't you been trying to find out who lived on the farmstead prior to the Gallows family?" Lindsay, who had just taken a bite of blueberry pancake, nodded. "Good. You spend the day continuing that search. We'll have a special tent or trailer for you to use to examine the bones once the coffins are opened. Didn't you say a local doctor will be assisting you?"

Lindsay swallowed. Lewis, as usual, was thinking about several things at once, and she had to concentrate to follow. "Yes. He and his wife own the cabin that used to be here on the site."

"Great. That will make a good story."

"Good story?" asked Sharon. "With all due respect, isn't this getting a little bit like a circus?"

Lewis smiled, showing rows of gleaming white teeth. "Circuses are a troupe of strangers who come to the community and present the local citizens with strange and sometimes bizarre things they probably haven't seen before. So do we." There was laughter. "Circuses also depend on the goodwill of the community . . . and so do we. They use publicity to inform the community about what they have to offer. And so do we. What we have to do is manage the circus and see that it doesn't get out of our control."

The phone in the living room rang, and Lindsay jumped up to answer it.

"This is Elaine McBride. May I please speak with Lindsay Chamberlain?"

"Elaine, this is Lindsay. How are you?"

"I'm just great. You'll never guess . . . I'm so excited."

"What?"

"Hope Foute did have other diaries, and I've found them."

"You did! How did you find them? Where are they?"

"Actually, I've found the person who has them. Another descendant. She lives in Virginia."

"Will she allow us to copy or borrow them?"

"I don't know. I got the impression she would like to sell them."

"Oh."

"I'm making arrangements to meet her."

"That's a long way."

"By plane it's a couple of hours."

"This is really above and beyond . . ."

"No it isn't. I'm having a good time. It's like finding a whole new chapter in the story of my home."

"We'll be excavating the coffins tomorrow. Will your husband be available?"

"Oh, yes. I'll be going to Virginia without him. He wouldn't miss the opening of the coffins."

"I'll give him a call when I know more."

"This is so exciting."

Lindsay said good-bye and hung up the phone. She stood with her hand on the receiver, getting herself lost in Elaine's enthusiasm. The McBrides had turned out to be good informants. She wondered why Drew hadn't pursued them after Claire alienated them. It wouldn't have been hard. They were very anxious to help. She turned to go, and the phone rang again, a loud, piercing ring.

"Did you forget something?" Lindsay smiled into the phone.

"Who is this?" The male voice sounded indignant, as if he had been accused of forgetting something.

"Who are you calling?" It never failed to make her bristle when someone called without identifying themselves and then asked who they were talking to.

"I was calling Drew Van Horne," he said. "Is this the site?"

"I'll get her. May I tell her who is calling?"

"Eric Van Horne. This is her husband."

"Just a moment, Mr. Van Horne."

Lindsay walked back to the dining room and tapped Drew on the shoulder. "Drew, you have a phone call. It's your husband." *I seem to have pissed him off,* she wanted to add.

Drew got up to answer the phone. Lindsay wished she could listen to the conversation. He was a document collector. She wondered if she should have questioned him while she had him on the phone. That really would have made him irate. She smiled at the thought, having taken an instant dislike to Drew's husband. He was too quick to anger . . . but then, she was one to talk.

"You look like you've been into a bowl of cream," said Marina.

"That was Elaine McBride. She's located someone who owns more of Hope Foute's diaries and is going to try to acquire them."

"You're kidding. How did she do that?" asked Marina.

"Elaine McBride? She and her husband own the cabin?" said Lewis.

Lindsay nodded. "She didn't give me any details. The owner is out of state. Elaine's flying to meet her."

Although she tried to listen to Drew's side of the conversation over the noise of talking around the table, she heard nothing, not even the sound of Drew recradling the phone before she returned to the dining room.

"My husband may be joining us later this week," said Drew. "He's between cases and thought it would be nice to have a look at all the fuss."

"Would you like to have your room back?" Lewis offered. "I can room with the guys downstairs."

Drew shook her head and smiled. "He would be more comfortable in a motel or maybe a mountain cabin. He doesn't like roughing it, and he'd definitely hate sharing the bathroom with a crowd of people."

Lindsay took her plate and utensils to the kitchen and washed them. Mrs. Laurens always did the dishes, but there was no automatic dishwasher, and Lindsay thought washing two loads of dishes a day was too much to ask. Afterward, she went upstairs to change out of her work clothes, since she wouldn't be working on the site today.

Claire's bed was made, as usual. However, Claire's part of the room looked vacant. Her computer was nowhere in sight. But like Lindsay, she might keep her valuables in her car. Her suitcase and clothes were gone, too. Lindsay looked around the room. Drew's things were beside her bed, Lindsay's by hers. Claire's were gone.

She would have said something, surely. Maybe she got up early and went to the laundry in town. That was probably it. With all the people coming, this would be the only time to get away to do personal chores. Lindsay should probably do the same.

Lewis met her at the bottom of the stairs when she came down. "Where you going today?"

"I thought I would visit the church cemetery."

"Sounds good. Let me get the crew started and I'll come along."

Chapter 25

THEY FOUND THE church with no difficulty by following the map in the survey reports. It would have been a lot harder had they needed to rely on verbal directions. A modern sign, the kind with changeable lettering, stood at the front of the drive. It read, *Kelley's Chase Primitive Baptist Church,* and beneath that, *And now abideth faith, hope, charity, these three; but the greatest of these is charity. 1 Corinthians 13:13.*

Lindsay parked her SUV, and she and Lewis got out. She stood looking at the church. It was a plain, rectangular vernacular building with white board siding and a simple steeple. A brass plaque next to the front doors said, *Founded in 1810.* The survey report said the original building burned in 1830 and a new one was built fifty feet away. Since then the church had been added onto and restored several times.

There were no cars around, but she knocked on the church door anyway. No one answered. She tried the door, but it was locked.

"Are you sure we want to be here?" asked Lewis. "We're really way back in the mountains."

"We're about five miles from the site as the crow flies."

"Unfortunately, we aren't crows."

"No one here." She stood back and looked at the building. "I have a question. If the curators of Thomas Jefferson's ax had to replace the handle, and fifty years later other curators had to replace the head, is it still Thomas Jefferson's ax?"

"What are you talking about?"

"This church. Is it its history that makes it the same church, or is it the building? Nary an original stick of wood or person remains."

"Don't get philosophical on me. It's too early. Do you know where the graves are?"

Lindsay opened the map and pointed to a spot. "Yes. The Gallows graves are here. I'm hoping the Foute graves are nearby."

Near the church were several rows of modern gravestones, thick, substantial, shiny granite ones with readable names, dates, and sometimes verses etched into the rock. The stones farther back toward the older church site were thin, covered with lichens, and worn so that the writing was barely legible. Even when they were new, they had been plain stones. Now, they leaned forward or backward with the pull of time. Each grave was marked with a headstone and a small weathered rock footstone.

The weeds were kept pulled. Lindsay could imagine the church members every Memorial Day, and sometimes in between, coming out and taking care of their ancestors' resting places. The newer graves had fresh flowers. But it hadn't taken long for the older ones to be forgotten, or for the nearest relatives to be buried beside them, leaving no one to bring flowers.

She found the graves of Rosellen and Josh Gallows side by side. She could barely make out Rosellen's name. Beside them was a smaller grave, marked only with two rocks at the head and foot. According to the map, they had walked past Elisha Gallows's grave, dated sometime in the 1900s. Lindsay went to the next stone and squatted down, trying to read it.

"Can I help you people?"

Both Lindsay and Lewis were startled. Neither had heard anyone approach.

A short, square-built man in jeans and a white shirt stood watching them through narrowed eyes.

"Are you the elder?" asked Lindsay.

"You'd be right about that. I'm Elder Timon Moore. Who would you be?"

"I'm Lindsay Chamberlain. This is Francisco Lewis. We're archaeologists from the Gallows farmstead site. We're looking at the Gallows graves."

"Francisco? Like San Francisco?"

Lewis nodded.

"Odd name. I heard you people are going to dig up graves. You're not thinking of digging up the Gallowses, are you? We won't have that."

"No," Lewis hurried to assure him. "No. We're just . . ." He looked to Lindsay, as if to say: "What are we here for?"

"We would like to see Hope Foute's grave. Is she buried here?"

"She's here. So's her whole family."

"Are you related to Broach Moore?" Lindsay asked. "The two of you favor each other."

"You'd be right about that. Broach is my brother. You meet him professionally?"

"He came out to the Gallows farm where we're working."

"He goes to Kingswell Baptist." Elder Moore eyed Lewis. "You from New York?"

"Yes, I am."

"Thought so." He turned to Lindsay again. "Where's your people from? You sound a little like you might be from Kentucky."

"Yes, Kentucky. Stearns. It's near Somerset."

"I've got people from Kentucky. Don't know any Chamberlains. Is that your married name?"

"No. I'm not married."

"I know where Somerset is. Who's your mother's people?"

"Ravinel," said Lindsay.

"I know some Ravinels up in the Bluegrass region."

"They might be related."

"Hope Foute's buried over here." He led them to the other side of the cemetery, near the foot of the mountain. "Her whole family's buried right here." He pointed to a cluster of graves near the side. She could make out the name Clarence Foute. She assumed Hope's grave was beside his. She brushed over the face of the stone with the tips of her fingers. She thought she saw an *H*, part of an *o*, a *te*, and one date that looked like 1778. Other stones were more legible—a daughter, Martha, who died when she was eight. Perhaps a son and his wife, both of whom died in their fifties. The most legible stone was for Faith Redmond, Hope Foute's sister.

Close up, Lindsay could read the numbers 1770–1860.

"Marina dated the clay pipes at the site between 1730 and 1820," said Lindsay. "The Gallowses held the property from 1831 to 1869. I know that the building techniques on the oldest side of the log cabin dated from the 1700s—so any stones with dates that fall in the times of the clay pipes were contemporaries of the people who were the first occupants. Josh Gallows bought the land from Clarence Foute, so I assume that Clarence's relatives might have lived there before him."

"So, do you know if any of Clarence Foute's people are buried here?" Lewis asked Elder Moore.

"I don't believe so. You trying to find out who owned the land before the Gallows family?"

"Yes," said Lindsay. "Do you know?"

"I can't say as I do. I always heard that was a bad place. Some say poor Mrs. Gallows killed her children."

"Do you think she did?" asked Lewis.

"Don't know. Doesn't seem like her neighbors would have stood for it—or let her be buried here at the church," he said.

"Do you know any stories connected to the Gallows place?" she asked.

"No. I don't pay much attention to stories."

"Have you ever heard older people mention a Cherry or an Eda Mae?"

"I went to school with an Etta May Ramsey. Her family was from Kansas, but I suppose you mean back in the 1700s. No . . . Wait. I do remember my granny saying something being 'as sharp as Eda Mae's tongue.' You mean that kind of thing?"

Lindsay nodded. "Yes, exactly. Do you know who she was talking about?"

"No. That's just something she said, like Raw Head and Bloody Bones."

"May we take a look at all the old gravestones?" asked Lindsay. "We won't harm anything."

"Just so long as you don't dig 'em up."

"No. We won't do that."

"Some of the old graves don't have headstones no more. They're just marked with rocks. Don't know who's there, exactly. Just old church members. Don't do any of those rubbings, either. They damage the stones."

"No, we won't. Thank you for allowing us to look at the graves."

Lindsay and Lewis watched as Elder Moore walked along the edge of the cemetery back to the church.

"These are hard to read, but maybe we can find something." Lindsay took out a pad and pen to write down names and dates.

"You did that very well, Lindsay. I'm impressed."

Lindsay had kneeled near a stone, trying to read the writing. "What?"

"Talking with him. I was about to get worried for a moment."

"These are religious people, Lewis. What did you think he was going to do?"

Lewis squatted down to help look at the stone. "I don't know. He just seemed very suspicious of us. But you handled it well. He wasn't interested in my relatives."

"That's because you're from New York. He doesn't know anybody in New York. He was suspicious. For all he knew, we were here to dig up some graves. He was actually being very nice. He was trying to find a reason to trust us, looking for some common ground, trying to place us in his context. The same thing as us looking at someone's vita. Does this look like Ezra Heaton?"

Lewis traced the indentations with the tips of his fingers. "I think so. You know Timon Moore's brother?"

Lindsay turned her head toward him and grinned. "He's the process server who came to serve Drew. The one I told you about. He drove across Feature 3 and Claire made off with his truck."

Lewis laughed. "I remember. Small world."

"Here in the mountains it is."

"You think his brother told him about serving Drew Van Horne with papers?"

"I would think they'd find us a popular topic of conversation. On the other hand, maybe there's some confidentiality code of ethics among process servers. Then again, I imagine their religious differences are a more hot topic of conversation between them."

"Why do you say that? They're both Baptists, aren't they?

Didn't I hear him say his brother goes to . . . what . . . Kingswell Baptist?"

"Broach is Baptist, Timon is Primitive Baptist. They don't hold the same beliefs by a long shot." She stood up, brushing her hands together. "I'm not sure we're going to find out as much as I'd hoped from these graves. Most of the stones are unreadable."

"Are there other cemeteries in the area with graves this old?" Lewis asked.

"The survey found none in the immediate area. There are old ones in the Smoky Mountain Park, but they're connected with settlements there. The survey doesn't say where in the cove the Foutes lived, or any of the other families, for that matter. This cove has really gone unnoticed. I think it would be fun to survey the entire cove, not just the Gallows farmstead."

Lindsay and Lewis went from stone to stone, writing down as many names and dates as they could make out from the years of weathering. Before driving away, Lindsay stopped and thanked Elder Moore and asked him if there were any other old cemeteries in the cove. He knew of none.

"Let's stop and eat before we go back to the site," Lewis said, "or does Mrs. Laurens make lunch as well?"

"Nope. We're on our own at lunch. We usually fix ourselves a sandwich, grab an apple." Lindsay drove in the direction of the diner.

"Did we learn anything this morning?" asked Lewis.

"I don't know. Nothing I saw on the stones struck me. I wonder if there are other private cemeteries in the cove, similar to the one at the Gallows farmstead. I'll ask Drew if the survey team found any other homesteads. I'll be a little surprised if they didn't. Hope Foute's diary mentioned several families."

They stopped at Ellie's Diner and ate a quick lunch. Lindsay looked over the list of names from the gravestones as they ate. Still, nothing stood out. Something, though, tugged at the back of her mind. Lewis paid for the meal and they climbed into Lindsay's Explorer.

"I may have wasted our time," she said, turning the key in the ignition. "I'm not sure what I thought . . ."

She looked at the blue-green digital display as the tape player activated. Just as the engine started, a tape began to play—"Every Breath You Take," by the Police. Lindsay stared at the tape player, unmoving. When Sting came to the words "I'll be watching you," she hit the eject button.

"I don't remember that being on when we stopped." Lewis looked at the dash and over at Lindsay. "Lindsay, are you all right? Lindsay?"

She didn't move. Her eyes were fixed on the tape, half out of the tape slot, like someone sticking his tongue out at her. She felt Lewis shake her shoulder.

"Lindsay, are you all right?"

"They did this." Her words came out a tearful whimper.

"Who?"

"I don't know who. If I knew, I would . . . I don't know who."

"Are you saying this isn't your tape? Someone put this here while we were eating? Could it be a prank?"

A prank. That's what she thought about the torn page. Who would do such a thing? Claire? She had been acting a little strange the last day or two. It was subtle, but something had changed in the new rapport they shared. Trent? He was gone. Wasn't he? She thought of the whiff of marijuana at the party. Could that have been Trent? What would he be doing lurking around?

She was overcome with nausea. "I'm going to be sick."

She opened her door, jumped out of her truck and leaned her forehead against the cool metal of the vehicle, trying to breathe normally.

"Here." Lewis handed her a glass of water. She hadn't noticed that he had gone inside. He had left her alone and gone inside.

"Thanks." Her hand shook as she took a sip.

Lewis scanned the parking lot, the woods, the highway. "I don't see anyone," he said.

After a minute, the nausea passed and she climbed back into the driver's seat. Lewis returned the glass to the diner and got back in.

"You want to go to the sheriff's office?"

"Yes. Maybe there are prints on the tape."

"I can drive if you want."

"No. I can drive." She started the engine and put it in reverse. "You know what really makes me mad? I like that song. When we were competing, Derrick choreographed a dance to it. It was fun, and we won. I have good memories about it. Damn them, damn them to hell. It wasn't enough for them to take away all my memories for a time, now they're corrupting the ones I have."

She backed out of the parking place and headed toward Kelley's Chase. Lewis sat in silence as she drove, his brow knitted in a worried frown.

"I wonder why they're doing this," he said when they were almost to the sheriff's office.

"What do you mean?"

"Why frighten you and not try and not . . . finish what they started? This exposes them. Someone could have seen them in the parking lot at the diner, or ripping the page from the library book."

Lindsay slowed down. "I should have asked at the diner."

"I asked when I went to get the water. No one saw anything," said Lewis.

Lindsay pulled up to the sheriff's office and delivered the tape in a sandwich baggie she found in her trash bag.

"You say someone put this in your SUV while you were in Ellie's?"

"Yes. And no one there saw anything."

"It may be just a prank, but I'll have it fingerprinted. Maybe something will turn up. In the meantime, do you think anyone you work with could be doing this?"

Lindsay shrugged, reluctant to accuse. She wished she had an answer. She wished he had an answer.

"Perhaps this Drew woman?" suggested the sheriff.

"We'll see if anyone left the site," said Lewis. Neither mentioned Trent. To mention Trent would be to mention his drugs, and that was a can of worms both of them wanted to stay closed.

"I don't have enough deputies to give you protection," said the sheriff.

"We'll be having people from the army come to the site tomorrow," said Lewis. "I'll see that she gets protection."

"I'll see what I can do with this. Don't get your hopes up."

On the way out, Lindsay saw a partial headline in the newspaper. Nigel had identified his two hikers. Perhaps she should go home and allow Nigel to examine the bones. That might be best. Maybe that's what they wanted, why they were scaring her and not trying to kill her. Maybe if she went home, she'd be safe.

Lindsay started to let Lewis drive back. She felt defeated, tired, and depressed. But she climbed into the driver's side—more from force of habit.

"You can't let them win," said Lewis.

"They are winning."

"No, they aren't."

"You've spoken with Drew. Do you think she could be involved?" Lindsay asked.

"I don't know. Then again, I'm not a particularly good judge of murderer personality types. Do you think she may be behind this, to get you to stop investigating the Tidwell thing?"

Lewis looked tired, too, Lindsay noticed. He ran his fingers through his windblown black hair to get it out of his face. Was he worried, too?

"Or, maybe they don't want me to clear her. Or, it may be something else—Trent or Claire getting even for whatever, and just using what happened to me because they know they can scare me with it. Claire's away from the site today."

Lewis raised his eyebrows. "So she is. I'll talk with her when we get back."

"I'll talk with her. You'd probably just make her break down in tears. Do you know Drew's husband?"

"No. Drew hasn't said much about him. Why?"

"I don't know. He called this morning, and I answered the phone. I didn't like him."

"Any particular reason?"

"No, not really. He just seemed self-important. I was just thinking. Maybe I should go back to Georgia. You can get Nigel to examine the bones. Get Kerwin to come up here. Historical archaeology is his field, anyway."

"The people are coming tomorrow. You can do it. Didn't your

mother teach you to get back on your horse after you fall off?"

Lindsay looked over at him, made a face, and started the Explorer.

The crew were still working at the site. When Lindsay stopped to let Lewis out, she counted heads—they were all there, except Claire. Even Marina, who usually worked in the tent on the artifacts, was helping out with the preparations.

She drove up to the house and parked her SUV. As she got out, seeing the crew's cars, she had an idea. She went to each one and touched the hood to see if any were warm. They were all cold, even Bill and Sharon's, who had driven from their motel early that morning—all except Adam's. His had a faint lingering warmth. Adam was one of the last persons she would suspect of a prank, or worse. It very well could have been innocent, probably was. There wasn't a law against leaving the site. She could ask him. And say what: Adam, I couldn't help noticing that your engine was warm—where've you been? Lose any tapes?"

She walked up the steps and into the house. Passing the closed door to the guys' room, she realized the house was empty; everyone was at the site. She made a sharp turn and tried the doorknob, then went in.

Chapter 26

THE ROOM WAS a mess. Four mattresses were arranged like the last four petals of a flower, using the four walls as headboards. The bedclothes were rumpled. One mattress, Byron's, Lindsay guessed from the Grateful Dead T-shirt visible on top, had clothes heaped on it in a tangled pile. Each mattress had a suitcase or duffel bag nearby. There were few other possessions in the room. Like Lindsay, everyone kept their valuables locked in their vehicles.

She went to Byron's mattress first. She took the ballpoint pen clipped to her T-shirt and gently rifled through the pile on the bed. She resisted the temptation to go through his pockets. She had to draw the line somewhere. She moved to each piece of luggage, going through its contents by lifting items with the pen, trying to leave things as she found them, feeling extremely ashamed of herself. Occasionally, she peeked out the one window that wasn't boarded up to see if anyone was coming.

She found nothing. What did she expect? She wasn't sure what she was even looking for—something incriminating, suggestive, what? Who had tapes? None that she remembered. When they had music it came from CDs on Powell's player, which he kept locked in his trunk. Lindsay sighed and turned to leave the room. She gasped.

Someone was standing in the doorway. An explanation quivered on her lips when she recognized the man with honey-colored long hair she had seen on the porch. Behind him stood the woman she had seen in the mirror. A scream stuck in her throat, choking her. She started to sink to her knees, and the couple vanished.

She was motionless, half kneeling on the floor, breathing hard, heart pounding, shaking with fear. Slowly, she stood and made her way to the door, grasping the frame for support.

Oh, God. What was that? Ghosts? Insanity?

She ran up the stairs to her room and closed the door. A suffocating darkness sucking the warmth from her body. Cold, dizzy, and sick, she collapsed on her bed, gasping for air, lost in utter panic with nothing to hold on to. She felt her memory slipping away.

Grasp something. Get back on the horse. She barely heard her inner voice calling from a distance. *Hold on to something before you're whisked away.* Hold on to what? *Some strong anchor, a strong root to who you are.*

She heard her father's voice spring out of the darkness. The admonition that *"perhaps you can't control what you feel, but you damn well can control your behavior."*

On shaky legs she rose from the bed, feeling as if she had just run a marathon.

"This has to stop," she said aloud.

This isn't going to be my life.

She looked at her watch. Whatever kind of panic attack this was, it had lasted about five minutes. She looked out the window toward the site. The crew were still working. She couldn't see the entire site, but she thought everyone was there.

Maybe she should just take a nap. Rest. She was so tired.

No. Rest later. Get back on the horse.

She looked around the room. Drew's things. Her suitcase contained nothing but preppy-looking clothes and a couple of paperbacks. She flipped through them. Nothing. What did she expect? A secret message? Drew's makeup case contained the expected personal items, nothing more.

She skipped Lewis's room and went to the one that Marina, Kelsey, and Erin shared. Marina's and Kelsey's areas were tidy. Erin was a bit messy. Feeling less guilty—nothing like stark-raving fear to push guilt aside—she searched their luggage in the same manner she had the guys'. Nothing but clothes, books, stationery, makeup, perfume—normal stuff. In Kelsey's she found a bottle of raspberry massage oil and felt her guilt coming back. What was she doing invading their privacy like this? She'd hate it if they did it to her.

The closet contained nothing but a couple of dresses on wire hangers. The top shelf was empty. Like the guys, they kept only the necessities in the house. She really needed to search the cars. Good luck trying to manage that, she told herself.

The storeroom door was locked. She wished she had acquired lock-picking skills. So far she had found nothing.

She had left the attic and basement for last—if she were caught, it would be much easier to give a plausible reason for being there than if she were caught in someone's room. She went back in her room for a flashlight and stood a long moment at the foot of the stairs to the attic before ascending.

Go. You can't spend the rest of your life with hallucinations, flashbacks, panic attacks, and looking over your shoulder.

She forced her legs to carry her up the stairs and through the door. The attic was a large rectangular room situated over the midsection of the house. Several doors led off the main room to storage areas where the slanted roof had reduced the useful headroom. The attic was completely empty, except for a brightly colored tropical-flowered curtain over the door to one of the storage rooms under the eave. She pulled back the curtain and revealed a mattress neatly made up with a white chenille bedspread. *Kelsey and Powell.* She smiled and dropped the curtain.

Out a front window of the attic she surveyed the site to see if the crew were still working. They were. She looked at her watch. They should be at it for another half hour. Probably longer if Lewis was there. He had a knack for getting overtime out of any crew.

Lindsay went down the stairs, heading straight for the basement. The door leading down to the basement was off the first-floor reception hall. She'd passed it many times but had never opened it, even to take a look. As she reached for the knob, her heart beat faster.

Now what? Calm down. It's just the psychological reaction to the thought of entering a strange dark basement.

This was where Dillon had found Trent's drug paraphernalia. Perhaps there were other things down there. She certainly hadn't found anything in the rest of the house. She opened the door.

The stairs were the kind she hated. Why did builders skimp on basement stairs? They were steep, without solid risers, the kind of steps you might wedge a leg under if you slipped. The handrails were also missing. She shone her light into the darkness and started down, hoping she wouldn't have a dizzy spell, hallucinate, or otherwise go berserk.

She stopped and sucked in a lungful of air at the bottom. The basement was pitch-black except for where she shone her flashlight. It was kind of like a cave. She shivered. Like most basements with dirt floors, it was earthy smelling. She stopped, stooped, and brushed the earth with her fingers. It was hard-packed reddish-brown soil. She was glad someone hadn't covered it over with flooring. Archaeologists can do a lot with dirt floors.

Just a few feet in front of her was the old furnace that once heated the house. Years earlier someone had converted the chimney of the fireplace in the main reception hall into a flu to vent the smoke and fumes from the basement cast-iron furnace. She examined the floor leading to it before she walked across the dirt. There was a vague muddle of tracks, probably Dillon's and Trent's, at least.

She walked to the furnace and opened the door, shining her light on the inside. If she expected anything like charred bones, she was disappointed. It was empty. Not even ash.

The basement was rather small, compared to the floor space of the house. She walked back and forth along it, looking at the ground. There were signs of activity, but nothing that suggested itself as a clue.

Several wooden skids leaned against the front wall next to a rickety door. Probably where fuel was brought in for the furnace from outside. She was reaching for the knob of the door when she heard voices. She jumped back and put a hand over her mouth, but the voices weren't behind the door. They seemed all around her. Her heart raced. *It's going to wear out,* she thought as she held her chest. She slowly turned and shone a beam of light around the room. It was empty.

Don't let me be hearing things on top of everything else.

She heard the voices again. No words, but one sounded male and the other female. She wasn't sure, but the quality of the tone sounded like Lewis. An oval of her light rested on the furnace. Of course. She walked back over and opened the door. If she remained very quiet she could just make out what sounded like Lewis making dinner arrangements with someone else. Next, she heard footfalls going up the stairs.

She shone the flashlight above her and saw the metal ducts that had carried the hot air from the furnace throughout the house. That's where the voices were coming from. If voices could be heard down here, she bet they would carry from the basement upward. She thought of Sharon and the voices she had heard and wondered if the house had been empty that day after all. If someone, more than one someone, had been in the basement.

She walked back to the rickety door and pulled it open. A long dirt hallwaylike room led under the living room and porch area, terminating at another door at the far end. Apparently, there was a door under the front steps that she had never noticed.

She examined the floor, staying next to the wall, trying to make as little disturbance in the soil as possible. Near the outside entrance she found impressions that she could identify. It looked like the wooden skids might have been on the floor, keeping something heavy off the ground. The impression had been disturbed, but enough remained that she could identify the marks of the wooden platforms currently leaning against the wall.

So what? Something was stored here. This is a basement, after all. No telling when these marks were made. She squatted on her haunches, examining the floor for impressions in the dirt and looking for anything that might have been dropped. People leave things behind, wherever they go.

Nothing had been dropped, but she did find a small square impression, about a half inch deep, near the entrance. Whatever had made it had straight edges and sharp corners. Okay—this was something. Perhaps not anything important or relevant, but something just the same. She examined it closely. It looked like someone had dropped whatever made the impression and then stepped on it before retrieving it. As she studied it, an idea came to her.

Lindsay retraced her steps and left the basement. At the top of the stairs she checked her feet for dirt, wiping them on the top step. It was quiet. The main crew hadn't returned. Lewis and probably Drew had come back early. Lindsay slipped through the doorway and walked up the stairs to her room.

Drew wasn't there, but out in the hallway she heard the sounds of running water. Good, she'd just as soon not have to look someone in the eye whose possessions she had so recently rifled through. She knocked on Lewis's door.

"It's me," she called.

"Hey, Lindsay, come in." Lewis was sitting at the table with his feet propped up on an extra chair, making notes on a yellow pad. He moved his feet and motioned to the chair. "How are you?"

Apparently, stark-raving mad, she thought.

"I'm okay. I've been doing a little snooping. I need to find some plaster or something to make a cast. Do you know when the scientists are due tomorrow?"

"In the afternoon. The plan is to set everything up and get started early in the morning, day after tomorrow. What are you making a cast of?"

"I don't know. Maybe nothing. Has Claire come back, by the way?"

"She didn't show up at the site."

"I wonder where she is?"

Lewis shrugged. "I'm taking everyone out to dinner tonight. Maybe we can find a place to get the stuff you need while we're out."

"Don't mention it to anyone."

His eyes twinkled. "No problem."

She was glad someone was enjoying this. The way Lewis kept his eyes on Lindsay, she wondered if he really believed she was okay. Perhaps she should have looked in the mirror before she talked with anyone. She raked her fingers through her hair.

"Where you taking us to eat?"

The group had voted for a steakhouse with a large salad bar to accommodate everyone's tastes. Drew rode with Lewis. Lindsay drove Erin, Kelsey, and Marina. Sharon and Bill took their own car. The guys—Powell, Dillon, Adam, and Joel—piled into Byron's van. Lindsay left a note on Claire's bed saying where they were going and asking her to join them, please. On the way, Lindsay passed a shopping center with a large craft store still open. She detoured into the parking lot.

"Don't lose them," said Kelsey.

"I know where we're going," said Lindsay. "I'll be just a moment." And she was out of the vehicle before anyone could protest further.

"What'd you get?" asked Marina when Lindsay came back with a large bag.

"I wanted to try some new casting techniques on bones. I didn't know if I'd be able to get away tomorrow." Lindsay was relieved to discover that they were more interested in talking about Lewis than what she might be up to, and she was happy to answer their questions about him.

It was late when they got back to the site. Everyone was tired and ready to get some sleep. Lindsay carried her casting material up to her room. Tomorrow when everyone was at the site would be the best time to make the cast. Just as well for no one to be in the house while she went about her sleuthing. As she put her stash in her suitcase, she felt a little foolish, going to this much trouble on something that probably wasn't connected to anything.

She got a towel and washcloth. This late she could get a hot shower with no waiting. She noticed that her note to Claire was still on the bed. She tossed it into the wastebasket.

Drew was getting ready for bed when Lindsay returned from the shower.

"Any ideas where Claire is?" Lindsay asked.

Drew shrugged. "She didn't say anything to me."

"I can understand why none of the crew are particularly concerned, but I would have thought you would be worried."

Drew gave Lindsay a sharp look. "What I don't understand is why you are so concerned, considering what a rough time she gave you."

"She's missing."

"She's not missing. She just went somewhere. Look, I like Claire and think she has promise, but you can't help but have noticed that she has problems. Lately she was concerned that with both me and Lewis here, she was losing control of her job as site director. You did notice that she's somewhat of a control freak?"

"Yes. I saw her problems. But I also know she was looking forward to the antique air project. And she wanted to watch me analyze the bones. I don't think she would just cut out. Where does she live?"

"I'm not sure. She gave up her apartment to work here."

Lindsay thought Drew was being deliberately evasive.

"Where *did* she live? She writes checks. Where's her bank?"

"Claire has been known to just leave when things aren't going her way. She did it in graduate school. She's probably shacking up with Trent somewhere. He came by the night of the party looking for her. Now, I've got a big day tomorrow, and I'm tired."

Lindsay stood and eyed Drew for a long time while she set her alarm clock and tucked herself in bed. Drew ignored her, but it made her uncomfortable. Lindsay could tell by the way she fumbled with the clock.

Sound Ecology would have all of Claire's personal information. She would call them tomorrow. Finally, Lindsay settled into her own bed, wondering what kind of person she was sharing a room with. She was uneasy about going to sleep.

Chapter 27

THE CASTING MATERIAL, though not normally bought for the purpose Lindsay was putting it to, was very easy to use. It was sold in craft stores for body sculpting—sticking a hand into the molding compound, for instance, then making a plaster cast of it. The molding and casting compounds were designed to be mixed with water and dried quickly. Lindsay decided to use the molding compound rather than the plaster material, hoping the smoother surface of the rubber would give greater detail in the cast.

After the crew had gone to the site, she raided the kitchen for measuring utensils, a Mason jar, and a spoon. Mrs. Laurens, who was busy washing the breakfast dishes, seemed a little out of sorts.

"What you doing with all that?" she asked.

"A special project for Dr. Lewis."

"He says a bunch of folks are coming today. Offered to pay me a whole lot extra for cooking. We can always use the money, but I'm going to have to have my daughters come help me. I told him I don't think this kitchen is big enough to cook the kind of meals he's asking about. I'm getting my daughter-in-law to fix some meals in her kitchen and carry them here."

"Lewis obviously likes your cooking."

"I just hope I can do a good job. You know, you don't just double the ingredients if you're cooking for twice the people. Cooking don't work like that. Jimmy is going to have to get hisself in here and help, that's all I can say."

Lindsay patted her shoulder. "I'm sure you'll do fine however you decide to organize it. Lewis thinks so, too, or he wouldn't have asked. He's the type of person who leaves it up to you to decide how much you can do. He'll keep piling the work on and tell you he wants it faster, until you tell him no. And it's all right to tell him no, or that you'll need to hire more help."

"He just seems so confident in me that I hate to disappoint him," said Mrs. Laurens, wiping her wet hands on a towel.

"Yes, that's part of his charm. He does that because it works. You'll do fine. Don't you worry about it."

"Thank you, Lindsay. You're a real nice girl."

Lindsay took her paraphernalia down to the basement and into the passageway. She mixed the molding compound with water in the Mason jar and poured it into the indentation in the soil, including the whole area of the footprint. The instructions said it took four minutes to harden into a rubber mold. She looked at her watch and waited.

The basement was silent and dark—like a cave. She'd been trapped in a cave. She looked at the small door and told herself that she was just a few feet away from the outside, or only a room away from the first floor.

This isn't a cave—I'm not buried.

She looked at her watch. Only forty-five seconds had passed. Maybe she should go upstairs and wait.

Don't be silly. It's only three more minutes. Get a grip. Her inner voice was losing patience with her.

She thought about Claire. Why was Drew so unconcerned about her? She wondered what time the office for Sound Ecology opened.

When I'm finished with this, I'll call and get Claire's home phone. They might have a number to call in case of an emergency. Maybe Claire went to visit her parents. Trent—Sound Ecology will have his phone number, too.

The idea that Claire was with Trent was a relief. Why was she so worried? Claire was concerned that she had become unnecessary—she told Lindsay that herself. Lindsay realized that she was worried because Drew, supposedly Claire's friend, was so unconcerned. Drew hadn't wanted to give Lindsay even the name of the city where Claire lived. That was odd. Lindsay looked at her watch.

Carefully, she peeled up the hard off-white colored rubbery mold. So far, so good. She could see that she had something. She quickly gathered up her supplies and headed up the steep steps for the first floor. After dusting off her feet, she made a beeline for her room.

In the light, Lindsay examined her creation. The shoe print was faint, only an impression of a print, no distinguishing marks. Other than size, there was probably no information she could gain from it. But the square protrusion in the center had what could be a design on its surface. The uniform color of the material made it hard to make out what the pattern was—if anything at all.

Lindsay walked down the hall to the storage room. Locked. There was a desk in the living room with supplies. She hurried downstairs and searched through the desk drawers. She found pens, pencils, pads of lined yellow paper, graph paper, and site forms galore, but not . . . She found a stamp with rotating numbers for numbering forms. If there was a stamp, there was an ink pad somewhere. She continued searching. Shoved to the back of a drawer was a black ink pad. If her luck held out, it wouldn't be dried up. She raced back upstairs with her find.

She dug her Swiss army knife out of her jeans pocket and sliced the rubber square away from the footprint. Using the mold like a rubber stamp, she pressed the patterned side on the ink pad, then on a piece of paper. Under the light of her lamp she studied the ink spot. It was something. Re-inking the stamp, she made several more impressions and examined them under the light, turning the paper around in her hand, holding it close and at a distance.

After staring for several moments, she decided the image contained what looked like part of a cat. One ear was distinct. The other, if it was an ear, had made only a partial imprint in the dirt. She saw what might have been a paw, but it was in the wrong place. She stared at the stamped images, trying to make sense of the design . . . and suddenly, it jumped out at her.

It was Chessie—the sleeping cat logo for the Chesapeake and Ohio Railroad. She grinned with pleasure that her method had worked. She didn't know what it meant, or if it was relevant to anything she was doing, but it had worked.

The secretary for Sound Ecology must have just walked in the door. She answered the phone on the fifth ring and sounded out of breath. Lindsay explained who she was and what she wanted. Fortunately, the secretary was all bubbly about the antique air project and asked few questions about why Lindsay wanted information on Claire and Trent.

"Keith called from China, and I told him all about the coffins and NASA, and everything," she said. "He was *very* pleased. We are all excited up here. It sounds like such fun. Okay, here's the information . . ."

It turned out that, rather than give up her apartment, Claire had subleased it. When Lindsay called the apartment, the female voice on the other end sounded as if she had been awakened from a dead sleep.

"Yeah? Hello?"

"Is Claire Burke there?" Lindsay asked.

"Claire Burke? No. She's working at some archaeological dig somewhere in the boonies."

"Has she called you in the last few days?"

"No. Why would she?"

"I'm one of her coworkers at the site. She had to be away for a few days, and we need to get in touch with her."

"She's not here. I hope she doesn't come here. This is a one-bedroom apartment, and I've paid the rent to stay here."

"If she calls, would you ask her to get in touch with Lindsay Chamberlain or Francisco Lewis at the site in Tennessee?" Lindsay gave her the number.

"Well, okay." She hung up the phone.

"Thanks," Lindsay said into a dead phone.

Probably too early to call Claire's parents or her brother. Lindsay dialed Trent's number. Trent was just as vague answering the phone, but probably for different reasons.

"Trent, hi. Is Claire there?" Lindsay thought it best not to tell Trent her name right off, lest he hang up.

"Claire? No. Who is this?"

Lindsay's heart sank. She hadn't realized how much she was counting on Claire being with Trent.

"This is Lindsay Chamberlain. I'm trying to find Claire."

"What do you mean you're trying to find Claire? She's at the site. Where are you? Or don't you know?"

"I'm at the site. Claire seems to have left without telling anyone."

There was a long pause. "Well, what do you want me to do?"

"Claire's your friend. She tried to stop you from being fired. I thought you might care."

"Hey, I care, but it's not like she really helped me, or anything."

"She did her best for you."

"I don't understand what you mean here. Claire is missing? Is that what you're trying to say?"

"Yes, she's missing."

"Since when?"

"Powell and Kelsey saw her driving away in her car at about three in the morning after the party the other night."

"Powell and Dillon—stupid clones. You'd think nobody ever smoked a little pot at a dig before."

"Drew said you came looking for Claire that evening."

"That bitch's not trying to blame me for something, is she?"

"No. She just thought Claire might be with you."

"That superbitch Drew firing me, that was so unfair."

"Claire thought so. She was on your side."

"Yeah, Claire's all right. Hey, you don't think she came looking for me and something happened—like a carjacking or something? Like what happened to you maybe happened to her? That'd make me feel real bad."

Lindsay paused. Her heart, which lately had seemed to habitually beat like a jackhammer, now felt like it had stopped.

"You didn't see her that evening?"

"No. I waited beside the house in the dark until I thought everyone was out front. Drew caught me coming in the back way. Told me to leave, or she'd call the police. I didn't need that kind of trouble. If Claire wanted to talk to me, she could call me later."

"She wanted to talk to you? Do you know about what?"

"Not exactly. I thought it had something to do with the other thing."

"What other thing?"

"You know how Claire was kind of down on you when you came?"

That's putting it mildly, thought Lindsay. "Yes."

"Drew told her you were this professor at UGA who had some kind of nervous breakdown. You weren't too swift to begin with, but now they had to find something for you to do, and Keith owed that Lewis fellow a favor."

"Drew told Claire this?"

"That and a whole lot more. Drew made out like you were coming to take Claire's job. Claire was real insecure because she didn't have a master's. Drew told her you were going to make some big deal out of that Tidwell complaint and get her in trouble. And Claire said Drew was really afraid of what you would do to her career. Like that woman has ever been afraid of anything."

"I wish I'd known."

"When you made Claire that offer to write articles with her, she checked out your vita and found out Drew had told her a bunch of lies about you. Drew told her the only way you could get published was if you coauthored with somebody else, but Claire knew that wasn't true when she saw all the stuff you got published, and that you were the only author on a bunch of it. Then added to that, you juried for some pretty big journals. Claire called me about it. She didn't know what to think. I told her that Drew was just jealous of you and to forget it. I told her to do the articles with you."

"That explains a lot. You don't know what this latest thing was she wanted to talk to you about?"

"I kind of think it was more of the same, but she said she found something that really disturbed her and she needed advice. I could tell she was upset, and I said I would come meet her."

Lindsay felt depressed and scared. This time, not so much for herself as for Claire. Drew was deep into something. No one tells that many big lies without being up to no good.

"I have her parents' and brother's phone numbers. Do you think she went there?"

"No, she wouldn't go to her father. Probably not her brother. Her father's an alcoholic, and she hates her stepmother. Her real mother died when she was twelve."

"Does Claire have a friend she would go visit?"

"I don't know of any. Claire's not very good at making friends. That's why Drew's been so important to her. Drew really played her."

"Trent, would you call me if you hear from her?"

"Sure. If you see her, tell her to give me a call."

Lindsay dialed Claire's father's number anyway. A woman answered.

"Is Claire Burke there? This is Lindsay Chamberlain."

"Claire? No, Claire's not here. I don't know where she is."

"May I speak with her father?"

"No. He's asleep."

"Would you call if . . ." The woman had hung up the phone.

Lindsay went ahead and called Claire's brother. He was more civil than her stepmother, but he hadn't heard from Claire in several months. Lindsay hung up the phone and sat there in the cane-back chair with her head in her hands for several moments. She picked up the phone and called the sheriff's office and explained everything to him.

The sheriff whistled. "That's quite a story. Doesn't make this Van Horne woman look very good, does it?"

"No, it doesn't. I'm beginning to wonder about a lot of things. But would you be on the lookout for Claire's car?" Lindsay gave him a description. "I don't know the license number."

"I can get it. I'll tell my deputies to watch for it. I understand you all are going to have company out there today."

"That's the plan."

"I think you may have a few protesters. Just thought I'd warn you."

"Thanks. We've had protesters before. We'll be on the lookout."

"I guess when your occupation is digging up graves, you're bound to upset a few people."

"Yep. Thank you, Sheriff."

Lindsay had hoped that calling the sheriff and reporting Claire missing would make her feel better. It hadn't. The morning's conversations had left her deeply worried—and wondering what she was going to say to Drew.

◆ ◆ ◆

Watching the trucks from NASA and the Armed Forces Radiobiology Research Institute was like watching the circus come to town. The train of vehicles was impressive, three tractor-trailer trucks and a convoy of four military vehicles and two SUVs. Behind them, three cars, one of which Lindsay recognized.

"Wow," said Joel. He stood with the rest of the crew watching the parade.

"I wonder how much this costs," said Marina.

"You don't want to know." Lewis bent down and whispered in her ear.

"I don't think the last three belong to the convoy," said Adam.

"Those must be the protesters Lindsay said were coming," said Drew.

Between the time Lindsay left the house and arrived at the site, she had decided not to tip her hand to Drew. She had to force herself to look at Drew and not challenge her, even when Drew gave her a mild rebuke cloaked in a joke about her not being at the site all morning.

The caravan drove down the dirt road and stopped opposite the site. Several men dressed casually in slacks and short-sleeved shirts hopped out of the SUVs and hurried across the grass toward the crew. Lewis stepped forward to greet them. Behind the men, members of the army reserve dressed in camouflage uniforms piled out of their dark olive vehicles.

"Dr. Francisco Lewis, I presume?" A thirtyish-aged man with wire-frame glasses and an impressive head of red hair held out his hand. "I'm Alex Jarman, Atmospheric Sciences and head of the team here. I appreciate your giving us the call."

"Our pleasure," Lewis told him.

"This is Peter Willis. He's hoping to get his dissertation out of this project."

Peter shook Lewis's hand up and down. He was of slight build with thinning brown hair and very excited. "I can't tell you what this means. The timing is perfect."

Jarman introduced the rest of the team—experts in geology, physics, structural engineering—and a host of graduate technicians in various fields. After the technicians, Dr. Jarman introduced Sergeant Stagmeyer of the army reserve unit assigned to erect the tents and protect the area. All in all, a rather spiffy group, compared to the rather ragged archaeologists.

"I told you we should have pressed our cutoffs," Lindsay heard Byron whisper to someone.

Lewis introduced the crew. While all the shaking of hands was going on, Lindsay noticed that the handful of people whom she assumed to be protesters were hanging back. Odd behavior for protesters, but they were an odd mix of people.

Luke Youngdeer, cousin to and employee of John West, grinned and waved. He wore an *X-Files* T-shirt and jeans and looked completely comfortable with the odd group.

Elder Timon Moore was among them, and Lindsay recognized Maxine Roxbury. Maxine had protested before, against the Archaeology Department's possession of ancient artifacts, and against the vet school's use of animals for teaching. Her latest protest at UGA was about the installation of level-four biocontainment facilities at the vet school. Maxine was typically low-key for a protester, preferring letter writing, court injunctions, and the like, to in-your-face confrontational tactics. Lindsay hoped she didn't have an injunction with her now. Probably not, or she would have served it.

Lindsay didn't recognize the other three. One older man seemed to be with Timon Moore. He and Moore appeared uncomfortable with the rest of the protesters, like the others might be making a deal with the devil, but they weren't sure. A much younger man was with Maxine. Ah, the younger man was the reporter Lindsay had accosted. She noticed that he was keeping his distance. If five were all they could come up with, that would be a good sign.

As Lewis and Drew showed Dr. Jarman and Sergeant Stagmeyer the locations of the coffins, the archaeology crew spoke with the other members of the government team, asking questions, giving information about the site. Lindsay watched the protesters. They all looked solemn, except for Luke.

"The first coffin is buried over by Helget Pond," she heard Adam tell one of the technicians. There was something about the way he said it that gave her pause. Her eyes followed Moore walking toward Lewis and the team leaders. There was something about him, too.

Lindsay wrinkled her brow, trying to coax whatever memory or thought was on the edge of her mind. She walked over to Lewis. Some of the others followed. Lewis faced Moore and held out his hand.

"It's good to see you again, Mr. Moore."

Lewis looked quizzically at Luke, who grinned and winked at Lindsay. *What is he doing here?* she wondered—supporting Maxine, who had often supported Native American claims? Moore shook Lewis's hand and introduced the man from his church, who nodded.

"Maxine," said Lewis, "haven't seen you in a while."

Moore started to speak, when Maxine inadvertently interrupted him. He frowned.

"We want you to know that we think what you're doing is wrong," she said. "You're upsetting the community's sensibilities, and you should let the dead rest in peace."

Lindsay heard several of the newcomers groan.

"You know that we hope to obtain valuable environmental information," Lewis said.

"It's wrong to disturb a burial," Maxine repeated. "You're offending the people who live here."

Buried well, by the gate to hell. It came into Lindsay's mind like a flash of light.

"This isn't a proper burial," said Lindsay, and everyone turned to look at her.

"What are you talking about? You are digging up coffins, aren't you?" Maxine had her hands on her hips in a classic stand of defiance.

"No culture buries its dead with the trash. This is a trash pit. If you look at the profile, you can see that it was a trash pit when the hole was dug for the coffin."

Lindsay hoped she could get them to focus their attention on Feature 2 and forget about Feature 3, which probably was a private cemetery.

"So?" asked Maxine, not sure what to make of what Lindsay was saying. "Are you telling us that it's just an empty lead coffin that was buried with the trash?"

"No . . ."

Lindsay didn't know what made it come to her, but another flash of insight electrified her brain and came out of her mouth.

"There's a young woman in the coffin . . . by the name of Charity Redmond."

Chapter 28

THE NEWCOMER SCIENTISTS didn't have much of a reaction to Lindsay's announcement, but the archaeology crew were stunned. Drew's mouth fell open. Lewis grinned from ear to ear.

"How could you possibly know that?" Drew demanded, almost angrily, as if Lindsay might have lapsed back into a nervous breakdown and was about to embarrass her. "There's no Charity Redmond in any of the documentation. I've read it. There was no grave marker with a name on it. We didn't even know the grave was here."

"She knows," said Lewis. "I've seen that look before."

"The point is," said Lindsay, "there is something abnormal about this burial, and it warrants investigating."

Maxine was loath to give up her position. "Abnormal?"

"She didn't receive the usual burial afforded to members of her community. She was thrown, in a manner of speaking, into the trash."

"We didn't come here to picket or cause trouble," Elder Moore finally spoke up. "We came to voice our objection to your disturbing a Christian grave. If you have a notion that something is wrong with this burial, then it might be that she needs a Christian service."

"If she's Christian," someone from the crowd behind Lindsay commented.

"She most likely is," said Lindsay. "And I never disturb the dead. I tell their story. It's only some of the living who are sometimes disturbed."

"But you must consider the living's feelings," said Maxine.

"I do. But if you also present yourselves as spokesmen for the dead—which you have—then you must consider their right to be heard."

"Right to be heard?" said Maxine. "They're dead."

"Precisely my point," said Lindsay. "They're resting in peace, whether they're in the ground or being examined by me."

"We are forgetting the enormous environmental problems we have," said Jarman. "The air in these coffins may provide us with a benchmark against which to compare our current atmosphere."

Maxine was clearly in a quandary. Her education was ecology. She understood very well the need to do something about the greenhouse effect.

Lindsay turned to Timon Moore. "These coffins may predate your church, but at a later time the relatives of these people were members of your church. When we finish gathering all the information we can, you can give them services and inter them at your cemetery with their family."

Moore conferred with his companion. "That sounds reasonable to us."

With the two representatives of the area in agreement, Maxine acquiesced, mumbling something about the consensus of the community being important in this case. Lindsay thought the whole thing odd. She'd crossed swords with her before, and Maxine had always been better organized and more committed.

Maxine and Moore drove away, but Luke did not leave with them. Lindsay grabbed him by the arm and pulled him away from the crowd as Jarman and Stagmeyer began giving orders, turning the site into an anthill of activity.

"Lindsay," yelled Adam, "you're not leaving without telling us . . ."

"In a minute." She waved him off and led Luke off to the side. "What was this about?"

"Good to see you, Lindsay."

"Luke, what are you doing here? These aren't your ancestors we're digging up."

"You know what they say, politics make strange bedfellows. Max has always come through for us when we need her."

"Yes, but . . ." She narrowed her eyes at Luke. "Are you here to protest or to watch after me?"

Luke looked at the ground, half smiling, and back up at Lindsay, his obsidian eyes glittering. "John had to think about what would make you less angry, protesting your digging up a grave, or protecting you. He went for the protest."

"That was a pitiful protest. Surely, John didn't arrange that to camouflage his intentions."

Luke looked over at the dust settling on the dirt road that Maxine's and Elder Moore's cars had stirred up when they l eft. "It was pretty pitiful, wasn't it? Not many people care about you digging up your ancestors." He shook his head. "Maxine called George to ask if anyone would come. Seems that she found out about this at the last moment. Some anonymous person called her and Moore and made it sound like you guys were railroading something through up here against everyone's wishes."

"An anonymous caller? That's strange."

"Maxine said so, too. She hesitated to come and wouldn't have, but she was coming near here anyway. She's from North Carolina."

"That explains why she didn't kick up too much of a fight. This really is odd."

"It worried George, and he called John. Got a place for me to stay?"

"You mind bunking in the living room?"

"Living room sounds fine. You guys staying in that old house I saw through the trees?"

"Yes. Do you have sheets and blankets?"

"Sure. Got everything I need. What are all the military here for? What exactly are you guys doing? Digging up aliens?"

Lindsay and Luke watched the army reserve unit putting up the tents as she explained what was about to happen. The archaeology crew hung back until it was time to do the actual excavation. They had nothing to do but watch the transformation of the north end of the site.

Marina had taken digital photographs of the site features from several angles, marked distances on them, and E-mailed them to Jarman. He had used her information to plan the location of the various tents and trailers. The preplanning was making the erection of the tiny scientific town go smoothly. First, they set up the porta-johns, three of them beyond Structure 4, close to the woods. Next, near Big Branch Creek they erected two large off-white heavy canvas tents, one to house the personnel and one to serve as a mess tent. After that, tents would go over Features 3 and 2.

Between the shelters and the personnel tents they planned to install a trailer where Lindsay was to analyze the bones, and another one to house the x-ray and other equipment. Later, with the structures in place, they would begin setting up their special equipment. Lindsay and the others got a look at some of it already being unloaded onto the ground—generators, vacuum pumps, special x-ray machines, along with wires, tubes, and mechanisms whose purpose Lindsay couldn't even guess.

"Wow," said Luke, watching the tents go up like a big top. "This is getting like the cofferdam site. Archaeology's becoming pretty high-tech these days."

"We are, aren't we? You see the number of people we have here? You don't need to baby-sit me if you have other things to do."

"I'll stay a couple of days, just the same. It will put John's mind at ease. He's never been comfortable with the authorities' inability to find out who hurt you."

Lindsay had been undecided about what to tell Luke about the current situation. She'd been going back and forth in her mind, listing the pros and cons. If he was going to stay a while, he needed to be informed. She told him everything that had happened. He listened as he watched the soldiers work.

"You've told the sheriff, and he takes it seriously?" asked Luke.

"Yes. So does Lewis. I haven't told anyone else—except the McBrides. They know." Lindsay explained who the McBrides were. "None of the crew know."

"Did the sheriff find any prints on the tape or the torn page?"

"No."

"You think it was someone in the house?"

"I'm trying not to think that. Don't tell John about all this. It will just worry him."

"I'll have to tell him. It's why he sent me up here."

"Luke . . ." Lindsay didn't say anything else about it. She knew she couldn't talk him out of it. "How's Bobbie. Seen her lately?"

"Right now, she's mad at me. It won't last. I'm sure she misses me already." He grinned at Lindsay.

She and Luke walked over to where the other crew were standing watching. They eyed Luke suspiciously. She introduced him.

"You remember John who came to visit me the other day? This is his cousin, Luke Youngdeer." Lindsay allowed them to believe that Luke's showing up with the protesters was a coincidence.

"Oh," said Adam, shaking his hand. "This is something, isn't it? I didn't know this was going to be so involved."

"We going to be able to do anything," asked Powell, "or just stand and watch?"

"As I understand it, you guys will be excavating alongside their geology people. Lewis or Drew will tell you about it this evening. I think they're going to excavate both coffins simultaneously, but I'm not sure. Right now, you know everything I know."

"Okay, Lindsay," said Joel. "Just how do you know who's buried in the coffin?"

"Yeah," said Marina. "Where did that come from? You are going to have to tell us."

"Do tell us." Lewis and Drew had walked over. Lindsay hadn't heard them for the noise.

"It's a tenuous connection."

"It has to be," said Lewis. "But you sure got everyone's attention . . . and Maxine off our backs. Good move."

"I've read all the documents," said Drew. "I've never come across a Charity Redmond."

Drew didn't look as pleased as Lewis. In fact, Lindsay thought she looked like she was under a strain.

"But you've come across a Faith Redmond," Lindsay told her.

"Hope Foute's sister? Yes. But . . ."

"Seeing the sign at the Baptist Church, and Elder Moore again today, made a series of pieces suddenly fall into place."

"What pieces?" asked Drew, unwilling to believe.

"First, the poem, '*Buried well, by the gate to hell.*' Helget Pond—It's the way I heard Adam say the words earlier. It sounded like he said *Hell Gate* Pond. Hell's Gate . . . the gate to hell. The pond has no bottom, according to local legend. Treacherous or unfathomable terrain is often named after the devil. It was probably originally named Hell's Gate Pond, but the name has become corrupted over the years."

"So, you think the poem is talking about the coffin being buried by Helget Pond?" Marina said. "Cool. It works for me."

"Once I made the connection—however tenuous—between the coffin, the pond, and the poem, then my mind made other connections with the poems. I remembered seeing 1 Corinthians 13:13 on the church sign about faith, hope, and charity. It clicked."

"What clicked?" Adam asked.

"We know that two sisters in the Redmond family were named Faith and Hope—I reasoned that there was a third, the oldest—*'the greatest of these is Charity.'*"

"That's a leap," said Drew. "There's no evidence of a third sister. And, why Charity? Where did that come from?"

"First, it was not uncommon at all for people to take names from the Bible. So, if there were two sisters named Faith and Hope, it's not at all unreasonable that a third sister, if she existed, might be named Charity."

"That's it?" asked Drew.

"No, that's not all. Remember the poem, *'Cherry's gone a looking, not at home a cooking.'* Cherry is a nickname for Charity."

"I love it," said Lewis.

"We know the farm was in the family. The Gallowses bought it from Clarence Foute—Hope's husband, so that fits, too. That's how I arrived at it. As I said, it's tenuous."

"Tenuous is right," said Drew.

"We'll see when it's opened up," said Adam. "It has to be a young female, right? Why young, by the way?"

"Because the poet seemed to be speaking about a young person. That was just my feel of it."

"It does make a kind of sense," said Joel. "Lindsay's right about the trash pit not being a place where a person would be buried. From the sound of those couplets, whoever is buried there was out of someone's good graces."

"Do you think the *he* in the poem refers to the person buried in the cemetery?" asked Erin.

"No way to tell," said Adam. "Unless Lindsay comes up with another remote association."

"Remote is right," said Drew. "I think they want to speak with us." She motioned toward the science team and took Lewis's arm.

"Would you tell them I'll be there in just a second? Thanks."

Drew dropped her arms to her side and walked over to Jarman and the others. Lewis watched her for a moment, then directed his attention to Lindsay.

"I didn't want to mention this in front of Drew. She seems to be on edge," Lewis began. It was a bad sign for Drew. She was principal investigator, and Lewis was taking her out of the loop. Lindsay wondered why. "The geologist voiced a concern that we haven't actually uncovered the second coffin. He wasn't overly concerned. He just had a question."

"What's his concern? That there may be only one?" asked Lindsay.

"Yes."

"I suppose that's a possibility, but I believe it's there. Why does he doubt it?"

"There appear to be no other graves in the cemetery. They're questioning whether it is a cemetery, and that perhaps the coffin in the pit is a throwaway."

"Something metal and the size of the coffin is buried in the cemetery according to the metal detector survey and the radar," said Adam. "Besides, we're the archaeologists. If we say it's a cemetery, it's a cemetery."

"Right now, that will have no effect on how we proceed, will it?" asked Lindsay.

"No. I just want to give them some assurance that they aren't wasting their time and resources," Lewis said.

"Tell them you have my assurance. Just leave out the part where I recently lost my mind."

A broad smile spread across Lewis's face, then he laughed. "I will reassure them." He turned to Adam. "And I will also reassure them that we do know what we're doing out here. Which brings me to the next thing I need to tell you. Adam, Byron, and Dillon will be excavating the coffin in Feature 2. Joel, Sharon, and Powell will excavate the one in Feature 3. Adam and Joel head the teams. I'm sorry I can't put everyone on it, but I'm going with experience. We'll be ready to excavate tomorrow." He left to join Jarman and Drew.

"What's up with Drew?" asked Adam.

"Her husband is coming up," said Marina. "It's probably that lawsuit thing."

"Has anyone heard from Claire?" asked Lindsay.

"No, and good riddance," said Joel.

"I agree," said Kelsey. "You notice how much nicer things are now?"

"But it's strange that she just left without telling anyone," persisted Lindsay.

"Not really," said Adam. "If she's not in control, she doesn't want to be involved."

A week ago Lindsay might have agreed. But lately, she really thought that Claire might be content just to have the title of Site Director at a site with an important find. That is, until the last couple of days before she disappeared. During those couple of days, there had been something different in her demeanor, but Lindsay had been so absorbed in her own problems she didn't pay enough attention to know what.

"I need to make a phone call. If Lewis wants anything, tell him I'll be right back."

"Sure. We'll be sitting here watching," said Powell.

Lindsay walked across the site, skirting around workers who were beginning erection of a fence around the compound. Briefly, she thought about seeing if there was room for her inside the fence, where it would be safe. When she arrived at the house, a couple of trucks were parked around the side. She hadn't noticed them arrive. Inside the house she got a whiff of the aroma of food. *Mrs. Laurens's relatives helping out,* Lindsay thought. She went to the living room and dialed Derrick's office number. She got lucky. He was in.

"Derrick, Lindsay here."

"Lindsay. How are you? Good to hear from you. I understand you have quite a find down there."

"The military and a team of scientists are here setting up. You should see it."

"When will you be able to analyze the bones?"

"Probably day after tomorrow. I'm not sure exactly what all is going to be done. I have a question."

"Sure."

"I found an impression in the dirt floor of the basement and made a cast of it. Actually, I used rubber molding compound, the kind you get in a craft store. The thing is exactly one inch square. It has very sharp corners and edges. I put ink on it and stamped the design on a piece of paper. Although it's not real clear, it looks kind of like Chessie . . . the logo for the Chesapeake and Ohio Railroad."

Lindsay could hear Derrick laughing. "Okay, I'll put aside for a minute what you were doing in the basement examining the dirt. Essentially, you made a rubber stamp, right?"

"Right. It looks like someone dropped whatever this was and stepped on it, pushing it into the dirt. There was a footprint over it."

"It sounds like a photo-engraved block."

"What's that?"

"It was used for printing newspapers. Engraved blocks were put into a chase—which is a frame for locking in place the blocks and type that made up the layout for a page of newspaper. The blocks would have pictures, advertisements, logos . . . stuff like that on them. The one you're describing sounds like a logo. Often they would be copper plated. It's a collector's item now. Does that help?"

"A lot."

"Should I ask what this is about?"

"Do you want to know the answer?"

"Are you all right? Really all right?"

"I don't know, Derrick. I've had hallucinations and I've been threatened. I think whoever did this to me is still after me, and I'm frightened all the time."

For several seconds, Derrick didn't say anything. "Lindsay, do you want me to come down there?"

"I've got a yard full of soldiers right now. Lewis is here, and John sent his cousin Luke. When I'm finished analyzing the bones in the lead coffins, I think I'll go home."

"What were you doing in the basement?"

"I have reason to believe that what happened to me is connected to this place. I think the attack on me was to stop me from coming here. One of the crew has disappeared, and I was looking for her, or some trace of her, when I found signs of activity in the basement."

"What! Someone has disappeared? I hadn't heard about that. Is it in the papers?"

"No one believes it's a problem but me. Most everyone thinks she ran away. But I don't."

"Have you talked to the authorities there?"

"Yes, and the sheriff believes me. He's as helpful as he can be."

"Does John know how serious this is?"

"He will soon. I told Luke, and Luke will tell him."

"Keep in touch, Lindsay. If you need me, I'll come down."

"Thanks, Derrick. Thanks for asking."

Lindsay hung up the phone and sat for several moments on the cane chair. It felt good to have told Derrick. It felt good that he wanted to come down. Whatever had happened to their romance, she always wanted him as a friend. She rose and started out the door and almost ran into a man in the hallway whom she had not met, but knew immediately who he was.

Chapter 29

You must be Drew's husband."

The man seemed to bristle, or perhaps he was already agitated. Had he overheard anything? Did it mean anything to him? Was he involved?

Documents are missing. He's a document collector. There has to be a connection. If Lindsay telegraphed her thoughts to him, he didn't show it.

"I'm Eric Van Horne. And you are?"

Eric Van Horne's hair was blond, like his wife's, and his eyes were such a light blue they didn't seem real. What Lindsay disliked about his face were his lips. They had an unsympathetic twist to them. She wondered how he did with jurors. He spoke as if he were dressed in a three-piece suit and had just caught her in his office. Perhaps she thought of him that way because she knew he was a lawyer. In fact, he was wearing tan slacks and a polo shirt, and he was not in his office. He was there to snoop—at least that was her fear.

"I'm Lindsay Chamberlain. I believe we spoke on the phone."

"Yes, I believe so." He was about an inch shorter than her, so he couldn't look down at her, though she got the impression he would have liked to. "I'm looking for Drew."

"She's at the site. You passed it on the way in."

"I thought perhaps she would be knocking off about now." He looked at his watch with some impatience.

"We're not on our normal schedule. We have a team of scientists setting up to run some tests. Did Drew tell you about them?"

"Yes, some nonsense about lead coffins."

"You aren't a fan of archaeology?"

"A fan?" He must have noticed that he was being rude, for he attempted a smile. "No, not really. But I do like history, and I understand this is a rather historic find."

"Yes, it is. You can come to the site and take a look, or you can wait here. Mrs. Laurens usually has some tea made. Would you like some?"

"Tea? No, thank you. I think I'll go down to the site and see what all the fuss is about."

As they walked out together, Lindsay felt a sudden relief. If he was here, then Drew would be staying with him at his motel. She would have her room to herself. She was suddenly glad to have him here.

They said little to each other on the way down to the site, banal prattle about how the site looked like a circus with all the big tents. The security fence now completely surrounded the tent city, and Lindsay had to get Lewis's attention to be allowed past the guard. After Lewis introduced Lindsay to the guard and gave her an ID pass, he led the two of them inside.

"This is Drew's husband, Eric Van Horne."

Drew looked up from a diagram she had been studying and seemed relieved to see him. Lindsay was surprised, but had no idea why she thought Drew wouldn't be pleased. He kissed her cheek, and Drew began explaining what they were doing.

"Looks like they're making quite a bit of progress," Lindsay told Lewis.

"We'll start excavating bright and early in the morning." Lewis guided Lindsay away from Drew and her husband toward the examination trailer.

"I thought you might like to see the facilities."

He took her inside. It looked like an autopsy room.

"Fancy," Lindsay said.

"All the best equipment."

She picked up a new hinged caliper and turned it over in her hand.

"Hey. Don't touch anything." Lindsay recognized the speaker as Peter Willis. "Dr. Lewis . . ." He put his spread hands out in front of him, as if trying to stop something. "Please, don't touch anything. We'll give everyone a tour when we've completely set up, but right now, please . . ."

Lindsay put the caliper down on the metal table. "We understand," she said, smiling.

Lewis folded his arms across his chest and started to speak. Lindsay threaded her arm through his and led him out of the tent.

"Peter's a little cocky. He's already gotten Adam and Powell angry enough to strangle him."

"And you as well, from the looks of it. How are the others? They cocky, too?"

"No. This guy Peter is really counting on getting a good sample of air, and he's a little on edge. You know how graduate students are. They can be very intense. It seems, even with the best of circumstances, the chances of getting uncontaminated air are not very great."

"So, I imagine the idea that there might be only one coffin instead of two was not a welcome one."

"No, it wasn't."

"Has Drew given you a hint as to what's up with her?"

"No. I didn't want to say this in front of the others, but the doubt about there being a second coffin came from her."

"What?" Lindsay was incredulous.

"She told them flat out that she didn't really know if there was a second one. The geologist and some of the others were mildly alarmed. I tried to explain about it being a cemetery, but . . . they aren't archaeologists, and antique flowers, berms, and the like aren't persuasive to them. Drew's not been particularly helpful." He glanced in her direction. "However, she seems to be getting better."

"You think she's the one who called Maxine?"

"What are you talking about?"

"Luke told me it was an anonymous call that got the protesters, such as they were, here."

"Sounds like she wants to stop the project, doesn't it?" said Lewis.

"It does. Why do you think she might want that? By the way, Luke's going to stay a couple of days, if that's all right with you."

"John send him to look out for you?"

"Yes. John's worried about me."

"Sure, he can stay. He can room with the guys." Lewis stopped and put his hands on her shoulders. "Lindsay, if *you* know anything about what's going on, tell me. I don't like surprises."

"I'm still fitting pieces together."

"Then you have pieces? You know I don't want to hand Keith a scandal."

"I'll be as discreet as I can."

"What does that mean? You think Drew really is involved with this Tidwell thing?"

"You tell me. Look at the way she's been acting."

Lindsay reminded him that Drew was an authority on historic documents and that her husband was a collector. She also told him about her interview with Trent and the lies he said Drew had told Claire.

"It could be something else entirely," defended Lewis. "She may have simply wanted to discredit you, in case you were here to check up on her. She could simply be worried about her career."

"Yes, that could be it. Accusations of murder and theft would definitely stand in the way of her getting a position at a top university. Would you hire her under those circumstances?"

"That's what I mean. She could just be caught in a bad situation. But I sense that you think she was involved in stealing the papers."

"That and other things."

"Do you think she was connected with what happened to you?"

"I don't know, but . . . let me continue to investigate. And quit worrying about Keith."

"Make sure you have an airtight case before you accuse anyone of anything."

"Trust me."

"I'm trusting you with a lot of things. Like there really being a second coffin. Do you know how I'm going to look if there's not one?" He looked at his watch. "It's about suppertime. I need to talk to Stagmeyer and Mrs. Laurens."

The presence of a second coffin had been the least of Lindsay's worries. But, standing amid the bustling enterprise, the expense of the operation dawned on her. *If that's all there is, one coffin will have to do. Why does Lewis put that much faith in me anyway?*

Lindsay went looking for Erin and found her with the other archaeology crew outside the perimeter. They were complaining about the newcomers. Luke was with them, enjoying himself, judging from the smile on his face.

"You'd think we're amateurs," said Adam. "Did you hear what that guy said to me?"

"He was trying to explain to me how to dig without damaging the coffins," complained Joel. "Me!"

"Hi, guys. Talking about Peter?" Lindsay asked.

"Is that his name?" said Adam.

"He just told me not to touch the bone measuring equipment."

"Who does he think he is?" Adam punched his hand with his fist.

"According to Lewis, he's a nervous graduate student who is really counting on a good sample of air."

"We have to have ID tags now, just to work on our own site," said Byron. "I'm not used to working like this. It's like we've been taken over by fascists."

"The equipment is very expensive," muttered Bill.

"It could be worse," said Kelsey. "Trent could be here."

"And Claire," said Joel.

"One thing about Claire, though," said Adam. "She'd tell that little pissant where to get off."

"Or steal one of their fancy trucks," said Dillon.

Everyone laughed, and Lindsay felt a pang of dread. Where was Claire? She hoped very much that she just ran away.

Suddenly, the sound of a bell ringing in the compound grabbed everyone's attention.

"What the heck is that?" asked Joel.

"I imagine, the dinner bell," said Lindsay. "Let's go eat. I think Mrs. Laurens got her entire family to help with supper tonight."

Supper was homemade beef stew in deep cooking pots, mountains of cornbread muffins, bowls of fruit salad, and sheets of blackberry cobbler and coconut cake for dessert. Almost everyone went back for seconds and thirds. Still, Mrs. Laurens was apologetic. Lewis hugged her and kissed her cheek.

"Wonderful job, Mrs. Laurens. Wonderful job. You can be proud."

He can be so charming, thought Lindsay. Amid all the clamor of dining with that many people, Lindsay did manage to get Erin apart from the others and ask her if they could go to her great aunt's house after dinner.

"Sure. Why?"

"I need to look around."

"Uncle Alfred and Mom will want to be there. I hope that's all right."

"No problem. I was going to suggest that. I need to know if anything else is missing."

"I'm not sure they would know. Aunt Sugar might."

After dinner, Lindsay, Erin, and Luke—who insisted on accompanying Lindsay—drove to Mary Susan Tidwell's house.

"Everybody is sure on edge at the site," said Erin. "I think it's exciting."

"As soon as they start the digging, they'll come around," Lindsay told her. "Right now, the crew's feeling displaced. I don't blame them, but we don't know how to hook up the equipment, much less use it. It's mostly the environmental scientists' show right now."

"Archaeology isn't like I expected."

"You expected it to be exotic and romantic?"

"I guess I did. It's better without Claire. Even Adam's nice to me now. We went into town together yesterday to get supplies."

Yesterday. Lindsay had forgotten. Adam's vehicle was the only one with the warm motor. "Where all did you go?"

"Hardware store. Adam stopped at the bank. He got several rolls of new pennies. He said Lewis asked him to get them for the site. I wanted to ask him what for, but I was afraid that was something I should know, and I didn't want him to make fun of me."

"They're to put in the postholes after the new fence is removed," said Lindsay.

"Why?"

"When archaeologists are leaving behind holes that in the future might be construed as features that belong to the site, they often mark them in some way. For example, some archaeologists put an empty drink can in the bottom of a survey pit so future archaeologists will know the hole wasn't contemporaneous with the site. We're doing block excavations of the structures at the farmstead. Someone later might want to look at the space between the structures. We'll drop a penny in the postholes before we cover them up, so if they're ever cross-sectioned, they'll know the postholes are an artifact of a past excavation process."

"I'd never have thought of anything like that."

"Lewis is a stickler for marking features left by the archaeologists. Early in his career he thought he had found a palisade around a village of a people not known to have them. He even published a paper on it with an elaborate hypothesis about the transitional nature of that culture. In the next issue of the journal, another archaeologist wrote a letter to the editor explaining that he had done testing at the site years earlier and had dug postholes to fence off a portion of it. It was his postholes Lewis had found. It was very embarrassing."

"I'm glad I'm not the only one who's made mistakes."

"No, we all make them. When you and Adam were out yesterday, did you stop by the diner?" Lindsay hoped her question sounded casual.

"No. We had sandwiches back at the house."

Erin's family was waiting when they arrived. Lindsay had expected the house to be more isolated, but there were three neighbors across the way. However, there was no one on either side of her house.

It was a beautiful house—a Queen Anne Free Classic style sitting on a cut stone foundation, with an asymmetrical complex of roofs and gables, turned columns on wooden piers, and a large porch. Lindsay pulled into the drive, and Erin directed her to the rear, which was completely isolated. Even if Mary Susan Tidwell had neighbors on each side, they would not have been able to see through the shrubs and trees around her enormous yard. She had several outbuildings—some metal, some wood—a barn, and a corral that was now empty, but Lindsay smiled remembering Broach Moore and the story about the goat. There was also a driveway into the back.

"Where does that lead?" she asked Erin.

"It eventually goes to the main road. Aunt Susan preferred it. She didn't like the neighbors to see her come and go."

They got out of their vehicle, and Lindsay introduced Luke to the Tidwells and to Bonnie Blake.

"Thanks for letting me come take a look," she said.

"We appreciate your doing something about this," said Alfred Tidwell.

Alfred unlocked the door and disabled the burglar alarm and they all followed him into an old-fashioned country kitchen. It was very tidy. Lindsay wondered if that was the way Miss Tidwell kept it, or if they had cleaned it after she died. Lindsay was hoping for some clue that would give Lewis the airtight case he was insisting on.

Erin touched the table by the window. "Aunt Susan and I used to have tea here. She'd tell me about the places she'd been looking for her finds, as she called them."

"See," said Bonnie Blake to Alfred and Sugar. "I told you she liked Erin."

"Now, don't start that, Bonnie," said Alfred. "We know she liked Erin. We all do."

"Aunt Susan was a health nut." Erin ignored her family's squabbling. "Any food she read about that'd help you live longer — orange juice, green tea, broccoli—she'd eat it." Erin continued. "She wanted to live as long as possible. I just don't believe it was her time."

"She lived here in the back of the house," said Sugar. They led Lindsay from the kitchen past the bathroom. Lindsay went into the bathroom and opened the medicine cabinet.

"We've taken out most of her perishables," said Sugar, "medicine and all that."

"Mostly, just drugs for hypertension," said Bonnie.

"Hy*po*tension," said Alfred. "She had hy*po*tension. If you paid as much attention to her as me and Sugar, you'd've known that."

"Her bedroom is in here," said Erin.

The bedroom was as tidy as the kitchen. The bed was made, the dresser tidy, even the mirror was sparkling clean.

"I cleaned up after the funeral," said Sugar. "We didn't know it might be a crime scene."

"The safe is over here," said Alfred, opening a door that looked like a closet but had a tall black safe behind it. He opened the safe to show Lindsay that it was indeed empty.

"You say she lived in the back here. What's in the rest of the house?"

"Her finds," said Bonnie. "The whole house is taken up with them."

"I'd like to know if anything is missing. Would any of you be able to look around and tell me?"

"Sugar might be able to," said Alfred.

They walked down a short hallway into the parlor. "She certainly had a lot of stuff," said Lindsay, on seeing the wall-to-wall shelves of possessions.

"Yes," agreed Alfred, "she did that."

"Junk, mostly," said Bonnie. "Just look at these old comic books. She even put them in separate bags. What was she thinking?"

"She was thinking about protecting them," said Alfred.

Lindsay glanced through the stack of comic books—old *Superman, Green Hornet, Batman, Archie.*

"Mrs. Blake," said Lindsay, "these are very old and probably very valuable."

"Those? You're not serious."

"She's right," said Luke. "There's a good possibility these might be worth several hundred dollars apiece."

"Comic books?"

"Yes, Mother. They're very collectible."

"I don't know what that means, 'very collectible.'" Mrs. Blake sounded as if her own unfamiliarity with things was a plot to annoy her.

"It means that these are things that a lot of people collect. Like these toys." Erin pointed to the shelves of toys, most still in their original boxes.

The room contained many obviously valuable things that could have been removed easily. Lindsay was beginning to doubt that anything had been stolen.

"She was open Fridays and Saturdays," said Sugar. "After her first heart attack, Alfred or I stayed with her while she was open, to help her keep an eye on the place. But she mainly advertised in collectors' magazines and sold things that way."

"She was thinking about starting up a shop on the computer," said Alfred. "She said some kind of virtuous store. I don't exactly know what that is."

"A *virtual* store, Uncle Alfred. It's a store on the Internet," said Erin. "I was trying to talk her into that. That way, she could just take photos of her stuff and post it. If anyone wanted it, they'd just click and pay by credit card number and Aunt Susan could mail it to them."

"Erin is so clever," said Mrs. Blake. "She really should be a lawyer."

"Internet stores aren't my idea, Mother. It's the way things are done now."

"Erin, don't hide your light under a bushel. You're a smart girl."

Erin's shoulders sagged. "I may be, Mother. But the Internet shop isn't evidence of it. That's just what people are doing nowadays." She walked off to another room before her mother could say anything.

Miss Tidwell didn't collect many pieces of furniture. There was the odd humidor, chair, trunks, and carousel animals. Most of her collections were things that would have fit in her station wagon. The rooms, both upstairs and down, contained things like old lanterns, glass insulators, bottles and jars, coffee grinders, radios, moldings from old houses, music boxes, snow globes, baskets, magazines, books, carvings, paintings, records, toys, porcelain bric-a-brac, and many things Lindsay had no idea what the purpose was. There could be a fortune contained in the rooms, or it could be mostly junk.

"Do you see anything missing?" asked Lindsay.

"Over here," said Sugar. She led them to one of the rooms. "This is where she had some of the stuff she collected from real old places that had gone out of business. Like old soda fountains. I like these glasses."

"Now don't you go claiming things, Sugar," said Bonnie.

"They're just glasses, Mother."

"You think something is missing?" asked Lindsay.

"She liked old newspaper and printing companies. She had stacks and rolls of old unused paper and some ledgers. They aren't here, and I know I saw them just a few days before she died."

"I told you about the ledgers," said Bonnie. "They can't be worth anything."

"Were they written in?" asked Lindsay.

"No," said Sugar. "It was mostly unused stuff."

"She must have thrown it away," said Bonnie. "Why would anyone steal worthless items like that?"

"Was there anything that looked like rubber stamps, with pictures or designs on them?"

Sugar nodded. "Now that you mention it, there was. I don't know about rubber, but she had a bunch of them that looked like they were made out of wood, and some looked copper. She kept them in boxes. They aren't here, either."

"You know something?" asked Bonnie.

"Maybe," said Lindsay.

"What? Tell us," she demanded.

"Now, just you wait, Bonnie," said Alfred. "Be patient. I think Miss Lindsay has found something. You believe us about the documents, don't you?"

"Yes," said Lindsay. "Yes, I do."

Chapter 30

LINDSAY WAS ALONE in her room that evening, the door locked, only one lamp on. She looked out the window over at the lit tent city. Luke, her protector sent by John, was downstairs with the guys. Drew and Eric had taken a motel room. She felt safe. She could think.

She opened a drink from her cooler and propped herself up on her bed with her back against the wall. What did it mean when valuable objects were left and worthless ones were missing? Were they worthless? They had to be. Surely there wasn't a collector's market for old unused ledgers. Who could she call and ask? Did she know any dealers in collectibles?

Alfred Tidwell had confidence in her, so did Lewis. *Why?* she wondered. She certainly must look more confident than she felt.

What did she know about the stolen documents? Not much at all. The words *Beau* and *Turkeyville.* The story about the man sick in a log cabin. And that she had something that would make Erin famous as an archaeologist. Not as a lawyer, but as an archaeologist. What kind of documents would make an archaeologist famous—at least in Miss Tidwell's eye? Famous to whom—the whole world, or only to fellow archaeologists?

Lindsay felt that sensation of something familiar lurking in her brain trying to make it to the surface. What? What was familiar? She was an archaeologist—what papers could she come across that would make her famous for finding them? It could be a multitude of things. History was full of lost documents. But they had a connection specifically to archaeology—not simply history. *You're an archaeologist, dammit, think.*

Lindsay took a long drink. Sleep on it. Maybe her brain would sort it out during the night.

◆ ◆ ◆

Lindsay wasn't awakened by any blinding revelations, but by banging on her door and Lewis calling her name.

"Yes?" She jumped out of bed. "Is the house on fire, Lewis?"

"No. Just making sure everyone is up. It's going to be a long day today."

Lindsay glanced at her clock—set to go off in two minutes. Lewis was probably already fashionably dressed and ready to go. She pulled on her jeans, sneakers, and a sweatshirt jacket over a T-shirt. She ran a brush through her hair before pulling it up into a ponytail, pulling the tail through the back of her West Construction cap. It was the first morning in a long time she felt completely rested.

Breakfast that morning was at the site. Inside the mess tent, Mrs. Laurens and her family set up a steam table with huge trays of bacon, eggs, ham, sausage, biscuits, french toast, pancakes, and orange juice. Lindsay couldn't imagine cooking this much food. After this site, Mrs. Laurens would either open a restaurant or never cook another meal in her life.

Lindsay made herself a ham and biscuit, got a glass of orange juice, and went to find someone she knew.

"Lindsay." Lewis was standing with Jarman, Posnansky, and Peter Willis near the tent exit. Breakfast in hand, she went over.

"Lindsay will be doing the analysis of the bones," Lewis told them.

"Have you ever done anything like this before? I'm going to need certain samples." Peter Willis shoved his glasses up on his nose.

Lindsay stared a moment and took a sip of her orange juice to keep from smiling. "No, but I have a chart that tells me how all the bones are connected. How hard can it be?"

Peter put his hands to his head and turned as if to walk off. "Oh, man I don't believe this." He looked at his watch. "Okay. It's early. It'll take a while to excavate the coffins. We won't be ready to open the coffins today anyway. We can get Crow or Lipsig here. . . ."

"Peter . . . Peter . . . ," said Jarman. "Calm down. She's putting you on."

"Dr. Chamberlain is a forensic anthropologist," said Lewis. "She's done this many times, she's conducted workshops for the FBI and the GBI on recovering skeletal remains; she knows what she's doing and will do a good job."

"Provided you let me handle the equipment," Lindsay said.

Peter's cheeks turned red. "Sorry, I didn't know." He looked at his feet for a moment before casting his gaze back up to Lindsay. "I need samples . . ."

"I've collected many a sample for pollen, entomology, soil. If there's a special kind of sample you need, you are welcome to tell me what you need, or collect it yourself."

"It's just that collecting accurate information is important to us."

"To us, too," replied Lindsay. She turned to Jarman. "Where do I go to get a special pass? One of the local physicians is observing the analysis of the remains."

"Sergeant Stagmeyer." Jarman looked out over the crowd eating breakfast. "There he is, second row, halfway down."

Lindsay spotted him. She also saw Drew and her husband coming into the tent and heading for the food. She excused herself to go tell Stagmeyer what she needed.

"No problem. I'll have one made up." He took the name down on a notepad. "I'll do it after I'm finished here. By the way, whoever's cooking the food's doing a great job."

"Mrs. Laurens and her family. I'll tell her."

Someone pushed past Lindsay and she leaned forward, holding a chair to keep from falling into the table.

"Sorry." A man in his late twenties was going between the tables filling a plastic garbage bag with paper plates, napkins, plastic utensils. "You guys enjoy your breakfast?" His dark eyes sparkled as he looked at Lindsay.

"Yes, Sergeant Stagmeyer was just complimenting the food," said Lindsay.

Lindsay thanked Stagmeyer and left to find Luke. He wasn't far, just outside the tent discussing baseball with Adam. She was surprised at how much relief she felt getting out of the crowded tent into the open. She hadn't really realized she was feeling so confined.

"Luke," she said. "Sleep well, I hope?"

"Pretty good. Food's not bad, either. Nice job you have here if you didn't have to get up before the crack of dawn." Adam caught sight of Joel and trotted off to meet him. "You doing okay? You look a little winded."

"I'm fine. Luke, you see how many people are here. I'm sure you must have other things you'd rather be doing?"

"Trying to run me off?"

"No. Just feeling guilty."

"Don't. John's been working my butt off. This is like vacation. Adam tells me you're digging up the bodies today."

"That's the plan."

Luke laughed as he looked around at the people, tents, the generators, the lights. You guys sure make a big deal out of it."

"Thanks for being here, Luke." Lindsay pointed out Drew and Eric getting up from breakfast. "I suspect those two are involved in some way. I don't have any concrete proof whatsoever."

Luke scrutinized them through the door of the tent. "Want me to keep an eye on them?"

"Stealthily."

"You got it."

It occurred to Lindsay as she watched Drew and Eric that perhaps she didn't need to find an expert in collectibles to talk to, but an expert in crime. After all, it was the theft of the items that she was curious about. As soon as it reached a decent hour, Lindsay knew who to call.

"We are going to start the excavation," said Lewis, coming up behind Lindsay. "Want to watch?"

"A little while. It's likely to get crowded in there, and I'm not really needed. You got Peter calmed down yet?"

"I don't think that's going to happen. He's been hoping for something like this to come along, and now he's depending on it for his dissertation." They started walking toward the tents covering Features 2 and 3 along with a crowd of other people. "Tell me, Luke, what kind of project is John working on?"

"He's building an aquarium in South Carolina—one of those where you watch the fish through glass. You'll have to come down for the opening. Lindsay, I'm going to hang around out here."

"Sure, Luke." She took his hand and squeezed it, then continued on toward the tent. On the way, she saw Eric Van Horne in deep conversation with the guy bussing the tables. There was something about him that Lindsay couldn't put her finger on. She was staring at him when he looked up and caught her eye for a moment and smiled.

An argument was already under way when they arrived at the first tent, the one over Feature 3, the cemetery, assigned to Joel, Sharon, and Powell.

"You're not digging with that shovel," said Joel. "In fact, you're not digging at all. You're the one that's been worried about punching a hole in the coffins, and you bring along a pointed shovel."

"You can't dig with those flat things," insisted Peter, holding his shovel with the tip in the ground.

"We are not digging a hole. We are excavating," said Joel. "And we're taking it down a layer at a time. We have to get a profile once we've uncovered half."

Lewis was about to say something when the geologist stepped in. "Joel's right, Peter. Let them work."

Powell leaned over to Sharon and whispered, "I think something happened to Claire, and she came back as this guy. Did we do some kind of shit in a past life, or what?"

Lindsay tried to ignore the dissension and study the contents of the tent—alien machines, cylinders, and all manner of containers. Several of the other graduate students were busy setting up, testing, and calibrating. As she looked at the tubing associated with the machines, Lindsay realized that these were the mechanisms they would use to capture the antique air. She wanted to go over and ask them about the process, but they looked very focused. She spotted a chart posted on the side of the tent, just inside the entrance, and went over to have a look. It was a diagram of the extraction system. It was complex, but essentially a sharp stylus, similar to a drill bit, imbedded in a boxlike structure with flexible tubing leading from it. Following its path was like working one of those maze puzzles. Lindsay put a finger on the start—where the stylus would fit into the coffin and traced the diagram to a container cooled in a tank of liquid nitrogen. Apparently, once the air was sampled, they were going to pump cold argon gas into the coffins—to keep the remains stabilized, Lindsay guessed.

"Impressive, huh," said Marina over her shoulder.

"I'll say."

"I still don't understand how they are going to penetrate the coffins and not let any outside air in."

"I think it has something to do with the design of this stylus and the box attached to it," said Lindsay.

"I guess."

Lindsay heard Lewis suggest to Peter that he go to the Feature 2 tent. "It will be going faster. Half has already been excavated once, and a profile already done."

Peter agreed, and Lindsay, Marina, and Drew walked with Lewis to the Feature 2 tent where Adam, Byron, and Dillon were already under way with the excavation.

"Won't the decaying body have contaminated the air?" Lindsay asked.

"There'll be a lot of gases we'll have to sift through for sure. But, we know what to expect from the decaying process." He grinned as though looking forward to the tedious procedure. "If this works, it will be one of the oldest air samples to date. Do you know what a find that is?"

It didn't take long to reach the part of the coffin that had already been excavated. Peter's eyes glowed with excitement.

"Now be careful."

"They will," said Drew, smiling at him. "Don't worry. We are going to take it back a little farther. You said you don't want it completely uncovered?"

"That's right. The dirt covering will help keep it stable," said Peter.

Lewis and Drew determined that sifting the fill could wait until after the project was completed. The dirt went on a pile beside the pit. It had just grown light outside when they got the coffin about halfway uncovered. They took whiskbrooms and swept the surface, examining it for writing or any kind of symbols.

"Look at this," said Adam.

Peter jumped down into the hole with him. "Damn. We're not going to get any air from this one."

Lindsay squatted by the edge of the pit. Lewis and Jarman were on either side of her. Jarman shook his head.

"Same thing on the other side," said Drew.

Peter looked at Lindsay. "I hope you're right and there is another one, or we've all come down here for nothing."

Lindsay barely heard his complaints. She was trying to figure out what the holes punched into the side of the coffin meant.

Chapter 31

THE SIX OF them, Jarman, Posnansky, Peter, Lewis, Drew, and Lindsay stood outside the tent discussing how to proceed.

Posnansky puffed on a brown cigarette. "Is there any need to x-ray the damn thing? Why don't we check it for weaknesses, haul it out of the ground, and concentrate on the second coffin."

"If there is a second coffin," Peter grumbled.

"We'll know soon enough," said Jarman. "Do you see any reason not to take Poss's suggestion?"

"Lindsay?" Lewis had that look she'd seen him use with other people. The one that asked the question: Are you about to make me look bad—this was a hell of a lot of trouble and expense.

"I believe there's another coffin, based on the archaeological and remote-sensing data I've seen. Like Alex Jarman said, we'll know soon enough. As for this one, I personally don't see any reason to zap it inside the lead coffin, though I'd like to take traditional x-rays when it's out. Can you guys do simple stuff?"

Posnansky grinned. "Yeah. We can do the simple stuff."

"Good," said Jarman, nodding. "Let's complete the excavation, see if this thing has any cracks, and get it out of the ground."

Juliana Skyler, expert in nondestructive evaluation, sat cross-legged in the pit with the coffin. "What we are going to do here," she told the archaeology crew with elaborate gestures, "is to see if the coffin is in good enough condition to be lifted out of the ground."

"If it isn't?" asked Drew.

"We'll have to open and analyze it here. Simply put, what we're going to do now is send different kinds of energy through the coffin. If the coffin is in absolutely perfect condition, whether it's heat, or sound, or electromagnetic currents being introduced, they will go through relatively undistorted." She moved her hands smoothly along the top of the coffin. "However, if there are flaws or weaknesses, the various currents and eddies will be distorted." She moved her hands across again, occasionally wiggling her fingers. "The degree or pattern of distortion tells us how serious the weakness is." Skyler spoke as if she had explained it a hundred times.

Lindsay was watching Skyler and her assistants monitor their equipment, when she suddenly remembered a call she needed to make. Lindsay slipped out of the tent and headed for the house.

On the way she met Phil McBride at the entrance. "I hope you haven't been waiting long."

"Just got here. I know you said it would probably be tomorrow, but I got a colleague to cover for me all this week and I thought I'd pop down early."

Lindsay took him to get his pass, which Stagmeyer had ready as promised, and Phil clipped it on his collar. "I didn't realize you had such security."

"Besides the very expensive equipment, they have some cobalt for the gamma x-rays of the lead coffins. It comes with its own set of guards, inspectors, and sacks of sandbags."

"I'm impressed."

"Me, too. And way out of my depth. They're good at explaining everything as they go along, but it is far more complex than I realized. The first coffin was compromised, so they are checking to see if they can lift it out of the ground. Come with me and I'll introduce you to Francisco Lewis."

Lindsay took him to the tent and motioned Lewis over to introduce him to Phil McBride. "Phil and Elaine own the cabin from the site."

"We appreciate your sharing your photographs," said Lewis, shaking his hand.

"I've got to go make a call. I'll be back shortly." Lindsay was off before Lewis could ask her any questions she didn't want to answer.

This time she decided to use her car phone. Inside the relative privacy of her SUV she dialed the FBI.

"Parker, hi. This is Lindsay Chamberlain."

"Lindsay, how are you? I heard about what happened. You doing okay?"

"Pretty good."

"I don't have to tell you how lucky you are."

"I try not to think about it too much . . . actually that's not true. I'm working on something that may or may not be related, and I need to ask you a question."

"Shoot."

"If you heard of a theft where the thief took some valuable historical documents and along with them took some items that didn't seem to have any value, is there anything you could make of it?" Lindsay explained about the missing paper, ledgers, and printer's blocks. When she finished, she felt a little silly. What could he possibly make of what she had told him? So she was surprised when he gave her an immediate answer.

"Forgery. Particularly, document forgery."

"Forgery? How?"

"One of the problems with forging documents is making the paper look old. Some do it by soaking it in strong tea to discolor it and by putting coffee grounds on it for the foxing—the speckles often found on old documents—then drying it in the oven. Some forgers make their own paper. But the best method is to use genuinely old paper. Same goes for using the engraver's blocks for graphics. If you have the real thing, you don't have to draw it and introduce mistakes."

"But the ledgers have lines on them. What would—?"

"Money."

"Money? I thought . . . I don't understand."

He laughed. "Can't spend it, but you can sell it to collectors. At one time, states and even companies printed their own money. Companies printed it to be exchanged for only their own goods.

Anyway, when paper was scarce . . . as it was from time to time, they used what paper was available . . . recycled old ledger paper was common. Very collectible stuff."

"How hard is it to forge documents and the like?"

"Depends on how talented you are."

"Is it hard to detect?"

"Sometimes very hard. Forgers can be very clever. There's hardly anything one person can make that another can't make just like it."

"But old things . . . aren't there tests?"

"Yes, but if you use old paper, chemically age the ink, have a good hand . . . One popular thing to do is to use a genuinely old document . . . like a letter written and signed by a president. Then add something, like a postscript about a notorious event in his life. You have a more valuable document, and most of it's authentic."

"Is there a type of person who is a forger?"

"Not one particular type, but a collection of possible traits. For example, some are artistic, but some are just good with a computer. Often they are very meticulous and detail oriented—have to be, to do what they do. Rarely women, but not completely unheard of. Some are motivated by the desire to prove they can do it. Some are people who feel they have been wronged in some way and want to show their ability. Or they are people with low self-esteem and success reinforces their self-image. Some like to match their ability against an expert—risk takers. Some are just greedy."

"This is something I never thought of."

"I can fax you some information, if you like. Got a number?"

Lindsay thought a second. "The library. I don't have the number here, but if you call Afton Phillips at the Marella Oliver Public Library in Kelley's Chase, Tennessee, and ask her for the fax number, I'm sure she'll give it to you. Do you mind?"

"Not at all. Glad to help. You think this has something to do with what happened to you?"

"I don't know. It's possible, but I really don't know."

"Be careful. People don't like getting caught."

"Right now I've got the army reserve camped out in my front yard." Lindsay told him about the site and what they were doing.

"Damn, that sounds interesting as hell. Let me know how it turns out. You know, once upon a time, I wanted to be an archaeologist."

"It's not too late."

"Maybe that will be my retirement vocation. Take care, Lindsay. I'll send this information right away."

"Thanks."

Lindsay got out of her Explorer and ran into the man who was earlier bussing tables in the mess. "Hi. My name's Mike Gentry. I thought maybe you and me could go out when I get off. I saw you making eyes at me." He winked at her.

"You saw me being polite, Mr. Gentry." Lindsay started around him, but he blocked her path.

"Call me Mike."

"They're expecting me to look at some bones right now. Don't block my path. I'm not going out with you."

He stepped aside. "Sorry, didn't mean to offend. I saw you looking at me and thought you were interested. I like girls with long legs and long hair."

Lindsay brushed past him. Her heart was pounding. She didn't know why she felt so afraid—there were plenty of people around. The crew and science personnel were eating lunch at different times, so Mrs. Laurens had had her people bringing trays of food to the mess tent since noon. But she didn't like that man. She didn't like the way he wore his hair, his gold jewelry, his voice. Especially, she didn't like presumptuous men. She would have taken flight if she could; she would have run if it wouldn't have made her look afraid—and vulnerable.

A shadow startled her as she walked past a copse of trees. "Hey," a voice said. "You okay?" It was Luke leaning against a tree out of view of the house.

"Luke." She put a hand to her chest. "I'm glad you're here."

"Just looking out for you. I saw you come up here and thought I'd follow. That guy's had a couple of intense conversations with Eric Van Horne. I've been watching like you said."

"I'm glad to know that you were there. He . . . well he frightened me."

"Have you ever seen him before?"

"No. Just here. He's just a type I don't like."

"I'll find out who he is. The people around here seem to like to talk to Indians. Maybe I'll become a private investigator." Luke grinned, showing even, sparkling white teeth.

She leaned over and kissed his cheek. "Have you talked to John?"

"Last night."

"I suppose you told him about what's been happening."

"He's not real happy. He wants me to stay here a while. I agree."

Lindsay felt very relieved, but a little disappointed that John didn't drop everything and come down himself. But she wouldn't have liked that, either. Somehow, she had to figure out how to get her old independent feeling back. Every time she seemed to be making progress, something set her back. *Unfinished business*, a voice in her head said. "Where did that come from?"

"What?" asked Luke.

"Nothing." As they crossed the bridge, they heard whooping and clapping coming from the tent over Feature 3, the cemetery. "Must have found something," Lindsay told Luke and increased her pace around to the gate.

"I'm going to ask about that guy," Luke told her as they parted ways.

"You be careful," she warned.

Most of the archaeology crew was crowded around the entrance. Lindsay squeezed through. "Find something?" she asked.

"Yeah. Second coffin." Kelsey was fanning her T-shirt in and out. "Hot in the tent. I think I'll go talk to some of the army guys."

Lindsay grinned and went into the tent. Lewis, Phil McBride, Peter Willis, and Alex Jarman were staring down into the pit at a lead coffin sticking out about a foot from the profile. Joel and Sharon were in the ditch next to it, with Powell sitting on the edge drinking a bottle of water.

"I didn't think we'd ever get to it," said Peter. Lindsay imagined that Joel and Sharon's painstaking excavation technique drove Peter nuts.

Lewis turned toward Lindsay, giving her one of his brightest smiles. "Looks like you were right."

"Lewis, you've known me what—about two years now? Have you ever known me to be wrong about anything?"

He laughed out loud, from relief as much as anything else, she guessed.

"Let's just hope punching holes in the sides isn't some kind of burial ritual here," said Peter.

"What happens now?" she asked.

"We need to uncover more before we try to get an air sample." Peter looked at his watch. "I think I'll wait until tomorrow for that. Everyone's kind of tired. Joel, let's go ahead and finish excavating this half and get a profile and soil samples, and we'll quit."

Lewis put an arm around Lindsay's shoulders, giving her a slight hug. "You had any lunch?"

"It's about suppertime," Lindsay told him.

"So it is. Did you eat?"

"No. Not since breakfast. How's the other coffin doing—passing the tests?"

"Don't know yet. Let's go take a look."

"Francisco told me you think our 'Cherry' is in this next coffin," said McBride. "I phoned Elaine." He patted his jacket. "She's very excited."

"She's welcome to come over," said Lewis.

"Right now, she's waiting for a call about Hope Foute's diaries. I have a feeling the owners are talking to a lawyer or an appraiser. Probably decided they can send their kids to college on them."

"How much would they be worth?" asked Lindsay.

Phil shook his head. "I have no idea. I have a feeling they are going to turn out to be Elaine's birthday and Christmas presents for the next ten years."

Just as they were about to go into the tent, Lindsay saw a car drive up and stop on the grass near the fence. It looked like Afton behind the wheel.

"Be right back." Lindsay trotted to the gate and over to meet her just as she was getting out of the car. She had a manila envelope in her hand.

Afton stared wide-eyed at the compound and people milling about. "My goodness. You putting on a circus?" She took off her sunglasses and put them on her head. "Double-O Afton here, librarian with a license to kill. Boy, don't I wish that were true." She handed Lindsay the envelope. "A man called saying he was with the FBI and would I mind receiving a fax for you. Who could turn down that, right? Couldn't help but glance and see what they were about. Please, when you finish whatever you're doing, fill me in. I know this is going to be a whole chapter in my memoirs about my life as a small-town librarian."

"Thanks, Afton. I appreciate this. You didn't have to drive out here. I would have come to pick them up."

"And miss all this?" Her gesture took in the entire compound. "It takes this many people to dig up two coffins?"

"Apparently. It's all pretty amazing. I'm sure Lewis will want to write it up for a newspaper article."

"I heard you had a couple of protesters," said Afton.

"A couple's about all. They didn't protest too much, fortunately. Do you know the reporter?"

"Yeah. He wants to date my younger sister. He told her some woman here attacked him. He thinks you guys are weird, so don't expect good press from him."

"Some of us are weird. Just as long as he gets the archaeology right . . ."

Afton glanced at her watch and sighed. "Gotta go. Good luck with whatever."

"Thanks again." Lindsay opened the envelope and peeked in. He'd sent about a half-inch stack of papers. *Looks like I'll be up late reading tonight.*

Lindsay tucked the envelope under her arm and made her way back to the tent at Feature 2. The nondestructive evaluation team was still testing, and since Lewis had mentioned food, her stomach started growling.

She found baskets of fruit in the mess tent. Taking an apple and a banana, she sat at one of the tables and propped her feet up on a chair. The only person in the tent was someone refilling the iced tea machine. Despite the fact that all the people around made her feel more safe, the solitude was relaxing. Lindsay looked out at Big Branch Creek longingly, wishing she could still hear the sound of the river over the hum of the generators. How nice it would be to just float down the river on a raft like Huckleberry Finn and Jim, escaping the bad guys.

"Taking a rest?" Drew sat down opposite her.

Lindsay tried not to show her annoyance at being disturbed—it might, after all, be a good opportunity. "Hey, Drew. No. I haven't done a thing all day to have to rest from. Just being lazy. I'm sure you were relieved there was a second coffin." Lindsay peeled her banana and bit into it.

"It was touchy for a while. That coffin was deeper than the other one, and Joel and Sharon are so slow. I'd have split them up."

"Why didn't you?" The question took Drew aback—and embarrassed her. She hadn't realized she was admitting that she had simply bowed to Lewis's judgment. A manipulator being manipulated. Lewis had that effect on people. Lindsay saved her from answering by asking her another question. "Have you heard from Claire?" Another question she didn't like. *That will teach you to interrupt my solitude.*

Drew hesitated. "Claire? No, no I haven't. Like I said—she's done this before. She's likely to show up tomorrow, in tears, asking to be forgiven. Tell me, how's your investigating coming?"

Lindsay bit into her apple with a crunch. "Dead end."

"What?" Drew looked startled.

"It's at a dead end. If the Tidwells don't know what their aunt had, they can't prove anything was stolen. Both the doctor and the sheriff say Miss Tidwell died of natural causes. That's the end of it. I've made a good-faith effort. I'm sure you'll be hearing from their lawyer that they'll be dropping the charges."

Drew brightened. "You think so?"

"Yes. I haven't told them yet, but I'm going to strongly suggest they do. No telling what their lawyer is milking them for."

"I really appreciate that, Lindsay."

"Nothing else to do. You could do the McBrides a favor."

"What's that?"

"You know that Elaine has a line on Hope Foute's other diaries." Drew nodded. "Phil said that he felt they saw dollar signs when Elaine contacted them, and I think Elaine is going to be too tempted not to buy them. Could you go talk to Phil and give him an idea of how much they are worth?"

"Sure. They will be worth more together than separated. It's in the McBrides' favor that the historical society has one of them. I'll talk to him and give him a range. I need to make up to him and Elaine anyway. Claire treated them pretty awful."

"Hi. I'm Luke Youngdeer, Lindsay's boyfriend's cousin." Luke sat down by Drew and held out his hand.

"Hi. I thought you were here protesting."

"No. I don't care if you dig your own people up. I'm visiting Lindsay. Being John's mother's brother's son, I have special responsibilities to his girlfriend."

"Oh, really." Drew turned in her seat toward him. Lindsay took another bite of her apple to keep from laughing. "I wasn't aware of that aspect of kinship."

Luke bobbed his head up and down. "It's kind of like a godfather."

"I'd like to hear about it sometime," said Drew.

Lindsay stood up. "I'm going to see if the coffin passed."

"I'll go with you." Luke stood, and the three of them walked to Feature 2. Lindsay hung back with Luke, allowing Drew to walk ahead.

"You anthropology types are really funny," Luke told Lindsay when Drew went into the tent and out of sight.

Lindsay laughed. "You aren't the first to think that."

"That guy who spooked you," said Luke. "He's not a relative of the Laurenses. He came to them. Said he heard they were hiring. They needed a few people to wash dishes and bus tables, so Mr. Laurens took him."

"I don't like that," said Lindsay. "Did they know anything about him?"

"Yes and no. He's worked at the diner up the street washing dishes for about a month. The diner's owner gave him a good recommendation. He's not very talkative."

"Luke, don't take any risks. I mean it."

"You're one to talk."

"I've not been taking any risks. They've been coming to me. So he's worked at the diner. How about before that?"

"Baltimore, doing construction work."

"Do you think that's true? Does he know anything about construction work?"

"I don't know. He wouldn't talk much. However, it's not unusual to find guys who've worked in construction who don't know anything about it."

"Thank you, Luke. And don't take any chances."

"We got all these army guys around. Don't worry."

Suddenly loud mechanical sounds erupted from the tent. "Sounds like a hydraulic jack," said Luke.

"I'd better go in," said Lindsay.

Another team, from the military, was driving a steel plate under the coffin as Lindsay entered. When it was fully in place, they carefully slid it onto a wooden and metal frame—like a cradle attached to a wench. Each had heavy metal framing inside. Lindsay could see now it was to support the heavy coffins. When the coffin was in the cradle, they secured it and slowly began lifting it out.

Lewis was there. So were Drew, McBride, the crew who dug up the coffin, and several members of the science team. The archaeologists hung back out of the way and craned to see as it cleared the hole. It was mesmerizing, watching the coffin hanging like a pendulum, realizing it weighed almost 1,300 pounds.

"I wonder how the settlers got it in?" whispered Kelsey.

They slowly moved it across to the awaiting trolley. It was like watching the tiny sojourner rover inch along on Mars. Lindsay let out a breath when it was finally settled securely on its transport.

"Well, who is that?" asked Juliana Skyler, standing on the edge of the pit, looking in. "The grave digger?"

Chapter 32

LINDSAY THREADED HER way through the onlookers to the edge of the pit and followed Skyler's gaze. There in the bottom, crushed, displaced, and the color of the surrounding brownish red dirt, looking like a macabre bas-relief Picasso, were the remains of a skeleton.

Were it not for the curve of a rib and the relative length of the femur, it would have been hard to tell they were the bones of a human, having been flattened for two centuries by the heavy weight of the coffin. Lindsay squatted for a closer view.

"Is it human?" asked one of the men who had just hoisted the coffin onto the trolley.

"Yes, it's human," answered Lindsay.

Lewis had come up and squatted beside her. "Who is it?" he asked.

Lindsay turned her attention to him for several seconds, a smile playing around her lips. "I don't know."

"Could it have fallen out the bottom of the coffin?" asked Kelsey.

"I think I would have detected that kind of breach in integrity," commented Juliana Skyler.

The inescapable truth was that the coffin had been put in place on top of other remains.

"Is it contemporaneous with the coffin?" asked Lewis.

"Lewis. I'm squatting here looking at the bones for the first time, just like you are. How am I supposed to know?"

Lindsay stood and dusted her hands. She glanced at the pit wall and the black charcoal layer only partially uncovered.

"Probably is contemporaneous," she said. "We're still in the trash pit."

"How about Joel and I start excavating it after dinner?" said Adam.

"Why don't Kelsey, Erin, and Bill do it tomorrow morning?" said Lewis.

Over dinner, Lindsay outlined how she wanted to proceed with the new remains. "There's been significant disturbance and damage from the metal sheet sliding under the coffin. Take pictures first. Do a grid and a relatively quick excavation. Put the skeletal pieces and any artifacts in a separate box for each grid. When it's up, go on down until you reach pit bottom. Sift everything."

"Is there any chance you can make anything of the bones?" asked Kelsey, pleased to have been put in charge of this particular excavation. "They looked pretty smashed to me."

"It depends. If there are some diagnostic pieces in good enough condition—maybe."

"But, you could tell it was human from a distance," insisted Erin.

"That was because of the rib and femur that are visible. Human ribs have a tighter arc than animals'. Humans also have very long femurs."

"And you don't know if it has anything to do with the coffins?" asked Jarman. "I've heard of one burial intruding on another one. Might it be, say, an Indian burial?" The entire archaeology crew who sat in proximity to Jarman glared at him. "What?" he asked, puzzled at the stares.

"That opens up a new can of worms they don't want to deal with," said Luke.

"I've seen numerous intrusive burials," Lindsay said. "Usually only a part of one intrudes on another. I haven't run across one burial exactly on top of another. That's interesting in itself. Besides, Indians didn't bury their dead in white settlers' trash pits. You got any glue among your supplies?"

"Glue?" asked Jarman. "You're going to glue it back together? All those pieces?"

"Not the whole thing, but if I find enough pieces of skull, I'll try to put some of the larger pieces together."

Agent Parker McGillis had faxed an entire book on document forgery. Fortunately, it wasn't a long book. Lindsay settled into bed, propped up with a pillow at her back against the wall, and her door safely locked. The book echoed what Parker had told her about the psychology of forgers. Everyone here could be made to fit some of the characteristics—including herself. Lindsay had noticed years ago that a great many archaeologists can draw, many quite well. How many artistic people were there at the site? Erin, Marina, Joel, Bill—to name the ones she knew.

How many of them felt a need to prove something? Claire—perhaps she ran away for fear of being caught. But, if Claire had any artistic tendencies, she hadn't shown them. Perhaps she knew someone who did. Claire could use a computer. Well enough to create documents? Surely, one couldn't forge a historic document with a computer. How was it done?

A sharp knock on the door startled her. "Lindsay, telephone."

Lindsay tucked the fax pages under her pillow and opened her door. It was Dillon, holding a beer, still moving to the tune on the radio playing downstairs.

"Cool about the extra skeleton, huh?" he said as she followed him down the stairs.

"A surprise, for sure."

"Think you can do anything with shattered bones?"

"Maybe. We'll see. I like your guitar playing. I hope you do more of it."

"Thanks. I will, now that Claire's gone."

"Do you have any idea where she might be?"

"Nope. Don't care."

Dillon took the radio out on the porch so Lindsay could hear the phone. Several of the guys from the science team were on the porch with Dillon, Adam, and Byron, drinking beer and exchanging stories.

Lindsay sat down on the couch with the telephone. "Hello?"

"Hi, babe. It's John. You doing okay?"

"John. It's good to hear your voice. Yes, I'm fine. Thanks for Luke."

"He's enjoying it. I'm sorry I can't be there myself."

"I'm pretty well covered."

"I know. I talked to Lewis last night. We're all looking out for you. Found out what's in those coffins yet?"

"Not yet. We're opening one tomorrow. We did find someone extra under one of the coffins."

"He must have been mashed flat."

"The crew's calling him H.D. for Humpty Dumpty."

"I miss you. How about when I'm finished here, I come visit you at your place? Just you, me, and the horse?"

"I'd like that. How's the aquarium coming?"

They shared tales of their work for almost an hour. It was good to listen to him talk. It was normal. She wanted to grab every normal part of her life and keep it surrounding her until her existence was comfortable again. She hated saying good-bye, hated hearing the click of the phone. She sighed and started for her room. As she was about to go up the stairs, she heard one of the guys talking through the open door. The voice sounded like Peter Willis.

"What's the story on the bone broad?"

She stopped still and strained to hear over the radio.

"Who?" asked Adam.

"The tall, good-looking bossy woman with the long hair."

"You talking about Lindsay?" asked Adam. "What about her?"

"Your guy Lewis says she has to be protected. The army's not only watching out for the cobalt 60, but for her, too. Seems that somebody's stalking her."

"Stalking Lindsay? You serious? First we've heard."

A loud piece of music came on the radio, drowning out their conversation, and Lindsay continued up the stairs, smiling to herself. Good old Lewis. Maybe if it got out that she was being watched, whoever it was would give up.

It was well into the early hours of the morning before Lindsay went to sleep. But she had learned a bit about forgery. She learned that many forgeries have been detected because the forger didn't know that different eras had different styles of handwriting. One forgery of a Daniel Boone letter was discovered by looking only at a photocopy of the letter because the writing was a modern style.

You have to be educated to be a successful forger.

She remembered Mrs. Laurens's story about Miss Tidwell bringing in an old letter to show her class, and Mrs. Laurens doubting its authenticity because it was in better condition than much younger documents she'd seen. Lindsay would have to tell her that paper in the 1700s was made from rag and could last a long time, whereas later nineteenth-century paper was made from wood, a process that produced a more fragile paper.

The most interesting part of the book was about detecting forgeries. Intriguing, perhaps because it was more like a model or theoretical construct, concepts she understood. Charles Hamilton, the preeminent detector of forged documents, said a document under examination must pass four tests.

First, a document must have provenance—as in artifacts, you must know where it came from. The document must possess both internal and external evidence of its authenticity—kind of like internal and external validity, thought Lindsay—no historical anachronisms or inaccuracies, or any inconsistencies in paper and ink. Finally, the paleographic evidence must be correct, as was not the case with the more modern writing in the forged Daniel Boone document. The handwriting must match the supposed author of the document.

A document must pass all of these tests. Both the forger and the forgery detector have a hard task. Lindsay could imagine the satisfaction a forger gets from trying to produce such a document. She could also identify with the document detective.

But then, what did any of this have to do with what happened to Mary Susan Tidwell? The only reason to be suspicious that there was a connection was because of the missing printing paper from her house. Slim reasoning. Miss Tidwell herself could have gotten rid of it.

No, the missing paper wasn't the only reason. There was the stamp impression Lindsay had found in the dirt floor of the farmhouse basement. Too much of a coincidence. Someone could have purchased things from Miss Tidwell and stored them in the basement. No. Why put them in the basement? It was musty and had an earthen floor. If the purchase was legitimate, no reason not to just store the items in the living room or the storeroom.

Lindsay finally drifted off to sleep. She dreamed about Daniel Boone carving messages into wooden floors and was awakened by Lewis banging on her door two minutes before her clock was to go off. Her first thought was to sneak into his room and set his clock back two minutes.

Lindsay and Phil McBride were outfitted with filter masks hanging around their necks, surgeon's gloves, and white coats. They stood back while the lid was being pried and hoisted off the trash pit coffin, which still sat on the trolley in the exam trailer. As the men worked on opening the coffin, Lindsay stared at the holes punched in its side. They reminded her of catching lightning bugs in a jar and punching holes in the lid. The thought made her head swim. She shoved it out of her mind, or tried to.

"Why do you think the holes are there?" asked McBride.

Lindsay shrugged.

"Maybe it's empty," answered Peter Willis.

He was there to give Lindsay instructions about sampling. He already had given her a long explanation of why he wanted samples from the trash pit coffin, even though they would be getting no antique air from it. For comparison, his long narration had finally come down to. Lindsay understood perfectly and wanted to give him a lecture on what archaeologists do. They don't simply have Ph.D.s in digging holes. Bone broad indeed. She ought to call him airhead.

The entire crew was there, with the exception of Erin, Kelsey, and Bill, who were excavating the unexpected remains in the trash pit—and with the exception of Drew. Lindsay assumed she was in the other tent watching the tests they were putting the other coffin through. Even Luke was there. So were several members of the science team who weren't busy with the other coffin. It was a crowd, but the trailer was big.

With a screech, crack, and a pop, the lid came loose and was lifted off with the hoist and gantry. When the heavy lid cleared the coffin, Lindsay got her first look inside a vessel that hadn't been opened in more than two hundred years. There was a skeleton, small and fragile, in the bottom of its huge lead sarcophagus. It lay faceup. The skull had rolled forward so that it looked as though the chin were resting on the shoulder in sweet repose. The rib cage was collapsed, the sternal ends of the ribs pointing downward. The bones were a mottled palette of color—cream, brown, dark red-orange. There was no sign of a wooden inner coffin that Lindsay would have expected. Odd.

Around the edges, where the holes had been punched, surrounding soil had entered over the years, carried in by water and insect action. Peter Willis, vial in hand, reached in to take a soil sample. Lindsay clasped his wrist in a firm grip. He looked at her, surprised.

At first, Peter had been an enigma. She had observed that most of the time he was a very careful and competent researcher. Then, out of the blue, he would seem to forget methodology altogether. Suddenly, seeing him reach inside the coffin, sample containers ready, Lindsay realized that he simply didn't care about her research. He was interested only in his own agenda.

"No," Lindsay said. "It stays untouched until it has been photographed and I have given every inch a visual examination. Mr. Willis, I know very well how to take samples. I understand about contamination, integrity, provenance, chain of custody, and a host of other considerations. Why don't you go take care of the cemetery coffin? Call me when you get ready to extract the air. I'd like to see it."

"Sure. Just trying to help."

She let go of his wrist, and he pulled his hand away.

"I'll be over in the other tent, if you need me."

Lindsay asked the photographer in charge of the fancy photography equipment, a small man with hunched shoulders, to take a series of photographs the entire length of the remains in the coffin. The images would be exposed on large plates, and the resulting photographs would be clear, detailed with a depth of field that would make them look almost three-dimensional. Good for teaching, she thought. The camera moved along the track above the coffin, making the remains look as if they were undergoing some kind of medical scan. As she watched the technician control the camera, she thought that his nasal spine must be very long to support such a large nose.

"Elaine has gone to visit her sister," Phil said. "She lives only about seventy miles from the woman who owns the diaries. She and her sister are driving down to meet her tomorrow."

"Did Drew speak with you about the value of the diaries?" Lindsay asked.

McBride shook his head. "Was she going to?"

"I asked her to. That's one of her specialties—appraising historical documents."

"Really? Did she mention what they might be worth?"

"No. Maybe you can talk to her about it over lunch."

"All done," said the photographer, pushing the tracking arm out of the way. "I can have pictures for you this afternoon. Also, if you like, I can stick around, in case you want some close-ups."

"That would be great." Lindsay slipped her mask on and bent over the remains, scrutinizing the bones.

"Okay," said Adam, coming forward to take a look. "You said they would be a young woman. How close are you? We have a pool going."

Since most of the technicians had gone, there was more room, and before she realized it, the whole crew was peering inside the coffin.

"Take a look, then step back a bit. So, are the odds in my favor?"

"Lewis here's pretty confident."

"Somebody pay up. The bones belong to a female."

"You have to explain how you know. Not that we don't trust you, you understand, but, well, it's money."

"Adam," said Lindsay, "you mean you bet against me?"

"Why are you and Dr. McBride wearing masks and we aren't?" asked Sharon."I mean, should we have them?"

Lindsay pulled down her mask. "Anytime something has been closed up this long, it's good to wear a filter—for the dust, if nothing else."

"They wouldn't have buried them in lead because they were contaminated or something, would they?" asked Sharon.

"No," said Adam. "I don't think they had any ideas about contamination back then."

"This is not an unheard-of burial practice for the time," said Lindsay. "You don't see it much, because at that time burials were primarily in cemeteries. We don't often dig in cemeteries."

"Why?" asked Luke.

Lindsay met his stare—very similar to John's when they were discussing the different way that Indian burials are treated by archaeologists, as opposed to non-Indian burials.

"Because they won't let me," she said, and he grinned at her.

"Going to tell us about these bones?" asked Byron. "If I'm going to be out some money, I want to know why." Byron had on his Grateful Dead T-shirt, and Lindsay had a twinge of guilt for rifling through his things. She decided then that she would never write her memoirs—she didn't want people to know some of the awful stuff she had done.

"Byron . . . you bet against me, too?"

"It seemed like a long shot, and I always play the favorite."

"Lewis," said Lindsay, "it looks like you're going to be raking in the big bucks. Okay, if the remains under examination contain certain critical bones, like the pelvis, sexing is pretty easy. Here we have a very well-preserved pelvis, and it's very female. Two main things you look at are the subpubic angle and the sciatic notch."

She pointed them out to the onlookers. "Females are wider in both. Also, look how graceful the skull is," she said, running her fingers across the forehead of the exposed skull. "Males tend to have more frontal bossing. Byron, feel your forehead, then feel Sharon's. Guys have squarer jaws as a rule. However, young guys can have very graceful features, so the skull isn't as reliable an indicator as the pelvis."

Phil McBride took a pen from his pocket and pointed to a patch of porous bone on the jaw. "It looks as though calcium deposits may have formed on some of her bones."

"You may be right," agreed Lindsay.

"What would cause that?" asked Lewis.

Lindsay thought a moment. "Diet, hormones . . . any number of things."

"What about her age?" asked Adam. "It has to be a young woman to win."

"Piece of cake," said Lindsay. "First, her wisdom teeth are just coming in. Look at her . . ." For a moment, Lindsay couldn't think of the name of the bone. "Humerus . . . ," she almost shouted. "The head of her humerus . . . you can see that the . . . the epiphysis . . . has only just fused . . . she's probably . . ."

"It looks like her arms are . . . ," began McBride.

"Lindsay are you all right?"

Lewis's voice was almost like an echo in her head. She could feel her knees giving way as she backed away from the bones and a tidal wave of fear washed over her.

Chapter 33

LINDSAY COULD FEEL the dirt being thrown over her . . . shovelful by shovelful. She heard the sound of the shovel hitting and sliding through the soil and the muffled thud as each shovelful dropped over her. She couldn't move, could barely breathe—she was going to slowly suffocate.

"Lindsay!"

A shout from the end of a cavern. She felt a hand on her arm, a strong grip pulling her from the grave, an Indian pulling her up out of a cavern.

"Lindsay."

"Luke? Luke. I'm okay."

She took a deep breath. She was sitting on a metal chair. Luke, Lewis, and Phil McBride were standing over her.

Dammit, they've claimed my memories, stalked me, terrorized me, and now I'm afraid of one of the things I love most in the world. I won't allow it. It stops here. She put her head down for a moment and felt the blood rushing back and pulsing in her temples.

She sucked in another breath, stood, and pushed her way back to the coffin. She concentrated on her legs to hold her steady and on her hands not to shake. But her heart thumping wildly against her ribs was on its own. She ignored the crew's puzzled stares.

"You were about to observe, Phil, that her arms are tucked behind her. Not a normal burial position." She took another breath. "The deposit of calcium on the bones is possibly indicative of slow suffocation." She heard an intake of breath . . . this time not her own.

"You're not saying . . . ?" whispered Sharon.

"The holes in the sides of the coffin, the hands behind her back, the calcium deposits, and the lack of an inner wooden coffin, all are very suggestive that she was put in the coffin alive."

She heard a gasp from one of the onlookers.

"The evidence suggests that she may have been held in the lead coffin for a time before it was buried. Otherwise, the oxygen would have run out sooner and we would not see the buildup of calcium deposits. There would have been enough air getting in through the holes to provide sufficient oxygen to keep her alive, though gradually asphyxiating her, for perhaps a week."

"Ouch," said Dillon. *Peter, Peter pumpkin eater, had a wife and couldn't keep her. Put her in a pumpkin shell, and there he kept her very well.*

"You think?" asked Adam.

"'*Cherry bell, bound to hell.*'" McBride recited one of the loft poems. "It does seem to fit, doesn't it?"

"There are other very reasonable explanations. If we're lucky, we'll know after I examine the bones . . . Or it will remain a mystery. In the meantime, Lewis, I think you're due some money." Ignoring her racing heart, Lindsay took a magnifying glass and started with the skull.

Cherry Redmond, if that was her name, was a delicate woman, possessing a fine forehead, pointed chin, high cheekbones, and a slight overbite. A snowflake design looking almost like a tatoo of fine dark lines on the collarbone caught Lindsay's eye.

"Here's something. Have a look at the left clavicle."

She handed McBride the magnifying glass. He leaned into the coffin and examined the one-half-inch-square section of bone Lindsay pointed out to him.

"A pattern?" he asked.

"It looks like it might be the remains of a bit of lace adhered to the bone." She turned to the photographer. "Could you take a close-up of this, please?"

Lindsay stood back as she watched him line up the shot. *He'll probably tell the others that I must be an amateur, getting all weakkneed over a set of bones. Stop being self-conscious, and do your work.*

After he took several shots of the design, Lindsay concentrated on the postcranial skeleton. She saw no evidence of breaks or disease. So far, the woman seemed to have died healthy, or if she had a disease, it hadn't reached her bones.

"Look here." Lindsay pointed to a section of pelvis. "Here, between the sciatic notch and the auricular surface, notice the preauricular sulcus."

"She's had at least one child," said McBride. "Right?"

"You can tell that from the bones?" asked Sharon.

"Any pull of your muscles on your bones will show up somewhere," Lindsay told her, "whether from hard work, lifting weights, or a pregnancy."

"You can tell all that from bones? I never knew." Dillon had inched closer and was now peering into the coffin. He straightened up and stepped back. "She's a tiny thing."

"My guess would be around five feet or less. I'll have a better estimate when I measure the lengths of the bones. What we're going to do now is collect some soil samples, then lay the bones out on the table here. This examination will take considerably longer. Each bone is going to be measured and given thorough scrutiny. So, it won't hurt my feelings if you don't want to stick around for the whole thing."

They, in fact, didn't want to stick around for the whole thing, opting to divide their time between the cemetery tent and this one. Luke winked at her on his way out with the others. "I'll be nearby if you need me."

Lindsay sensed a restlessness in the crew. They wanted to work. She motioned to Lewis as the crew left the tent.

"You need something?" Lewis asked.

"A couple of things. One is a sandbox." She indicated the approximate size with her hands.

"Of course. I'll have Mr. Laurens make one. And the other?"

"Why don't you have the crew work on the barn area? It's away from this compound, near the artifact tent. There's still a lot to do, and I think they would appreciate working."

"You're right. I didn't realize the barn excavation isn't finished. Drew should have seen to that," he added, and started to leave. He stopped for a second and turned to Lindsay. "You're doing a great job. Your analysis of the survey data and your discovery of the second coffin impressed Jarman and the others. Me, too."

Lindsay had the feeling he was going to say something else, but he left without saying anything more. Secretly, she was glad to see Drew's continued slip from Lewis's favor. Though she had no direct proof, she was convinced of Drew's implication in the theft of items from Miss Tidwell's house. And she felt that Drew was somehow involved in the acts of harassment against her. What she didn't know was how far and how deep her illegal activities extended. She wasn't about to protect Drew for Keith's sake or to prevent any tarnish on the name of Sound Ecology.

"Mind my asking what the sandbox is for?" McBride asked.

Lindsay powdered her hands and slipped on a pair of latex gloves. "I expect to do some reconstruction of the skull from the skeleton found under this coffin. Sand is a good medium to hold the pieces upright while the glue is drying."

"Do you think you can really fit those pieces together?" McBride reached for a pair of gloves from their box.

"Sure. Some of them."

"This is absolutely fascinating. To actually stand here and examine someone who lived in my home over two hundred years ago is just amazing." A plume of powder hovered over McBride's hands as he donned his gloves. "Did I hear Lewis talking about doing a facial reconstruction?"

"Yes. He loves those. Actually, I do, too. Remind me to show you the ones he brought with him from a Spanish galleon site we worked on."

She took several samples of dirt from around the sides of the coffin and sealed them in glass bottles the size of baby food jars while McBride labeled each with a marker on the side of the jar.

"He said you do sketches."

"Yes. I can do the reconstructions, too, but I'm not nearly as good as the artist who did the ones from the galleon."

"Elaine and I'd love to have a sketch of the people here."

"Sure." She stored the samples in two boxes, one for Peter Willis and another for the archaeologists. "Now, we'll take the bones and put them in anatomical position on the table." She gently lifted the skull from its place and set it on a donut ring. "I'm also going to take a soil sample from the auditory meatus. You never know what you can find sometimes." She used a thin wooden Popsicle stick she had fashioned herself to take the sample from the ear canal and stored it in a vial. Whether excavating around bones or poking around in the skull, Lindsay preferred to use wooden tools to metal ones when soil conditions allowed—less of a chance of doing damage.

"Was that a flashback earlier?" McBride asked. "Elaine told me what happened to you."

"I suppose that's what they are. I've had a couple of small episodes like that since I've been here. They haven't lasted long."

Below the skull set the atlas, the vertebra that holds up the head, like Atlas holding the world, and the axis on which the head is able to turn.

"Are you seeing anyone about them?"

"I've had my brain scanned. The doctors say everything is just fine."

"I mean a psychiatrist."

"No. I'll deal with it myself." Lindsay picked up a small arc of a bone. "Here's the hyoid bone. It's intact. Good chance she wasn't strangled."

"I don't suppose the argument would work that you wouldn't take out your own appendix, or defend yourself in court?"

"No. It's not the same. Medical doctors and lawyers possess expertise I don't have."

Phil McBride smiled as he placed the rest of the cervical vertebrae on the table. "You're a psychiatrist, too?"

"No, but I am an expert on myself . . . at least I know more about me than anyone else."

"You're an independent sort, aren't you?"

"I used to be. Now, I don't know. Now I seem to need people watching out for me."

"Elaine also told me about the torn page from the Edgar Allen Poe book someone sent you. Do you think it's related to the attempt on your life? Are those people here, you think?"

Phil McBride's brow made deep lines of concern, yet his voice was calm. *Good bedside manner,* Lindsay thought, as she picked up the sternum, which over the years had come to rest on the anterior surface of the thoracic vertebrae, then had slid off to the side.

"We'll take the vertebrae and ribs out first, then remove the shoulder girdle and bones of the arm." Lindsay gave the breastbone a quick look before she set it down on the table. "I've been trying to tell myself that what's happened to me here was just pranks, but I've been avoiding the obvious. Denial goes a long way with me. After what happened today, I think it's time to face it. They aren't going to make me afraid of bones."

"I haven't meant to pry," he said. "Elaine and I like you. After the way she was treated by Claire Burke, Elaine very much appreciated your treating her with respect. By the way, I haven't seen Claire around. Is she still here?"

"No, and it worries me. She left in the middle of the night a couple of nights ago, and no one has heard from her."

Phil raised his eyebrows. "You expect something might have happened to her?"

"I don't know. Drew says she's behaved like this before when things got uncomfortable for her. But . . . I don't know. Not a lot that's been happening fits together. But I'm going to make it fit." The skull and vertebrae lay on the table like a head with a long tail. "Notice that the epiphyseal ring on the vertebrae are almost, but not quite, fused."

"I see that. What would that make her in years?"

"Probably under twenty, over sixteen."

McBride shook his head. "So young."

Lindsay took out each rib, lightly running her fingers over each before setting it on the table.

"What are you feeling for?"

"Any nicks or cuts that might indicate injury or any other abnormalities."

"Do you appear in court a lot as an expert witness?"

"A fair amount."

"Is that why you don't want to see a psychiatrist?"

"It's true that an attorney will jump on anything that might weaken my credibility. However, that's not the reason. I believe that if I am to really get over this, I have to do it myself."

"If you change your mind, I can give you the names of some good people."

"Thanks, but I hope it won't come to that."

She and McBride had just placed the final phalange of the left foot on the table when Lewis and Posnansky came in with x-rays of the cemetery coffin.

Posnansky hung them for Lindsay to look at. "Great images," he said. "You can see the inner coffin."

"That lends some credibility to your hypothesis about the trash pit burial," said Lewis. "They did use wooden coffins in proper burials."

Lindsay examined the clear image of the skull and shoulders. "Nice shot. Looks like we may get some material besides bones. Maybe some hair and tissue. With that kind of preservation, you may have an airtight container."

"We're very hopeful," said Posnansky.

"Can you tell us anything about this person from the x-rays?" Lewis asked.

"My first impression is male. But we'll have to wait." She pointed to the bottom of one of the x-rays. "Looks like we may have a piece of jewelry here. Is that what it looks like to you?"

Lewis and Posnansky got close to the picture. "Like some kind of bow," said Posnansky.

"That's what it looks like to me," agreed Lindsay.

"Isn't that what you'd find with a female?"

"Maybe," said Lindsay. "Or it might be something a female would put into a coffin."

"Would the two of you like to break for lunch?" asked Lewis. "They're setting up right now."

Lindsay started to shake her head. Work was going to be piling up on her when the remains under the trash pit coffin and the cemetery coffin were ready. But a glance at McBride told her that he would welcome lunch.

"I'd like to take a break and call Elaine. See how she's coming with the diary hunt."

In the mess tent it looked like everyone except those working on the cemetery coffin had arrived for lunch. Mike Gentry, the repulsive man who had approached her, was helping serve. As Lindsay made herself a sandwich from the fresh-baked ham she had smelled early that morning, an idea occurred to her. Was it an idea, or a memory? It felt like an idea. If it was a memory, it was still deeply hidden in her mysterious subconscious. She looked around for Luke and spotted him in line only two people behind her. He was never very far away.

She waited until he had his meal in hand and pulled him aside. "I have something I want you to do."

"What's that?"

"The guy serving food, the one who calls himself Mike Gentry . . ."

"You don't think that's his name?"

"Maybe, but I would like you to take a photograph of him—without him knowing it—and drive up to the hospital where I was treated. I'll give you the address. Show the nurse." Lindsay hesitated. "Damn, I can't remember her name. I'll go make a call and find out. Anyway, show her the photograph and see if she recognizes him."

"You think he may be the one who tried to take you from the hospital?"

"Yes."

"Does he look familiar?"

"No, but my memory of that time is hazy-to-none. If he is the one, I can have the sheriff hold him."

Luke nodded. "Probably get him to spill his guts. Good plan, except for the part about me leaving you here."

"I'll be fine. Everyone knows Lewis asked the army guys to look out for me. Luke, I know this Mike person has something to do with what happened to me, and I know Drew and her husband have been up to something here, and I've seen Drew's husband talking to him on a couple of occasions."

"Yeah, me too," said Luke.

"Eric Van Horne is not the type to associate with the working class unless he has business with them."

"Makes sense, but why would they be so blatant? Would they count on your not remembering? Would Van Horne risk being seen with him?"

"When I told Drew and the others what had happened to me, I

explained how I had no memory of the period during my spell of amnesia. I think his running into me in the mess tent was a test."

"I don't like this."

"Luke, I want to be free of this. Please do this for me."

Reluctantly, Luke agreed, and Lindsay went to the artifact tent to get the camera, eating her sandwich along the way. She stopped by the crew working on the barn.

"How're things going?" asked Adam.

"I just saw some x-rays of the cemetery coffin. Looks good. May be airtight. How about you guys?"

"With all of us working on it, we ought to have this area excavated in no time. It's good to be doing something besides watching and being told we're in the way. Lindsay, are you being stalked? If you are, we want to know about it."

"You got that right." Powell dropped his shovel and came over, followed by Byron, Joel, and Dillon.

"We heard that Lewis asked them to watch out for you." Dillon motioned his head in the direction of the compound.

"I've had a few things happen while I've been here."

"Why didn't you mention it? We'd be on the lookout. You don't suspect any of us, do you?" asked Powell.

"No," Lindsay lied, well, only half-lied. She suspected Drew for sure. Maybe someone else, but standing facing them, they all seemed innocent and concerned. She wanted to tell them about Mike Gentry, but she couldn't be sure that no one among them was involved. "I asked the sheriff not to come out and question anyone here. I didn't want him to meet Trent."

"Good plan," said Byron, smoothing his beard. "That's all we'd need is a rural sheriff getting wind of Trent."

"We'll keep an eye out for you," said Adam. "If you have any problems, give us a holler."

"Or bang on your floor," added Dillon.

"I will. Thanks."

"You think it might have been Claire? She sure had it in for you," said Adam. "Not that she didn't have it in for all of us."

"She did," agreed Dillon. "Have you had anything happen since she left?"

"No. No, I haven't. But Claire was getting so much better the past few days before she left and . . ." Lindsay looked out over the site. "You guys better get some lunch before it's picked over." For a moment Lindsay thought of telling them about Drew poisoning the well with Claire, so to speak, but decided against it. Better to keep that information to herself.

"I smelled a ham baking this morning," said Byron. "Those reserve guys will have it picked to the bone, unless we hurry."

"Thanks for your support, guys. I really appreciate it."

"You just remember it if an application to graduate school comes across your desk," said Adam.

Lindsay laughed. "I will, indeed."

The guys broke for lunch and Lindsay proceeded to the artifact tent where Marina was absorbed in cataloging artifacts.

"Hi, Marina. Lunch is being served up."

"Oh, that ham, I'll bet. I'd better go get some."

"I'd like to borrow the Polaroid. We have one, don't we?"

"Sure. It's always useful to have an on-the-spot photo." Marina slipped off her stool and retrieved the camera from an overhead cabinet.

"My thoughts exactly. I'm going to have some really fancy photos of the bones, but I'd like to have some to take up to bed with me tonight to look at. They have x-rays of the cemetery coffin, by the way. Come by the tent and look at them after lunch."

"Really? Who's in it, do you know?" Marina handed her the camera.

Lindsay shook her head. "Male, maybe. He's in an inner wooden coffin, unlike the one from the trash pit. Elaine McBride is trying to acquire some other volumes of Hope Foute's diary. I'm hoping they'll contain information we need."

"The diaries, the cabin, and the coffins. This is going to be so neat when it's written up. Lindsay, I've been meaning to ask you. Lewis mentioned that you do facial reconstructions—drawings mostly." Lindsay nodded. "I'd like to acquire that skill. You think when you're free, you can show me how? Maybe let me work with you on the skulls here?"

"Sure. With your talent, you'll pick it up easily. It's a matter of following the structure of the bones. There are a few tricks, like knowing how long to make the nose."

"Yeah, that's what I want to know."

"I'll let you know when I do the sketches. Oh, looks like we may get some tissue samples with the second coffin."

"I'm not sure I want to see that."

"It'll be like a mummy."

"That would be better."

"We'll probably find some bits of clothing, buttons or something from the cemetery coffin."

Lindsay walked with Marina back to the compound. When they parted, Lindsay snagged Luke and shoved the camera into his hands. "Don't let him see you taking a picture. I'm going up to the house to call the hospital."

"Better hurry, before I have second thoughts about this."

Lindsay took him at his word and hurried off. As she approached the house, she heard hammering toward the rear. She cut around to the back and found Mr. Laurens constructing a device that looked like it was going to be a box, about a foot and a half square.

"That for me?"

Mr. Laurens grinned, showing missing premolars. "You the one getting the tiny sandbox?"

"Yep, that's me. Thanks for making it."

"It's what you all pay me for. I've got you a bag of sand to go in it, too. Didn't buy any little buckets, though." He laughed. Someone opened the door, and the aroma of food wafted past them. "Lord, don't that smell good?"

Lindsay agreed. She must tell Mrs. Laurens what a good job she was doing. On the way in the back door she met someone coming out with a container of food to take to the site.

"Hand me that clean apron on the rack there," Mrs. Laurens's voice came from the kitchen. "I've done spilled gravy all over this one."

Lindsay took a full-length apron from the rack and picked up a jacket with it that had dropped to the floor. She reached to hang it up, when she noticed that one of the jackets on the rack was one she'd seen Mike Gentry wearing in the cool mountain mornings. She took the apron into the kitchen.

"Oh, is that you, Lindsay? I thought it was Jimmy coming in. Thank you, dear." Mrs. Laurens took off her soiled apron, tucked it in a corner, and tied the other one around her.

"I wanted to tell you how good the food is. I know this isn't exactly what you signed up for."

"No, but it's always good to rise to a challenge. I'm just glad we've fixed enough for all those people."

Lindsay slipped back to the coatrack and in one swift movement pulled the jacket off the peg, rolled it up, and tucked it under her arm.

Chapter 34

LINDSAY WALKED AS calmly as she could through the kitchen with Mike Gentry's jacket tucked under her arm. When she reached the dining room, her intention to dash through to the downstairs bathroom was checked. Two of Mrs. Laurens's daughters were busy at the dining room table organizing the food to be taken to the site.

She could hardly make a mad dash past them without at least arousing their curiosity. She muttered something she hoped was a compliment on the food as she walked past them to the far side, finally making it to the reception hall and across to the bathroom. The door was locked.

"Just a minute," someone called out.

Lindsay didn't wait around. She bolted up the stairs and locked herself in her room. Her hands shook as she unzipped the right front pocket of the jacket. Not much there for her effort—Gentry's car keys and a cheap folding knife. She opened the knife and looked at the blade. It was dull.

Once when she was sitting by a campfire with her uncle and her grandfather deep in the Kentucky woods, eating the fish they'd caught and fried, her uncle told her, "You can judge a man by how he keeps his knife. A dull knife says something about a man."

She never understood what exactly, but then she was only five at the time. She still didn't know what it meant. She folded the knife and picked up the keys. Dodge, it said on the key ring. Unfortunately, it didn't say green truck.

The left pocket contained a paper clip, spray breath freshener, five gold dollars, and a gold piece of eight. The inside pocket was empty. No, it had something in the very corner. She dug down and brought it out. A tooth, or rather, a temporary cap made of gold—a molar.

The guy likes gold.

That was it. Not much for the mad dash she'd made. She started to put the items back in his pockets, when it hit her—the piece of eight, pirate treasure. Hadn't Mrs. Laurens mentioned that Mary Susan Tidwell had a gold treasure coin? Mrs. Laurens had made a rubbing of it as a child. Lindsay grabbed a piece of paper and rummaged through her things for a pencil.

For a second she considered making a mold. How long would that take? Four minutes for each side. No, better not risk him finding the jacket missing. A rubbing would have to do.

A number three pencil with a broken tip was in the side pocket of her suitcase. She unfolded Gentry's knife and did a hurried sharpening of the pencil. It *was* a dull knife. When she had some lead, she did a quick rubbing of both sides of the coin and hid the paper under her mattress.

Putting all the items back in their proper place, she checked the bed to make sure she hadn't left anything. She rolled up the jacket and pulled her own sweat jacket from her suitcase and put it over the one she'd purloined—just in case she ran into anyone. Out of habit, she looked out her window.

"Oh, shit," she swore out loud. A crowd of Mrs. Laurens's staff were walking across the parking lot from the site. Mike Gentry was among them.

Lindsay raced out of her room and down the stairs. She barely slowed down going through the dining room and kitchen to the mudroom. She hardly heard the footfalls on the wooden outside steps above the pounding of her heart in her ears. She hung the jacket on its peg at the same moment she heard the doorknob turn. She didn't look back as she made it through the door into the kitchen just as the back door opened.

"What you rushing around about, Lindsay?"

She jumped at the sound of Mrs. Laurens's voice.

"I'm looking for the phone book. Have you seen it?"

"It wouldn't be in here, I don't think, unless one of you all moved it."

She heard them talking in the mudroom, ready to come into the kitchen. She was safe now, but she couldn't face him. He'd probably be able to read her thoughts.

"I may have overlooked it in the living room. I'll go back and have another look."

She collapsed on the sofa, her cheeks burning and stomach hurting. *Calm down. So what if he had caught you? You could just say it dropped and you picked it up. No big deal. There were lots of people around. This was nothing. You've done more daring deeds than this little escapade. The phone book—Luke's waiting.*

The phone book was where it should be, under the phone. Lindsay had gone over in her mind the question of who to call: the detectives in Athens, hoping they'd have the nurse listed as a witness, the sheriff in Mac's Crossing, the hospital? The sheriff. She picked up the phone book and started to flip through the pages. What was she thinking? The number wouldn't be in here, only local numbers. She'd have to call information. The unexpected appearance of Eric Van Horne had taught her not to use the phone in the house. She went out to the privacy of her SUV.

Lindsay had to explain who she was and what she wanted to three different people before she got the name of the hospital nurse—Mary Carp. A call to the hospital revealed that Mary Carp would not be on duty this evening, but would be tomorrow.

She was making progress. Mike Gentry was the link between Mary Susan Tidwell, Eric Van Horne, and the attack on her—tenuous links with gossamer threads, but links nonetheless. She felt she almost had the thing solved. On the way back she met Luke on the bridge.

"I was coming to look for you." He held out a snapshot of himself standing next to one of the servicemen. Just behind them setting a tray of rolls down was Mike Gentry, frowning at the camera.

"Clever ruse, to get someone else to take the picture."

"It's not easy to take surreptitious photographs with an instant camera. It's not like it has a telephoto lens. Did you get the nurse's name?"

Lindsay gave him a piece of paper containing the information. "I thought maybe you could go tomorrow morning."

"I'll go. But you stick with someone you know and trust. Don't go off alone."

"There's no place here I can be alone."

"You have a knack for getting into trouble. You don't promise me, I won't go."

"I promise. Believe me, I don't want anything to happen to me. I'll be working all day. I've got bodies piling up, and I haven't finished the first one yet."

Phil McBride was already in the tent looking over the data forms when she arrived. "You fill all these out on each of the bodies?"

"Yep."

"That's a lot of measuring. I had no idea. I'd always thought you needed tissue to understand anything about a body. I thought once you get down to the bones, there's little you can discover."

"You do get more information from a fleshed-out body. But there's quite a bit you can get from bones. Some things, like handedness, I'm not sure how you could get, except from bones."

"I do thank you for this experience. It's fascinating work. I got ahold of Elaine. She's meeting with the people tomorrow. Drew gave me a range of prices that the diaries might be worth. Rather high, I thought, but I have a feeling that Lewis is going to pitch in to buy them. At least he hinted at it."

"Once he gets involved in something, his curiosity takes over. He wants to know about these people as much as we do."

Lindsay and McBride sat on stools on each side of the table. Starting with the skull, she examined each bone and recorded her observations. McBride actually made the task longer, as she explained everything to him, but she was glad for the company. By the end of the day, she was halfway through the remains. She looked up to see Lewis coming in the tent.

"How are you progressing?" He leaned over the table next to her to get a close-up look.

"Moving right along. How about the other coffin?"

"Jarman's going to wait until tomorrow to try for the air extraction. He and Peter've been looking at the x-rays, making a plan of attack. Peter's very nervous."

"How about our skeleton in the trash pit?" Lindsay stopped for a moment to take off her latex gloves and tuck back a strand of hair that kept falling in front of her face.

"Kelsey and her crew are having a great time. They've uncovered a belt buckle that's made them excited. They're happy as clams."

After McBride left for home, Lindsay confided her suspicions about Mike Gentry to Lewis, and she told him about Luke's trip planned for the next day.

"You really think Gentry's the one who tried to kill you?" Lewis's brow was wrinkled.

Lindsay was disappointed he didn't immediately accept her suspicions. "At the least, he may be the one who tried to claim me at the hospital."

"But you don't recognize him?"

"No, but right after the incident happened, I told John about the man who pretended to be my fiancé and tried to take me out of the hospital. Later, after I could no longer remember that episode, John told me the description I had given him of the man. I just have this feeling." She looked down at the wooden floor of the tent. "I also went through the pockets of his jacket."

"You did what? Why? Isn't that illegal?"

"I don't think so. It's nosy and pretty awful, I'll admit, but I did find a gold piece of eight that could be part of Miss Tidwell's estate."

Lewis shook his head in confusion. "A piece of eight? I haven't heard anything about that."

"It's information I got from Mrs. Laurens. She told me Miss Tidwell owned one."

"Pieces of eight are not exactly rare. We have a few thousand of them."

"Lewis, I know all my connections are weak at this point, but we'll know something tomorrow."

Lindsay went to bed with a giddy feeling that everything could be solved by this time tomorrow. If the nurse identified Mike Gentry as the one who tried to claim her from the hospital, then the dominoes would start to fall. She would be free and life would be good again.

Morning came quickly and she was out of bed as soon as her eyes snapped open. Lewis wasn't even up yet. She took a quick shower, dressed, and bounded downstairs to the kitchen where Mrs. Laurens was organizing breakfast.

The aroma of sausage made her mouth water. Eating in the mess tent with a hundred others didn't hold any appeal this morning. She took a biscuit and sausage from the waiting trays and a bottle of orange juice from the refrigerator and sat on the front porch, looking out over the pond to the site, lit up like a county fair. It only lacked a Ferris wheel in the background. People were already moving around like ants, but then they probably never slept. Someone always had to stand guard.

"You're up early." Luke Youngdeer squatted beside Lindsay's wicker chair.

"It's a good day."

"You're counting on this identification, aren't you?" He took her hand and squeezed it.

"If I can turn him over to the sheriff with a positive ID, he'll roll over on the others."

"You're sure?"

"Yes. He's not the type to go down alone."

"You know this, do you?"

"Yes."

"Lindsay, I believe you'll solve this thing, but don't be disappointed if this isn't the path."

"It will be. Eat breakfast before you go. It's not that long a drive, about eighty miles, and it's very early yet."

Lindsay absorbed herself in finishing her analysis of the bones from the coffin and tried not to let her mind wander to Luke's mission. Other than the calcium deposits, there weren't any remarkable pathologies on TPB1, as the trash pit coffin burial was designated. TPB1 was right-handed. Her handedness showed clearly in her glenoid fossa, even at so young an age. She must have worked hard at something that required repeated reaching. If her work had been hard, it didn't show up in her spine, which appeared normal for a person her age—no signs at all of wear.

She had just written the last entry of her analysis when Lewis came to tell her and McBride that Jarman and Peter were ready to extract the antique air. The two of them hurried to the other tent, already filled with people.

There was no room near the pit for any of the archaeology crew. Alex Jarman and Peter Willis were in the pit, and a host of technicians were around it, monitoring equipment and operating the various instruments and valves involved in the process. The archaeology crew had to stand toward the back of the tent. Lindsay strained to hear over the noise of the machines and the focused chatter of technicians.

"I guess one person can't do this job," whispered Byron to no one in particular.

Occasionally, Lindsay got a glimpse of Jarman's red hair when his head cleared the pit as he went about the duties of supervising the complex procedure.

"Okay," Jarman said. There was a hum and a sound like a loud dentist's drill.

Lindsay held her breath with the others but didn't know exactly what she was holding it for or for how long.

"Okay," she heard Jarman say again. The sound of the drill stopped and the sound of the vacuum pump increased.

"It's holding a vacuum," said Peter.

Lindsay took that to be good. She craned to see inside the pit, but all she could see was tubing leading to the pit, the bald spot on Peter's crown, and Jarman's thick shock of red hair.

"What do you think, guys? Did we get it?" Alex Jarman stood up, and from the smile on his face, he knew they did.

The activity of the technicians didn't decrease after the acquisition of the air sample. They were still just as busy. Jarman explained that while the rest of the coffin was being excavated, they would pump chilled argon gas into the coffin to replace the air that was taken and to preserve the remains. Then Juliana Skyler would test the soundness of the coffin to be lifted out of the pit.

With the main show over, Lindsay left the tent and stood at the chain-link fence, her fingers curled over the wires as she watched the road for any sign of Luke. He had left at seven. It was conservatively about two hours each way. Giving him a generous one hour to get the task done, he should be back by twelve. She looked at her watch. It was 10:14. She turned and went to her bones.

While Lindsay had been watching the air extraction procedure, Mr. Laurens had delivered the sandbox. It was sitting on a table against the wall of the tent. A small bag of sand sat on the floor under the table. She started to fill the box, but the photographer showed up to complete the photographs of the bones.

McBride came back from the cemetery tent as she and the photographer finished setting up a shot on a special table for that purpose.

"Will you make your sketch from these photos?" McBride gestured toward the skull sitting on the donut ring.

Lindsay checked her watch again—10:20. "What? Yes. I usually start the sketch on a light table, then fill in the shading after I have a basic face."

"I read a book about that once." The photographer lined up the shot for a profile. "I forget the name. But it was about sketching and sculpting faces from skulls. You do that?" As he moved the tripod to the 45 degree mark Lindsay had made on the table, the aroma of cigarettes and body odor wafted past.

"Sometimes," she answered. "I'm going to make sketches of these."

"Funny about the skeleton under that first coffin. You think he was alive when they dropped it on him?"

"We'll probably never know." Lindsay shuddered at the thought. "I think that's all the shots I need of the skull. We'll get some of the postcranial skeleton, and that'll be it for this set of remains."

"I heard someone say you're going to glue that fellow together. How long will that take?"

Lindsay was starting to get a headache.

Why is the photographer being so annoying?

She was growing tired listening to his running questions as he snapped his pictures.

He's just curious and asking perfectly natural questions.

She realized as she looked at her watch again that she was

counting on the nurse to identify Mike Gentry, counting on Luke returning with news that would make her nightmare come to an end. She was starting to resent any other thoughts that interfered with that one goal.

Dammit. Relax.

"I want to get close-ups of these calcium deposits." She indicated the area to the photographer.

"You really think this poor kid was suffocated in that coffin? I've read about kidnap victims buried alive. That's about the cruelest thing I can think of."

Lindsay had to agree.

"You ready for another one?" Erin, grinning proudly, entered the tent carrying a tray of boxes. "Bill and Kelsey are coming with more—where do you want them?"

"On the table next to the sandbox."

Erin set the tray on the table. Kelsey, smelling like hot perfume, came in behind her. Her hair, like Erin's, was stuck to her head in damp locks, and her T-shirt was hiked up in front and tucked under the bottom of her bra. She had rolled up the sleeves to her shoulders.

"Whew, it's hot inside the tent down in the ditch. You won't believe the stuff we've found." She set her tray down next to Erin's. "If you like, we can arrange the boxes like the grid."

"That would be great. We're almost finished here. What did you find?"

Bill arrived with boxes of long bones. Shattered, but distinguishable. Kelsey picked up several boxes and brought them to the examination table.

"I asked Dr. Lewis to join us." Kelsey almost giggled with delight, and it was catching. McBride was about to laugh, and Lindsay felt like she could crack a smile. She tried to look in the boxes, but Kelsey put her hands over them.

"Okay, what'd you guys find?" Lewis strode into the tent mopping his damp forehead with a red bandanna, which he then stuffed in his back pocket. Sharon hurried in behind him, slipped her arm around her husband's waist and kissed his cheek. "What'd you all find, honey?"

"First." Kelsey held up a brass belt buckle. "We found it near what might have been his midsection, only displaced a couple of feet. If you look real close, you can see the initials W. K."

"Which happen to be my initials." Bill took off his glasses and cleaned them on his shirttail.

"Yeah, he's got a covetous eye on it. We're going to have to search his luggage when he leaves here." Kelsey set the oval buckle on the table.

"Erin found this," she continued, gently taking out what appeared to be a knife with an antler handle. She set it beside the buckle on a cotton cushion.

The photographer whistled. "Now, I like that."

"The blade's about gone," said Bill, "but look at that handle."

Lindsay stroked the carved antler. "It's in very good condition. We're lucky it isn't smashed."

"Okay, I found this next thing," said Bill.

Kelsey pulled out a wad of cotton with a six-inch V-shaped metal object on it and placed it beside the others.

"It's a compass," said Lindsay. "A hinged compass."

Kelsey nodded enthusiastically. "I think the guy may have been an engineer or some kind of surveyor. We figure it's a guy, because these were guy things back then."

Lewis bent down and scrutinized the compass. "I like this. Now, if we can just figure out what he was doing under the lead coffin."

"We've come up with several creative scenarios while we've been digging," said Kelsey, "but none that are sensible. So tell me, what do you think of our little excavation?"

"I think it's as interesting as the coffin burials," said Lewis, and Lindsay agreed.

"So do I," said McBride. "I particularly like the compass. It would be kind of like finding my bones with the metal parts of my stethoscope. You'd know something about me."

"Or me with a camera," added the photographer. "A man is known by his tools. We can photograph these here where we did the skull."

"Okay," agreed Lindsay. "Someone got a quarter for a reference size?"

The photographer patted his pockets. "Alex took all my bills and my change last night for beer."

"What did you say? Alex took your bills?" Lindsay frowned.

The photographer looked at her, puzzled. "It's just a figure of speech. He didn't steal them. I gave them to him for beer."

"I didn't hear what you said," Lindsay said with a faint laugh.

What can I say—something about what you said made my brain itch? They'd know for sure I've gone nuts. What was it, though?

It was one of those thoughts that flashed lightning fast through her brain, too fast to see, too fast to catch. She mentally shrugged. Maybe it would come back around and slow down.

"I like what you guys found," she told Kelsey. "We've got a job description and initials for TPB2. That gives us a good chance at identifying him." She turned her head toward McBride. "Think Elaine's up for going back through the historical documents at the library?"

McBride nodded vigorously. "She'd love it."

"Here." Lewis handed Lindsay a coin.

It was a shiny new State of Georgia quarter, the one with the peach. Personally, she preferred Delaware's with the horse, but Georgia was known for its peaches. She flipped it to the photographer.

"Let's get some good shots of these artifacts."

As they were setting up the first shot, Luke Youngdeer walked into the tent.

Chapter 35

Lindsay stared at Luke a moment, trying to read his face. She excused herself and pulled him out of the tent and away from ears that might overhear them.

"Did she identify him?"

Luke's keen dark eyes bore into hers compassionately. "No. I'm sorry."

"No?" Lindsay was utterly surprised. "She said it wasn't him?"

"She said she didn't recognize him."

Luke was fading away in a blur as tears formed in her eyes. "Did you ask around?"

"Yes. I talked to several of the nurses, the receptionist, the people in the business office who did remember that the guy who came to fetch you wrote them a bogus check."

Lindsay stood still for a moment. She was so sure they were the same person. She squeezed her eyes tight, trying to remember her time in the hospital. There was nothing there, just empty space. She felt the tears running down her cheeks. "I'm sorry I wasted your time on such a wild-goose chase."

"I don't feel I wasted my time. For what it's worth, Mary Carp didn't want to talk to me. I don't know if she was afraid you were going to sue the hospital, if she'd already received a lot of flak about the incident, if she didn't like talking to an Indian, or if she was lying."

Lindsay opened her eyes and looked at him. "You think maybe she lied?"

Luke shrugged. "She may have. I know you were counting on this. I'm sorry."

"Me, too. There were two men who came to take me. One didn't go into the hospital. He waited on the sidewalk. Maybe Gentry is the second one—except he fits the description I gave John for the other one. I shouldn't have counted on this so much."

"You have police detectives working on it. Tell them your suspicions, and let them talk to this guy."

"That's what I'll have to do. I was just hoping to wrap it up myself. Go get yourself something to eat. I know you must be hungry."

"I will when I know you're all right."

"I'm fine." One side of her lips turned up in a lopsided smile. "We're finding lots of interesting things associated with the guy under the coffin."

"You don't say."

"They're being photographed right now. Come in and take a look."

On her way in, Lindsay met Lewis coming out, and she couldn't avoid telling him the disappointing news. Of course, it wasn't as great a disappointment to him. He hadn't hung his future on the outcome.

"This should be a relief then," he said.

"It's not."

"It was a long shot."

"I didn't think it was." Lindsay pushed past him and went into the tent, wondering what could be her next move. She had to solve this. The idea of going through life not knowing who had tried to kill her, and never knowing if they might try again, was unbearable. If she could solve murders that happened almost five hundred years ago, for heaven's sake, she could solve this.

The photographer was setting up the shot of the knife. That was his favorite, she could tell by the way he handled it and the delighted expression on his face. Lindsay was content to let the others take care of the photos. She walked over to look at the shattered bones in the boxes. Erin, in a halter top and dirty ragged cutoffs that her mother would hate, was organizing the boxes according to the grid numbers.

"You found some interesting items," Lindsay told her.

"We did, didn't we? I'm glad Dr. Lewis put us on that burial.

We had a good time. The best time I've had here. I feel like this is what archaeology is like, not what Claire showed me."

"Like anything else, you have good and bad times."

"We haven't sifted the soil yet. There's probably some other great stuff just waiting for us to find. Who do you think he was?"

That question again. Lindsay had to laugh. "I believe Kelsey's right. He was a surveyor or some sort of engineer. I don't have a clue as to how he got where he was."

Lindsay spotted the curve of an innominate and picked up its box and several others with pelvic bones and set them aside.

"Lewis, you want to help me with the sand?" asked Lindsay as she squeezed past him to grab the glue from the box of supplies.

"Sure." He and Luke opened the sack of sand and poured it in the newly made box, courtesy of Mr. Laurens.

"You going to glue the whole pelvis together?" asked Erin.

"No. Only as many pieces as it takes to determine sex. Like Kelsey said, it's probably male, but we need to confirm it with the bones."

All the pelvic bones were completely shattered and mixed with fragments of other bones. Lindsay first picked out the bones that belonged to the pelvis and sorted out the fragments with obvious diagnostic characteristics—a piece with a curve, part of the acetabulum, part of the auricular surface, part of a tubercle, or a piece with a fossa. She glanced at the other boxes, looking for more pelvic bones, and found several more fragments from a distant grid.

"Can I ask you a question?" Erin asked.

"Shoot," said Lindsay.

"Aren't you mixing them up?"

"Yes, and in most situations you don't want to do that. But we know we severely disturbed the fragments when we lifted the coffin. Having the bones taken up in a grid will help me quickly locate the bones that go together."

"It's like working a jigsaw puzzle." Luke bent over her shoulder, watching her work.

"Exactly." Lindsay put two pieces together, separated them, then glued them together. She found three more pieces that fit.

"Hey, Chamberlain." Alex Jarman stuck his head inside the tent. "Want to see inside the coffin? We're ready."

Lindsay, McBride, Jarman, Lewis, Peter, and Posnansky crowded around the small screen watching the trek through the inside of the coffin as the technician snaked the fiber optics borescope through the hole.

"We have some hair." Lindsay pointed to the screen.

"I'm losing mine at twenty-six, and this guy's over two hundred and dead and still has his hair. It's not fair." Peter Willis had loosened up considerably now that the pressure was off and he had his sample.

"When will you know if you have uncontaminated air?" asked Lindsay.

"Not for several months. But I'm very optimistic. I've examined some trapped gases in ice cores. But this will be the oldest air sample I or anybody's managed to capture—if we have it. Like I said, I feel really good about it. What's that dark stuff on the bones? A fungus or something?"

"Desiccated skin," said Lindsay. "What's that?" She tapped the screen at a distant fuzzy image. "Can you get closer?"

They watched the view as the borescope moved farther into the coffin and maneuvered to an object.

"It looks like glasses," said Jarman. "Did they have glasses back then?"

"You ever see a portrait of Ben Franklin in glasses?" Lindsay asked.

"Oh, yeah. How about that. Looks like they might have been stuck in a pocket or something the way they're situated."

"We can get an idea about his vision," said Lindsay. "Nice."

"Okay." Posnansky straightened up from his bent position and rubbed his lower back. "We're going to pump argon gas into the coffin while your guys finish the excavation. If all goes well with Juliana's tests, we'll lift it out of the ground late this afternoon."

"All this is pretty amazing," said Lindsay.

"We've enjoyed the opportunity to play with our toys," said Posnansky. "Looks like we got something to write home about. Alex here's ordering us a tub of beer tonight, and we're going to have a good time."

Lindsay tried to smile, but it froze on her face. She ducked out of the tent while Posnansky was giving the technician instructions and headed back to her bones. Their work was over. It had caught her off guard. They would be leaving. Her examination trailer would stay, she was sure. But the servicemen were here to guard the expensive equipment, not her. And they would go with the equipment.

"Lindsay." Lewis caught up with her and put a hand on her shoulder.

"Are you all right? You left looking kind of pale."

"I just realized they will be leaving soon."

"Yes, but a few will stay until you finish. It's their equipment you're using. I'm staying a while and so is Luke. I'm sorry things didn't turn out the way you wanted. But maybe you were counting too much on it."

"The whole idea of it being over was just so . . . so peaceful. I'll be fine. Just need another plan." Lindsay walked with Lewis toward the mess tent.

"Good. That's the spirit. Let's go eat lunch. You're looking a little thin, too."

"Lewis . . . never mind. Where is Drew? I haven't seen her lately."

"She had to go somewhere with her husband. There she is at the mess tent. I guess I'll go fill her in. Not that it'll make a difference."

Lindsay watched Drew and her husband going into the huge tent. "What's with her, can you tell?"

"I don't know. I'm beginning to think you're right about her. Since her husband showed up, it's hard to keep her attention on task."

"Has she said anything about Claire?"

Lewis shook his head. His gaze stayed on the tent opening Drew had just entered. "Just apologized for the way Claire treated you."

"She was the cause . . . It's true that Claire was hard to get along with, left to her own devices, but Drew really played on that."

"You believe what this Trent fellow told you?"

"Yes. On this I do. And I'm very worried about Claire. The sheriff hasn't found a trace of her."

"How hard is he looking?"

"I'm sure he's not treating her like a missing person. But he did contact her parents just like I did, and he's had his deputies keep an eye out for her car."

"She wouldn't leave the site and hang around Kelley's Chase, would she? That wouldn't make any sense."

No, Lindsay admitted to herself, *but if she is somehow involved in all this, she might. It would be easy to rent a cabin somewhere in the Smokies.* Oddly, that thought was a relief. Lindsay preferred to think of Claire as a criminal, rather than dead. *Dead.* She hadn't thought the word so blatantly, but had kept the idea at a safer distance in her mind. But she was very much afraid that Claire had gone out in the dead of night and met a fatal end. Lindsay shivered.

Lewis went off to see Drew. McBride was with Jarman, Posnansky, and Peter. The three of them were coming out of the cemetery tent heading for the mess tent and deep in conversation. Luke was with Adam, Byron, and Dillon, laughing and joking with some of the reservists. She wished she felt as happy as they all looked. She entered the tent and paused just in the doorway. It was noisy as usual for this time of day, filled with the sounds of a myriad of conversations going on at once. She surveyed the food line and looked over the crowd for Mike Gentry. He wasn't there. She ducked out of the tent and headed for the house.

Mrs. Laurens was relaxing in the kitchen, drinking a glass of iced tea and talking with one of her daughters who was washing dishes.

"Hello, Lindsay. Aren't you eating with the others?"

Lindsay pulled out a chair and sat down. "I was kind of taking a break from the others."

"I know what you mean. You have to take your respites when you can. I was just telling Darlene we're getting a break for supper. Dr. Lewis is getting shrimp. Going to serve it on a big tub of ice. He wants us to boil some corn on the cob and make some key lime pies."

"Those are Lewis's favorites."

"It sounds like you all are having a party." When Darlene turned her head a certain way, she looked exactly like a younger version of her mother.

"Most of the work the scientists came for is finished. This is a celebration. I suppose they'll be packing up and leaving tomorrow."

Trickles of condensation ran down Mrs. Laurens's iced tea glass. The caramel-colored liquid over ice looked cool, an invitation too good to pass up. Lindsay got up and poured herself a glass. She'd been thinking about how to ask about Mike Gentry without arousing any suspicion. She wanted to say something like: "Doesn't Drew know Mike Gentry, the guy who works for you?" But she didn't want it getting back to Drew. She wanted to keep Drew and her husband in the dark.

"Are you a little short-handed? It seems like I didn't see as many people serving." Lindsay sat down and sipped her tea.

Darlene was putting a large pan in the dish drainer. "That Mike Gentry didn't come to work today. He's the only one, and if you ask me, we can do without him."

"Was he a problem?"

"Not a problem, as such," said Mrs. Laurens. "He was one of those people who look for every opportunity to get out of work. Ellie at the diner recommended him. She said he was a good worker."

"Mama, that's because he'd stayed there a couple of months. It's so hard to get good people to work in the restaurant business, they're grateful for anyone who sticks around for more than a couple of weeks."

So he was gone. Had he gotten wind of what Lindsay was up to? How? Did he get suspicious of the picture after all? Did he know she went through his pockets? Lindsay would like to be glad he was gone—if she really thought he was. He was too good a suspect to let go of.

"Mrs. Laurens. Didn't you say you made a rubbing of that treasure coin Miss Tidwell brought to your class?"

"I was in third grade. We all had to do a project. She let me make a rubbing because she knew I was careful and knew to use the side of my pencil and not bear down hard. You couldn't trust boys with something like that, leastwise, not nine-year-old boys."

"Do you still have it? I'd like to see it."

"Lord sakes, Lindsay. That was almost fifty years ago."

"You know, Mama, that trunk in the attic has some of your old report cards in it and that scrapbook of leaves you collected when you was in sixth grade. You might still have it."

"I don't want you to go to any trouble, but I really would like to see it."

"This have something to do with Miss Tidwell and what Erin's people asked you to do?"

"Yes, but I wish you wouldn't mention it."

Lindsay left and went back to the site, leaving Mrs. Laurens and her daughter puzzled, she was sure. People were streaming out of the mess tent and back to their posts. She went straight to her trailer and continued reconstructing the pelvis. She stopped when she determined it to be a male pelvis, though she wanted to go on. There was something restful about fitting bones together. She stood the glued pieces in the sandbox and looked for boxes containing skull fragments.

"Did you eat lunch?"

"Lewis—I didn't hear you come in. I had some business to take care of, and I wasn't hungry. I'm having fun, so leave me alone." She took two pieces of the right ascending ramus, glued them together, and stood them up in the sand to dry.

"I see you have a big piece of the pelvis finished. Is it male?"

"Yes."

"Is there anything else you can tell about him?"

"He was mashed flat."

"Is that how he died?"

"Lewis, I almost hate telling you this, but there are limits to what I can find out from bones. I don't know who he is, I don't know the cause or manner of his death, and I don't know what he was doing under the lead coffin. In fact, I don't know any more than Kelsey has already discovered."

"When you do find out all those things, let me know."

"Did I hear my name?" Kelsey came in.

"I was just about to tell Lewis what a nice job you and your crew did on the excavation."

Kelsey grinned. "We had a great time. So, can you put Humpty Dumpty back together?"

"Yes, I think so."

Kelsey turned to Lewis. "Some of the guys tell me you and Jarman are throwing a party here tonight."

"We thought a little celebration was in order."

"Great, I'm ready." Kelsey danced her way out of the tent, her arms over her head, snapping her fingers to a tune in her head.

Lindsay thought it would be nice if John could come. She found the several pieces of the occipital, the back of the head, and glued them together.

"If you're doing okay here, I'm going to see how the coffin is coming."

Lindsay barely heard him leave as she sorted through the bones looking for a piece that fit with the fragment of temporal she had in her hand. She located it and several other pieces in another box and glued them together.

"So," she said to the pile of fragmented bones, "now I have your cause and possibly the manner of death."

Chapter 36

"OKAY, WHAT AM I looking at?"

Lewis sat perched on the stool at Lindsay's left. Phil McBride sat on the other side. The trash pit coffin's skull sat on a donut ring in front of them.

"The left parietal bone of the skull." Lindsay touched the side of Lewis's head with her fingertips. "Right now I'm touching your right parietal." She pointed out the same bone on the coffin skull.

"Hey, guys. Kelsey told me she and her crew found come interesting artifacts." Marina had used the pause in the site excavation to catch up on her cataloging and had missed most everything but the highlights.

"She did indeed," said Lewis. "We'll show them to you in a minute. Lindsay's found something in the bone fragments here."

"Oh, great. I've wanted to watch Lindsay with the bones." She stood next to McBride and leaned on the table.

"This is a bullet hole," said Lindsay, indicating a hole in the right side of the reconstructed bones. "It bevels inward. That means it's an entrance wound. There's no crack pattern around the hole, which means it's a low-energy wound. There's been a lot of postmortem damage and deterioration, but it appears that the bullet traveled a path starting from the left parietal bone, terminating at the lower right quadrant of the occipital—the back of the skull. We don't have an exit wound, which also suggests the bullet lost energy during its travel." She took the occipital from the sandbox. "See this small indentation? I think it's where the bullet hit the cerebral surface of the occipital, probably bouncing off and doing more damage in his brain." Lindsay demonstrated the path with the trash pit skull. "During the sifting, they may find the bullet."

"So someone shot him," said Lewis.

"The angle is a little difficult for suicide. And we'd probably see some cracks around the wound. The bullet would have more energy if the gun was pressed against the skull or the shot was fired from close range."

"So whoever shot him was at some distance?" said McBride.

"Probably."

"Wow," said Marina. "Shot him dead, in the head."

"Of course, the poem," said McBride. "I should have thought of that right off."

"You think it refers to this guy?" Lewis asked.

"The other poem seems to refer to the trash pit coffin, but who knows? It's somewhat of a coincidence," Lindsay added.

"I'll say," said Marina.

"So, you were able to determine the cause and manner of death," Lewis said, showing his white teeth in a broad grin. "You see, I'm learning your forensic terminology."

"But do you know which is which?" Lindsay grinned back.

"Cause of death is homicide and manner is gunshot?"

"The other way around. The cause is gunshot and the manner is either homicide or accident."

"Oh, yes, accident. I've been hanging around you too long. I'm starting to think everything is murder. So, what do we know?"

Lindsay backed up from the table so she could see the three of them and counted on her fingers. "We have one skeleton who may have been suffocated, one who was shot in the head. Each may fit one of the loft poems in the McBrides' house. Elaine and I searched the historical documents in the library for any reference to the Cherry or Eda Mae mentioned in the loft poems. We haven't found anything, but some of the older residents in town do remember some sayings from childhood about Eda Mae being someone with a sharp tongue or someone their parents or grandparents warned kids against emulating. Also, there was a ghost story of sorts about an Eda Mae being haunted by a witch who would slap her during the night, among other things."

"You and Mrs. M've been busy," said Marina. "That's quite a collection of findings."

"If the poems are about these people, taken as a whole, it's very suggestive." McBride rocked back and forth on his heels as he spoke. "It looks like some kind of love triangle, maybe more than one. Two poems suggest that Cherry and Eda Mae went somewhere when they should have been somewhere else—*'Cherry gone a looking, not at home a cooking,'* and *'Eda Mae gone all day, wouldn't say which a way.'*"

"Sounds like assignations to me," said Marina, perching herself on the stool vacated by Lewis.

"Perhaps the girl in the trash pit coffin is Cherry, like Lindsay suggested," said Marina. "She was married—maybe to the guy in the other coffin—and made her husband a cuckold by sneaking off to see this guy. Oh, this is perfect." Marina rubbed her hands, warming to her topic. "Kelsey said the Humpty Dumpty guy may have been a surveyor—the kind of guy who's just passing through and looking for a little action with the local girls. The husband catches the two of them, shoots the guy in the head, but wants to make his wife suffer. So, he holds her in the coffin until she dies of slow suffocation, then he buries them together in the trash pit."

"That's certainly a scenario," said Lewis.

"It does fit," said McBride. "Perhaps the poem, *'not my sin, the hell he's in,'* refers to him. What do you think, Lindsay?"

"Who wrote the poems?"

McBride shrugged. "Perhaps Hope Foute. She seems to be the writer."

"Mmmm, not the same handwriting," said Marina.

"Besides, I think Hope might have been too young," suggested Lindsay. "She probably lived with her parents."

"The poems have something of a tattling nature to them," said Lewis. "Whatever happened, someone was watching."

"They're ready to lift the cemetery coffin out of the ground." Drew stood in the doorway backlit by the bright daylight, a dark form blocking out the sunlight.

The exam trailer was crowded and hot. For most of the scientists and technicians, the cemetery coffin, the one that gave them what they came for, was the big show, and they wanted to see what was in it. The lid was lifted off and set aside in the same manner as the first coffin. Inside, like nesting dolls, rested a smaller wedge-shaped coffin built from walnut. Its deep, brown smooth surface looked almost like new. This burial, unlike the first, was for a person who was cared for—at least after death.

While Joel and Adam were removing the inner coffin lid, Lindsay stood in front of the assemblage of people, most of whom were sitting in chairs they'd taken from the mess tent, some siting on the wooden floor, others standing. She took a sip of iced tea and looked out at the crowd of faces.

Drew and her husband stood by Lewis off to the side. Her gaze brushed over their faces, but didn't linger. Eric Van Horne's face was impassive. He didn't even look particularly interested in what was going on, but he didn't exactly look bored, either. Why was he here? Visiting? Maybe, but Lindsay didn't think so.

Why have I wasted so much time? I should have gone headlong into investigating Drew and her husband while the army reserves are here. Now, tomorrow they will be gone.

Joel and Adam lifted the wooden lid from the coffin and set it aside. An acrid odor rose from the coffin as everyone stood and craned to get a look inside. At a glance it wasn't easy to make out the bones among the rags.

"It looks like we have remarkable preservation," said Lindsay.

Sparse wires of dark hair stuck to the top of the skull. Adhering to the bones were patches of darkened desiccated skin and dark tattered cloth. It was difficult to tell flesh from fabric. While the photographer took the photographs, Lindsay addressed the group.

"As a result of the rather spectacular excavation of a Spanish galleon off the coast of Georgia by UGA's Archaeology Department, the department now has a new Conservation Research Laboratory directed by Carolyn Taylor. Because these remains will deteriorate quickly, after the photographs and collecting samples for Peter, I'm going to give the bones only a brief examination. Then we'll ship the remains to the conservation lab where I'll be able to do a more thorough examination after the conservators remove the fabric.

"The material has lots of microbes attacking it, making it fragile, and it will have to be handled carefully so it doesn't deteriorate any further. The conservators will remove the fabric from the bones and, after a sterilization procedure, will store it between glass. From a study of the cloth, we'll be able to know what it's made from, how it was woven, and possibly how the articles of clothing were sewn together."

"Didn't they make their own clothes out of cloth they made from plant fibers?" asked Jarman. "Didn't I hear someone say they grew—what was it, flax, for that purpose?"

"Yes, they made linen from flax."

"Linen? Linen is made from plant matter?" said Jarman.

"Yes, flax makes a very tough cloth. However, it doesn't take dye very well, so it is usually a white to off-white color. These clothes are dark—men were typically buried in dark suits—I assume it's probably cotton or wool, but I don't know."

The photographer finished the shots along the length of the remains, and Lindsay showed him where she wanted close-ups.

"We have an added bonus," she said, "of having a pair of glasses with this one." She pointed to an object amid a heap of cloth. "We'll be able to get some idea about this fellow's eyesight, which I think's kind of neat."

"So, it's a man?" asked Marina.

"The skull looks male."

"All done for now," said the photographer.

Lindsay slipped on her mask and took a pen and gently lifted pieces of fabric away from the pelvis. "It's a male pelvis."

"How old is he?" Adam asked.

"Let's see. His wisdom teeth are in, and that usually occurs between seventeen and twenty-five. His epiphysis in his humeri and femurs are fused."

Lindsay carefully lifted the pubic bone and luckily found no hindrance in examining the pubic symphysis. She explained to them, as she did her students, that the surface of the pubic symphysis changes as a person matures and ages, so that it can be used as an indicator of age. However, there is such overlap in stages of change that, as in sexing, other bones should also be used, when they are available, to arrive at a more accurate age estimation.

"Because the act of childbirth causes changes in the pubic symphysis, this method is not valid on female skeletons."

Lindsay examined the sternal ends of several ribs. "From a quick examination of the ribs, pubic symphysis, teeth, and epiphysis fusion, I would say he was in his early twenties, no more than twenty-five."

"Maybe he's the one who was *shot dead in the head,*" said Joel.

"No, Lindsay found him," said Marina. "He's the shattered skeleton."

"You found a bullet hole somewhere in those skull fragments? Well damn, a murderer can't get away with anything with you around," Adam said.

"No." Lindsay's voice was strong and unwavering. "No, they can't." She resisted looking at Drew and her husband in particular, but focused her gaze on the crowd.

"Now, I'm going to take some samples of detritus around the skeleton for Peter and us, look over the bones again for any features, then we'll close it up."

"What about that bow we saw in the x-ray?" asked Posnansky.

Lindsay took her pen and gently teased back some of the material and found a jeweled bow lying in the midsection. "It's a broach. It looks like marcasite."

Marina came forward and examined the piece of jewelry. "It is. Very typical of eighteenth-century jewelry. Perfect condition."

"Are you sure about the gender?" Eric Van Horne asked, his mouth curled in what Lindsay supposed for him was a smile.

"Yes. Bones are far more diagnostic for sex determination than associated artifacts."

"I'll bet," said one of the female technicians, "that his wife or girlfriend put it in his coffin, so that something of her would always be with him."

"That's what I would imagine," said Lindsay.

"Someone said something about them being reburied?" asked another technician.

"When we finish the analysis," answered Lewis, "the bones

will be reburied in the cemetery of the Kelley's Chase Primitive Baptist Church near who we believe are relatives."

"I believe that a member of the congregation who is a cabinetmaker is going to make new coffins from wood he has on hand—which, I might add, is befitting the customs of these people." Lindsay gestured to the remains in front of her.

"Are you going to bury the jeweled bow with him? It would seem that if you believe the woman who loved him wanted something she cherished to stay with him always, you would have to." Lindsay looked up to see John West standing near the rear with Luke, his arms folded, his face rigid. Everyone turned to look at him, then back at Lindsay.

"I suppose that's true." Lindsay smiled at him for a long moment and his stern face broke into a grin as he stared at her.

Chapter 37

"Did you come all this way just to harass me?"

John kissed Lindsay on the cheek as she collected the samples from the coffin. "Indeed not." He looked down into the coffin. "Is this what I'm going to look like after a couple hundred years?"

"Depends on what happens to your body after you die. Close you up in an airtight case with no embalming, and you might look something like that."

"John, good to see you." Lewis grabbed John's shoulder and shook his hand. "He wasn't embalmed?" Lewis asked Lindsay.

"Actually, after I said that, I realized I don't know. We'll be able to tell when the samples are analyzed."

"I think I would prefer to be cremated and have my ashes scattered to the wind," said John. "This does not look good."

Lewis introduced John to Phil McBride and the others gathered near the coffin as Lindsay finished collecting the samples. Anyone who wanted to see the remains, which was almost everyone, came up to take a peek.

"Very interesting," said Eric Van Horne. "Never knew you could tell so much from a pile of bones."

Out of the corner of her eye, Lindsay saw John take Lewis aside and whisper something in his ear and Lewis whisper something back.

"All that and more," said Lindsay. "I hope you're enjoying your visit. This is quite a show we have here, isn't it?"

"Quite different from the primitive digs that Drew usually works on. Didn't know archaeology could go so high-tech."

Lewis and John rejoined the group. "John designed and built

the cofferdam for excavating the Spanish galleon." Lewis began an elaborate explanation of what a cofferdam is, holding the audience spellbound at the thought of working in a dry well in the ocean.

"Okay, we can close him up." Lindsay helped Adam and Joel put the lid back on the coffin.

"Lindsay." Lewis pulled her aside as the others filed out of the tent, ready to party. "I've decided to send all the bones back to the lab. Is that all right with you? You have enough for a preliminary report don't you?"

"Yes, that's fine."

"Alex is going to pack up tomorrow, and I thought it would be more efficient if everything went at the same time. I'm going to stick around a couple of days. So is John."

There was that tickle in her brain again. An itch she couldn't scratch. What exactly did Lewis say that caused it?

"You and John've been planning things?" she said.

"I hope you don't mind, but he's convinced me that you are in danger here."

"He has?"

"Don't go getting angry with either of us. That tape in your SUV and the torn page worried both of us."

"I'll be fine. I think I'll stay until I've solved this thing."

"No." John's whisper was almost a shout. "No, you won't," he said more softly. "Luke's spoken with the sheriff here, and he's looking for Gentry. You are going home."

Lindsay looked back and forth at the two of them. "Has something else happened that I don't know about?" They stared at her a moment, looked at each other, at the ground, at Luke who came to join them. "What?" she asked.

"They found your old Explorer in a pond near Mac's Crossing."

"Too bad about the Explorer. I liked that vehicle and now it's waterlogged."

They stood still, like they were waiting to have their teeth pulled.

"There's more?"

"Another car was with it," said John. "Claire's. She was in it."

Lindsay put her hands over her mouth, her eyes filling up with tears. "Oh, no," she whispered. "No. Tell me she's not dead."

John put his arms around her and held her tight. "I don't think we should tell anyone just yet." He stroked her hair. Lindsay bit her lip to hold back the tears.

She pushed away. "How did it happen?"

"We don't know yet."

"I was afraid something had happened to her."

"I know," said Lewis. "I'm sorry I didn't take her disappearance seriously."

"It wouldn't have mattered," Lindsay told him. "What could we have done?"

"I don't know." Lewis handed Lindsay his handkerchief to wipe away her tears. "As John said, we don't want any mention of this now." Lindsay nodded and wiped her eyes.

Lewis and Jarman had tubs of shrimp on ice and a keg of beer delivered to the site. Mrs. Laurens had piles of corn on the cob and rows of key lime pies in large rectangular cake pans laid out on the table. Tables and chairs were set up both inside and outside the mess tent. The music was compliments of Dillon Gavin and Luke Youngdeer, who had brought his acoustical guitar—plugged and unplugged. The music was set up near the cemetery tent so Dillon could plug into its generator. Adam, Byron, and a couple of reserves, with the help of Mr. Laurens, had scrounged up a huge piece of throwaway linoleum that they spread on the ground for a dance floor under the stars. Lindsay would have found it heaven, if it weren't for the news about Claire.

She didn't know how she was going to get through the party acting jovial. Everyone was so happy. They talked, took pictures of each other, laughed. A site that Adam had described as archaeology hell was now something they were all proud to be a part of. And the visiting scientists got what they came for—or at least there was a good chance they did.

The only unusual thing at the party, at least to Lindsay, was the appearance of the sheriff and one of his deputies. They were out of uniform and brought their wives, and the sheriff made a point to thank Lewis for inviting them. They were guests, as far as anyone knew. But Lindsay wondered how they could investigate without arousing suspicion. Maybe it wouldn't arouse suspicion. The crew knew Lindsay had told the sheriff that Claire was missing. It would be only natural for him to ask questions.

John brought Lindsay a loaded plate of food and set it in front of her. "Try to eat something."

Lindsay nodded. She was trying to hold Claire's death to the back of her mind, but there was only so much that would fit there. Lewis, Phil McBride, and Alex Jarman sat down with her and John. They were laughing.

"You should have seen this, Lindsay. Alex took Phil's picture and . . . ," began Lewis.

There it was again, the tickle in her brain. This time it slowed down so she could grab it.

"That's it. I know what at least one of the documents is. Erin . . ." Lindsay called over to the next table where Erin had just sat down with Adam.

"What?" asked Lewis.

"Something you said."

Erin hopped up and came over. "What's up?"

"Did your great-aunt Susan speak French?"

"Yes, it was one of the things she taught."

"Sit down a second. I think I know what one of her missing documents is about."

"You do?" She pulled a chair over and sat down on the edge of the seat.

"What did I say?" Lewis asked.

"It's been running through my brain for a couple of days. People have been saying these phrases that sound like something vaguely familiar, and it just now came into focus."

"What do you mean?" asked John.

"First the photographer said, 'Alex took all my bills'; then Lewis said, 'Alex's going to pack up'; and just now Lewis said, 'Alex took Phil's picture.'"

"I'm afraid I don't see," said Lewis.

Alex Jarman laughed. "Have I done something?"

"Coincidence of name." She explained briefly to Jarman about the missing documents. "The only thing Erin and her relatives remember are the names Turkeyville . . ."

"That was me," said Erin. "I remember something about that name when I was a kid."

". . . and Beau. And Erin remembers her aunt reading from a document about a man sick in a log cabin during a blizzard with wind blowing through the cracks in the logs. Get it?"

"Not in the least," said Lewis.

"In 1831 the Frenchman Alexis de Tocqueville and his friend Gustave de Beaumont traveled through the eastern United States writing about their observations on American democracy. They arrived in Tennessee in December during one of the harshest winters in history. Alexis de Tocqueville took ill in Sandy Bridge, and they were forced to stay at an inn built of logs. He and Beaumont were miserable because the spaces in the logs were so wide that the wind blew through."

Erin clapped her hands. "That's it." She hugged Lindsay. "I don't believe you figured it out."

"It's just a matter of having studied about Alexis de Tocqueville. I believe the document was a letter in French written by de Tocqueville, or Beaumont."

"I can't wait to tell Mom and Uncle Alfred." Before Erin could jump up and head for the house, Lindsay grabbed her arm. "Wait until you see them face to face."

"Why? Oh. Okay." She bounced back to her seat beside Adam.

"Okay, how about me? How do I fit in?" asked Jarman.

"Your first name is Alex, and people kept saying phrases that vaguely rhymed with Alexis de Tocqueville—at least, enough to set my brain to going."

"Dr. Chamberlain," said Jarman, "you have a strange brain."

"She does, doesn't she?" said Lewis.

Eric Van Horne collects postrevolutionary documents? How tempting would a de Tocqueville letter be to a collector?

Lindsay felt a bit of comfort that her brain was functioning at a reasonably normal level. Apparently, so did John, for he slipped his arm around her waist and hugged her to him and kissed her cheek, unusual behavior for either of them. Lindsay and John seldom expressed affection in public. One of the things for which they were well matched. *John must be deeply worried,* she thought.

"Hi, guys. Guess what I have?" Elaine McBride stood beaming, clutching a package to her breast.

"You were right, Lindsay. Hope Foute had an older sister, Charity—called Cherry. Her full name was Charity Belle Redmond. Her married name was Warfield."

Elaine sat down in the chair Lewis offered, while McBride went to get his wife a plate of food.

"Whew, I'm tired. It's been quite a trip."

Lindsay introduced her to John and Alex Jarman. She unwrapped two diaries. They looked very much like the one in the library, leather bound, dark cream pages, neat handwriting in brown ink.

"My sister's husband has a friend who has a client who knows about old documents. He came with us. The people turned out to be very nice. Not sharks at all."

"Did you purchase the diaries?" asked Lewis.

"Yes." She made a face.

"Don't tell me the damage now," said her husband, setting down a plate of food. "Let me enjoy my meal." She leaned over and gave him a kiss.

"They had these two journals of hers, and I think there were only three altogether. That's the sense I get from reading them. The one at the library is in between these two. They cover kind of like her young, middle and elderly years. The ones I got in Virginia are the young and elderly."

"Don't keep us in suspense," said Lindsay. "What do they say?"

"Keep in mind that Hope Foute was born after her parents built the house in 1775. The journal entries about the early part of her life are partly constructed from her memory years later and partly from others' recollections.

"The story starts in Pennsylvania with a man named Sheldon Warfield. I believe he was a man in search of a kingdom. He should have been in the history books here, but I'd never heard of him. Warfield was in politics in Pennsylvania, and I get the idea that things weren't going well for him, or at least not the way he wanted, so he came down to North Carolina, South Carolina, then to Tennessee. He was among the first settlers in this part of the mountains, especially the first settlers with money. He set up a trading post and built a house close to what's now Sevierville and went in with mining, smelting, and sawmill ventures. Hope remembered a lot of the pretty things he and his wife had in their house when her parents took her visiting."

Elaine stopped to peel some shrimp and take a bite of her corn. As people finished eating, many drifted out to the dance floor and the music got louder. A few, Marina, Drew, and her husband, came and sat down with Lindsay's group.

"Elaine has Hope Foute's other diaries," said Lewis. "She was just telling us about them."

Elaine wiped her hands on one of the pile of napkins and shook their hands. "I remember you," she said to Drew. "Good to see you again."

Drew apologized for the way Claire had treated Elaine. Lindsay almost said something, but she felt John's arm tighten around her waist as he pulled her and her chair closer to him. Lewis looked impassive, under hooded eyes. She'd seen that look before—at faculty meetings. Elaine took a drink of tea and continued her story.

"When Warfield came down, he brought several families with him, not only from Pennsylvania, but also from Ohio and North and South Carolina—handpicked families who could build the kind of community he had a vision for." She stopped and grinned at Lindsay. "This is one of the best parts."

Lindsay smiled back, willing herself not to look at Drew and her husband, thankful for the dim light.

"I can't wait."

"Yes, dear. You have our attention," Phil said. Elaine opened her mouth to speak.

"Did you get a good buy on the diaries?" asked Eric Van Horne, picking one up and looking through it. "You really need to keep these wrapped."

John had a hand on Lindsay's shoulder, and she felt him squeeze. But the warning didn't work. Lindsay, on bad days, and this was a very bad day, believed in using negative reinforcement to control rude behavior.

"Oh, I meant to tell you, Drew, the Tidwells have had some good luck. One of the documents missing from their aunt's collection has been identified as a letter from Alexis de Tocqueville's visit to Tennessee, describing his illness."

Lindsay wished she had a camera at that moment. The reaction was brief, only a second. But the Van Hornes were clearly stunned. *So,* thought Lindsay, *try to sell something like that now—or even show it to anyone.*

Lewis looked at her from under a pair of knitted eyebrows. But she could tell he was amused. Lindsay had thought Jarman was probably clueless about what was going on, but he appeared not to be in the dark, the way he looked at the Van Hornes' faces. When Lewis had asked the reservists to keep an eye on her, he must have explained to Jarman parts of what was going on.

"So . . ." Drew cleared her throat. "So, there were documents, then?"

"Yes, It turns out that Miss Tidwell may have hidden a photo album of her documents among her things." Lindsay was not above lying to people she believed to be murderers.

"That was smart of her," said Drew.

"But I apologize, Elaine. Please, go on with the story. You have me on pins and needles." Lindsay squeezed John's leg, and he squeezed her shoulder again—private communication. She was glad he was here.

Elaine looked over at Lindsay and cocked an eyebrow and gave her a hint of a smile before she continued.

"Two families in the Warfield party are of particular interest. One is a farmer and lay preacher named Garrett Redmond and his wife, Prudence, from Ohio. The Redmonds were to have three daughters, Faith, Hope, and Charity, the oldest of whom was Charity."

Phil McBride clapped his hands. "Beautiful. And who is the other family?"

This time Eric Van Horne, a man Lindsay guessed liked to be the center of attention, kept quiet.

"A man from North Carolina by the name of Brodie MacIntyre, his wife, Erlina . . ." She paused dramatically. "And their daughter Eda Mae."

"Elaine," said Lindsay, "you found them."

"I found historical documents, but you found Cherry—literally."

"Have you read both diaries?" asked Marina.

"On the way to the airport and on the airplane. Fortunately, Hope Foute had very neat handwriting, and it's easy reading."

"How do the Warfield, Redmond, and MacIntyre families connect to the site?" asked Lindsay. "And do you know who wrote the loft poems?"

"Yes, I know who wrote the loft poems."

Chapter 38

"ARE WE GOING to have to drag this out of you a line at a time?" Phil McBride asked his wife.

"Just enjoying my dramatic pauses. The MacIntyres and the Redmonds homesteaded land in the cove. Garrett Redmond and his wife built the first pen of our log house in 1775. The parents slept downstairs, and the three girls slept together up in the loft. Charity and Faith on each side, Hope in the middle. Both the Redmonds could read and write, and they taught their daughters. They wanted them to be able to read the Bible. On bright nights, when the moon was at an angle to shine in the window, Faith liked to take a nail and scratch poems on the floor on her side of the bed."

"So, Faith Redmond wrote the poems," whispered Lindsay. Elaine nodded.

"Please, honey, don't wait for an invitation," said McBride. "We've been waiting to hear about this."

"The Redmond household was a happy one. Hope stayed mostly around her mother or Cherry. Cherry Belle, as her father called her, was petite and pretty like her mother . . . and outgoing. She apparently loved the mountains and streams and was fearless in the woods. She would sometimes take Hope with her berry hunting. Cherry preferred to go off walking in the woods and watch wildlife rather than help her mother."

"Ah," said Lindsay. *"'Cherry gone a looking, not at home a cooking.'"*

"We got that wrong," said Marina. "We thought the poem was talking about a love interest for her."

"Don't jump ahead." Elaine grinned. "Faith was left to do the chores, and she resented it. Unfortunately, according to Hope's diary, *'Faith bore more a likeness in complexion and figure to our ruddy robust father than our fair delicate mother.'"*

"Oh, no," said Marina, "homely, and forced to do the chores."

"Yes, and that plays a part in what eventually transpires. From the time Charity was a little girl, she had made trips with her father to the Warfield trading post for supplies. Sheldon Warfield had an only son named Nathan who clerked for him. Nathan was just three years older than Charity, and over the years of seeing each other, he and Charity fell in love.

"Then, in about 1782, a tragedy occurred. The girls' parents had a fatal accident while visiting neighbors deep in the cove. When her parents died, Charity and Nathan married and he went to live on the farmstead with her and her sisters. Hope was only five at the time, Faith was twelve, Charity was sixteen, and Nathan Warfield was nineteen. Now, Charity and Nathan slept downstairs and Hope and Faith slept upstairs."

"Where were the parents buried?" asked Lewis. "There's only one grave in the farmstead cemetery."

"There's no mention of that," said Elaine. "There could have been another church with a cemetery somewhere in the cove."

"Then, is Nathan Warfield the one buried in our cemetery?" asked Marina.

"Chances are, he is," said Elaine. "Nathan Warfield was a good hunter and provider for Charity and her sisters, by all accounts. On one of his hunting trips he came down with what I believe was appendicitis." She turned to her husband, who sat leaning on the table with his palm propping up his head. "You can look at the symptoms, hon, and see what you think—fever, vomiting, pain in the right side."

"That sounds like a reasonable diagnosis."

"He was brought home by a relatively new friend, a surveyor named William Kinkead who had been hired by the brand-new State of Franklin."

Marina jumped up and whooped. "Yes! We got him here on the premises with his bone-handled knife, hinged compass, and belt buckle with the initials W. K. Not to mention a bullet hole in the head."

"You do!" said Elaine. "You found him, too?"

"Under the first lead coffin," Lewis told her.

"I take it Nathan died?" said Eric Van Horne.

"Yes, and his father, Sheldon Warfield, was devastated. Hope says in the diary that it frightened her the way he carried on at the funeral. His son was not just his son, but his heir to the dynasty he wanted to build. The really sad thing is that Cherry was pregnant, and now she was alone with her two young sisters on a farmstead in the middle of the wilderness."

"Her skeleton indicates she bore a child," Lindsay commented.

One of Mrs. Laurens's daughters came around offering more pie. All of them gladly helped themselves to another piece.

"I love key lime pie," said Elaine. She took several bites before she continued. "I'm going to catch us up on Eda Mae MacIntyre. Her and Faith's families were neighbors in the cove. She and Faith were friends—about the same age. When the surveyor came to the cove, both girls got a crush on him. Eda Mae even sneaked out to see him, telling her parents she was visiting Faith. She swore Faith to secrecy, but wouldn't tell her where she was going."

"'Eda Mae, gone all day, wouldn't say, which a way,"' Phil McBride quoted.

"That's what I figure," agreed Elaine.

"Charity's husband, Nathan, died in the summer. The baby was born in the dead of winter. Eda Mae's mother, Erlina MacIntyre, delivered it—a little boy, and naturally Charity's father-in-law was very happy that he had a new heir. Charity and her sisters were getting along fairly well—the neighbors helped, of course. William Kinkead did some hunting and chopped wood for Charity and the girls. The Indians . . ." Elaine stopped and looked at John.

"You don't mind if I call them Indians, do you?"

"No. Like the man said, I'm just grateful Columbus wasn't looking for Turkey."

Elaine broke up giggling. Jarman had to think for a moment before he broke out laughing. The others laughed out loud, except for Drew and her husband, who only smiled.

They look worried, thought Lindsay. *Good. I hope I worry them.*

"Anyway," continued Elaine. "The Cherokee brought them

dried pumpkin and fur to last through the winter. Hope wrote their names—Catahe and Ewaynah."

Another incident of the kindness of the Indians helping the settlers through the winter, thought Lindsay.

"On one trip, they brought her a doll carved from wood and dressed in leather. It was a happy moment in a very frightening time for her as a five-year-old girl, and she remembered it always. Over fifty years later, during the forced removal of the Indians in the years around 1838, she wrote in her diary that she remembered the kindness of the Indians to her and her sisters when they were little girls, and she and her husband, much to the anger of some of the cove folk, spoke against forcing the Indians to leave. She, her husband, and a few of the other residents of the cove sneaked food to the Indians hiding in the mountains. A little Indian girl touched her heart, she said, and Hope gave her the doll she had kept and treasured all those years. Hope Foute seemed like a very nice lady."

"What happened to Charity?" asked Marina.

"According to her diary, Hope didn't know. Charity just disappeared. Hope remembered the day Charity's baby died. That was in March. Charity's father-in-law, Sheldon Warfield, came to see to things. The death of the baby, his last living heir, devastated him all over again. She remembers there was a lot of commotion, with lots of people around for a while, but after the baby died, and Mr. Warfield and the other people came, she never saw Charity or William Kinkead again. Some folks thought they left together.

"According to what she wrote years later, she asked the adults where Charity was, but she was just a child and no one would tell her anything. Faith was apparently just as upset as she was and couldn't tell her anything, either. Hope didn't remember much more about that time. She wrote that she had nightmares and thought she saw a ghost running in the woods outside her window in a flowing white dress. She was only seven at the time and was terrified. Faith carried her to the MacIntyres, who took both of them in and raised them."

"That's not the end, is it?" asked Jarman. "After all that?"

"Most of that was in the first diary. In the second diary, as we know, she writes about the Gallowses and their neighbors. In the third diary she writes about her sister's death, and about her life with her husband. I tell you, you get a span of a whole lifetime reading the diaries. I really cried when I read some of the passages. She writes better than I tell it."

"Did she write any more about what happened to her sister Charity?" asked Lindsay.

"Not exactly. If anyone knew, no one ever told her. But there was a curious entry. Let me read it." She pulled a pair of white gloves from her purse and opened the diary.

"'Faith is fading from me, going to God. I think she'll be happy in his bosom. She found no serenity here on earth, except, bless their souls, in my children, their children, and their children.'" Elaine turned the page. "'In the end, she lay in the pillows like she was lying in clouds, like an angel with skin as thin and pale as the skin of a pearl onion. She told Robert and Melanie' . . . Those were her great grandchildren," said Elaine, "' . . . to never give in to envy and covetousness.'

"'When she and I were alone in the room, I thought peace would come like a dove, but it did not. She looked at me with her clouded blind eyes—seeing with clarity something, I was sure. *"Forgive me, Hope and Charity. I didn't know, I didn't know, I didn't know . . . poor Eda Mae . . .'"*

"'I'd not heard Eda Mae's name for many a year. Eda Mae . . . When we lived with her family, an evil came upon her, provoking her to awaken in the night screaming. Her poor parents would rush up the loft steps to Eda Mae's bed and shake her awake. In the morning her face would be swollen and red. Once I saw the mark of a hand, like the devil's thumb on her smooth plump jaw. At first, Eda Mae's good people thought we were to blame . . . but the same evil happened when she stayed with a neighbor. They brought her back and told her parents to keep her away from them, she was done possessed of the devil. Cruel people."

"'Now after all these years, I'm reminded of her. *"Please,"* my sister said to me, *'"Will God forgive me and Eda Mae? We didn't understand . . . but we should have . . ."* She passed before I could tell her God always forgives. I didn't ponder what it meant. I reckoned to find out soon enough.'"

"That's full of possibilities," said Marina. "What do you think, Lindsay?"

Lindsay hesitated a long moment, aware that all eyes were on her.

"Guilt, it sounds like," said Phil McBride. "Deep guilt."

"Was it Faith really slapping Eda Mae, you think?" Marina mashed her fork on the graham-cracker pie crust, bringing the crumbs to her mouth.

"No," said Lindsay, "Eda Mae was doing it to herself. Like Phil said, it's all about guilt." Her gaze rested on Drew and her husband.

"How do you know she was doing it to herself?" asked Jarman.

"It happened when she was at home with only her parents. It happened when she slept with Faith and Hope, and it happened when she stayed with neighbors. The only person present at all those times was Eda Mae herself. And there is the evidence of the thumb print on the jaw. If it were done by someone else, the thumb print would most likely be on the cheek."

"Could guilt really make a person act like that?" asked Marina.

Phil McBride nodded. "Guilt can manifest itself in a host of physical and psychological ways."

"What do you think she did to feel that guilty about?" asked Marina.

"Eda Mae and Faith caused Charity's death," said Lindsay. "I don't think they meant to. They were only fourteen. Even though girls married at that age then, fourteen is still fourteen."

"You'll have to spell it out for me," said Jarman. "I'm purely an empiricist. If I can't measure it, I don't know it."

"Faith and Eda Mae had a crush on William Kinkead the surveyor. He may have had a thing for Charity, or he may have just been helping a friend's widow through the winter. The two teenage girls became jealous, especially Eda Mae, who had apparently sneaked off with him a time or two. They may have put some spiteful bug in Sheldon Warfield's ear that made him believe that Charity and William Kinkead had killed his son, Nathan, perhaps poisoned him, so they could be together. Or they could have confided their spite in someone else who told Warfield. Anyway, there are poisonous plants all around the place here. And Nathan's symptoms of appendicitis could have been construed as a poisoning. Being the self-centered egomaniac he was, Sheldon Warfield didn't see two silly, jealous fourteen-year-olds. He could only see his own lost dynasty. He got even. He was the rich guy. He was from Pennsylvania, a more urban and longer-settled place at the time. The lead coffins probably represent his family's burial practices."

"Those poor little girls," said Elaine. "I'm sure they didn't have any idea he would react that way. They probably somehow saw or found out what he had done, but for some reason couldn't stop it or tell anyone."

"Other people knew, too," said Lindsay. "Perhaps men who worked for Sheldon Warfield. That lead coffin weighs thirteen hundred pounds. It took several men, horses or oxen, and a wagon to move it. They could have been sworn to secrecy, but word would get out. That's why the place had such a mysterious reputation for being evil, but no one could put a finger on what it was—they'd talk about evil, but not the specific act of it."

"That's a big leap—saying the father killed Charity and the surveyor," said Eric. "It's a leap to say the girls said those things."

"Yes, it is," agreed Lindsay. "But something like that happened. If Sheldon Warfield did it, it would've taken something that important to him to make him murderous."

"He went back to Pennsylvania soon after," said Elaine. "I think you're right. I think he killed Charity and William Kinkead."

"We've accounted for all of the loft poems," said Lewis, "except one." He paused a moment and put a hand to his head. "'*Not my sin, the hell he's in.*' What about that?"

"Probably refers to Sheldon Warfield," said McBride. "Faith felt guilty, but tried to deny it by saying if Warfield goes to hell, it's not her fault."

"We may never know," said Lindsay. "But it all sounds reasonable." She looked out over the dark Smokies. *Oh, God,* she thought, and shifted her gaze to McBride, who looked her in the eyes.

"You all right, hon?" Elaine asked her husband. "You look kind of pale."

"Been sitting here a while. I think I'll go use one of those porta-johns." Lindsay watched him go not to the portable toilets, but into the crowd.

The music was going strong, and people were dancing and having fun. Lindsay wished she could, too. She stood up and stretched.

"I think I'll turn in."

"You look as exhausted as I feel," Elaine said. "I'm going to find Phil, and we're heading out."

"I'll give you a call tomorrow," Lindsay promised.

"I think we need to be heading back to the motel, dear," Eric told Drew.

"I agree. See you tomorrow, guys." Drew waved as she and her husband left.

Jarman walked with Marina over to the dancing.

"Let's go to bed," said John. "I know you're tired." He brushed a strand of hair out of Lindsay's eyes.

"I'll go to the house with you," said Lewis. "I'm tired, and tomorrow's a long day."

They walked back to the house silently. When they got to the bridge, out of earshot of everyone, Lewis turned to Lindsay.

"What passed between you and McBride. Where did he go?"

"Probably to the sheriff to tell him to get an exhumation order for Mary Susan Tidwell's body."

Chapter 39

LEWIS STOPPED AND stared at Lindsay openmouthed.

"Phil McBride is asking the sheriff to exhume the Tidwell woman? Did I fall asleep and miss an entire conversation?"

"No, you didn't. Phil McBride and I possess information that you don't. Mary Susan Tidwell suffered from hypotension—low blood pressure. Anything given to her of a toxic nature that would further lower her blood pressure would bring on death—her heart would just stop."

"This is the woman whose death you believe started all this?" John asked.

Lindsay nodded, looking over the side at the moonlit creek overgrown with green flora, wild, beautiful, inhabited by snakes.

"Yes, I believe everything started as a result of her death and the theft of her documents. When we were discussing what Nathan Warfield's father might have thought about his son's death, I remarked that there are poisons all around, and it hit Phil and me at the same time. Look around at the woods. Rhododendron, mountain laurel—the woods are thick with them."

"And they're poisonous?" asked Lewis.

"Several species contain a toxin called grayanotoxin, which, among other things, lowers blood pressure. Tea can be made from laurel leaves. Miss Tidwell drank green tea daily, maybe several times a day, for her health. Someone could have made tea from laurel leaves for her instead."

"So, you think Drew did murder her?" Lewis asked.

"There's enough reason for suspicion to test her body for the presence of grayanotoxin or other poisons."

"And what's her motive?" John asked.

"Drew and her husband both have reputations to keep. If they stole her papers and she knew it, she would have to be killed in order to protect their reputations. When your professional reputation depends on your integrity, you can't afford to be accused of something as serious as theft."

"But she is accused, by the relatives," said Lewis.

"Relatives squabbling over an estate that they don't know for sure even exists is different from having the owner herself accuse you. Miss Tidwell had a good reputation of her own for collecting valuable things. People around here would believe her if she said something was stolen."

"You said a record of her documents has been found," said Lewis.

"I lied. I wanted to scare them."

"Lindsay . . . you lied?"

Lindsay looked up from the flowing creek to Lewis's face."Yes, I lied."

"They could be innocent," said Lewis.

"Then that won't scare them." The three of them continued on across the bridge and up to the house.

"This is where you stay?" John stood in the middle of Lindsay's spartan room.

"These are really pretty good accommodations compared to some of the digs I've been on. The only problem was not having a door. Even that wouldn't have been a problem had I not felt so vulnerable."

"I imagine that was the point. Unlike Lewis, I'm not inclined to believe the Van Hornes are innocent."

"Me neither, but I suppose I need to keep an open mind. I don't like her husband, and I think that might be coloring my viewpoint a little." She put her arms around John. "I meant to thank you for Luke. I hate it he's had to watch over me all the time."

"I doubt he's done it all the time, but he needed a break. I try to rotate breaks for my crew when we're doing some of the intense work we do. I have a good record for crew safety, and I like to keep it that way." He wrapped his arms around her. "Let's get a good night's sleep. Tomorrow we're going home."

"John, I don't like keeping you away from your job."

"You're not," he interrupted. "A component of the aquarium is a cylindrical tunnel." He put the tips of his fingers together, making a circle with his hands, and smiled as though the thought of the tunnel gave him such pleasure. "The tunnel will wind through part of the aquarium so that visitors can walk among the fish."

"You mean they can look up and see fish swimming over them?"

"Yes, over them, around them. The materials for the tunnel aren't ready yet, so I've got some free time."

"In that case I'm glad you're here. But . . ."

"Lindsay, let the authorities finish this. You don't have to solve everything."

The party at the site was still going strong. She could hear the music drifting up through her window. "You're right. The authorities will have to make the airtight case that Lewis wants."

"What's this?" John picked up a large envelope and handed it to her.

"I don't know." She opened the flap and pulled out what at first looked like a charcoal drawing. It was Mrs. Laurens's rubbing of the piece of eight. "She had it after all."

"She had what?"

Lindsay explained about finding the Spanish coin in Gentry's pocket, and about Mrs. Laurens's rubbing of the treasure coin when she was in Miss Tidwell's third-grade class.

"You searched his pockets?"

That's not all I searched, thought Lindsay—still feeling ashamed of herself every time she thought about invading her co-workers' privacy, but still wishing she could search their cars.

"Yes, I searched his pockets."

"Is it the same coin?"

"It's the same type of coin. They're both pieces of eight." Lindsay took the rubbing from under her mattress, stretched out on her bed, and compared the two. "When the Spanish minted this kind of coins, they weren't particularly careful about doing a perfect job. The insignias were often off center, the coins weren't necessarily round, often misshapen, and flaws were not uncommon. So, theoretically, each coin could be different."

John stretched out beside her and examined the two rubbings—actually four. Mrs. Laurens had done both sides of the coin also.

"What do you think?" Lindsay asked John.

"Not a lot of detail." John put his arm around her waist and pulled her close in beside him.

"But they are offset the same amount, and the design is in the same direction."

"A magnifying glass might uncover some significant detail."

"I think they are the same. If they are the same coin, that means Mike Gentry somehow got it directly or indirectly from Miss Tidwell, possibly after her death—possibly as a result of her death."

Lindsay put the two rubbings in the envelope and tucked them under her mattress. "I have some Dr Peppers in the ice chest. Want one?"

John nodded, and she took out two cans and lay back down beside him. He opened the can with a pop and drank several swallows.

"I love you." He brushed several strands of wayward hair out of her face. "I know I've never said it."

"You've shown it in many ways." Lindsay took his face in her hands and kissed him. "I love you, too. And I'm sorry that I get into so much trouble."

"You do that." He sighed. "I like your independence, but at the same time I'd like it if you did what I told you to do."

"Not much of a chance there."

"I know. Dad likes you a lot. So does my sister."

"How about your kids, do they like me?"

"My kids don't even like me much these days. I can hardly get Jason to talk to me, he just grunts and mumbles. I tell you, whoever started the notion that Indians only speak in grunts must have come across teenagers when they landed."

"I think that characteristic of teenage boys is a constant across all ethnic groups."

"Actually, both Jason and Shelly do like you. You aren't around very much, and you treat them like adults when you are. Besides, they like it that you get into more trouble than they do."

Lindsay laughed and kissed him again.

Lindsay lay with her back against John's chest, his arm around her waist, feeling the rhythm of his breathing, remembering what it's like to feel safe. The thing that she wanted, though, was to feel safe when she was alone. Fear had overtaken her life, and she wanted to rule it again. Unless she herself solved this, she might never get back her feeling of security and independence.

Then, think, her inner self told her. *Think.*

First, what is this about?

Miss Tidwell's stolen documents.

More than that.

Yes, more than that. Her death.

That's the result. What is the wellspring of all the violent behavior? What is going on? What do you know?

It has something to do with forgery—I think. At least that's a good possibility. Why else steal old paper and ledgers, worthless to anyone other than a forger? *Was* it worthless to anyone other than a forger? Was it stolen? But also, it's about collectible historical documents. The two could go hand in hand.

Lindsay changed her position, causing John to move in his sleep. Ideas darted in and out of her brain like sparks of electricity. What stuck was the notion of forgery and the information Parker had sent.

The personality characteristics could fit anyone, she told herself.

Then think about what is needed to do the job.

Knowledge and ability. Drew had the knowledge—she could also supply the provenance. Easy for a historical archaeologist. So could her husband, a lawyer and a collector.

What was it she read in the book Parker sent? One way of falsifying a document's pedigree is to find a library copy of a little-known auction catalog and give it a new page showing the forged document up for auction, listing the document's bona fides. In other words, apply forging talents to the catalog itself, then refer to the library's copy in the authentication papers.

That would take ability with graphics, or an artist, or a computer expert.

What catches a forger?

Not knowing internal evidence about—paper, ink, anything testable connected with the document. That can be learned. Lindsay knew a little herself after reading one book. Drew, her husband, or anyone else could learn just as easily.

What else catches a forger?

Not knowing about external evidence of a document. Not knowing history. Not knowing about the person who was supposed to have written the document. Drew could handle that, too.

The final possible trap for a forger is wrong paleographic evidence—understanding handwriting. That means the historical styles of writing and the specific writing of an individual. Possessing authentic historical documents would go a long way toward providing that information. And what did Parker say? One method of forgery is to add a little something to the bottom of an authentic document that would make it more valuable.

How much money would forged documents be worth? Potentially a lot. Even letters of minor historical players can fetch quite a sum.

One more thing is needed. A person with artistic ability.

What was clear to Lindsay was that a small group of people with certain abilities and knowledge could produce documents that would be very hard to detect—especially if one of the group authenticated documents. The group could put a document into the market . . . then Drew could come along to authenticate it. No one would need know the two were connected. She could even expose documents as a forgery on occasion to enhance her reputation. This explanation was working, and there was potentially enough money involved to make murder worth risking.

You need proof.

"Yes, proof," she whispered. "Where am I going to get that?"

Find the other person, the artist.

Where?

A workman is known by his tools.

Lindsay's inner voice could be very annoying. She fell asleep.

There was no problem in the morning getting the bathroom. With the site mostly finished, most everyone was sleeping in. Lindsay and John were down for breakfast before anyone, but Lewis was up.

"I suppose we should go and eat at the site," said Lindsay as John pulled her toward the dining room.

"No, I asked Mrs. Laurens to make you something special."

"You didn't! John, she has enough to cook without making a special dish for me."

"Now, Lindsay, I didn't mind. It's something me and Jimmy like, too. I thought we'd sit down and eat it with you."

Mr. Laurens came in carrying a huge platter of fried mush. One of Lindsay's all-time favorite foods.

"You did say you made some for you, too," said Lindsay, laughing at the size of the platter.

"What've you made this morning?" asked Lewis, sitting down beside Lindsay.

"Ambrosia," answered Lindsay.

"Fried mush," answered John. "Fried, boiled cornmeal."

"Boiled cornmeal?" said Lewis. "That's it, cornmeal and water?"

"You got it," answered John. "Lindsay loves the stuff."

"It sets overnight," said Mrs. Laurens. "In the morning, you slice it, fry it up, and serve it with oleo."

"It's a Kentucky thing," said Lindsay, buttering a slice. "This is great, Mrs. Laurens."

"You know, it isn't bad," said Lewis.

After stuffing herself to the point of embarrassment, Lindsay walked down to the site with John and Lewis.

"It looks like the truck is here to take the bones back to campus. I've called Carolyn. She's getting ready to receive them."

"What about the lead coffins?" asked Lindsay.

"I've decided to re-bury them here where they were excavated. They're too heavy to haul around the country."

There were far fewer people at the site. Lindsay guessed that many were still in bed. In a way, she was relieved to be going home—home to her own research, her own house, her horse, her friends. Perhaps that was the key to her getting well and freeing her mind of ghosts. Go home to a safe, familiar environment.

Lindsay made her way to her excavation tent to pack up TPB2—the bones of William Kinkead. Lewis brought in some old newspaper to stuff around the boxes. John came in carrying three cartons of orange juice.

"I thought you might need more nutrition than just cornmeal." He handed one to Lindsay and one to Lewis.

Lindsay opened hers and drank several swallows. "Thanks."

"Need any help?" asked John.

"I've just got to pack these bones. I think Lewis has already loaded TPB1 and CB1."

"Don't you call them by their names?" asked John. "Seems to me you know these guys."

Lindsay took a newspaper off the stack and started to stuff it in the space between one of the smaller boxes inside the larger packing box. She stopped, stark still, staring at the pictures on the front page.

"Lindsay? Lindsay . . . ," said John.

"Lindsay?" said Lewis.

They both sounded far off.

John's father was right. Her brain was working right, she was just reading it wrong. She was right. Ghosts are the unfinished business of the living.

"Oh, no. Oh, no. Oh, no."

She felt herself crumbling to the floor, plunged into deep grief, and horrific guilt.

"Oh, God."

Tears streamed down her face, and her body was racked with sobs.

"I'm so sorry."

"Lindsay!" yelled John. "What is it? What are you sorry about?"

"Where are you, Lindsay?" asked Lewis.

"I'm so sorry."

She felt herself lifted onto a chair. She heard John and Lewis beseeching her, but she couldn't stop crying. She remembered everything, and she had unfinished business to take care of.

Chapter 40

THERE WAS NOTHING John or Lewis could do but wait until Lindsay stopped crying. John took the newspaper from her hand, and he and Lewis looked at the front page.

"It must have something to do with this story," she heard Lewis say.

The headline was one Lindsay had seen several days earlier, but she hadn't seen the photographs that went with it. She tried to think back. Was Claire already dead when the story appeared? She couldn't remember.

If I had read the story and seen the pictures, maybe I would have known then what I know now. If I could have told someone then—everyone—maybe Claire would still be alive. Would knowing about the pictures really have made a difference? Maybe. Maybe they would have chosen to run and not kill again. Or maybe not. No way to know now.

Lindsay stopped crying and tried to breathe evenly under the heavy guilt.

"Can you tell us about it?" asked Lewis.

He and John sat down facing her. She took a breath.

"Nigel Boyd at the University of Tennessee identified these two lost hikers," she said, touching and rubbing the pictures with her fingers. "They're the ghosts I've been seeing—the one in the mirror, on the porch, and again in the house."

"You've been seeing ghosts?" said Lewis. "I didn't think you believed in ghosts."

"I believe in memories and unfinished business." She looked at John. "Your father told me that the hallucinations might be my brain sorting things out. He was right. It was trying to tell me something, and I couldn't understand."

"Did they have something to do with what happened to you?" asked John.

"They tried to save me. When I was chased into the woods by the two men who forced me off the road, I tripped on some barbed wire and they caught me. I fought them off and escaped again, and ran deeper into the woods. They caught me again. I screamed for help, hoping someone would hear me. The hikers, a man and a woman, did. I remember being so relieved.

"The guy fought one attacker off and seemed to knock him unconscious. The woman and I tried to overcome the other one, but he shot her in the chest. I put my hands over the wound to keep the air from escaping her lungs. Her companion ran to her, but the attacker he had fought off recovered too quickly and hit him hard in the back of the head with a piece of dead tree limb. The other one must have shot at me, and I suppose the bullet creased my skull. I don't remember.

"When I came to, I was buried with the two bodies. I was on top with my face in the crook of an arm. The arrangement of limbs created a space for me to breathe. That's why I didn't suffocate. When I clawed my way out, they . . ."

Her eyes filled with tears. She paused for several moments.

"They were dead. They tried to save me and died for it. I lived, and they died."

"Lindsay, it wasn't in the least your fault." John's voice was so gentle. *He deserves better than someone who is always getting into dire trouble,* she thought.

"He's right," said Lewis. "The men who did it are responsible, not you."

"I thought I was going crazy, seeing those phantom faces." She shook her head. "I owe them a debt. I have to try to find their killers."

"Now that you remember, you can tell the authorities what happened. That is the extent of your debt," said John.

Lindsay took the paper from John's hand.

"Are you sure you want to read that?" he asked.

"Yes."

She read the article out loud. She was disappointed it didn't have much forensic information in it, but news articles rarely do. There was one paragraph, however, relating how Nigel had made the identification, that gave her enough information to be reasonably sure who one of the killers was and how to prove it.

"I'll call Sheriff Ramsey and the sheriff at Mac's Crossing and tell them what I remember."

"That's the best thing," said John. "Tell them what you know, and let them handle it. It's time to put it behind you and go home."

Most of the remainder of that day the site crew watched and helped the science crew take down and pack up their tents and equipment. Drew and her husband weren't there. Lindsay overheard Sharon and her husband telling Adam that the Van Hornes' cars were gone when they left the motel to come to the site that morning. So they skipped out. Rather incriminating.

Lindsay watched the trucks pull out, leaving the site as bare as before they came. And she watched the archaeology crew with a cold, objective suspicion, wondering if any of them was a member of the gang of forgers she believed to exist. Sharon Kirkwood and her husband were possibilities. Bill Kirkwood was very good with a camera and a computer—two talents a good forger needs. And why was his vacation so long? How long had he been here? Three weeks? Sharon's penmanship on the site forms was like an engineer's—very neat and uniform.

Joel was a possibility. He was so meticulous at everything he did. Erin said he was an artist. Marina and Erin were possibilities, both artists. Maybe the others had hidden talents. For that matter, Elaine McBride was artistic. But a good forger had to be more than artistic. He . . . or she . . . would have to be an accomplished artist. And there was Claire. Perhaps she had been in with the forgers, too, and there was a falling-out among thieves.

Ideas occurred to her as she watched the crew, ideas she should have thought of before if her brain had been working on all cylinders. It was working again now. Remembering about the hikers had removed that smothering fog from her mind and freed up brain cells for other work.

For instance, why had Drew kept Miss Tidwell out all day doing things that had already been done during the survey? Because, Lindsay answered herself, to allow someone all-day access alone in Miss Tidwell's house to look for the documents and anything else worth stealing.

It would be so easy to come in the back way to her house, back up a truck or car to load anything heavy, and not be seen by passersby or neighbors. Drew probably knew the security code of the alarm system. Miss Tidwell had no reason to suspect fellow scholars of anything so heinous as murder.

Could Erin have been the one in the house, looking for the thing that would make her famous? Or, to get money to get away from her parents? Surely not. Her mother wasn't that bad, but perhaps Erin's greed was. That explanation left a bad taste in her mouth. She liked Erin. Lindsay always preferred that her criminals be someone she didn't like. But she'd been fooled in that respect before.

Mike Gentry had been in the house. She was sure of that. Just as she was sure that he stole Miss Tidwell's coin. She was also sure the nurse, Mary Carp, lied to Luke. But Lindsay no longer worried about Nurse Carp. The sheriff at Mac's Crossing would deal with her.

"Okay, gang," said Lewis. "Can I have your attention?"

"We going to be digging today?" asked Powell. "He looked at his watch. It's really too late for that."

"I'm kind of beat," said Kelsey.

"Do you know where Drew is?" asked Byron.

Lewis didn't answer any of their questions. He looked over their faces a moment. Lindsay wondered if he was contemplating them as suspects or simply feeling sympathy for a crew who were about to get some sad news.

"Claire Burke was found dead in her automobile. She has been murdered."

Lindsay watched their faces. Their mouths fell open. Everyone was surprised . . . or seemed to be. Bill found his voice first.

"What happened? How? Why, for heaven's sake?"

"I don't have any details, but I think it would be fitting to have a moment of silence here at the site in her memory. I'm aware there were issues with Claire and the way she directed the site. But that's over now."

After the moment of silence, they looked at one another in bewilderment.

"What happens to the site now?" asked Byron. "Claire's gone, Drew's AWOL. What the hell's going on around here? Claire was murdered, you say? Someone killed her?" It was as if what Lewis had told them just now sank in with Byron.

"Yes, someone killed her. The authorities are investigating. I'm sure they'll want to speak with each of you. But don't be alarmed in any way. They just have to gather as much information as they can about Claire's last days. As for the site, I've been in touch with the state archaeologist, and I'm taking over the remainder of the excavation. Adam, you are the new site director. I hope that sits well with everyone."

"Work's for me," said Powell.

"This evening we all need to sit down and discuss how to finish up here. I know there were issues about the excavation, and we need to iron those out so we can proceed. This is a good dig. Good things have happened here, too. The antique air project is significant, and we all can get articles from what we've done here."

"Did Drew have anything to do with Claire's . . . with Claire?" asked Kelsey.

"I don't want to speculate," said Lewis. "I know this has to be preying on your minds, but let the authorities handle it."

"It's some coincidence that she left just as Claire was found murdered," said Dillon. He put a hand on his brother's shoulder as if for comfort.

"Did she kill my aunt?" asked Erin.

Lewis looked to Lindsay. She wished he hadn't, for everyone looked her way for an answer.

"Erin, have you talked with your parents today?"

"No. Why?" Erin looked at her suspiciously. "What's happened?"

Might as well tell some of the truth, Lindsay thought. *They all need some kind of debriefing after news like this.*

"Sheriff Ramsey is going have your aunt's body exhumed and an autopsy preformed at the request of Dr. McBride."

Sharon gave a sharp intake of breath. "Oh, my God. Did Drew really . . .?"

"I don't know," said Lindsay. "There have just been new developments. I know all of you have questions. I do, too, and so does Lewis. None of us have many answers. When the authorities ask you questions about Claire or anything else, try to remember everything you can that seems even remotely suspicious. That's the best way you can help."

"We can't help but speculate," said Joel. "I mean, like Byron said . . . Claire murdered, Drew skipped out, our survey informant, Miss Tidwell, is being exhumed. Things like this just don't happen in real life."

"I know you need answers," repeated Lindsay. *Jump in any time, Lewis,* she thought. "Neither Lewis nor I have any, right now."

"Does anyone suspect us?" asked Kelsey.

"Not as far as I know. The sheriff will question all of us about Claire, including me, Dr. Lewis, and the Laurenses."

"Who was the last person to see her alive?" asked Dillon.

"I suppose I was," said Lindsay.

"But that doesn't mean anything," said Erin. "Does it?"

"Of course not," said Marina. "Any of us could have been the last person to see her."

"Let's get things back on track with the site and take all this other . . ." Adam groped for the right words and failed. "Let's just do the best we can with the situation. Lewis is right. We need to discuss how to proceed with the site. I know we have some money to do some extra excavation, like in the outhouse, for example, and maybe get Marina some help in cataloging the artifacts."

"Now there's an idea," agreed Marina.

They trooped back to the house, mostly in silence. Occasionally someone exclaimed their disbelief. Mrs. Laurens had an early dinner on the table when they arrived.

"I thought some food would do you all some good," she said. "I was real sorry to hear about Claire. It's so sad when the young die."

Lindsay wasn't particularly hungry. Something was nagging at her. What she really wanted to do was sit quietly and think.

Luke was leaving after dinner. She walked outside with John to see him off.

"Thanks, Luke. You've been a great friend. Really going above and beyond." She leaned through the window and kissed him on the cheek.

"You'll be sure to tell Bobbie what a great, sensitive guy I am, won't you?"

"I certainly will."

Lindsay felt safer somehow, now that Drew was gone and Miss Tidwell was being exhumed. Regaining her full memory was like finding an old friend—her self-confidence.

When Luke was gone, she and John joined the others in the living room. John actually seemed to find discussing the site interesting. John, an archaeologist—she smiled at the thought.

"Is it true you're leaving?" asked Marina.

"What?" Lindsay hadn't been listening.

"John said you're leaving."

"Probably. My work left with the skeletons. After the conservators do their work, I need to analyze the bones again."

"I wish you would stay," said Adam.

"I appreciate your wanting me to. I'll think about it." She stood and stretched. "I'm going to turn in early. This has been kind of an exhausting week."

"Certainly emotionally exhausting," said Sharon. "I think Bill and I are going back to our motel. Bill's going to have to go back to work, so I'm moving back here in a couple of days. I hope that's all right."

"Sure," said Kelsey. "You can room with us again, or in Lindsay's room. Is that okay with you, Lindsay?"

"Fine. It's a huge room, and I'm not sure I'll be in it."

Lindsay, John, and Lewis sat on the floor in Lindsay's room drinking Lindsay's Dr Peppers, which it turned out was Lewis's favorite soft drink, too.

"How about you?" Lindsay asked Lewis. "When are you leaving?"

"I don't know. I feel like now I've stuck my hand in a tar baby. Can't seem to let it go. Probably when I see things are going smoothly and we get some new folks in, I'll leave it to them. Adam seems to think that some of the people Claire ran off will be willing to return."

"Claire sometimes seems not to have left us," said Lindsay.

"When did you last see her?" asked Lewis.

"After the party. After the fire scare. She was already in bed."

"Why do you think she ran out in the middle of the night? Did you hear anything?"

Lindsay hesitated a moment. Why would she get up in the middle of the night and leave? Did Claire just wake up and decide to go somewhere? It didn't make sense. Then it hit her.

"No, I didn't see Claire then. I thought it was Claire, but I never saw her face, just a form, and the rising and falling of the covers. It could have been anyone."

"What do you mean?" asked Lewis.

"I mean, the fire was not a protest about our digging up the coffins. The whole protest thing was a sham. The only purpose of the fire was to cause a commotion to get everyone out of the house, so they could get Claire. She wasn't part of the party, and she was the only one upstairs. In all the confusion of running to the fire, someone took Claire."

"But didn't Kelsey and Powell see her leave?" asked Lewis.

"No, like me, they thought they did. They saw her car leave. It was dark, 3:00 A.M. Whatever happened to Claire was premeditated. Someone planned to do away with her."

"Who was in Claire's bed?" asked John.

"Whoever is in it with Drew and her husband."

"You believe strongly then that Drew is guilty?" asked Lewis. "And there is another guilty party still here?"

"I don't have proof of Drew's guilt, but I'll get it. And I don't know who else is involved, but I'll find out."

"No," said John. "No, you won't. We are going home tomorrow."

"I need to solve this."

"Fine. You didn't have to be on that Spanish galleon five hundred years ago to solve that murder. You don't have to be here to solve this one. Just think it through back home."

Lindsay had never seen John so determined. She wondered if just once she should give in. When he was on a job, which, fortunately, was a lot these days, he was away from his kids. Now that he had a moment of free time, he was still away from his kids, here with her, trying to keep her safe. Maybe that could be a gift to him—peace of mind.

She put her hand over his. "Sure, we'll go home tomorrow."

He flipped his hand over and grabbed hers and squeezed it. From the look in his eyes, Lindsay saw that her agreement meant a lot to him. Perhaps he was right, perhaps she did have enough information, and all she needed to do was put it together. Besides, if the police could find Mike Gentry, they could make him turn over on the others.

Lindsay lay awake again, unable to sleep. John, however, was sleeping peacefully beside her. She slipped out of bed and went to the window, looking out at the empty site. Surprising how accustomed to the lights and tents she had gotten. She hugged herself against the cool air and wondered how the hikers' families were. If knowing what happened made it better or worse for them. When some time had passed, she would have to write them a letter.

As she turned from the window, something occurred to her. The evening of the party—or was it the evening before—she came upstairs and had a vague notion that Claire was coming out of Lewis's room while he was downstairs with the others. Maybe there was something she could do before they left in the morning. She slipped back into bed and snuggled her back against John, glad for the warmth.

Chapter 41

IN THE MORNING John and Lewis went to turn in John's rental car and gas up Lindsay's Explorer. Lewis had wanted some time to speak with John alone, Lindsay guessed. He had this idea of building a scale model of the cofferdam in a tank of water, allowing visitors to see through the glass walls of the tank to where the bottom of the dam was anchored to the ocean floor. He'd gotten the notion from John's telling him about the aquarium he was building. Lewis wanted to stock it with live fish and have the bottom littered with scale models of cannons and other artifacts from the ship. Lewis was never at a loss for expensive ideas.

The crew got a late start to the site as they lingered over breakfast talking about the day's work ahead. Despite the uncertainty and bad news, they were on the whole in good spirits. Life went on. But not for the hikers, or Claire, or Mary Susan Tidwell.

With Lewis out of his room, Lindsay went in and searched. If Claire was in his room, it was for a purpose. Maybe it was to hide something. She started with the mattress, looking between the mattress and the box springs, under the box springs—nothing. Nor was there anything hidden behind the one picture on the wall. She shone her flashlight inside the fireplace and up the chimney as far as she could see. Nothing. She examined the closet, even the pockets of Lewis's clothes, in case Claire had stuck something there. They were completely empty. Nothing on the top shelf of the closet, either. The balcony was fragile, but she looked out there anyway, in every place Claire might have secreted something away. She pulled open the drawer to the desk and searched the contents. It contained office supplies, nothing Lindsay could make into a clue. Perhaps she was wrong and Claire hadn't left a clue, evidence, or anything, after all. The last thing Lindsay did was feel the bottom of the desktop from inside the drawer. There it was, taped in place—a three-and-one-half-inch computer disk.

She raced downstairs to where her bags sat in the living room, took out her laptop, and plugged it in. She slipped the disk in the drive and looked at its contents. There were two graphics files labeled "before.psd" and "after.psd." She called up the paint program and opened the first file in the directory—after.psd.

Though her memory was blurry, she knew what she was looking at. When she was in her amnesia state, on the way home from Tennessee to Georgia she had described the picture in detail to John. It was of Lindsay and her fake fiancé, Mark Smith—the man she now knew as Mike Gentry.

More accurately, it wasn't her body, but her face on someone else's body. She had observed even then that whoever's body it was, she was shorter than Lindsay, as were her fingers, seen here threaded through the crook in Smith/Gentry's arm. Lindsay recognized the photograph of her face as one on the Department of Archaeology's Web site.

She called up the before.psd file from the directory. As it came up on the screen, she stared at it in surprise, realizing for the first time that in her heart she hadn't really believed it was one of the crew.

The woman on Mark Smith's arm was Marina. Of course, it made sense. Marina was an excellent artist, had done archaeological illustrations for site reports and a textbook. A workman is known by his—or her—tools. In Marina's workroom upstairs was everything needed to make a forged document. Paper, ink, tea to soak the paper in to make it look old, coffee grounds to supply foxing, an oven to dry it. Not at all incriminating, not even circumstantial enough to have an impact in court—nevertheless, Lindsay could go in there right now and come out with an old-looking document, a forgery.

Lindsay hadn't taken note of it at the time, but Marina knew how the writing on the loft floor could be made to look old. And she was the one who looked at photos of the writing on the floor and said it might just be the real thing, and she was the one who quickly said Hope Foute's diaries weren't in the same hand as the loft writing.

After reading the book Agent McGillis had faxed her, Lindsay now understood that Hope Foute and her sister wrote in round hand, not in modern Palmer style. Marina had known that. That's how she knew the writing on the floor was probably authentic. Why hadn't Lindsay put those little things together before now? These pictures were what Claire had discovered when she thought she had borrowed a blank disk from Marina's computer supplies.

Lindsay started clicking away at the keys as quickly as she could before calling Sheriff Ramsey. She looked at the gray plastic incriminating disk in her hand as she waited for the phone to pick up.

"Sheriff Ramsey, please. This is Lindsay Chamberlain. It's very important."

Ramsey was out so she asked the receptionist to tell him to meet her here, that she had proof of the identity of the killers, as well as of her attackers . . . that she and one of them would be at the house on the Gallows farmstead site.

She slid the disk in the pocket of her jacket and turned around. Apparently, she hadn't learned from Eric Van Horne's eavesdropping not to use the telephone in the living room. But then, John had her SUV. Marina stood in the doorway, her arms folded under her breasts.

"So, you know."

"I'm surprised."

"Why? I'm very talented. You've seen my work."

"I'm surprised because I liked you."

"Liked? Past tense?"

"Are you aware of what you've done?"

"Are you aware of the money involved?"

"But murder?"

"Claire was a head case. Drew hired her because of her ignorance—and the fact that she could control her. If anything happened, she was to be the scapegoat. It didn't quite work out that way, but that was your fault. The Tidwell woman was very old. We probably only shortened her life by about six months or so."

"And what you did to me? What's your rationale for that?"

"You were an accident. They were only supposed to leave you hurt in the woods, to scare you, to make you want to go home. We knew you were coming here to investigate. Drew had read about you and your crime solving in the paper. According to Francisco Lewis, if one Neanderthal conked another on the head, you'd find him out, plus his motive. If it hadn't been for the hikers, things would have gone different for you—and for them."

"You blame the hikers?"

"Sometimes people should just mind their own business. That's why all this happened. If the hikers and you and Claire had simply minded your own business, everyone would be all right."

"Except Miss Tidwell."

"She was old and in poor health. She had already had two heart attacks and was waiting around for the next one. She had a much better death than if nature had taken its course."

Lindsay had confronted murderers before, but never one who denied responsibility with such self-assurance. She had no doubt that Marina believed what she said.

"Do you know what she had?" continued Marina. "She can't have appreciated it the way Drew, Eric, and I do."

"What?" asked Lindsay.

"You were right about the Alexis de Tocqueville letter, but that was minor, compared to the other things. On one of her trips buying a pig-in-a-poke, the old lady came away with Thomas Jefferson's papers."

"Thomas Jefferson's papers? His presidential papers?"

"No. You know that he collected Indian vocabularies and excavated part of an Indian mound?"

"Yes, but those papers were destroyed by the thief who stole his trunk when he was moving back to Monticello."

"They were never found. They found the thief and the trunk, but not the contents."

"Didn't they find a few destroyed vocabularies?"

"Yes, but Miss Tidwell happened on a trunk with twenty-seven remaining vocabularies out of Jefferson's original fifty. The trunk also contained several sketches he had made of the mound he excavated, along with his observations. It also contained a pocket telescope that was listed among the contents of the original trunk."

"She had Jefferson's papers? Are you sure?" Lindsay was so surprised, she almost forgot that a murderer was standing in front of her.

"Drew and Eric both authenticated them. The old lady had them and sat on them for over thirty years, waiting for God knows what. Maybe to make one of her descendants like little Erin famous. Can't you see that those were too tempting not to take and put on the market? Do you know what linguists could do with those? The vocabularies are unique."

"Murder was a little harsh, don't you think?"

"Go ahead and joke about it, but she had those things hidden away, not really knowing how to take care of them. Fortunately, much of the eighteenth-century paper is rag and better quality. She even had a copy of the first written constitution adopted by native-born Americans. You've heard of the Watauga Compact? It's absolutely beautiful, written on creamy vellum in a lovely hand, and just sitting there in her safe. Eric admired her as a collector." Marina gave a little laugh. "Said she'd done a damn sight better than he had. If you could have seen the papers, you'd understand and not be standing here judging me, Drew, and Eric."

Lindsay was concerned that Marina was telling her so much. That wasn't a good sign. It meant she was probably going to try to kill her. But why was she waiting? Was she waiting for someone?

"Did Claire discover the doctored photographs and tell Drew?" Lindsay asked, casually edging toward her. She was taller than Marina—and heavier. She could push past her and run to the site. Or, if she backed up carefully, she could run through the dining room and out the back door. Marina kept her hands in the pocket of her jacket. Did she have a gun?

"Exactly. Sneaking around in my things and tattling to Drew. Fortunately she hadn't guessed that Drew was in on everything. I didn't know the little witch had made a copy of the disk and hidden it away somewhere. Clever of you to have found it. But that's the whole problem with you, you're too damn clever, you know too much, you can figure out too much."

"Who is Mike or Mark, or whatever his name is, to you?"

"It's Mike . . . and Marina's my cousin." Lindsay felt a hard grip on her arm and a gun in her back.

"Take the disk out of her pocket," said Marina.

Mike slid his hand in the pocket of her sweatsuit jacket, pulled out the disk, and tossed it to Marina, who then picked up Lindsay's laptop from the couch.

"Who was the other guy?" Lindsay asked.

"Barrel? He's a cousin, too. Mine, not Marina's." Mike put his lips to Lindsay's ear. "Baby, if you'd just played along with us a few months ago, all this would be over and you'd be home safe and sound now. Instead, you got that poor couple in the woods involved, and now they're dead."

The Marina Lindsay liked had completely disappeared. This Marina's eyes were like black ice—dark, treacherous, and cold. "The Laurenses are in the kitchen. I know you like them. You don't want the crew to come back to the house and find a massacre. I want to impress upon you how far both Mike and I will go to protect ourselves—and we have little to lose now. One or two more won't make any difference. You are the last loose end. You do see the logic of our position?"

"Yes," said Lindsay, "your logic is very clear."

"Now I want you to go out the front door," said Marina. "Don't give either of us any problems. I know you're inclined to be altruistic and won't want anyone else to get hurt."

"It's not true that one or two more won't make a difference," said Lindsay. "You can still cut your losses. And you need to know that . . ."

Lindsay felt a sharp blow on the side of her head. The pain blinded her for a moment. She put a hand to her cheek, expecting to see blood, but she wasn't cut.

"Keep your mouth shut and get out the door, or I'll hit you again with more than the barrel of this gun. Don't think I don't mean it. Keep your mouth shut."

They took her down the steps and toward the woods. Lindsay wished that John would drive up. She watched the road to see if they were coming, but they hadn't left that long ago. They probably weren't even to the car rental place yet.

"No one's going to come to the rescue," said Marina, watching Lindsay's gaze. "Go on, Mike, I'm going to dump the disk and computer into our bottomless pond, and then I'll walk a ways through the woods with you."

Lindsay watched Marina go toward the pond with her computer. She thought about Claire and her admonition to back up her hard disk.

"I have research on that," said Lindsay.

"You won't need it," Mike snapped at her. "I told you to shut up." He jabbed the gun in her ribs and marched her into the woods. Marina caught up with them.

"Okay, the evidence is gone. I'm going along this trail by the tree line so I can enter the artifact tent by the back. Take her really deep into the woods and try to do something to muffle the noise. I mean it. This is supposed to take care of all our problems, not create more. And don't get any blood on you."

"How can you talk so casually about . . ."

"Shut up," said Mike.

"I do need to tell you something important . . ."

He hit her in the middle of the back, and she fell to the ground on her hands and knees, gasping for air.

"I don't want to hear your voice. Say one more word, I'm going back to the house and shoot Mrs. Laurens and her husband. Nod your head if you get it."

Lindsay nodded.

"You should've just taken all the hints we gave you to leave." Marina walked off down the trail.

"Get up and walk, bitch. You've been nothing but trouble. I had to come down here and take a job in that greasy spoon just to stick around to see what you were up to."

Lindsay didn't say anything but simply walked. When she was on the ground, she had gotten a glimpse of his footwear—cowboy boots. Not good for hiking. He wouldn't be going far. Lindsay hoped they would go far enough to cross over into the national park.

They walked for about fifteen minutes. It could have been a beautiful walk, with the bright bluets and deep blue spiderwort, and intense red firepinks along the way. They went farther than she thought he could go in those boots. *Must be broken in better than I thought.* She guessed they had already crossed over into the national park. At least that was some small comfort. The forest had become so dense only an occasional shaft of sunlight penetrated the canopy to make a small pool of light on the ground. She considered calling out for help, but that had gotten the hikers killed.

"Okay, stop a minute. I've got to think."

Lindsay stopped and turned around. *Can't think and walk at the same time. Great, was that a good or bad sign?* A cool mountain breeze blew through her hair. For the first time she got a good look at the gun he was carrying.

"Okay. Turn left and off the trail and keep going."

They walked through the forest another five or ten minutes, up and down small hills while he looked for a place where she wouldn't be found for a while.

"Okay, stop."

"Can I say something?"

"Sure. Go ahead. I'll give you a last request. We can do more than talk if you want."

"You have several problems to deal with."

"Don't try to snow me. I've got everything pretty well covered . . . deep in the woods, unregistered untraceable gun, all the computer evidence is floating to the center of the earth. You are the last problem."

"No, you and Marina think you've come up with an organized plan, but there are several mistakes you've made. Do you want to know what they are, or would you rather walk back to wherever you parked your truck wondering if maybe you should have listened?"

"Sure, go ahead. Shoot." He laughed. "But that's your line."

"The Internet."

"What about it?"

"I sent out the photos in E-mail messages to a couple of lists in my address book."

"What the hell are you talking about?"

"Do you know what E-mail is?"

"Yes, I know what E-mail is. Do you think I'm ignorant or something?"

Well, yes, Lindsay thought. *Anybody who would do a job like this with a black powder revolver has to be a little ignorant.* Not that she was complaining. Occasionally, Lindsay let her gaze dart around, looking for any kind of weapon, without him seeing what she was up to. Difficult with him looking straight at her.

"I sent out the photos to all the faculty members in the Department of Archaeology and Anthropology, and to all the FBI agents of my acquaintance."

"You what? You what?" For a moment, he looked frightened. "You're lying. The thing has to be plugged into a phone line, I know that much."

"It was. I was in the living room using the phone jack in there."

"You're lying. That old place wasn't wired for computers."

"I did send those pictures out, but let's move along to your other problem."

Lindsay spotted a limb, possibly a discarded walking stick, under a rhododendron. Could she dive for it before he shot her? No. Getting to it would require that she move toward him. There was a laurel thicket to her right. She might make it, but she needed more information before she acted.

"And what would that be?" he asked.

"We're in the Great Smoky Mountains National Park."

"Yeah, how's that a problem?"

"You're now in the jurisdiction of the FBI. It's they who will be hunting my killer, and not the local sheriff." That gave him pause, and Lindsay continued. "Now, I'm open to a solution that will get us both out of here. If I'm dead, I can't disavow those photographs I just sent all over the country."

"You can forget that argument. I don't believe you. You're just trying to talk your way out of this." But he did hesitate a moment. "You may be right about the FBI thing." He brightened. "Marina said you'll just disappear. The wild animals will drag your body off."

Unfortunately, he could be right about that. "Maybe. Provided I didn't drop anything on the way through the woods. Were you watching me the whole way? Did you know if I had a ring that I might have slipped off my finger?"

"You're reaching. No one would ever find it. If they did, they'd never know who owned it. Is that all you have?"

"Where did you get the gun?"

"I'm getting tired of this." He raised the gun and cocked the trigger.

That was the information she needed. She turned and sprinted around the laurels, leaving him cursing his gun. The admonition to not go off halfcocked sprang to mind. She stopped still, thankful that the forest was dense and the light was dim. Now what? She looked around for a path. There—through a copse of trees. She might be able to make it. She picked up a rock and tossed it and ran. He fired. She jumped and rolled into the bushes, scrambling deep in the thick of them. He had learned to cock his gun, but he had only five more shots remaining. After that, even if he had anything to reload with, she could be halfway to the Chimneys before he got the thing loaded. Maybe there was some way to get him to use up the remainder. She stayed still.

"Come out, dammit. If I have to find you, it won't be a quick kill."

"Mike . . ." She heard a far-off call. "Mike . . ."

"Barrel, is that you?"

Oh no, the other one. She needed a weapon.

"Barrel. Over here."

"Did you have to go so deep in the woods? I've been trailing you forever. Where is she?"

"She ran for cover. This gun you gave me don't work half the time."

"You have to cock the hammer, but that's what I came to tell you about."

He takes his advice on guns from a man named Barrel? Maybe she had more than half a chance to get out of this.

"Better not use that gun. That's what I came to tell you."

"Why not? You said it's not registered."

"It's not. But I didn't realize—Clayton said he loaded it last week."

"So? What's the problem?"

"That kind of gun—it's not good to leave it loaded. He didn't mean to leave it like that."

"Dammit, Barrel. We've got to get her, or we're in trouble."

"You know, Mike, I don't like this. They found that couple."

"Exactly. That's why we need to get rid of her."

Lindsay listened to them talk. They seemed to be standing in one place and not looking for her. She slowly turned her head to one side, then the other, looking for a quiet way out of the bushes. Behind her was the best bet, then up the slope. The only drawback was that part of the path would be in the open before she could escape down the other side. She eased backward until she could stand.

"What's that?" said Mike.

Lindsay started running up the hill as fast as her legs would go.

"There she is," yelled Mike.

"Wait, don't shoot," Barrel yelled.

Lindsay didn't hear a shot. Maybe he took Barrel's advice. She topped the ridge, slipped on the leaves, and went sliding down the other side, just missing a huge oak. Unhurt but hearing her pursuers, she scrambled and hid in another thicket of bushes.

"It didn't fire, dammit," yelled Mike.

"Don't go waving that thing around. It'll fire and you'll hit me, or yourself."

"It won't fire. I don't have my finger on the trigger. Think I'm stupid or something? I wouldn't climb a hill with my finger on the trigger."

"No, I don't mean that. I mean, after it clicks like that, sometimes it don't fire right away after you pull the trigger. It waits a while."

"Waits a while? What the hell kind of gun is that?"

"Put it down. You don't know when it'll fire."

"Barrel, I told you, I need an unregistered gun, not some kind of maniac gun. What is this thing?"

"I told you, it's a black powder gun. It's not the same as a gun that uses bullets."

"Barrel . . . What do you mean, not the same as a gun that uses bullets? What am I shooting at that woman with?"

"They're bullets, but . . ."

As much as Lindsay wanted to wait around and listen to the

conversation, she decided to take a chance. Farther down the slope it leveled off to a place of large moss-covered rocks and huge trees. If she could find a good place to hide, she could wait them out. It was doubtful they knew anything about the woods. She had just started to run when the gun fired, and she heard a scream.

"Barrel, you son of a bitch. I'm hit."

She heard several explosions and another scream. This time, she imagined, the other four rounds went off.

"My hand. You son of a bitch! Oh, God, my hand. Barrel . . . help me."

"It don't look that bad."

"What do you mean, it don't look that bad? My hand is burning off."

"Go stick it in that creek. The cold water will stop the pain."

Lindsay started running. She heard gunfire behind her. This time it was an automatic. Barrel must have brought another gun.

Chapter 42

LINDSAY STOPPED BEHIND an outcropping of rocks to catch her breath. It would be better not to run deeper into the Smokies but to double back toward the site. John and Lewis would be coming, sooner or later.

"Stand up."

Lindsay looked behind her to see a man with dirty blond hair and cornflower blue eyes holding an automatic pistol on her.

"Barrel?" she said.

"You got her, Barrel? You got her? Shoot her, dammit, and let's get out of here. My hand's killing me."

"No, Barrel. You seem smarter than he is. You know this is a national park. The FBI will be all over you."

"I don't know what you're talking about."

"Think about this, Barrel. Don't get in any deeper. The hikers were an accident. You hadn't intended to kill them. This is intentional. In court there is a big difference."

"None if we don't get caught," he said.

"Shoot her, dammit, shoot the bitch." Mike came up with a wet handkerchief wrapped around his hand.

"You still have a problem, Mike. Why don't you quit screaming and listen to me? You and Barrel are both in trouble."

"What do you mean?" asked Barrel.

"Do you know your way back? Mike, did you think to keep track of where you were while you were leading me into the woods? Barrel, did you just follow the trail, then the sound of the gunshot to locate Mike? Did you watch for landmarks?" They looked around, then at each other. "I do know the way out," she said.

"So do we," snarled Mike. "We just follow the trail back."

"Which one? The woods are full of animal trails. You've made too many mistakes for me to believe you kept track of where you are, and you're bleeding. Go ahead, Barrel, tell him what that means."

Barrel looked at her, hair falling in his face. "What are you talking about?"

"Don't listen to her, Barrel, she'll say anything to stay alive. Shoot her, dammit." He grabbed for the gun, but Barrel pulled it away.

"Marina was right about the wild animals," Lindsay said. "You do know there are bears in the woods?"

"Everybody knows that. The rangers keep them away from people. Drive them back into the mountains. That's what Marina said."

"Do you see any rangers here? This is where they drive them to. Do you see any tourists?"

"You know, she has a point, Mike."

"You're bleeding and they've probably already smelled your blood. That's why they have those long pointed noses. They're as good as bloodhounds."

Lindsay didn't tell him that in the park's history, no one had ever been killed by a bear. Mauled when they'd provoked one, but never killed.

"However, the bears are not the worst. The wild boars are the worst. Did Marina tell you about the wild hogs?"

"What about them?"

Mike was getting tired and scared. That meant he was getting either more dangerous or less. She wasn't sure which.

"Lots of people have disappeared in the Smokies and have never been found again—not a trace, not a piece of clothing, nothing whatsoever is ever found of them. Do you know what the park rangers think happened to them?"

"What?" asked Barrel.

As Lindsay spoke, she was forming a plan. If she could surprise them, it might work.

"Wild hogs. Some of them weigh five or six hundred pounds and run like a horse. They eat everything that has blood on it, bones, clothes, even a stick with blood on it. If you don't get out of the woods and get help, you're going to be sniffed out, run down, and eaten by a wild boar and the only thing that will be left of you is pig shit—but perhaps I'm being redundant."

Lindsay watched Mike get angry and Barrel start to laugh. She made her move. She shot her arm out hard and shoved two fingers in Barrel's eyes. He yelled and she grabbed his gun. He held on. Mike lunged at her and she grabbed at his hurt hand and hit his nose with the heel of her hand as hard as she could. He fell to the ground, stunned. Barrel was still rubbing his eyes and yelling. She picked up a rock and hit his gun hand. He still held on and squeezed the trigger. It missed her by a fraction. She ran as fast as she could in the direction of the site, leaving them yelling after her. Gunfire behind her kept her running faster. She hadn't been in this part of the woods, but she did know which direction she needed to be running. The important thing was to leave the two maniacs behind her, especially now that they were very angry.

Lindsay was in better shape than the two of them, and she was wearing sneakers. She stopped to catch her breath, gulping down lungfuls of air. Her sense of the sun was that she was heading away from it, though it was climbing rapidly overhead. She wasn't really sure where she was or which direction to go without stopping to think about it, and she had no time to stop and figure it out.

The way sloped down abruptly, terminating at a rock overhang and a creek. Growing near the creek was something she could use as a weapon. She fished her Swiss army knife out of her pocket. It would take forever to cut a devil's walking stick with this. "Damn," Lindsay said as she scanned the ground near the edges of the grove. There—a pile of them felled, perhaps by winter ice. If she lay flat, she could reach one lying just inside the grove. She didn't hesitate, even when the thorns tore the skin of her arm.

They're called devil's walking sticks because of their shape. They would make good walking sticks were it not for the sharp, prickly thorns covering them from end to end. She took her knife and shaved the thorns off the parts she wanted to hold and slipped her knife back in her pocket. She took the stick and followed the creek, which went more or less west.

Lindsay walked thirty minutes before she came out on Highway 129. She knew where she was. She wasn't that far from the dirt road leading to the site. She walked along the Little Tennessee River side of the road toward the turnoff. Just ahead of her, Mike and Barrel stumbled out of the woods.

They saw her just as she saw them. Lindsay looked down the embankment to see if there was any safe haven. Nothing but sharp rocks. This was a major highway. Surely, they wouldn't shoot her here. She was wrong. Mike had the gun now. He raised it and fired. A car came by, and she tried to flag it down. They didn't stop or even slow down. Instead, they gunned the engine.

Mike shot again. This time, Lindsay had another plan. She fell onto the grass and slipped down the embankment as if she'd been shot. She grabbed a piece of driftwood, threw it in the water with a splash, hunkered down among the jagged rocks and a fallen tree, and waited.

"I got her. I got her, didn't I? Did you see?"

"No, man, I can't see a damn thing. Look at my eyes. Did she poke them out?"

"No, stupid. You saw well enough to get out of the woods and cross the road, didn't you? You want pain and misery, you should have my hand and nose. I'm going to need plastic surgery on my nose. I can't breathe through it. I tell you, the money Marina's offering isn't worth this."

Lindsay waited until she saw the gun and then Mike's head, as he leaned to look for her in the water. Without hesitation, she struck his hand with the thorned walking stick. The gun went flying into the rocks, along with a spray of blood from his wrist. She briefly took note of where the gun landed, stood, and struck him again across the kneecaps. Mike yelled, cursed, and fell into the water.

"What is it, Mike? What's happening?"

"Help, she's killing me. Find the gun." Mike clung to the rocks, his legs dangling in the river. "Help me, Barrel. I'm going to drown."

"I'm getting out of here."

Lindsay heard tires squeal and braced herself for a thump. It didn't come. Instead, she heard Sheriff Ramsey telling Barrel to put his hands behind his back.

The sheriff took Barrel and Mike to the farmstead to pick up Marina. The three of them were in the dining room sitting at the table. Marina was cuffed to Mike. Barrel, squinting around him with deep bloodshot eyes, had his hands cuffed behind him. Lindsay sat across from them. Mr. and Mrs. Laurens stood by the kitchen door, behind Lindsay, looking very cross at Marina. The crew were in the living room gathered around the door.

"You can't prove anything," said Marina.

"This is the same caliber gun that killed the woman hiker," said the sheriff. "What're you willing to bet the bullet that killed her matches this gun?"

"Damn you, Marina," said Barrel.

"Don't say anything. That's what the Miranda warning is about. What you say can be used against you. Just pretend you have lockjaw. They have to have proof beyond reasonable doubt, or they can't even go to court."

"Little lady, you're dreaming if you think I don't have enough to take you to court. Miss Tidwell didn't die of natural causes, for starters."

"You can't connect me with that." Marina looked defiantly at the sheriff.

"We can connect you with Dr. Chamberlain's attack, for another thing."

"How?"

"The photograph of you and Mike, the one you changed to put Dr. Chamberlain's face on your body to fool her into leaving the hospital with Mike."

Lindsay could see the faces of the crew wide-eyed with disbelief.

"You just have her word that there was such a picture, and I understand she has no memory of the time she had amnesia."

"You're wrong there, missy," said the sheriff. "We have Mary Carp's testimony. The sheriff in Mac's Crossing convinced her to tell the truth. Besides that, every FBI agent on Dr. Chamberlain's mailing list has a copy of the pictures, along with the UGA faculty, I understand."

Marina opened her mouth and shut it. "You're lying," she whispered.

"She told me in the woods she E-mailed it. I didn't believe her. You should have destroyed the thing," said Mike. "Sheriff, I'm really hurting. I need to go to the hospital."

"Mike, will you and Barrel please keep your mouths shut? Anybody could have doctored those pictures."

"Which leads us to you," said the sheriff. "Let's leave off for the moment that we have Lindsay's testimony against all of you." The sheriff placed the bagged contents from Mike's jacket pocket on the table. He picked up the baggie containing the coin. "This is Miss Tidwell's."

"You can't prove it."

"Is that some kind of—what you call it—a mantra?" said the sheriff. "You can't prove it? You think saying it over and over'll make it true? I damn well can prove it." He put a piece of paper on the table. "This here's a rubbing Mrs. Laurens did of Miss Tidwell's coin in 1952 or thereabouts. I believe it's the same coin."

"I don't believe you . . . Is that proof?"

"Damn near it." The sheriff picked up the bagged tooth and handed it to Lindsay. "Why don't you tell him about this?"

"You like gold, don't you, Mike?" she said. "This is a temporary cap for a molar. It's gold. Not particularly valuable, but gold nonetheless. I'll bet when you hit the hiker in the back of the head, you saw it pop out of his mouth and just couldn't help yourself. He had a temporary cap put on just before he went hiking. Nigel discovered the cap missing and used dental records of some missing persons to identify the body."

"That's my cap. You can't prove it's not."

"Mikey, Mikey, Mikey," said the sheriff. "The woman is a forensic anthropologist. Listen to her."

"When a dentist makes a temporary cap for a person, he makes it fit the tooth like a glove. This cap will only fit the person for whom the dentist made it, no one else. It's like a fingerprint. When Nigel puts this cap on the hiker's tooth, he's going to know it's his cap, without a doubt. And the jury's going to know the sheriff found it in your pocket."

Mike's frown looked comical with his swollen nose and black eyes.

"We're getting close, aren't we?" The sheriff leaned forward with his hand on the table. "Barrel, we going to be able to match that gun to the bullet in that woman hiker? I'll have to tell you, son, we already matched the bullet that came out of the hiker with the bullet that came out of Claire Burke." Barrel put his head down and mumbled something. "That's okay, boy. We can wait for the results."

"You don't have anything on me," said Marina. "Just because that photograph is of me doesn't mean I altered it."

"No, you're right about that. It doesn't. However, we have these boys' testimony. We got them, and they're going to be looking for a deal. Chances are, they aren't going to be that loyal to you. Put their testimony with the photograph, and all the little circumstantial evidence that keeps adding up. With Dr. Chamberlain's testimony to boot, I know the D.A. and he's going to be as happy with this case as he can be."

"It's not proof."

"Miss," said the sheriff, "we have enough proof to send you away. You can be as stubborn as you like, but your partners in crime are going to turn on you. Drew and her husband have already taken steps to distance themselves from this whole mess and lay the blame on you. They've sent Miss Tidwell's documents back with a letter saying when they bought them from you, they didn't know they were stolen, that you told them they had been obtained legally."

That got Marina's attention. "Drew, she killed Miss Tidwell, and her husband told her to do it. I heard him. I saw her crush the poison leaves and make the tea and put it in the Thermos to give to her. I'll testify to that."

The sheriff had been gone with his prisoners for about thirty minutes when the phone rang. Lindsay was in the living room, looking at Elaine McBride's photo album of the cabin. She picked up the phone.

"Lindsay, it's John. Lewis and I got tied up and are running late. I didn't want you to worry."

"I'm not worried at all."

"Everything okay there?"

"Sure. Everything's fine."

"We'll be there in less than an hour."

"No problem."

"Stay in the house and don't do anything dangerous."

"I won't. I'll stay right here on the couch. See you in a while." She hung up the phone and went back to the album. "Adam," she called into the dining room. "I have an idea."

It took a little bit to get Lewis to do it, especially without telling him why. But Adam had agreed, so Lewis signed off on excavating the well. This was not normal excavation procedure, and she and Adam gave it much discussion, pro and con, before deciding to do it. They excavated down to ten feet, a layer at a time, photographing a profile and sifting the dirt. At the ten-foot level, Lewis was growing uneasy.

"I think that's as deep as we should go," he said.

"Give me the rod," Powell called up from the bottom.

He was handed down a four-foot steel rod with a handle at the top that is used to probe beneath the surface of soil.

"No more than that," said Lewis, squatting beside the hole.

John had agreed to stay and help with the safety of digging a deep hole. Lindsay actually thought they would have to go deeper. He looked at her quizzically and stroked her bruised face, just as Powell said he had found something.

In less than an hour, Powell uncovered part of a tiny coffin.

"What?" said Lewis. "Another one? How did you know?"

"The loft poems," said Lindsay. "I looked at the photograph of the floor scratchings again and decided that the one that said, *'Not my sin, the hell he's in'* actually read, *'Not my sin, the well he's in.'* That particular poem was printed, and the capital *W* looks like a capital *H.* I think that Sheldon Warfield was given the impression, just before the baby was to be buried beside his son, that it was not his son's baby, but the surveyor's. In his anger, Warfield had it thrown, coffin and all, down the well. Another thing that Faith hadn't meant to happen and felt guilty about."

"But there had to be something else to make you think it was there," said Lewis.

"The Gallowses' bad luck. Their infant mortality, the baby who lived for a while only to die when he came back home, the miscarriages, Mr. Gallows's gout, both their heart conditions, Rosellen's hallucinations and paranoia—they are all symptoms of lead poisoning. Rosellen didn't kill her babies, she had a poisoned well."

About the Author

Beverly Connor weaves her professional experiences as an archaeologist and her knowledge of Southern culture into interlinked stories of the past and present in her Lindsay Chamberlain mystery series. Originally from Oak Ridge, Tennessee, she now lives in Oglethorpe County, Georgia, with her husband, her dogs, her horse, and her cats. *Airtight Case* is the fifth book in this unique mystery series.